The Scarlet Codebreaker

The Scarlet Codebreaker

A Russian Revolution Love Story

by L.M. Sizemore

This is a work of fiction. Names, characters, places, and incidents either are the product of the author's imagination or are used fictitiously. Any resemblance to actual persons, living or dead, events, or locales is entirely coincidental.

First paperback edition 2022

Cover Design by Tawnie Hansen

ISBN 978-0-578-32803-4

Dedication

To my darling mother, for never giving up on me

You are all that I am and hope to be.

and

To Jesse Vega. This one is for you, too.

Acknowledgments

First and foremost: my beloved best friend and editor, Emelie Lora. Thank you for everything. I couldn't have done it without you. I was moments away from giving up everything I worked for, but you helped me fall in love with my book again. Thank you for your countless hours of editing, revising, and listening to me talk hours about characters, plot twists, and storylines. Thank you, my darling. I cannot express my love and gratitude enough!

Thank you to my nonbiological sister, Kristina Iwasko, for always believing in me, especially when I didn't believe in myself. Thank you for having faith in me.

I want to give special thanks to my partner in crime, Anya Bannatyne, for teaching me Russian words and culture. It helped me bring my characters to life.

I want to give a big shout-out to Amanda Galloway for being my biggest cheerleader. Amanda, thank you for pushing me to keep going. Without you, I would have never had finished this book. Thank you for teaching me, "If it is not broken, do not try to fix it."

To my beloved, Pat Smith, thank you for listening to my crazy book ideas and giving your opinion and input on many things.

Lastly, I want to thank the little thirteen-year-old girl I used to be. Thank you for being brave and strong during our darkest hour. It was that hour that made me the woman and writer I am now. Thank you for teaching me how to be brave. Without you, my love, I wouldn't have met Ivan Mikhailovich at all.

Author's Note

Dear Reader,

I conceived the idea for this book when I was fifteen; however, I did not start writing it until a couple of weeks after turning 16. I thought writing this book would be easy, but I was wrong. I started from scratch seven times before I got the story right. It took me nearly half a decade to write this book.

Before writing this, I did in-depth research on the Romanov family through letters and the diaries of the Grand Duchesses, including the people who loved and knew them best, such as ladies-in-waiting, tutors, and even the Tsar himself. I learned all that I could about their personalities and daily habits, and hobbies. I learned all I could about what happened during the revolution and after and how it affected this family forever. My goal was to bring them back to life.

As I continued through this journey, I noticed that not only was my writing changing; I was changing as well. I was not the person I was when I started this project. I became someone else through the chaos and trauma that somehow became my life. When I thought I could not go on anymore, I picked up a pencil and started writing.

This book saved my life, representing everything I did not say through my tears and frustration. This book gave me hope, and with that hope, I found a will to live again.

This book was written by the girl I used to be. I am proud of that girl. She was strong when she had no reason to be. Without that girl, there may not be a book at all.

I hope that you love this story as much as I do.

L.M. Sizemore

For want of a nail, a horseshoe was lost
For want of a horseshoe, a horse went lame
For want of a horse, a rider never got through
For want of a rider, a message never arrived
For want of a message, an army was never sent
For want of an army, a battle was lost
For want of a battle, a war was lost
For want of a war, a kingdom fell And all for want of a nail.
— Unknown

"Remember that the evil there is now in the world will become yet more powerful and that it is not evil that will conquer evil—only love."

Grand Duchess Olga Nikolaevna

THE COVERT OPERATIONS

THE COVERT OPERATIONS

THE COVERT OPERATIONS

Chapter 1

Operation Dragonfly

I regret to inform you that I am dying. It is a slow and painless death, and the days are passing quickly. In fact, I am not sure how much time I have left.

My mother told me that I should never judge another human being without walking a mile in their moccasins. And I intend to do just that every day before I die. It seems like the right thing to do after all.

In the middle of the beautiful, twisted mess I call my life, I found a young man named Ivan Mikhailovich. Or perhaps, he found me. He told me his story. Every word and character, down to the slightest detail, were engraved inside my heart. I must share his story with you before I go. There is so much that I need to tell you, yet I possess so little time to say it. With the time I have left, I am going to tell you a story that has been retold throughout the decades. You will laugh and cry. Just always keep your tears within the margins. I cannot promise that you will not fall in love. For your sake and mine, try not to. That was my first mistake. And if you do fall in love, do not say that I did not warn you. I promise to tell you everything and not leave out a single detail. And if you choose to judge anyone in this beautiful story, please, try on a pair of moccasins or two.

This story starts with a man named Vladimir Lenin.

He was a man in his early forties. His head was nearly bald, but you could never tell because he always wore a black hat. His suit and shoes were also black. His eyes were deep brown. His goatee was dark and carefully trimmed. His face and chin were round. Lenin was not a very tall man. About one hundred sixty-seven centimeters. What Lenin lacked in height, he made up for in ego.

Lenin was not an ordinary man you would find walking in the streets of Chicago or London. He was much more complex than that. You see, Lenin had a one and only true love. In fact, it was the only woman that he ever loved. Her name was communism. Lenin had loved her more than half his life. He worshipped her. He would kill for her, die for her. His cold heart belonged to her.

There was something else about old Vladimir that you must understand. Lenin carried with him a bitter, hollow feeling buried deep inside his chest. He did not know how it got there or how long it had been there. It made him miserable, so miserable that Lenin could not remember a time when his heart was not affected by this heaviness. It was a cold, empty sadness that Lenin could not understand or shake.

It was a miracle that he even loved such a thing as communism at all.

It was August 1913. Lenin somehow found himself in Austria, where he spent several months gathering disciples. However, it was not all hard work. Lenin found his exile from Russia quite enjoyable. He ate and lounged at small Austrian cafes with his loyal wife, Nadezhda, who was not afraid to speak her mind. He sipped on black coffee and had passionate conversations with her. He grew fond of taking long walks in the park, not having to look over his shoulder. And, of course, Lenin spent this time spreading God's work: Communism.

It was a chilly Sunday evening when Vladimir Lenin climbed in the back of a black Austrian taxi. The driver was a blond man, about thirty-five, with a smug look on his face.

"von der Reis castle, please," Lenin said quietly in German.

The driver pressed his foot gently on the accelerator as the taxi drove smoothly out of town and through the Austrian countryside.

Lenin glanced down at his watch. It was half-past six, and the sun had just begun to slide into the mountains, creating golden orange hues in the Austrian sky. The meeting would start just as Lenin walked through those doors. But still, there was great anxiety lodged deep in his chest.

These kinds of meetings always had Vladimir Lenin walking on a tightrope. He never knew which man would fire the first threat or insult. He never knew which man would leave the meeting with a new revenge plot or another reason to kill again. These men were dangerously brilliant. Two of these men especially captivated Lenin with their prowess and accomplishments. With a sharp mind and wit, John von der Reis built a banking empire out of nothing. The other man was a lesser-known scientific genius who designed a weapon that could destroy the world. Lenin admired them, envied them. Lenin wanted to be them.

You could probably understand why Lenin would be anxious. I certainly would.

A half an hour later, Vladimir Lenin stepped from the black cab. He gasped at the gloomy, four-story, sixteenth-century manor that stood proudly behind a twisted iron gate. The crested roof slanted down at a sharp angle. As his feet stepped onto the pavement, he noticed the neatly trimmed hedges and delicate marble fountain. He walked toward the manor down a dirt path to a scarlet door. Lenin knocked three times and let out a small huff, waiting for someone to answer.

A hauntingly beautiful woman opened the door. Fear painted her face as soon as she opened it.

"Helen, you look well," said Lenin.

"You're late," muttered Helen. Her accent had small traces of German. Her dark auburn hair was thick and wavy, hanging just below her shoulders. Her lips were crimson red. Her velvet-colored dress was a silk chiffon embroidered kimono that fit tightly to her waist and hips. Helen knew how to pull off red; she wore it well. Helen von der Reis was the kind of woman that every man wanted to be with, and every woman wanted to be. She was beautiful, charming, and wealthy—the perfect combination for trouble.

Vladimir Lenin was surprised to see her at the meeting. Her husband usually had her locked up inside their bedroom so no other man could look at her. Helen was more his prisoner than his wife. But she had her ways of escaping, which I will tell you more about later as it is not important right now.

This meeting would not be like the others.

Helen held the door open for him. Better late than never, thought Lenin as he walked through the castle threshold. He hoped he did not come all this way to step into some sort of trap. Helen slammed the door behind him

Lenin swallowed nervously. "You're still not upset about that poor woman's death, are you?" Helen did not answer and rolled her eyes. Lenin scoffed. "You told me to wake you if she needed you. She died. She didn't need you."

Helen gave him a deadly glare. Her eyes flashed with anger. "That poor woman helped raise me after my parents died." Helen locked the door and continued, "And you would be angry, too, if it were Nadezhda who died."

Lenin took a step forward and crossed his arms, "Oh, darling. If it were Nadezhda, you would be dead."

Helen's eyes widened. As much as his words were frightening, they were true. Helen would be dead ten times over if Nadezhda had died instead of her aunt. "We should go," she muttered quietly. "My husband is expecting us. As you know, he is not a patient man." Helen took several steps forward, walking through the exotic drawing-room.

"Do you really think your parent's death was an accident?" said Lenin coolly. Helen stopped and turned, her whiskey eyes flashing in fear. Then she continued walking through the parlor.

Lenin took several brisk steps forward, following close behind. He stole a glance around the castle. The gray marble floor of the entrance gave way to a mahogany stairway that climbed to the top of the ceiling. The royal purple curtains framed the high arched, hand-crafted windows. The stone walls were covered with a silk coverlet. Lenin followed Helen to her husband's study.

John von der Reis reclined in a brown plaid sofa with heavy oak arms, dressed in a dark and costly-looking suit. His gray beard matched the color of his hair and eyes, and his skin was olive in tone. At six and a half feet tall, muscles rippled through every part of his body; his stomach, arms, and legs were perfectly cut. He closed his eyes, listening to the warm fire crackle. A newborn baby boy slept peacefully in his arms. According to Austrian birth records, this boy did not exist. John von der Reis would like to keep it that way.

As soon as the door cracked open, John von der Reis opened his eyes. His eyes darted to Helen. "Get this baby out of my arms, now," he said darkly.

Helen's whiskey-colored eyes flashed with fear and concern. She carefully took the baby out of her husband's arms and cradled him against her chest.

"And shut that door!" hissed John, his voice shaking with rage and frustration.

Helen huffed and quietly shut the door.

As soon as that door closed, the name John von der Reis was left outside. John was known by a different name. A name that people are afraid to speak. *The Chupacabra.* His identity outside that room was kept secret, of course. The very few who knew it would take the secret to their graves.

Helen retreated to her husband's favorite leather armchair, She cradled the baby there, and silently prayed with every ounce of her being that he would not make a sound.

The Chupacabra's eyes landed on Lenin, and he tossed his comrade a wicked smile. "Vladimir, you must be wondering why I have summoned you this evening," he said coolly, his American accent thick and heavy. He was a New York City banker who inherited the castle and a banking empire from his late German father.

Of course, the thought did cross Lenin's mind several times.

The baby suddenly let out a hungry wail.

"Helen!" shouted The Chupacabra. "How many times must I tell you to keep that baby quiet?"

Helen quickly stood up and bounced the baby in her arms. If she did not keep the baby quiet, her husband's gun certainly would. But he would not dare do that. You see, the child was of more use to him alive than dead.

The Chupacabra turned his attention to the fire, and he became quiet. His cold eyes were captivated by the fire dancing inside the flames. "I want to start a war," he said, lost in thought. "A big one."

"What?" gasped Lenin, his dark brown eyes flashing in horror. "How?"

The Chupacabra turned his gaze to his friend and comrade, giving him a devilish smile. "I—" The Chupacabra paused, thinking of the right words. The less Lenin knew about his master plan, the better. "I have some boys in Serbia who'd get the job done."

"Why?"

"Banking is a messy business," said The Chupacabra darkly.

Helen just had to have fallen in love with his friend and fellow oligarchy member, Mikhail Mikhailovich. She could not keep her hands to herself. And neither could Mikhail. He never learned not to touch what was not his. The Chupacabra hired an assassin to teach Mikhail that lesson. But when the killer got there, Mikhail vanished, as did those blasted plans for that bomb!

Mikhail thought he could hide those plans away in a bank somewhere in Europe. He was sadly mistaken. A war was coming. A big one. All the governments in Europe would fall, and the economies would collapse right into The Chupacabra's hands. Then, he would buy all the banks in Europe. And he would find those plans for that atomic weapon; no one would be able to stop him.

First, The Chupacabra would need Mikhail to come out of hiding, and he would use Mikhail's son to do just that! Of course, the boy would need to be broken. He planned on making Ivan's heart as cold as snow. He would rip the humanity right out of him, making him the epitome of evil. After he was done, The Chupacabra would make Mikhail wish that he had killed him when he had the chance.

Lenin loved the plan. Russia did not have the military strategy to fight a massive world war. The country would fall apart, the government would destroy itself, and civil war would surely break out. And Vladimir Lenin would be there to pick up the pieces as he could easily get Russia out of a war using his charm alone. Vladimir Lenin could sell the devil a block of ice. He would be their hero, their new leader, and he would not only be feared but respected. Ruthless but cunning, Lenin would paint the Tsar a picture with his blood! He would be the face of the revolution!

If only Sasha could see him now.

Sasha.

Sometimes names, places, or events will take you back in time further than you would like to go. And you cannot help but relive every moment down to the tiniest detail, from every breath down to the teardrops escaping your face. But it all happened in your head. Has that ever happened to you before?

His mind went back in time. Almost against his will. He looked different. He was a sixteen-year-old boy again, with a head full of shiny dark hair. His surroundings were different. He lived in that tiny house in the middle of town, where his mother raised six children. It was a different time. A different person. A different Russia.

Those were the best but also the worst times of his life. Those were the times that broke him and nearly destroyed him. But they were also the times that made him.

The air was cold and crisp that day. The sky was dark and cloudy. And by some miracle, young Vladimir had passed his geometry test. He had to tell his mother. It might put a rare smile on her face. She grieved deeply for his father every day, but she had no time to feel sorry for herself. She had six children to feed. She did the hard thing and continued, although it hurt. There was something called the new normal. No one ever liked adjusting to that.

Vladimir dashed through town, past the bakery, and past the blacksmith. He crossed over the bridge as fast as his legs would allow him. He heard screaming and wailing from outside his home. He entered the house and found his mother on the kitchen floor, tears running down her face. He felt so helpless at that moment as he watched his mother.

After she somehow found the strength to pull herself together, she could not speak. Her vocal cords were raw. His sisters told young Vladimir what happened to their brother, and he locked himself in the bathroom and cried.

It was not much of a funeral—closed casket. No body. Sasha was found with a rope around his neck, and his body dumped in an unmarked grave.

It was times like that when you clung to prayers as if your life depended on them, begging God for answers to complicated questions. Those questions kept you up at three in the morning crying, clinging to your pillow, because you might have discovered the solution to all of them. But there were none.

Sometimes you might even dare wonder if there was a God out there, why wasn't he listening? Perhaps the greatest answer to that would be that he was listening all along, and you were the one who was not paying attention. Or, maybe, you were not emotionally ready to handle what he had to say just yet. The pain still ripped through your chest like a bullet either way, if God was listening or not.

It was grief that became part of his identity now. And because of that he did the hardest thing that he ever had to do in his life. Young Vladimir left the Christian faith of his childhood behind and grew up a little more than he should have. There was no warning, and there was no stopping it. He woke up one day, and it was gone.

He was the man of the house now, and he helped care for his depressed mother and sisters. He could only somewhat cook and clean, but he ensured his sisters stayed out of trouble and finished their schoolwork on time. He became the father figure and somehow the emotional husband to his mother. He also spent hours at a time in Sasha's bedroom; everything was just the way he left it. The blankets on the bed were untouched. The schoolwork on his desk would forever be unfinished, and the books on the shelves began collecting dust. That was a colossal shame! Lenin picked a book from the shelf. As soon as the book touched his fingertips, it captured his interest, transforming it into an obsession. He was the author's prisoner.

The situation in Russia was unacceptable.

Bread was scarce. Children starved in the gutters with bloated stomachs as famine spread like some sort of disease. Skeletons walked the streets. Peasants and Jews were being brutally beaten and murdered. Russians were half-dead but still continued on. And the few who dared to act ended up dead just like Sasha. Lenin's anger built inside. *Why wasn't the government doing anything about it?*

The time for silence was over.

Vladimir Lenin enrolled in law school, where he wrote illegal articles and gave public speeches. He hosted secret revolutionary meetings, rallying the heart of the Tsar's broken, beaten down, and emotionally dead people. If the government was not going to change on its own, then they would force it to. But Lenin was arrested, thrown in jail, and sent into exile. But that did not shut him up. It only added fuel to the fire.

As of now, Russia was not ready for the revolution. Not yet. A few more things needed to happen before the people took arms against the Tsar and his government. Fortunately, Lenin was a patient man, and he would continue to work in the shadows for now. He did not care how long it would take, and he did not care who he had to kill. Nothing was going to stand in Lenin's way. Nothing.

His thoughts were interrupted. The door to John von der Reis' study flung open.

Lenin turned his head sharply. It was Jackob Goldstein, or what was left of him. His hair had completely fallen out, and his bushy eyebrows were thick and gray. His eyes were darker than Lenin remembered, with even darker circles around them. The man looked like he had not slept in days. He looked like he had lost about fifty pounds and aged twenty years and his suit barely fit around his waist. Wrinkles existed around his lifeless brown eyes and thin lips. Jakob Goldstein was completely unrecognizable.

That is what nine months in hell, also known as the asylum, does to you. His own brother declared him legally mad and locked him up in a mental institution. But Jakob was not insane. He was a brilliant genius who planned complicated disasters beyond your comprehension out of boredom. What would be discussed at the meeting tonight was one of them.

"Hello, Jakob," said Lenin quietly, fighting to hide the tinge of shock in his voice. "The asylum looks good on you."

Professor Goldstein ignored Lenin and stepped forward, his fists clenched into balls. His eyes were fixed on the man who nearly destroyed his brother's marriage—The Chupacabra.

"Where is it?" shouted the mad doctor.

Where was what? Lenin thought to himself. He had the strange, unsettling feeling in his stomach that in a few short moments, he was about to find out.

The Chupacabra ignored Professor Goldstein's screams. His gray gaze rested on Helen. She sat quietly in the leather armchair; her whiskey-colored eyes stared at the red carpet. She brought the baby closer to her chest, holding him tighter. The small child somehow slept peacefully through his screaming. Professor Goldstein noticed Helen and took another step forward.

"Give it to me!" shouted Professor Goldstein, raising his voice louder.

The baby woke up and began to cry.

Helen glanced over to her husband, asking with her eyes and not her lips. The Chupacabra's eyes shined with disapproval. Helen swallowed hard; her arms wrapped protectively around the baby which made the German angrier.

"Give that thing to me now!"

That thing? Lenin thought. Did that man just call the baby *that thing*?

Lenin felt a tinge of anger, and he wanted to take his fist and thrust it into Professor Goldstein's face. But something held him back. Normally Lenin would not allow something like this to bother him. But his wife could not have children, which made things more personal.

Professor Goldstein raised his hand over his head. Helen covered the baby's face with her arms as The Chupacabra stood up quickly. His fists were balled, and his eyes flashed with cold anger. The message was clear: If you touch her, I will cut you to pieces.

Jakob Goldstein lowered his hand.

The baby wailed louder.

"Helen," barked The Chupacabra, with his arms out.

Helen did not want to hand the child over. She wanted to hold him for a few more minutes. But that was an order. As she slowly rose from the armchair, the baby screamed louder. She carefully walked to her husband and placed the baby in his arms. The Chupacabra cradled the boy against his chest.

"Did the mad man scare you, little one?" said The Chupacabra childishly. Helen's husband looked down at the baby almost lovingly. The child's small hand wrapped around his big finger. And for a small moment, her heart slightly broke. Why wasn't he this good for their own child?

"I am tired of waiting! Give me that baby, or I'll—"

"Or you'll what?" The Chupacabra challenged the Professor with his eyes. For a moment, there was a terrifying silence. "Considering what you did to your own daughter, I don't think so."

Lenin cleared his voice. "I'm sorry to interrupt, but I am confused."

"Well, you see," said The Chupacabra. He paused for a few moments, choosing his words carefully. "Do you remember Operation Dragonfly?"

"The operation that you aborted because Jakob went to the asylum. I remember that." The Chupacabra and Professor Goldstein exchanged awkward glances.

"You didn't abort it," said Lenin nervously.

"The less you know, the better," replied The Chupacabra.

Lenin blinked a few times, slowly grasping his words. He could not believe his ears. Lenin swallowed hard, his palms sweaty.

Professor Goldstein could not remain silent a second longer. He stepped forward again and grunted loudly. "Now give me the boy!"

The Chupacabra took a step back and gave Professor Goldstein a mocking grin. "I don't think so." The Chupacabra could not let a man like Professor Goldstein walk out of that room with the baby. The Chupacabra would never see the child again, and that he could not allow. He needed the child alive. Children were a lot like dogs. They needed to be broken.

The Chupacabra turned his attention to Lenin, tossing him a charming smile. "Vladimir, you wanted to know why I summoned you this evening. You will take the child," he said calmly.

"What?" gasped Lenin.

The Chupacabra ignored him and placed the baby in Lenin's arms. As soon as the baby touched his arms, he squirmed.

"For how long?"

The Chupacabra gave Lenin a cold, stern look. And for a second, Lenin thought that perhaps The Chupacabra might take the child back. Instead, he opened his mouth and said the words, "For as long as I say."

"Would you bet your life on that?" asked Professor Goldstein darkly.

Now Professor Goldstein had The Chupacabra's attention. "Do you remember those scandalous letters with the most incriminating content in them?" said Professor Goldstein almost childishly. "I believe you wrote them."

"John, what is he talking about?" said Helen fearfully.

The Chupacabra turned to his wife and gave her a blank stare. He wanted to keep her out of this. If Helen knew, she would leave him without a second thought. If the world knew what he did, he would lose his business and everything he worked for his entire life. He would rot in prison. Those letters must never see the light of day! But they were missing—stolen.

Professor Goldstein gave the most wicked smile. "You mean, you never told her."

The Chupacabra turned sharply, his cold eyes flashing murderously. "Shut up!" he shouted. "What do you want?"

"I want to play a game," Professor Goldstein whispered playfully.

The Chupacabra raised an eyebrow.

Professor Goldstein was a big man-child who liked to play games. What he liked more than games was to win them. There were no rules, just mayhem, and chaos. His games were like fire: uncontrollable, and a dangerous thing to play.

"What kind of game?"

Professor Goldstein took another step forward and gave The Chupacabra a mocking smile. "If I find those letters first, I will destroy you and take the child. If you find them first, you can do whatever you want with me."

The Chupacabra liked the sound of that. He imagined Professor Goldstein's lifeless body hanging from a tree, his cold eyes staring at the ground. He fantasized about murdering the man many times before. Professor Goldstein deserved to be hung.

"If I find those letters first, I will kill you," said The Chupacabra viciously.

Professor Goldstein let out a burst of bellowing laughter. "Do you really hate me that much?"

The Chupacabra tossed Professor Goldstein a twisted grin, and the two men shook on it.

He then turned his attention to Lenin and gave him a stern, cold glare. "I did not give you all that money for you to fail," he said, pointing his index finger at him.

The Wall Street banker, John von der Reis, financed the coup. The Chupacabra cared little for what happened next after the empire crumbled. He only cared about Russia's natural resources, which Lenin promised in exchange for money. And lots of it.

"No," muttered Lenin quietly, clearing his throat. "Of course not."

"A word of advice—" The Chupacabra glared at the child that was now nestled close to Lenin's chest, sleeping. The baby was a very handsome lad but looked too much like his treacherous father. His father would pay for his sins soon. Starting with his son. "It's good to punish children," said The Chupacabra cheerfully. "Or else they'll never learn."

Lenin nodded. How was he ever going to explain this to Nadezhda?

Later that night, Helen spiked her husband's wine with a potent, tasteless, untraceable sleeping drug. The Chupacabra would be out cold until morning. Until then, it did not matter what Helen did.

Helen walked quickly to the basement, the one no one knew about. As she unlocked the basement door and opened it, there was a slight creak. She let her hand fall on the wooden rail as she walked down the old stair boards. When she reached the bottom, she whispered softly, "Greta."

There was no answer. A small deafening silence echoed in the darkness.

"Greta!" whispered Helen again a little louder.

She took several paces forward, walking deeper into the darkness. She suddenly felt a cold pistol against her back.

"Not another sound," whispered the cold voice of a woman.

"Greta," choked Helen. She slowly turned around with her hands in the air. Greta was a sickly woman, with thin honey blonde hair falling from her scalp and lifeless green eyes. She was a twenty-nine-year-old German but looked closer to sixty. She wore a black maternity dress, with the bones sticking out from her hips. She had been trapped in that basement since the birth of her child only three days ago. You see, this woman was the guinea pig for the project called Operation Dragonfly. She had been kept alive for the past nine months, but just barely.

"I know that you must be angry, considering what my husband put you through, abducting you and taking your child. But think about what you are doing. If you kill me, you are never going to see your son again," Helen said slowly.

It was clear that Greta was not the slightest bit interested in what Helen had to say so

Helen stepped in and grabbed Greta's wrist. She twisted the gun with her right hand, pushing it down, and this broke Greta's finger. Helen then grabbed the gun and aimed it at Greta.

"I didn't come down here to fight with you," she said. She lowered the weapon and gave Greta a sharp look.

"What do you want?" asked Greta coldly.

"If you want to survive this war, then you'll have to do exactly as I say."

Chapter 2

Operation Lock & Key

Ivan Mikhailovich was about to be killed.

His hands were tied behind his back. He had been beaten until he was unconscious. Then, Ivan was beaten even harder. He was beaten with a cane until it broke in half, forcing The Chupacabra to use his legs and fists. He had broken Ivan's nose and ribs and dislocated his arm and shoulder. And now, The Chupacabra was about to take Ivan's life. And Helen was forced to watch.

"Enough, John! Enough!" screamed Helen, her deep amber eyes pleading. "Can't you see that the boy has suffered enough?"

The Chupacabra punched Ivan in the jaw and grabbed him by the collar. He looked down at him with disgust, his dark, cold glare gazing through Ivan's pale blue eyes. There had been a flicker of life that didn't belong there. Ivan Mikhailovich wasn't broken, not yet. He released his collar and thrust his foot into Ivan's gut. The Chupacabra then lifted his gaze, turning his attention to his wife. She wore a soft pink negligee that night. Her golden eyes swelled with fear and concern. Helen had lost weight; her hips were much thinner. Her face looked paler, with fear written all over it. Helen belonged to him, and she needed to be reminded of that.

"You're right," said The Chupacabra quietly. His lips slid into a terrifying grin. "He has suffered enough." He pulled a pistol out of his greatcoat. He took the safety off the weapon and aimed the gun at Ivan's head. He wrapped his index finger around the trigger.

Helen stepped in front of the pistol, her expression hardened.

"Get out of the way," said her husband emotionlessly.

Helen shook her head. "No. No!" she said, sounding half frightened and half hysterical.

Ivan lifted his head up, staring at Helen with a blank expression. He didn't know whether she was very brave for jumping in front of a weapon like that or very foolish.

"Get out of the way if you know what's good for you." Her husband warned.

"If you do this, I am going to walk out that door. I will take our son, and you will never see him again!" said Helen darkly.

The Chupacabra lowered the weapon and looked down. He balled his fists and rammed his foot into Ivan's chest.

"What's wrong with you?" roared Helen, her voice shaking with powerful emotions that The Chupacabra couldn't begin to grasp or understand.

"What's wrong with me?" said The Chupacabra, sounding appalled. "What's wrong with you? You're the one with the secrets and lies!" There was a fire in his voice. But Helen was used to being burned, and she couldn't feel the heat anymore.

"What are you talking about?" hissed Helen. Her tone was low and dominating, and her eyes flashed with anger. It took all she had in her not to grab a lamp and throw it against his head.

The Chupacabra's mind was no longer in the present. In that very room six years ago, a deal was made. His marriage, his career, and what was left of his sanity depended on those letters. And that man in front of him threatened to tear it all apart! Anxiety was lodged deep in his chest, and there was no digging it out. This was about matters created long before Ivan was born, things that he couldn't begin to understand.

Ivan's father had betrayed The Chupacabra. The pain cut deeper than any blade ever would. He could only imagine Mikhail's fingers running through

Helen's fawn hair, his lips exploring her mouth. The thought made The Chupacabra want to run his fists to the wall until they bled. Mikhail seduced his wife. And because of that, The Chupacabra nearly lost everything. As soon as The Chupacabra saw Ivan that night, somehow, it resurrected the anger and jealousy.

"You don't think that I don't know?" asked The Chupacabra, sounding hysterical. Anger and anxiety coursed through him. His finger fidgeted with the trigger on the gun.

Helen took a step back and held her breath. Her heart stopped for one terrifying moment. How did he discover her secret? All who knew what she did were either deep undercover or dead. "Do you know how crazy you sound?" she said.

"CRAZY. . . CRAZY. . . I'LL SHOW YOU CRAZY!" roared The Chupacabra; the rattling of his vocal cords shook the room.

Helen braced herself as her heart hammered harder.

"Can I say something?" said Ivan quietly, coughing through his words. The room became silent. Helen and The Chupacabra's eyes were locked on him, and he now had their full attention. "I was just the distraction."

Before The Chupacabra could finish raising an eyebrow, a truck crashed through the window. The sound of glass shattering echoed through the room. The Chupacabra pushed himself and Helen out of the way, his hand losing the grip on the gun.

The driver of the truck was a young woman. She was a nineteen, with a button nose, rosebud lips, and doll-like features. Her light blonde hair was straight, hanging below her back, and her eyes were the color of winter. She was a slender girl with beautiful curves and a small diamond-shaped birthmark on the corner of her right wrist. She wore a pintuck blouse and a dark peasant skirt. Her name was Anya, and she learned to cope with unspeakable things in her own way. Anya had scars that only she could see, and they were the battle scars of a warrior.

Her light blue eyes flashed in horror, her heart beating faster than ever before in her life. And for a moment, a slight grin appeared at the corner of her mouth.

As The Chupacabra and Helen lay on the carpet groaning in pain, Ivan had somehow managed to untie himself from behind. He made several steps towards the truck and exchanged glances with Helen. Helen turned her head around. Her husband had his back turned, wanting to hide his bruised and bloody face. Her eyes glared at the gun on the floor as she turned her attention back on Ivan. Her hand slid the weapon across the floor, and it stopped at Ivan's feet. Confused, he picked it up and gave her a perplexed look. Her eyes flashed with loving tenderness.

Ivan opened the truck door and climbed inside. Before he could sit, Anya backed out onto the lawn and gunned it over a curb. Ivan gazed at Anya from the passenger seat. He noticed her blood-stained fingernails. He could only guess how she acquired the stolen vehicle, but it didn't matter. That was the thing about Anya. No one knew what mattered until it was too late.

"Are you alright?" asked Ivan.

As her blue eyes fixated on the road, Anya took note of a hidden worry inside his voice. No man ever cared for her the way Ivan did.

Ivan cared for Anya much more than he'd like to admit, but he couldn't have her know that. She might walk out on him, too, just like everyone else did, and Ivan would have no one to blame but himself.

She quickly glanced at him, then settled her eyes back on the road. "I am fine," she promptly dismissed his question. She glanced at him again and noticed the blood and bruises. "But you're hurt."

"It's nothing. I've been through worse."

Anya pulled over and faced Ivan, and she suddenly popped his arm back into its socket. Ivan winced at the sick cracking sound and grunted in pain. With that taken care of, Anya headed back onto the road again.

He looked out the window, trying to distract himself from the pain.

Ivan was a nineteen-year-old soldier with a square jaw and soft blue eyes. His short hair appeared light brown, but when it grew out, it was a wave of chestnut curls. He wore a beige tunic jacket and breeches, with a dark belt around his waist. His leather boots were black and well-worn. Inside his pockets were two identification cards, one being fake, a single pill of potassium cyanide, and a letter that was never sent.

He must have had some sort of death wish. He defected the Bolshevik army last week, escaped Russia with forged papers, and never looked back. He took a train from Moscow to Kyiv, where he met up with an old friend and spent two days there before taking another train to Vienna. At the Viennese train station, Ivan was caught by his enemies. Instead of sending Ivan back to Moscow, they did something far worse. He was sent to von der Reis castle, where it appeared that Ivan had caught The Chupacabra in a bad mood.

"I am glad that we got this over with," he said.

As Anya continued racing down the street, a man suddenly jumped from a thick tree branch and landed in the bed of the truck. There was a loud bang as the man's boots made contact. He was tall, just over six feet. His face was diamond-shaped, with wide cheekbones and a defined jaw. His grey eyes were cold and captivating, and his thick, wavy jet-black hair was slicked back. His dark beard was carefully trimmed. He tipped the scale at over two hundred pounds of pure muscle. He wore a dark blue tunic with breeches and black boots. His name was Konstantin Petrovitch.

Upon hearing the loud bang, Anya jumped, fear twisting in her stomach. Ivan pulled out the gun and turned sharply. As soon as he saw the face of their hitchhiker, Ivan took a sharp breath of relief and stowed his weapon.

"Don't scare us like that!" shouted Ivan, his voice shaking with frustration.

Konstantin grinned, sticking his head through the back window. "I wanted to make a dramatic entrance," he said coolly.

"Did you get the key?" asked Ivan.

As Konstantin nodded, a tall man jumped in front of the truck. The man looked about forty years old, with a round face and an overgrown beard. His thick brown hair fell past his shoulders. His eyes were dark brown, and they flashed with insanity. He wore a bronze tunic and breeches, with dark boots.

Anya slammed on the breaks, sending Konstantin's body jerking forward, nearly losing his balance.

Ivan glared at the man. He looked oddly familiar. "Volkov?"

"There's no time to explain," said Volkov, his tone laced with urgency. He walked around the truck and climbed into the bed. "They are coming."

"Who?" asked Anya.

The sound of motorcycle engines blared in the distance. Bullets started flying. Konstantin and Volkov ducked for cover.

"Drive!" screamed Volkov.

Anya gunned the truck.

Volkov slipped his hand inside his pocket and pulled out a gun. He aimed and fired the weapon, hitting a man in the leg and knocking him off the motorcycle.

Konstantin covered his ears with his hands, formulating a plan. His thoughts were interrupted when a particular object tempted his eye. A stolen M1919 Browning machine gun was laid in the metal bed. He felt a maniacal grin cover his face. Dodging the storm of bullets, Konstantin crawled to the other side of the truck and quickly loaded the weapon. He aimed the gun at the motorcycle tires and pulled the trigger. A loud roar echoed around him. He felt a deep power rise inside him, and he liked it.

Ivan glanced in the side mirror to see a man in a motorcycle closely following beside the truck. Ivan had an idea. He climbed through the truck window, hanging his body halfway out.

"I am coming with you," said Anya.

Ivan turned his head, nearly speechless. This young woman had more nerve than any man he'd met. "No, it's too dangerous," he argued.

Anya's expression softened. "Trust me. I have an idea," she whispered, her blue eyes reassuring.

Ivan wanted to say, "You're the only one I have left. I can't lose you, too." But he didn't. He couldn't bring himself to say things like that anymore. "You better keep up with me," he said darkly.

Anya flashed Ivan a triumphant smile. "Yosef Volkov!" she shouted.

Volkov just fired his last bullet. "What?" he asked impatiently.

"Take the wheel," the young woman demanded.

Dodging the typhoon of bullets, Volkov climbed through the back window, over the seats, and grabbed the steering wheel from Anya's hands.

Ivan jumped out the window and mounted the motorcycle, knocking the rider off. Anya followed Ivan out the window, climbing on behind him. She positioned herself facing the cyclists. Lifting her skirt, she revealed a hidden gun in her garter holster. She grabbed the weapon, aimed, and fired several times. Three men dropped like flies off their motorcycles. Anya turned herself around and wrapped her arms around Ivan tightly. Ivan was, indeed, impressed. She was not the same helpless orphan he'd met in Ekaterinburg.

Konstantin gazed his eyes upon a tan tarp in the back of the truck. Curious, he lifted it to reveal a crate. He opened it and found several dozen sticks of dynamite.

Ivan maneuvered the motorcycle in front of the truck, and he felt Anya's grip tighten.

Konstantin lit the dynamite and threw it. A thunderous roar echoed in their ears, and the sound of the motors ceased. Konstantin's gray eyes gazed upon a pillar of fiery smoke and a dust cloud getting smaller in the distance.

After driving for roughly half an hour, they abandoned the truck on the side of the mountain road and walked to the home of a mute hunchback named Heidi.

Heidi lived alone near the mountains in a cabin her husband built many years ago. She got married in that house and gave birth to her two children there. Everyone she ever loved lived inside those walls, and now they were gone. The hollow trees appeared old but somehow were still standing, with icicles hanging from their thick branches. The roof of the cabin was slanted, forcing the door to hang from its hinges. The windows had small cracks. Inside Heidi's humble shack were only these things: a tiny kitchen with a wood-burning stove, a small wooden table with four chairs, three beds, and a small attic. It was isolated, the perfect place to lay low until the train left early that morning.

"Thank you," said Konstantin quietly in German.

The old woman gave him a sharp look and continued washing dishes.

Konstantin sat at the small wooden kitchen table, sipping on a cup of tea. The cold air cut through his nose and cheeks like daggers. He rubbed his hands together rapidly to keep them warm. There wasn't much heat in the little cabin, just a small fire burning on the kitchen stove.

Ivan limped to a small wooden bench with elegant carvings and collapsed on it. It hurt to breathe. His chest and back were tender, and he thought his ribs were going to crash into his lungs.

"Ivan," said Anya, coming behind him. "I am a nurse. Please, let me help you."

Ivan hesitated for a short moment and let out a small huff. He removed his shirt to reveal a beautiful eight-pack on his abdomen. His pectoral muscles were well-defined.

The sight took Anya's breath away, and her heart hammered hard against her chest. Then she noticed the massive purple and red bruises covering his body and frowned. She sat up close to Ivan and looked deep into his brilliant blue eyes, trying to ignore his beautiful chest, abdomen, and biceps. His pupils appeared normal, and there were no signs of a major concussion.

"Can you, please, tell me your name and the year?" asked Anya softly.

"My name is Ivan Mikhailovich. The year is 1919," Ivan said emotionlessly.

"Can you, please, move your arms, fingers, and legs?"

Ivan stretched, raising his arms in the air. He wiggled his fingers and moved his legs back and forth.

Anya gazed at him again and frowned. "I'm sorry," she muttered.

Ivan lowered his arms and asked, "For what?"

Anya placed her hand on Ivan's broken nose and pulled it down, popping the bone back into place. It made a loud sickly sound, and Ivan grunted in pain. Anya tossed Ivan a beautiful smile. "Again, I am terribly sorry," said Anya.

Ivan gazed back at Anya. Her smile was so gentle, and it was difficult to stay angry with her. She wrapped his arm and ribs into place with medical tape and checked his arms and legs for broken bones. Then she examined his back for signs of injury. "It looks like nothing else is broken," she said gently.

Ivan grabbed her hand and pulled her close. "Thank you," he said.

It appeared that Ivan wanted to say more, but then he pulled away. It was a nasty little habit of his, and it had been safer that way. Somehow though, Anya saw everything he didn't say in his eyes.

"I think it is me who should be thanking you," she said nervously, her whisper cold and low.

"Why?"

"Because you're the best thing that has ever happened to me," said Anya compulsively, then wishing that she hadn't. Ivan looked at her emotionlessly, studying her. Anya frowned and shrugged, slightly embarrassed. "I'm sorry. Excuse me."

As she turned away, Ivan grabbed her hand again. Anya looked back and stared at him, remembering the reasons why she fell in love with him. Ivan went still. It was a few more moments before he said, "What could you possibly be sorry for?"

I am sorry that I am not her, thought Anya. Instead, Anya glanced at him, with a hint of fear and love flashing across her eyes. Did it love to hurt, or did it hurt to love? She didn't know anymore.

"For being such a burden," said Anya, her voice shaking with raw emotion.

Those words twisted Ivan's heart into a deep knot. He stroked his fingers through her blonde hair, and with his other hand, he caressed her face. For a small moment, Anya thought that Ivan might kiss her.

"If you are a burden, then you are the best burden that I've ever had," teased Ivan.

Anya couldn't help but smile and gently punched Ivan in the arm. He chuckled and looked deep into her eyes.

I love you, thought Ivan.

Whether she knew it or not, her clear blue eyes flashed the words: *I love you, too.*

Ivan could not replace what he had with Anastasia. That would feel like a complete betrayal. He was still in love with her. Now, more than ever. But somehow, he loved Anya, too. If anything ever happened to her, he wouldn't be able to live with himself. There was something Ivan needed first before he could allow himself to feel that way again. He needed closure, and he could only find that in England.

Volkov smoked on a small bed. The air was cold, but he was scarcely aware of it. His thoughts were dancing elsewhere. He paid a heavy price for deserting, and it had cost him everything; his career and home. Fewer still knew, if not for Volkov's actions, three Latvian men would have been involved in the murder of innocent women and children. In the end, Volkov knew he had made the right choice. He could never go back to Russia. Not after what he did.

The image of his former lover flashed in his memory. Her name was Darya. No one knew how broken and damaged her mind truly was, but Volkov had no one else to blame but himself. Darya had the face of the most beautiful angel but the mind of a sinister devil. There were no lines she would not cross—none.

And the letter—he had almost forgotten.

Volkov slipped his hand down into his boot. The letter was still there. The guilt returned. Volkov could give the letter to Ivan now, but the man would probably shoot him in the face. No, he will have to wait until after England.

After all of this was over.

Chapter 3

Operation Yurovsky's Note

Miles away in the great city of Moscow, a telephone echoed into the darkness. A man named Yakov Yurovsky rolled out of bed. He was a tall, strapping, forty-one-year-old with wavy dark hair and piercing brown eyes. He had a diamond-shaped face and high cheekbones, dark bushy eyebrows, and a beard. Who could be calling at this hour, he thought. Yurovsky yawned deeply and answered the telephone, half-conscious. He expected to hear the rough voice of a man. Instead, he heard the soft but furious voice of a woman.

"I thought you told me that there would be no more incidents, Yakov," said Helen sharply.

"Helen," gasped Yurovsky.

At the sound of that name, the woman sleeping next to him opened her deep brown eyes slightly. Nothing good ever came from that name. Nadia listened carefully, pretending to be asleep.

Nadia was Yakov's wife. She was a short woman, with thick, long, dark hair that fell past her waist and a slender nose. She had a round face, elegant cheek structure, full crimson red lips, and a beautiful figure. She was thirty-eight years old but looked twenty younger than that.

"Ivan Mikhailovich showed up at the castle tonight and stole the key," explained Helen.

Yurovsky held his breath, his hand clenching a pillow.

Helen continued, "He escaped and should be long gone by now."

Yurovsky had two questions; why did Ivan Mikhailovich leave Russia days ago, and why was he just now hearing about it?

"You promised me that nothing like that fiasco in Ekaterinburg would happen again," said Helen darkly.

Yurovsky wanted to say that what happened in Ekaterinburg was not his fault. First, the men were drunk. And second, nothing could have been done to keep Ivan Mikhailovich away that night. He would have done anything to save the girl, even turn against his own comrades. And nothing could have prepared anyone for the bloodshed.

"Yes, I remember," whispered Yurovsky, his voice slightly brittle. "Had I known the boy was planning on leaving Russia and deserting the army, I would have taken extra precautions."

Helen sighed heavily. "That doesn't matter now. Long ago, you promised me one more thing, and the time has come for you to keep your promise."

Being a man of his word, Yurovsky nodded and swallowed hard. "Yes, but I hope you realize that this puts me in a very awkward position."

Nadia's hands clenched the covers, and she held her breath. She wanted to pound her fists against the bed in protest. Instead, she kept her mouth shut and listened. She'd done that for years, and tonight would not be any different. Fifteen years ago, shortly after she put on his ring, Yurovsky spent months in jail for opening his mouth. Then, he came back to her a different man. Nadia had friends and family members disappear for uttering a peep. They were dragged from their homes, never to be seen or heard from again. Naturally, Nadia kept her mouth shut.

"Then you know what to do," said Helen coolly.

Yurovsky sighed heavily, thinking of the four words he swore he would never say. "The Nightingale has fallen." Yurovsky then heard the telephone click. This could not be happening, he thought. How could he let this happen?

Nadia could feel tears begin to gather in her brown eyes. She kept waiting for the man she loved to return from prison, but there was some part of him that never left that jail cell. He became obsessed with communism and creating a different world for their children. A world other than the life he had as a glass maker's son. He was consumed by it, loved it like it was his own, shaped, and molded by it. This obsession had destroyed the boy she met in a clock shop and replaced him with someone she hardly knew.

Nadia rolled over, pretending to wake up from a deep sleep. "What's going on, Yakov?" she moaned, barely opening her eyes.

"Nothing to worry about, my love. Go back to sleep," he reassured. Yurovsky threw on a red bathrobe and kissed her forehead.

Nadia gave him a perplexed look and felt her heart sink. After a small moment of sadness, she was filled with anger. The time for silence was over. Nadia grabbed a pillow and beat her husband several times in the arm.

"Stop lying to me!" she screamed. "Stop lying!"

"Nadia!" gasped Yurovsky. "What's gotten into you?" His voice was full of worry and confusion.

"Ever since Ekaterinburg, every word I hear that comes out of your mouth is a lie," said Nadia darkly.

Yurovsky wrestled the pillow out of his wife's hands and tossed it onto the bed. He grabbed her shoulders and shook her gently. "Nadia, what do you expect me to do?" he scoffed. "I'm creating this life for you and our family to be better than the one I had."

"You didn't do this for your family. You did this for you and that fancy promotion." Nadia grabbed the pillow and hit him again – harder.

"I did what I had to do, Nadia!" shouted Yurovsky.

Nadia's eyes widened, and her heart pumped with fear.

There was a lethal silence.

Yurovsky was the son of a glassmaker and a Jew. He wanted a better life for his family. If he had to murder again to get it, so be it. His mother and father worked until their backs were nearly broken and their fingers bled, providing for their ten children. They lived in a crowded apartment above a butcher's shop that smelled of meat and blood. They did not choose that life; it was chosen for them. The employees were the ones working their fingers to the bone, so someone else could live better than they did. That made Yurovsky angry. The working class had the real power. And they were going to take it back, even if it was by force!

"I did what had to be done," he said again, bringing his voice down a notch. "I'm sorry you're ashamed of it, but. I'm not proud of it either. And I'm sorry for raising my voice."

It took all Nadia had in her not to cry. "I am tired of pretending that things never happened, and words were never said," she said, her voice shaking.

"After tonight, my love, I am going to make things right."

A thousand thoughts danced inside Nadia's head as she saw her husband walk out the door. He husband looked the same, with the same dark chocolate eyes and curly hair. He had the same nose and smile. But somehow, it was not him. Maybe he never changed at all. Perhaps, he was simply better at hiding his thoughts.

Loving a broken and damaged man was the bravest thing you could ask a woman to do. But the most challenging part was not staying; it was leaving. There had been a part of Nadia that stayed because she was still in love with that young, ambitious man she met in that clock shop when she was eighteen years old. And the other part of her did not have the strength to leave.

She rolled over again and threw the covers over her head. As soon as she heard the bedroom door shut, she cried herself to sleep. It wouldn't be the first time, and certainly not the last.

Frightened, Yurovsky walked briskly to his office, where he emptied out his desk. His dark eyes rapidly skimmed through document after document. Desperately, he searched for evidence proving Ivan Mikhailovich was in Ekaterinburg during the summer of 1918. Yurovsky burned photographs, diary entries, and official reports holding precious secrets that linked Ivan to the murder. Next, Yurovsky would travel to St. Petersburg and destroy all evidence of Ivan Mikhailovich there, too. By the time he was through, it would be like the boy never existed, and his obligation to protect him would be done.

The mission last year nearly destroyed him. It was not entirely his fault that things went wrong. The room was small, and the windows could not conceal the noise. There were a lot of questions from the locals the next morning, and he did not have time to answer them all. The firing occurred in chaotic and disorganized circumstances. The men were young, incompetent, and drunk. And one man had the audacity to bring Yurovsky only one shovel.

He probably would have killed that man, too, if he weren't so busy cleaning up his mess. Yurovsky had a new mission tonight that had been in the works for years: protect Ivan Mikhailovich and take down the most powerful man in the world, The Chupacabra.

After he returned home, there was a hard pounding against the front door. Yurovsky jumped. His eyes glanced at the clock. It was three hours after midnight. Who would come to his home at this ungodly hour? It did not matter. He was not taking any chances. He grabbed the Brownie pistol on the desk. With his gun aimed, he prowled to the front door, hiding in the darkness. As his hand turned the doorknob, he held his breath and felt his finger shaking on the trigger. He opened the door and took a sharp breath of relief. Yurovsky stowed his weapon.

"Expecting someone else?" his guest asked.

"Filipp," whispered Yurovsky in relief.

Filipp Goloshchyokin was a fifty-something-year-old man with thin gray hair, light blue eyes, and a salt and pepper beard. His nose was long and slender. He wore a heavy trench coat with black leather boots that night. Nothing happened in Moscow without him knowing about it.

He pushed the door open, letting himself into Yurovsky's house. He stood in the foyer, with his arms folded and a smug look on his face. It appeared that he did not plan to stay long. There were too many spies these days.

"A train leaves in one hour, and we're going to be on it," said Filipp quickly, his deep blue eyes full of concern. "Don't worry about getting dressed or packing. Everything you need is already on the train."

"Let me at least get my coat," said Yurovsky quietly. He walked to the closet, slipped on his trench coat, and buttoned up. "How long will we be gone, Filipp?"

Filipp stared blankly at the window, watching the snow falling to the earth. He turned to Yurovsky, his gaze hardened. "For as long as it takes."

Yurovsky looked at Filipp nervously and shut the closet door. He grabbed a pen and scribbled a small note in a notebook. He explained to his wife that he left on business unexpectedly and would be gone for a couple of days. Yurovsky opened the front door and followed his former boss to the sidewalk. His dark eyes noticed a taxi parked by the curb. The driver had been following him since he left work.

"We'll be walking to the train station," retorted Filipp.

Yurovsky shrugged his shoulders. The train station was only a ten-minute walk from his house. He followed his comrade down the sidewalk and onto another street. Suddenly, Yurovsky let out a sharp breath and swallowed hard.

"Does the boy know?" he asked compulsively. A few moments later, he wished that he had said nothing.

"If the boy knew, Yakov," said Filipp. He stopped and turned to Yurovsky and gave him a sharp look. "Then he would never have gone to von der Reis castle." Filipp continued to walk quickly down the sidewalk and turned down another street, and Yurovsky followed, his strides swift.

Yurovsky took another sharp breath. "Does The Chupacabra know that—"

Filipp nodded slightly.

Yurovsky's heart almost stopped, and he held his breath. "What?"

Yurovsky remembered the promise that he made to Helen a long time ago; he would protect the boy at all costs. If The Chupacabra knew about their dirty little secret, then Ivan would be in more danger than he was with what happened in Ekaterinburg. Filipp made that same promise.

"How could he possibly know?" asked Yurovsky, his brown eyes flashing with horror.

It was a simple answer.

"Gabriel."

"Gabriel," repeated Yurovsky. That did not surprise him in the slightest. Whatever love and respect Gabriel had for his father was gone. "How does Gabriel know?"

"That doesn't matter. If he could find out, then anyone could." Filipp paused for a few moments collecting his thoughts. "We need to destroy every single piece of information that Helen. . . you know."

The two men turned down another street. There was another promise that Yurovsky made to Helen. Ivan could never learn about that cursed sheet of paper tucked away in City Hall. It unlocked a secret that must always remain buried. And it must be destroyed.

"I agree," said Yurovsky, stroking his beard. He looked at Filipp sharply. Since they met, there was a question nagging Yurovsky that he never had the courage to ask. He cleared his throat. "How do you know Helen?"

Filipp stopped again. For a small moment, there was an awkward silence. "I used to clean her teeth," he muttered as he walked across the street.

Yurovsky quickly darted behind him. "There has to be more to the story than that!"

"Well," said Filipp nervously. He continued, "Helen is an extraordinary woman with beautiful teeth." Filipp turned to Yurovsky. "How long have you known Helen?"

Yurovsky thought about it. He met Helen in Berlin many years ago. After his second banishment, he found himself in financial hardship, and Helen was kind enough to loan him money. He used that money to open a photography studio and had provided well for his family. It was through Helen that he met The Chupacabra.

"I've known Helen for fifteen years."

"Then you know what she will do to us if we fail," said Filipp sharply. "Where is Ivan?"

"On the run," recalled Yurovsky.

"Good. That means he has not killed him yet," said Filipp. Filipp was tempted to ask where Ivan might be. It would be better if he did not know, so no one would be able to torture the information out of him.

The two men had arrived at the train station. Filipp glanced at the watch around his wrist, his blue eyes squinting through the darkness. It was already twenty minutes after three.

"We could just be walking into a big trap," scoffed Yurovsky.

"Oh," A wicked grin came across Filipp's face. "I am counting on it."

A couple of hours later, a demon emerged from the shadows and crawled out of society's ashes, hungry for his own slice of revenge. Scarred with the memories of hell, the angel of death raged war against the enemies of God. The passionate hatred he had fought hard to bury had been summoned, and the demon had been called to battle once again.

The demon was Borsylov Vashlyshyn. He was a thirty-year-old Ukrainian with dark blond hair, piercing blue eyes, and a scar that went from the top of his head to the bottom of his lip. He wore a gray flannel suit, with a red tie and expensive leather shoes. No one could have picked a man who hated Ivan more, but he did follow orders.

He boarded the seven o'clock train. His orders were simple; Find Ivan and bring him back to Moscow, alive.

The image of the Tsar's lifeless body flashed in his mind. A devilish grin slid across his face. Vashlyshyn knew the sins committed in Ekaterinburg were for a holy purpose. Forgiveness was assured.

The demon traced the scar from the top of his head to the bottom of his lip and felt a flash of anger. Vashlyshyn imagined repaying Ivan the favor.

Chapter 4

Operation Wolf

Darya Lisanova had two great loves: her work and a man named Yosef Volkov. The first great love of her life was, indeed, her work. Darya Lisanova had been a private detective for the past twenty-five years. It was a great excuse to push things out of her head that did not belong there. You can call it her insurance policy. Her second greatest love was Volkov. For almost twenty years, she tried to push that man out of her head but somehow couldn't bring herself to do it. After leaving Ekaterinburg the second and final time, she thought she would never see him again. But exactly nineteen years later, on the other side of the dining car, was the only man she ever loved. He was also the man she betrayed.

The early morning was dark and crisp, with snow falling lightly on the ground. The train moved rapidly against the tracks. The ride had been bumpy, but it didn't matter to Darya as she planned on getting off somewhere soon. She sat awkwardly in one of the dining chairs, with her red lips closely pressed together. Volkov preferred standing, with his arms crossed and a hardened expression on his face. He had been in deep thought.

"Please, say something," whispered Darya, her bright green eyes pleading.

Darya was a forty-one-year-old woman with the emotional capacity of someone much younger. She had a tall, slim body, with dark brown waves that hung past her hips. She wore a blue coat that morning and a pair of black boots. Overall, she was a beautiful, manipulative, and dangerously damaged woman.

Volkov had nothing to say to her. This woman ripped out his heart, abandoning him half a lifetime ago. He never thought he would ever see her ever again. What do you say to a woman like that?

"I honestly don't know what to say," he sighed heavily.

Darya leaned forward, her eyes begging again. "Say anything," she cried, her soft voice shaking with emotion.

"What would you like me to say?" asked Volkov, his voice low and quiet.

Darya honestly didn't know either. She felt the anxiety rise and wrapped her arms protectively around her. For a few moments, she lost control. Darya balled her fists and grunted loudly. "Be angry with me! Hate me! Throw something at me! Scream at me! Anything!" Darya's heart hammered quickly, tears gathering in her eyes. "PLEASE, say something."

Volkov made quick paces towards her and stopped midway. Volkov stared at her piercing green eyes, something he thought he'd never see again. "I thought you were dead," he said quietly. He spoke like he wasn't interested.

"I am dead," whispered Darya, her lips breaking into a tearful smile. "I have been dead for a very long time." She buried her face in her hands. No one knew how broken Darya's mind was until it was too late.

When Darya discovered she was pregnant twenty years ago, it pushed her over the edge. Volkov would not understand until he met Anna, her other personality. The weaker side of her. Then maybe he would understand, just a little. Anna had been pregnant before—it was before the child was cut out of her abdomen by her jealous stepmother. Anna's father was a heavy drunk who did terrible things when under the influence. After Anna lost her child, she met Darya. She was much stronger than her. Darya was going to protect her from now on. But after Darya found out she was expecting Volkov's child, she left Anna for a while. Anna gave birth, faked the death of her child, called things off with Volkov, and left Ekaterinburg without another word. When Darya returned, it was too late.

"Why did you do it?" asked Volkov.

Darya sniffled and lifted her head. "I was a different woman then. I was scared, and I wasn't ready to be a mother." Darya covered her mouth with her hand and sobbed. Volkov knelt and took her hand. As soon as she pulled herself back together, she opened her mouth and continued, "I am so terribly sorry that I did this to you," she whispered tearfully. Volkov felt her grip on his hand tighten. "If I could go back in time and do it all over again." *Things wouldn't have turned out any different,* she thought.

Volkov gazed into her watery green eyes. Then he looked at the tears dripping down her face and wiped them away. He moved a strand of dark hair behind her ear and lifted her chin. "I spent many years hurting, and it was like a big rock inside my chest. One day, I woke up, and the rock was gone. I forgave you a long time ago, Darya."

"Really?"

Volkov nodded. "I am not the one who you should be apologizing to," he said darkly, letting her hand slip through his fingers.

Darya's heart sank. Her mind drifted to the past again, although they weren't her memories anymore. Anna's child had a birthmark in the small shape of a diamond on the edge of her right wrist. Anna had only known her daughter for a couple of hours before switching her with another baby that simply forgot how to breathe. Anna buried the baby a couple of miles away from Ekaterinburg and never returned. Whatever happened to Anna's child, Darya did not know. But she had nightmares about that night ever since.

"What was it?" asked Volkov, his voice masking emotion.

Darya sniffled again, snapping out of her trance. She eyed him carefully, her emerald eyes filled with confusion.

"The baby, what was it?"

The image of a baby girl flashed in her mind; her daughter, her sweet, tiny, perfect daughter. Perhaps Anna made the right choice, after all. Darya would have had to care for the baby. And unfortunately, she was born with no maternal instinct. But somehow, the baby was just as much her child as it was Anna's. But how could someone so broken love something so perfect?

"A girl," whispered Darya, tossing Volkov a genuine smile. "It was a girl."

Volkov felt a strange sense of relief. He had a daughter. And he had so many questions. What color were her hair and eyes? Did she look like him at all? Did she have his smile? How could he walk around for nineteen years and not know that he had a daughter? He had been alone for so long. He'd run away from home when he was fourteen as his Russian father beat him. His Latvian mother had been a drinker since he was born. One day, Volkov packed a bag and never looked back. He lived on the streets, joined gangs, and somehow became a goon for Gabriel. Volkov never felt at home. He had always been cold and lonely. But right now, he didn't feel alone in the world anymore.

"Do you ever regret loving me?" asked Darya bluntly.

Volkov fell back on a chair and looked at her lovingly. "I used to think that loving you was the biggest mistake of my life—it wasn't," he said frankly. "I don't regret loving you, and I never will, not for a second. I regret not being the man you needed me to be when you needed it. That's what I regret the most." Darya listened, soaking in every sound and syllable. "I am grateful that I met you when I did. You were just what I needed at the time, even if it didn't last long," he said.

Darya reached over and grabbed his hand, squeezing it gently. She smiled tearfully at him, with tears streaming down her face. Volkov kissed her hand. He stared deeply into the green eyes of his former lover, his heart beating quickly. There had been a small part of him that never stopped loving her.

Darya looked down and frowned. "But this is not why I have come."

"I know," said Volkov, his tone hardened.

Darya let her hand slip through his fingers. "I need your help," she sighed. "A woman's life is on the line, and you're the only one I can trust." My client—." Darya stopped herself, choosing her words carefully. "My client would like this woman found before—."

Volkov looked at her sharply. "Who is this woman?"

"Her name is Greta. She played a dangerous role in Operation Dragonfly. She knows what it is, and she knows how to stop it. And she knows who is behind it," said Darya, her eyes flashing with urgency. "We need to find her before someone else does."

There were only a handful of people alive who knew the existence of Operation Dragonfly. Volkov was one of them, but he did not know much. It was made to do one thing; kill.

Volkov got up and paced the floor, muttering things to himself in Latvian. He turned to Darya and sighed heavily, "This is suicide."

"If we don't do this, then thousands will die."

"Why should I ever trust you again?" asked Volkov slowly.

"You can't," muttered Darya.

Volkov sighed deeply. There was no reason why he should ever trust her again. He already had one mission on his plate: find Ivan and bring him to Gabriel. If he failed Gabriel again, he would be killed. But no matter how hard he tried, he had a hard time saying no to Darya.

"There is something else you should probably know," whispered Darya fearfully. "Broyslov Vasylyshyn is on the train."

One hour left.

The demon swallowed hard, the Vodka burning down his throat. He held his cigarette in between his fingers and took another drag. Vashlyshyn had hunted down his prey ferociously, leaving a trail of blood behind him. One hour left before revenge was paid.

Vashlyshyn stared into the mirror and straightened his bowtie. His lifeless brown eyes gazed at his reflection, and he glared at his scar. He had been the most handsome man that came out of Ukraine before his looks were stolen from him. Ivan Mikhailovich was going to pay for it. Then when he was through with Ivan, he would take back what rightfully belonged to him. He thought about Anya and that little souvenir he'd given her. Soon, he'd be reunited with Anya and his child. And then, they could finally be a family.

Vashlyshyn reached for his revolver on the dresser. His cold eyes glared down at the V carved on the bottom of the handle. He felt a sense of pride that he had used that gun to place a bullet in the Tsar's torso. Vashlyshyn stowed it away in his coat and took another drag of his cigarette. He walked out of his compartment and slammed the door behind him. He followed the jazz music, the beautiful women, and the smell of expensive champagne—the demon's hour had come.

One hour left before revenge was served cold.

Chapter 5

Operation Shattered Glass

Ivan Mikhailovich was tired. He was tired of quietly dying every day, and it was the kind of tiredness that sleep couldn't fix.

He walked down the train corridor, the wheels rattling against the tracks beneath his feet. He had the strong urge to smoke, stopped, and reached inside his coat for a cigarette and his lighter.

Just as his fingertips touched the lighter, a woman brushed past him, bumping into his shoulder. She was a short young woman with long copper hair, and she wore a brown wool sweater, a velvet skirt, and a hat.

Ivan looked at her darkly and thought about saying something about how she had bumped into him. Just as he took a step forward, the woman turned her head. Ivan took a step back. His heart dropped into his stomach.

Anastasia.

Ivan closed his eyes briefly before opening them again. He realized that he was dreaming of her again.

"Ivan," said a voice from behind.

Startled, Ivan jumped. He put his fists up and turned sharply, his heart beating rapidly. It was Konstantin, and he stood still like a mountain, his face unreadable. Ivan took a breath of relief and put his fists down.

Konstantin put his hand on Ivan's shoulder, his eyes flashing with regret. "Ivan, there is something that I should have told you a long time ago," said Konstantin, his tone low and serious.

Ivan swallowed hard.

Konstantin reached inside his coat and pulled out a crumpled piece of paper folded into four parts. Ivan grabbed the note and read it:

If the key is in your possession, then The Chupacabra has found me. I am afraid my desire to reunite with my family may have placed them in extreme danger—The Bolsheviks are now in bed with The Chupacabra. If I know my enemy well enough, they may try to go after me by recruiting my youngest son. I have no one to blame but myself, but may I ask one more favor?

If you could watch over and protect Ivan, I would be grateful.

Mikhail Mikhailovich

Ivan reread it and felt nauseated. The rough train ride didn't help. "Where did you get this?" he asked, his blue eyes flashing with anger. Konstantin didn't answer, and Ivan felt anger boil inside him. "Where did you get this?" he shouted. Konstantin gave Ivan a blank stare. Ivan grabbed Konstantin by the collar and slammed him against the wall. "I will not ask a third time," said Ivan slowly. "Where did you get this?"

"I have a contact," muttered Konstantin.

Ivan let go of his collar. "A contact," he repeated. "Who?"

Again, Konstantin didn't answer.

"Was it that Countess woman?" asked Ivan darkly.

Konstantin's silence seemed to give the answer away. Ivan turned and walked quickly to the Countess' train compartment. Countess Sofia Volkensky was Konstantin's new special friend. After Ivan twisted her arm a little, she agreed to finance the trip and accompany him to London. Konstantin made quick strides, trying to keep up with him. He grabbed ahold of Ivan's wrist, swinging him around. They locked eyes and Ivan and gave him a testing glare.

"Ivan, be kind," warned Konstantin.

"You're not my father!" Ivan scoffed, snatching his hand away, and continued to walk down the corridor.

Konstantin followed close behind. "Ivan, I mean it."

Ivan ignored him as his mind traveled to a different time.

Spring was disguised as winter.

Ivan was an eleven-year-old boy. It was a critical age when a boy needed his father. He woke up early that day because loud, heavy footsteps trudged past his door. Ivan rolled out of bed and darted downstairs. He saw his father with one foot out the door. There was a suitcase in one hand and a train ticket in the other. It appeared that he might be leaving for a while. Ivan took a step forward. As he was closing the door, he saw Ivan. Mikhail would never forget the look in his son's eyes; horror, regret, betrayal. Mikhail knew he had let his boy down. For a small moment, Ivan thought his father would stay. Instead, he left on the train that morning and never returned.

Svetlana, Ivan's fragile mother, screamed for hours after her husband left. She had a bottle of vodka in one hand and a letter from Mikhail in the other. You could walk a mile away from the house and still hear her screaming. She cried until she felt her lungs would burst.

Konstantin stepped in front of the door, blocking Ivan's way.

"Move out of the way," warned Ivan.

Konstantin would not budge.

Ivan pulled out his gun and pointed it at Konstantin's torso. "Don't make me do this, Konstantin," begged Ivan. "Please, move."

"No."

Ivan released the safety on his weapon, but Konstantin quickly kicked the pistol out of Ivan's hand before he could fire. Ivan threw a punch, but Konstantin ducked and tackled him to the ground. Konstantin pinned him down in a leglock and a headlock to the point where Ivan could not move.

"I am not going to let you in there when you are like this."

Ivan snarled. "I am not going to hurt her. I just want to talk to her."

"It's not her that I'm worried about, my friend."

As Ivan struggled to break free, Konstantin's grip tightened, though he didn't know how much longer he could hold Ivan down. And if he tensed up his grip any more, he might kill him. Finally, Ivan relaxed.

"I am going to let go now, my friend," said Konstantin slowly. "You are going to go in there, and you will be calm and respectful. And if you aren't, I am going to make you wish you had shot me."

Ivan nodded firmly. Konstantin released his grip and stood up. Ivan gave Konstantin a perplexed look. For a small moment, he felt like he had an older brother again. Konstantin took Ivan's hand and pulled him up off the floor. He picked up the gun and handed it back to him. Ivan took a sharp breath and stowed the weapon away.

He then opened the door to the private compartment. A woman reclined on a velvet sofa, pouring herself an expensive glass of tea as the smell of jasmine filled the room.

The woman looked up and grinned, bringing the cup to her ruby red lips. "Ivan, what a pleasant surprise," she purred.

Ivan took a step forward and looked at her sharply. "Where is my father?"

Meanwhile, Anya walked around the train alone watching the way the sunrise illuminated the coach floor.

Vashlyshyn's time had come. As the Ukrainian demon moved through the shadows, he cursed the lives of his enemies. He'd waited for this moment for many months, shivering in the cold, starving for the fresh taste of blood. After today, his holy vengeance would be paid.

Anya stopped. There was a familiar smell that danced in the air. Cologne;

it smelled of pine and the devil. The image of a Ukrainian demon flashed in her mind.

"Oh, no," she muttered. *How did he find me?* She thought.

Suddenly, Vashlyshyn came up behind Anya and grabbed her in a headlock, his arm squeezing tightly around her neck. Before she could react, she heard the click of a pistol.

"Hello, darling," he said with a menacing smile. "Did you miss me?"

"You?" whispered Anya.

Vashlyshyn swung her around and placed the gun against her waist. "How's my son doing, darling?" he boasted.

He suddenly released her head, moving the gun barrel to her chest. Anya slapped him in the face so hard that his head swung to the side. Vashlyshyn looked at her with his coal-like, lifeless eyes and smiled with menace. He slammed her body against the wall and laughed hard.

"Look at me."

Anya's eyes stared at the red carpet. She'd rather die than let him have the satisfaction of winning at his own game.

"Look at me!" Vashlyshyn swung his hand back and slammed her head against the wall. Anya lifted her gaze, revealing a perfectly red handprint stamped across her face. Vashlyshyn smiled. "Better. This is how it's going to work," he explained. "We're going to get nice and comfortable for a while until Ivan Mikhailovich finds you."

Anya tried to break loose, but his grip tightened. She moaned in pain, summoned all the strength left in her, and smashed her heel into his inner foot. She thrust her elbow upward, breaking his nose. Then she clenched her fist, striking his groin hard.

Vashlyshyn released Anya as he screamed in pain.

Anya made a run for it.

Vashlyshyn's evil smile flashed again. "I like it when they run," he said to himself.

The demon darted after her. At that moment, the hunt had begun, and his sacred vengeance had come.

Ivan stared blankly at Sofia, his mind traveling back to a small village on the Lena River called Yakutsk. There sat a wholesome wooden house surrounded by the permanently frozen tundra. As winter howled, snow danced in the bitter wind. The firewood froze in the hearth. Ivan shivered and sniffled inside a fur blanket with his brother and sister. The cold carved into their skin, but no one had been thinking of the arctic winter and runny noses. Babushka had been cooking reindeer meat in the kitchen, and its delicious smell filled the air.

Those were the times when things were simple, but those times were now gone.

Ivan never wanted to become a soldier. He wanted to become an artist. He watched his mother, Svetlana, paint for hours. She had taught him how to paint with different colors and textures. But Mikhail Mikhailovich was made from a tougher material than his gentle wife. He molded his son like clay, twisting him from the root, creating the perfect machine. Ivan had been trained in the art of deception—and codebreaking.

After Mikhail set his family aside like a forgotten newspaper, Svetlana married the village drunk who later shot and killed Ivan's brother in a state of inebriation. The next day, Svetlana's new husband disappeared and was found dead several days later, face down in the snow. And then Ivan's sister died from a botched abortion. The grief landed Svetlana in a mental institution.

Leon Trotsky, who had just been given command over the Bolshevik army, was Ivan's savior. He found and recruited Ivan into the red army, and Ivan never looked back. There was nothing—no one—to return to. Trotsky used Ivan as his tool of revenge. He played Ivan like a fine-tuned fiddle, breaking codes and foiling the plans of his enemies. Ivan had become a soldier—a Bolshevik. He was loved for it, hated for it, envied, even respected for it. Stripped of his desire to paint, Ivan slowly became a different person: a hero, a traitor, a monster, and a coward.

"I think you should be the one to tell him, Sofoshka," said Konstantin quietly.

Countess Sofia Volkensky was a dangerously beautiful woman with wild raven curls that dangled below her waist. Her grey eyes were cold, and her lips were red and intoxicating. She wore a lace gown with sequins perfectly stitched into floral designs onto the fabric. The dress came alive with every step she took. The lace and sequins tightly clung to her bust line, accentuating her tiny figure.

Sofia nodded nervously and paced the floor, not sure what to say or how to explain. It was a long story that had started long before Ivan was born. And it was far from over. Where to begin?

"Tell me what?" asked Ivan.

Sofia turned and looked at Ivan; her expression was unreadable. Suddenly, her hands went cold. She rubbed them together, thinking of the right words. Sofia hated the cold, and her hands were always cold—her heart was cold as well. Of course, life had made her that way.

"Your father took something from The Chupacabra, and he wants it back," said Sofia slowly.

"What did he take?"

Sofia ignored him, her eyes gazing upon a black and white photograph of her father. Her fingertips touched her father's face with loving sadness. It had been one year since her father's sudden death. It was amazing what a year could do to a person. Sofia never stopped grieving. She grieved for a man she barely knew and the relationship they never had. She abandoned all feelings and wrapped herself in a blanket of grief.

When her father went to St. Petersburg, he returned home a different man. Arguments erupted, doors slammed shut, and her parents slept in separate rooms. He became easily angered, kept to himself, and ignored his wife and daughter. Sofia tried to be loved by her father and, most importantly, keep loving him after getting hurt countless times. It was hard for her to understand. *Why did he stop loving her?*

Sofia turned to Ivan and said, "He stole the plans for a deadly bomb and locked it away in a safety deposit box in London."

The story didn't make any sense to Ivan. What was his father doing with plans for a bomb?

"The key we stole the other night. . ." Ivan glanced over at Konstantin, then back to Sofia. "Was that. . ." Ivan fell back on an armchair, Sophia's words slowly sinking in. "Why would my father do that?" asked Ivan, his blue eyes begging for answers.

Indeed, the key did unlock that safety box tucked away somewhere in a bank in a small corner of London. The Chupacabra had killed to get his hands on it. Once he had it, he would sell it to the highest bidder. Sofia could not let that happen. In exchange for Sofia's help to get close to the Dowager Empress, Ivan needed to break into von der Reis castle and steal the key. Sofia couldn't explain everything. The knowledge that she had would get them all killed.

"Because," she sighed deeply. Her thoughts were buried with her father. "The Chupacabra killed someone Mikhail deeply cared about."

"Who?" asked Ivan.

"It was his oldest son, Yuri."

Ivan's eyes widened, flashing in anger. "His what?" he stood up, shaking his head. "I don't have an older brother named Yuri." How could he have an older brother that he never knew about? The thought was absurd.

Sofia's light grey eyes flashed with a mixture of pity and sadness. Yuri had been at the wrong place at the wrong time. That bomb was meant for Mikhail, not Yuri. "How well did you know your father, Ivan?" she asked slowly.

Ivan's heart pounded, and his breathing accelerated. He felt a surge of panic, and he thought that he was on the verge of having a heart attack.

"I need a drink," he said, his voice full of panic.

Ivan eyed the alcohol cabinet and darted towards it. He opened the cabinet doors and poured himself a glass of Mamont vodka. He swallowed it all in one gulp. There was a subtle vanilla flavor with a fruity after-taste. Ivan surprisingly liked it. He thought about his whole life being a lie and laughed hysterically for a moment. Then, he felt a flash of rage and smashed the glass against the mirrored wall. Something had taken over, and he lost control. He grabbed another glass and threw it across the room. He then grabbed the bottle of vodka and slammed it against a mirror.

Sofia brought her tea to her lips and swallowed, glaring at Ivan. She set the cup down on a table and pointed her index finger at him, glaring darkly. "Need I remind you that you are my guest, and this is my private compartment," she said, her voice heated. "I would hope that you would show a little more restraint and respect."

Ivan scowled at the shattered glass scattered across the floor. He felt just as broken. He turned his attention to Konstantin, his heart beating faster. "The day I met Trotsky," he began, holding back a fit of seething anger he never knew existed, "that was no accident." Konstantin didn't answer. Ivan took deep breaths, on the verge of losing it again. "Where is my father?" he cried, his blue eyes begging for answers.

The Countess leaned forward. Her cold eyes softened and beamed with hope. Ivan noted they were the most beautiful eyes he'd ever seen; brave, virtuous, and broke. But they were not broken. They were the eyes of a warrior—the eyes of Mother Russia herself.

"Your father is in—"

Suddenly, the door flung open. It was Volkov, his face full of horror. "Where's Anya?" he asked, his eyes darkening with fear.

Konstantin looked perplexed. "Somewhere on the train," he said slowly.

Volkov cursed in Russian.

"Why?" asked Ivan fearfully. "What's going on?

"Ivan!" screamed Anya, her heart beating quickly.

Ivan let out a breath of relief. "Anya," he whispered.

She darted inside the private compartment and then stopped halfway, realizing she had given Vashlyshyn exactly what he wanted. She had led the demon right to Ivan. Anya gazed at Ivan fearfully. "No," she cried.

Ivan gathered Anya in his arms. He noticed the hand mark and purple bruise on her face, and a flash of anger surged through him. He was going to murder the man responsible for this. Anya shook in his arms, and her breaths were quick and heavy.

"Who did this?" asked Ivan angrily.

"He is here," she said hysterically. "He is here."

"Who's here?"

"Hello, Ivan Mikhailovich," said the voice of a demon.

Ivan's heart dropped. *No, not that*, thought Ivan. *Anything but that*. How did he find them?

"You have stolen some of my property." Vashlyshyn glanced at Anya and gave her a wicked smile. "I want it back."

"You're not taking her anywhere," said Ivan.

"That remains to be seen." Vashlyshyn looked around the room. His eyes noticed Volkov, the traitor who couldn't shoot a bullet to save his country. He glanced over at Konstantin, another traitor. He seemed to have skipped over Sofia, pretending that she was not in the room. He stepped inside the private compartment where Ivan pulled out a gun and aimed it at his torso.

"This is somehow familiar. Where have I seen this before?" Vashlyshyn gave Ivan a devilish grin. "Oh, that's right! The night that you killed the Grand Duchess."

"Ivan, what is he talking about?" whispered Anya fearfully.

Vashlyshyn continued, stepping an inch closer, "She is dead because of you. You killed her."

"Shut up!" said Ivan.

Vashlyshyn ignored him and took another step closer. "She would be alive today if it weren't for you. You failed her."

Ivan released the safety. "I said shut up!"

Konstantin grabbed Ivan's arm. "Ivan, don't. He is baiting you, my friend."

Ivan looked into the black eyes of his enemy. They were dark and cold, with not a speck of humanity left. Perhaps, he was staring at his future if he pulled the trigger. He lowered his weapon.

Vashlyshyn smirked. "I hope to see you soon, Ivan." He made a run for it down the corridor.

Ivan had held his anger in for too long, and now it was rearing its ugly head with renewed strength and ferocity. He could not let that demon get away. Ivan darted down the hall, and Konstantin dashed after him. He chased Vashlyshyn to the luggage car, but he jammed the door before Ivan could make it through. His hand jiggled the doorknob, but it would not open. He slammed his foot against the door and cursed in Russian. Ivan turned, glaring darkly at Konstantin.

"Don't try to stop me!"

"I am not here to stop you, my friend. I am here to help you."

Ivan's face froze. That he was not expecting. At the corner of Ivan's mouth, a malevolent grin appeared.

With his gun at aim, Konstantin released the safety and kicked the door down. Vashlyshyn stood on the balcony, tossing the two men a playful smile. Then he hurried up the ladder, climbing to the train's roof. Konstantin and Ivan rushed up after him, hoping to catch him before it was too late.

As the train rapidly kept its pace, Vashlyshyn stood on the other side of the roof, with a psychotic smile plastered on his face. The demon appeared pleased with himself. He had served his master well today. He had successfully hunted down his prey, but the hunt was far from over. Now it was time to pay.

"You have run out of places to hide!" shouted Ivan.

Vashlyshyn ignored Ivan. He appeared to be in his own little world. "You should have never left Russia, you know. Now, someone might get hurt," he sighed.

Ivan took a step forward and glared at him sharply. "Who sent you?"

Vashlyshyn turned sharply, glancing over his shoulder. His heavy, repulsive laughter thundered across the frozen landscape. "I thought you could tell me that."

Ivan stomped his foot and balled his fists in frustration. "Enough games," he roared gruffly.

"What games?" asked Vashlyshyn innocently, sounding almost surprised.

Ivan slipped his index finger around the trigger of his weapon.

"No. Can't you see that he is baiting you again?" whispered Konstantin. "You need to be smart about this."

Ivan reluctantly lowered the weapon. "Why are you here?" asked Ivan calmly.

"Isn't it obvious? I'm here for you," the demon declared, his tone hardened. "And you and I will be on the next train back to Moscow."

"I am afraid that's not going to happen," remarked Ivan.

Vashlyshyn felt a heavy grin slide over his face. He pulled out a knife that had been concealed in his sleeve. "I was kind of hoping you might say that," he said slowly. His orders were more than clear: bring Ivan back to Moscow alive. He will keep Ivan Mikhailovich alive, but just barely.

Konstantin noticed the knife, and his eyes flashed with horror.

Vashlyshyn threw the knife in the air.

Konstantin jumped, pushing Ivan out of the way. The blade tightly caressed the side of Konstantin's face, leaving a little scratch. As Ivan tried to stand up, the train hit a large bump on the tracks, causing him to lose his balance slowly stumble off the roof. Konstantin leaped forward and grabbed Ivan's arm, pulling him back up.

Ivan stood up again and balled his fists. He took a swing at Vashlyshyn, but the demon ducked. That made Ivan angrier. He spun a roundhouse kick, knocking Vashlyshyn to the ground, and pinned him down. He drew back his fist, punching his face repeatedly, causing blood to gush from his nose. Vashlyshyn reached for the gun inside his coat and used it to strike Ivan in the jaw. Ivan released his grip and screamed in pain. Then he heard the click of a pistol. He gazed up to see Vashlyshyn pointing the barrel at his head. Ivan shut his eyes tight and heard a gunshot. He flinched as his heart hammered. He expected to feel a cold bullet burrowing through his head and brain matter, but nothing of the sort happened. Ivan slowly opened his eyes.

Vashlyshyn dropped his gun and screamed, his empty eyes flashing with shock and pain. Ivan glared at the blood pouring from his enemy's leg. Then he looked over his shoulder to see Konstantin holding a revolver, aimed at Vashlyshyn.

"Are you all right?" asked Konstantin, his heart beating faster.

"Never better," muttered Ivan. He regained his faculties and kicked Vashlyshyn off the train. The demon fell about a hundred feet into an icy lake. The two soldiers gazed down at the watery grave, watching anxiously for any signs of life. After several moments, Vashlyshyn emerged from underneath the icy prison and struggled to swim to shore.

"Of course, the swine survived," said Konstantin darkly.

Vashlyshyn crawled out of the water and onto the shore, coughing up blood and lake water. The demon stood up, fighting through the pain. He watched the train disappear into the distance.

Those fools, thought Vashlyshyn. They think they are done with me, but I am far from done with them.

Chapter 6

Operation Petrograd

Near the beautiful Neva River was a large city on the corner of Russia and the Finnish border. It was the city where everything started; the revolution, the civil war, the blood bath. It all somehow started in the city once called St. Petersburg. Then, the war against the Germans interrupted everyone's lives. And old Nicholas thought St. Petersburg wasn't Russian enough. He decided to change the city's name to Petrograd. He hoped it would distract from the fact that he was, indeed, the grandchild of a German princess. Then, the revolution happened, and many people broke their silence. Nothing could have stopped it. Lenin took over, and the name of the white night city was changed, yet again. Leningrad, simply because he was egoistic, and he had the power.

They waited until nightfall.

Filipp drove around Leningrad with Yurovsky in the passenger seat. He parked the car across the street from City Hall, a large three-story building with a slanted roof, beautiful white columns, and a square-shaped courtyard. It was surrounded by a black iron gate. The building had been a palace back in the day of Catherine the Great before it was turned into a school for girls. After that, Lenin transformed it into City Hall and his personal office.

Filipp pulled out a cigarette, lit it, and took a long drag. The smoke made Yurovsky's eyes water. Filipp looked at Yurovsky sharply. "Get out."

"Why do I have to be the one to retrieve the documents? This was your insane idea," complained Yurovsky.

"It is because you are much younger, and I outrank you," said Filipp frankly.

Yurovsky sighed deeply and opened the car door, stepping onto the street.

"And by the way," added Filipp. "You'll find the documents in Lenin's office."

"I'll do what?" gasped Yurovsky fearfully. He never imagined that he would be looking for those records in the office of the most powerful man in Russia. He might as well be signing his own death warrant. "You didn't mention that before."

Filipp took another drag of his cigarette. "It's in his safe," he said indifferently.

Yurovsky slammed the car door and hurried across the street. He stopped in front of the iron gate and sighed heavily. He was too old to be doing this. He scaled up the gate and jumped down onto the courtyard. He used the darkness as cover as he moved among the shadows. He walked up to the door and wiggled the handle. Of course, it was locked. Yurovsky reached inside his pocket, pulling out a paperclip. He straightened it out and pinched the end of it. He did that several more times, making three ridges at the end. He inserted the paperclip into the keyhole and applied a little pressure. He gently moved the paperclip back and forth in the keyhole until he heard the door unlock. Yurovsky opened the door and entered City Hall.

He quickly moved across the marble floor and climbed up a steep staircase. He found the door to Lenin's office and opened it, stepping inside. Lenin must not have been much of a decorator. His office consisted of a neat, clutter-free desk in front of a window, several stools scattered randomly around the office and a red banner awkwardly placed in a corner. The room also contained a worn-out leather sofa, a cabinet with books, a safe, and a small clock.

As soon as he opened the cabinet doors, Yurovsky heard a soft voice.

"What are you doing here?"

Yurovsky turned sharply. It was Lenin.

"I am doing something that I should have done a long time ago," he whispered fearfully.

Lenin stood in the doorway, looking surprised and disappointed at the same time. He sighed and shut the door. With his hands in his pockets, he took a step forward and studied Yurovsky.

"You know that I can have you killed for this," he said quietly.

"If you wanted me dead, I would already be dead."

Lenin laughed hysterically. "The moment I met you, I knew that I liked you."

"Open the safe."

Lenin stopped laughing and glared at Yurovsky darkly. No one gave the Communist Leader orders. Surprisingly though, he walked briskly to the safe and opened it. He pulled out an old folder of documents. The records belonged to Ivan Mikhailovich and included the most crucial piece of information: his birth certificate, and it needed to be destroyed.

"This must be very valuable for you and Gabriel von der Reis to come after it."

"Gabriel?" asked Yurovsky.

"Over a year ago, Gabriel was looking for it because he discovered an interesting piece of information. There was a baby born in Berlin twenty-one years ago," explained Lenin. "The dates on the birth certificates matched exactly, except the names were different. The name on this birth certificate is Ivan Mikhailovich."

"Do you mean to say—"

Lenin scowled at Yurovsky. "Don't say it," he muttered as if someone was listening.

Yurovsky grabbed the folder from Lenin and walked towards the door.

Lenin continued, "Tonight, you have caught me in a good and generous mood, Yakov." Yurovsky stopped fearfully. "If you ever come to my office again unannounced, I won't be so forgiving."

Yurovsky turned slowly and nodded. "Yes, Sir."

As soon as he stepped back onto the courtyard, Yurovky heard a growl. He turned sharply to see a big German Shepherd aggressively barking at him. He didn't think twice before darting across the courtyard. The dog chased after him, gnashing its teeth, quickly gaining on him. Yurovsky promptly climbed up the fence and jumped onto the sidewalk, escaping the dog. He dashed across the street and opened the car door. Before he could sit down, Filipp gunned the engine, and they took off.

They were at the hotel in less than ten minutes. Filipp locked himself in his hotel room and read over the documents. His eyes stopped on the date written on the birth certificate: *July 9, 1898.*

Filipp chain-smoked and anxiously paced the floor as he contemplated what to do. Anxiety twisted and turned inside him, creating unbreakable knots. It was like a dagger had been plunged into his chest, and some strange, unknown force was twisting the blade even deeper. It pierced through his ability to feel, making it impossible to breathe without peace.

Filipp was going to make sure those records never saw the light of day again. He threw them into the raging inferno of the fireplace, including the birth certificate. He watched the documents disintegrate until every last ember was out, and the remaining firewood was cold to the touch. That still wasn't enough.

He drank his last bottle of vodka and smoked his last cigarette before writing a disturbing suicide note explaining his decision. With the pen in mid-sentence, Filipp suddenly stopped his writing. He realized he didn't need to explain. The right people would understand. His death wouldn't matter anyway, as no one would mourn for him. Not a single woman would be wearing black for him.

Filipp's wife died the previous year. In some ways, when Bertha died, Filipp died with her. He buried whatever was left of his heart when he buried her. The grief shook him like an earthquake, and the aftershocks never ceased. He wanted to crawl into a little corner and scream at God. Not like that would do him any good because God stopped listening long ago. The new reality had been difficult for Filipp to live with. Simple things became impossible; getting out of bed, eating, bathing, and breathing. He couldn't even feel his own heartbeat in his chest or the air filling his lungs. He felt lifeless.

Filipp knew he had better put himself out of his misery before this dirty little secret placed him in an unmarked grave. He pressed the cold pistol against the side of his head. The image of his wife's beautiful face flashed in his mind. He winced in pain, his heart breaking beyond repair. He wanted to cry until there were no more tears left as memories danced in his head; her smile, her laughter, her bright blue eyes, the taste of her lips, and the softness of her silky chestnut hair. The world was suddenly spinning. Filipp felt nauseated and fell back onto the sofa. *Why can't something buried stay buried*? he thought.

Time seemed to slow down as a cold blanket of grief surrounded him. His sobs went still, and a dangerous silence echoed around him. His heart hammered against his chest harder than ever, the pain excruciatingly unbearable.

Filipp placed the gun against his heart. He closed his eyes and reminded himself of the advice he gave the boys before the massacre; one in the head and two in the chest. Filipp slipped his finger around the trigger as his heart beat faster. His blue eyes glanced at the gold wedding ring around his finger. It filled him with a sadness he would never shake. He tried thousands of times but could never bring himself to take it off. The ring had been a loving reminder of what he had lost. He exhaled a painfully heavy sigh.

Filipp closed his eyes again. Buried memories from his youth resurrected from their coffin. The clock went back thirty years. Time had changed; Russia had changed; he had changed. He was a young man again. His fair hair glistened in the sunlight as he boarded a train to Siberia, with a small suitcase in one hand and his papers in the other. His blue eyes held back more emotion than he could bear. He was betrayed by his own blood. Through the train window, he saw his mother breaking down into tears, burying her face into her hands. He turned to his father, who angrily shook his head at him. From that day onward, Filipp no longer had a family. He felt utterly abandoned once more, taking him down an old, familiar path he couldn't escape.

These memories slashed through Filipp's heart. He couldn't scream or fight back as he had been forced to endure endless torture. Struggling through the pain, Filipp saw her face as clearly as he did all those years ago.

He got off the train, their eyes met, his heart jumped, and the world came to a complete stop. Bertha smiled radiantly at him as if she knew something he didn't. Without realizing it, Filipp shyly smiled back.

For a moment, he felt completely happy. Nevertheless, grief soon crowded his thoughts again, causing him to gasp in pain.

The clock flashed forward a couple of months. Winter had just begun. Snow quietly blanketed the ground around them. Bertha tenderly pressed her lips against his. Time stood still. His heart melted at her touch as he slowly ran his fingers through her hair. Bertha gently pulled away, gazing lovingly into Filipp's light blue eyes. He proposed. Filipp slid an arm around her tiny waist, pulling her close and kissing her lips gently.

Yes.

The clock flashed forward to the end of March—his wedding day. Filipp felt his heart leap out of his chest as he watched her walk down the aisle. Bertha wore nothing fancy, just a simple white gown and antique earrings. Nevertheless, he thought she was the most beautiful bride in all of Russia.

Time flashed forward again. Filipp graduated from dental school. Bertha pulled him aside and whispered: I am pregnant. Filipp's heart fluttered with excitement and joy. He wrapped his arms around his wife and kissed her softly.

That same year, she'd lost his child. Filipp held Bertha in his arms as she cried. The sight was unforgettable; her blue eyes were swollen shut from crying, and her cheeks were damp for many days. Her face was red, and her voice trembled with disappointment. That would have been the first of many miscarriages.

The clock flashed forward again, this time much farther than before. Filipp had been permitted to return to Moscow with his wife, who'd been expecting another child. After opening a dental practice in Moscow, his wife had given birth to a long-awaited daughter. He didn't know how something so small and precious could make a human being capable of so much love and devotion. Filipp cradled his daughter for an hour before she died in his arms. It had been the happiest moment of his life, and then it turned into the most heart-shattering.

It seemed fitting that his daughter had died in December. The air felt cold and bitter, depicting what his heart became that day. The trees were covered in layers of ice, and the streets had frozen over. The sky had been dull and gray. Russia appeared to be grieving with him.

He went to the synagogue often, grasping at the Jewish faith of his childhood. As he prayed, his cold fingers clutched to a tiny hat that was supposed to be hers. As he sat in the back pew, choking back a thousand tears, he re-read the simple phrase: *Thy will be done.*

Eventually, Filipp buried his grief in his work. He became too busy to grieve. And undoubtedly, too busy to console his depressed wife, who desperately needed him. Bertha became quiet, distant, and cold to the touch. She barely ate and slept most of the day. Her hair had turned gray, and her skin appeared waxy. She became a very sick and frail woman.

Filipp would never forget the day Bertha asked him to sleep in another room. Her words broke his heart into a million fragments. He tried to mend the pieces back together, but that would only push them farther apart. He loved his wife and wanted to make her happy. He left their bed without another word and started sleeping on the sofa. Every night, loneliness filled the absence of his dear wife. He continued loving her from a distance, but they had become strangers living under the same roof.

Time flashed forward yet again. The years of agony felt like an eternity as Filipp morphed into a different person. He was older, wiser, and gained the reputation of being the best dentist in Moscow.

His idiotic younger brother showed up on his doorstep one night—the same brother who'd betrayed him years before. His brother begged to stay the night with them and not ask any questions. Filipp felt a surge of anger, and he wanted to drive his fist into his brother's face. The last time he helped his brother, he'd been banished to Siberia and disowned by their father.

"Please, Isaac," his brother said, "trust me."

Isaac—the name his mother had given him.

He had been a fool to trust his brother. He had been arrested the next day for harboring a fugitive. Once again, he'd been banished to Siberia.

Filipp felt buried anger rise to the surface. His fingers released his grip on the gun. It all happened in flashes; it had been like a demon had possessed him. He suddenly flipped over a table and threw books off their shelves. He broke a window, a mirror, and teacups. He threw a glass across the room, shattering it beyond repair. He picked up the framed photograph of his wife and prepared to throw it across the room. But when his eyes glanced at the picture, his wife was smiling back at him through a captured memory. He never left town without it. He set the photograph down, unwilling to destroy that beautiful memory.

Filipp gazed around the room; everything was destroyed. He fell back onto the sofa again, his eyes welling up with tears. He wanted to scream until his throat was raw, throw more things, and hit people, but he didn't have the strength. He curled into a small ball on the sofa and screamed into a pillow, his cheeks wet from tears and his face red from crying.

The clock flashed back again. He'd escaped Siberia and fled to Prague, where he'd met Lenin and joined the oligarchy. He changed his name to *Filipp*. He returned to his wife a different man, a broken man. He had lost himself, his faith, and his heart.

Time flashed forward. After the first gunshots of the revolution, Bertha started running high fevers. Filipp spent every waking moment nursing his beloved back to health. Bertha gazed deep into Filipp's light blue eyes, as she'd done before many years ago. She held his hand, and he felt their fingers entwine. She uttered, "Thank you."

Sick with fear and confusion circling his mind, Filipp assured his wife that the doctor was on his way. Bertha smiled radiantly as if she knew something he didn't.

"I love you," she whispered. Filipp's heart hammered rapidly as he watched the light leave her beautiful eyes. He cried until his eyes were swollen. Grief slowly tore him apart, and he felt numb from the agony.

The pain of losing Bertha suddenly ripped through Filipp's heart once again. He grabbed the gun and placed the barrel against his chest. He let out one last painful breath. He summoned all his courage, his heart beating faster.

He pulled the trigger.

Filipp expected to feel the bullet piercing his heart, ripping through tissue, and relieving him of years of endless pain and heartache. But nothing happened.

Puzzled, he opened the chamber. There was not a bullet in sight. He had forgotten to load the chamber! Filipp rummaged through his luggage, looking for ammo.

He was interrupted by an insistent pounding on the door.

"Filipp, are you in there?" said a muffled voice. There were only two people alive who would dare call him by that name.

Filipp opened the door. "Yakov?" he uttered impatiently.

Yurovsky appeared worried. "I heard quite the raucous going on in here." Then, Yurovsky noticed the big mess through the doorway and wondered if he should have said anything at all. He eyed Filipp with caution. "What happened here?" he asked nervously.

Filipp stared at him blankly as if nothing had happened. "I don't know what you are talking about."

Yurovsky paused. He opened his mouth and waited again. He nodded his head towards the inside of the hotel room. "You mean to say that you don't know what caused all this?"

Filipp turned around, then back again. He cleared his voice nervously. "I was destroying those documents, and I realized—." Filipp stopped in mid-sentence. He almost spoke of a secret that could get him killed. "I realized that I am a terrible man. Then things got out of hand."

"You're a pretty good liar," said Yurovsky. "What seems to be troubling you?"

Filipp let Yurovsky into the hotel room and locked the door. He turned and looked at him sharply. "I haven't been honest with you, or anyone for that matter."

Yurovsky eyed Filipp carefully. He had a couple of secrets of his own, and all of them would most certainly get him killed.

Mikhail had betrayed The Chupacabra. Because of their past friendship, Yurovsky allowed him to escape Russia with the plans for the atomic bomb. Mikhail defected, and Yurovsky would have probably done the same if he didn't have a family to care for. Mikhail had been brave but foolish. He returned to Russia three years later, hoping to reunite with his family, only making them targets. Yurovsky smuggled Mikhail out of Russia before it had been too late, but not without the notice of The Chupacabra. Mikhail tucked the plans away in a safety deposit box in London. Then, foolishly, he gave the key to the Tsar, who took the secret of its location to the grave.

"I have done something that cannot be undone," cried Filipp.

"What is it, Filipp?"

Suddenly, there was a small knock on the door.

Puzzled, Yurovsky gave Filipp a sharp look. "Were you expecting anyone?"

Filipp shook his head. He unlocked the door and opened it slowly. Somebody had left a briefcase outside the door, with a small note left on it. Filipp picked up the letter and read it.

I know what you did.

His eyes widened. Fear pumped through his veins. How did someone know what happened that day? Only one other person knew his secret. And she wouldn't tell a soul. He brought the briefcase inside and put it on the bed. He opened it and, to his horror, saw that there was a well-made bomb inside.

And it was set to go off in thirty seconds.

Chapter 7

Operation Nightingale

It was late morning in London—*10:58* to be exact. Anya was curled into a little ball under the bedsheets, drifting into a deep sleep. This had been the first time that she slept since she left Ukraine. Leaving her eighteen-month-old son on a Ukrainian farm made her sick. Anya did what had to be done, and it nearly killed her to do it. As she drifted deeper into a much-needed sleep, her mind wandered to a place she no longer belonged.

Anya walked quickly but carefully, her footprints imprinting into the snow as she carried blankets for the other children in the orphanage. She took a shortcut through a shady part of the city as it was a couple of minutes shorter than taking the main road, and she didn't want to freeze. Russian winters were cold and unforgiving. Silence echoed in the background, and a gust of wind brushed against her face and fingers, making her shiver.

As Anya picked up her pace, an eeriness seemed to fill the air. Something wasn't quite right, and when she felt the hard barrel of a gun being pressed against her back, her heart froze.

"Put that down and come with me," said the demon's cold voice.

Anya didn't move.

"You will obey me if you know what's good for you," said Vashlyshyn darkly.

Anya heard a clicking sound as he released the safety on the gun. It took a few moments for her to realize that she was holding her breath. She blinked several times, her heart beating faster, and pulled the blankets down. Vashlyshyn held her close, with the gun at her side. He took her to an empty tavern and slammed her body against the table. He pointed the gun at her head.

Anya closed her eyes. The nightmare had only just begun.

Anya woke up from the dream, her heart racing. Her body shook uncontrollably. Tears gathered from behind her clear blue eyes as she let out a blood-curdling scream.

Ivan had been in the bathroom shaving his face when he heard her terrifying scream. *Anya!* He wiped his face with a towel and threw it on the counter. He swung the door open and darted to the bed. Anya was curled up in a ball, shaking and crying. Ivan gazed at Anya, grabbing her hand. Horror was etched in her eyes. He had never seen her like this before.

"Anya, please, calm down," said Ivan.

Anya kicked and punched into the air, screaming louder. "I hate you! I hate you so much!" Her mind was not in the present. It was still in places it no longer belonged. Anya threw the back of her fist in the air again, making contact with Ivan's nose. He grunted loudly as pain shot all over his face. Though he was somewhat impressed with her skill—he taught her that move. The agony lasted only a small moment, and Ivan pulled Anya close and cradled her like a child.

"Anya, you are safe now. I am here," reassured Ivan.

Anya sobbed into his shoulder, letting out an agonizing scream.

"You are safe now. I am not going to let anything happen to you," promised Ivan.

Anya had never been the same.

It had not been fair. She was just sixteen then, practically still a child. He used her, played her, manipulated her. The rules were never fair. It was just a nasty little game called power.

"I hate him so much," she wailed.

Ivan remembered what Vashlyshyn did in Ekaterinburg. It all came back in small bursts of memory. Ivan heard the terrifying gunshots again and smelled the smoke and vodka. And Vashlyshyn bragged about killing and raping like he'd won some sort of trophy. Ivan lost it. He gave Vashlyshyn that horrible scar. He held him down and carved a knife into his face with pleasure

"Me too," said Ivan. "I hate him, too."

Downstairs, a beautiful nightingale was nestled under the thin layer of bed sheets. Her arms clenched a pillow tightly. She wished with every ounce of her existence that she could close her eyes and not wake up. The Nightingale pulled the sheets over her head, burying her face deeper into her pillow. She closed her eyes, her mind diving into a pool of time.

She imaged a face somewhat like her own; long, light brown hair, deep blue eyes, and light skin. And it was all tied together with an angelic smile. This woman, a Serbian from the gutter, crawled into bed with a wealthy banker. The affair lasted two years, but it ended when the woman felt a threat move inside her; a baby.

The woman fled from Germany to Serbia. A child was a threat to the banker's son—the heir to his father's fortune, estate, and his position in the oligarchy. Serbia had changed, the seasons changed, and the woman had changed. She was now heavily pregnant.

She walked alone that night, cold, tired, and hungry, leaving behind bloody footprints in the snow. The waves of pain were endless. She had been steps away from the house of God, a place of refuge. The pain stopped, but only for a minute.

The woman opened her blue eyes, exhaling deep, long breaths. Her fists pounded against the door several times before a nun finally answered. The woman felt her baby beginning to crown, ripping through her flesh. Without realizing it, she gave an ear-splitting scream. The nun ushered the woman through the door and offered her a bed.

The woman began to push, her face white and her skin clammy. She pushed harder the second time, holding her breath. She pushed a third time and felt her baby slide into the waiting hands of the nun. Hearing the baby cry had been music to the woman's ears, but the blood kept pouring from her abdomen. She felt the fever rise; she didn't have much time. The baby taking the name of her father had been out of the question—too dangerous.

Jana Kovacevic

That had been the name of The Nightingale for eleven years.

The Nightingale's misty blue eyes opened slightly, staring at the plain, barren wall. She rolled to the other side of the bed. She closed her eyes again and pictured the face of her father: dark hair, olive skin, a well-trimmed beard, and eyes that glistened like diamonds, just like her own. After The Chupacabra learned of her existence, he added her to the list of his many possessions. He had been obsessed with turning her into a killer. He played her like a deck of cards. He manipulated her mind. After destroying that good, little Catholic girl, he took it further. He branded her left shoulder with a hot iron in the shape of a nightingale—the mark of death.

She painfully rolled out of bed. A strong rush of guilt punched through her thin gut. Tears swelled in her eyes—a deep hatred raged war against her body and her heart. It had been an addiction as overpowering and bitter as vodka and as cold and lonely as her father.

It had been twelve years, and still, she was haunted by what her father had done to the people she loved most. She imagined the looks that might have been on their faces, the tears they might have shed, and the prayers they would have prayed. The blood-stained floor and scattered brain matter had been permanently embedded in her mind. She would never forget the frozen fear plastered on their faces and their eyes, not a speck of life left.

Sadness ripped through her heart. Those nuns were her family. They were the women who loved and raised her and gave her a home after the death of her mother, who had died and left her nothing but a name - Jana Kovacevic. No one would miss them. He made sure of that.

The Nightingale. That's what he renamed her. Jana Kovacevic was the property of The Chupacabra. She killed for him, worshiped him, lived, and breathed for him—and she hated him.

The Nightingale closed her eyes and imagined a bullet piercing through her father's skull. But in her line of work, she had to be patient.

She walked to a full-length mirror and gazed at her reflection. Her white dress was open-weaved and laced. A string of pearls dangling below her long, slender neck would give others a false sense of innocence. She added an extra pin through her hair and sighed heavily. The psyche knot was still not good enough. Without thinking, she grabbed the lipstick on the dresser, tracing another coat of dark red around her full lips. She rubbed her lips together, her beautiful clear eyes gazing through the mirror, admiring and criticizing every inch of the body her parents had given her.

The Nightingale glared at the bathroom door through the mirror. She thought of the smell of vomit and felt a rush of guilt. It had been a special kind of self-hatred that few would understand.

She dashed to the coat closet and pulled a trench coat off a ~~coat~~ hanger. The lining inside the coat concealed a rifle, an Arisaka Type 44 Cavalry. She slipped the jacket on and straightened her hair one last time.

"I would reconsider your plan if I were you," said a familiar voice.

Gabriel.

He leaned against the mantle, smirking. His deep brown curls had salt and pepper streaks. He had lost weight but gained muscle. His Saxony Tweed suit was a light shade of gray. Saying he was tired would be an understatement. Gabriel was exhausted, fatigued from taking orders from his father—a man he despised. He was exhausted from sleeping every night with one eye open and from cleaning up after his father's messes. Every night, he wedged a chair against the door, fearing his enemies would murder him in his sleep.

"It's been a long time, brother," hissed The Nightingale. She spat out that last word as if it was cursed.

Gabriel took a step forward, his eyes locked on her, challenging her. He stopped and glared around the room with his hands in his pockets. His eyes stopped at the bathroom. The Nightingale looked skeptical, and her heart pounded. She fought hard to keep her secret, and she had even sprayed the bathroom with expensive perfume to bury the incriminating evidence. If her father knew, he would put a stop to it. He didn't invest so much time and money just to see one of his most prized possessions and his only daughter wither away. She was more beneficial to him alive than dead—and all she had to do was simply behave.

"What do you want, Gabriel?" said The Nightingale impatiently.

Gabriel straightened his jacket before sitting down on the white sofa and crossing his legs. Gabriel motioned her to sit next to him. The Nightingale hesitated slightly, then took a step forward. Her heartbeat quickened, and fear tunneled through her body. She placed her hand inside her pocket and grabbed ahold of her knife. She gingerly sat on the edge of the sofa, paranoia invading her mind. Gabriel moved closer; his eyes locked on hers. She thought about jamming the knife into his throat.

Gabriel reached inside his jacket and pulled out a telegram folded on four sides. The Nightingale snatched it from his fingers and read it:

The Nightingale has fallen.

"Gabriel, what's this?" asked The Nightingale, her tone emotionless.

"I was hoping that you could tell me," retorted Gabriel.

She folded the paper and ripped it in half. "This little paper means nothing to me."

"Is that so?" he said quietly. He leaned forward and gave her a wicked grin. "I tapped into Helen's telephone and heard a coded conversation regarding plans to kill Father. I intercepted this telegram and interrogated a person who is involved in the assassination plot."

The Nightingale's eyes widened. "Who?"

"You. Just now. You just confirmed your own involvement." His sister opened her mouth to say something, but Gabriel cut her off. "You never had a good poker face, Jana. I think that's why I was able to beat you at every card game when we were younger."

The Nightingale felt a rush of anger. "Gabriel, what do you want?" she hissed.

"You and I want the same thing. We want Father gone, and I want to help you bring him down," said Gabriel coolly.

"What's in it for you?"

"Bring me Ivan Mikhailovich. Or I will tell Father that his wife, daughter, and the oligarchy were planning to get rid of him. What do you think he'll do after that?"

The Nightingale swallowed hard. Her father would burn Europe to the ground, looking for those who betrayed him. Then, for those who survived, he'd pick them off one by one. He'd kill them slowly, savoring every moment.

This is a set-up, thought the Nightingale. If the plans to take down her father failed, Gabriel would allow her to take the fall. "You're blackmailing me to protect yourself. Why?" she asked slowly.

"Those are my reasons. We both want father gone. I don't need you to do that, but you need me," said Gabriel. "Ivan in exchange for my silence."

Volkov had somehow abandoned him, and Gabriel was running out of time. He could do this without Volkov, but not without his half-sister. Of course, he didn't want her to know that.

The Nightingale could smell a bluff over a mile away, and Gabriel had been, indeed, bluffing. Somehow, he needed her, or else he wouldn't have come all the way out to London to find her and offer help. Gabriel had something to gain over this, but the Nightingale hadn't figured it out yet.

"How far are you willing to go, Gabriel?" challenged The Nightingale.

"I am willing to do whatever it takes," he said darkly.

The Nightingale was a dead woman either way, but she wasn't done playing yet. If she played her cards right, she'd make it out of this game alive. "All right," she sighed heavily. "What's your plan?"

Gabriel leaned forward and smiled again. The Nightingale thought about using that knife about now, but something held her back.

"I have a plan. I just need you to follow my lead."

Chapter 8

Operation Metropole

Across the street, on the corner of Whitehall Place and Northumberland Avenue, stood a large triangular building called the Metropole Hotel. During the war, the hotel was used by the government, housing generals and soldiers, and hosting secret societies. Last night, the hotel celebrated its grand reopening.

A short, slender Danish woman made quick strides down Trafalgar Square. She stuffed her wispy, gray hair into a round burgundy hat. She had an expensive taste which was evident by her posh coat had big red buttons carefully stitched on the front, a wide leather belt around her waist, large cuffs around her tiny wrists, and a roll collar around her slender neck, making her figure appear small and slim. She didn't need her apparel to illustrate her small figure when she was with her husband, though; she paled next to his bear-like stature. What no one knew, not even her own sister, was that the woman had sewn a secret pocket inside the coat, concealing a revolver. She felt a sly grin spread across her face. A Danish woman must keep her secrets carefully.

Her sister kept pace behind her. Her long dress had been a vibrant shade of green at one point. The color was now faded, and the fit had loosened over the years. The dress fluttered around her as she quickened her step to catch up with her sister. They shared the same fondness for expensive things. Her brown fur coat had cost an arm and a leg, along with the small, round wool hat that framed her long, oval face.

"Minnie!" her sister panted, using her pet name. "Minnie—wait. Please listen to me!" She grabbed hold of her sister's arm. "Marie!"

Marie stopped, glancing over her shoulder, her blue eyes darting towards her sister peevishly. "I've already made up my mind, Alix," Marie barked in rapid Danish. "So, let go!" Marie seized her arm from Alexandra, tossing her a pleading look that only her sister could understand: *go home, please.*

Alexandra grabbed her sister's hand. "I am not here to change your mind," she whispered slowly in English, her eyes pleading. "When have you ever done anything stupid without me?"

Marie tossed her sister a devilish grin, locking arms with her.

Marie Feodorovna's ocean blue eyes were alert. She walked with purpose, taking a left on Northumberland Avenue. She glanced down at her tiny, slender fingers wrapped around her purple clutch. She clung to the clutch the way she clung to her past, with uncompromising firmness. She opened the latch, slipping her fingers inside and pulled out a small hand mirror, and gazed at her reflection. The brown color in her hair had faded and turned into a dark gray. Her flawless skin was now loose and waxy. But her eyes never changed; deep, piercing, and blue, just like her sister's. She angled the mirror slightly to the left, gazing at the reflection of a handsome young man with jet black hair, who had been tailing her for half an hour. The woman thought of the gun hidden inside her coat and drew a sharp breath. She silently wished she would never have to use it. After today, that wish might come true.

"What's going on, Minnie?" whispered Alexandra, so low only her sister could hear.

"Trouble," hissed Marie.

About five yards behind her, Konstantin ducked his face behind a newspaper he'd been pretending to read. He cursed in Russian under his breath. *My cover's blown*, he thought.

Konstantin was dressed in a gray flannel suit. It had been the first suit he'd worn in a long time. Inside his coat pockets were two revolvers and a dagger for self-defense. He glanced down at his watch. It was thirty minutes past twelve. Anxiety boiled inside of him. The plan had been far from simple; find the Empress, bring her to the rendezvous spot, and try not to get caught.

The Danish women picked up their pace, getting closer to the Metropole Hotel. Marie had an appointment with Mikhail Mikhailovich, a man she only knew by reputation. And a poor one at that.

Twenty-five years ago, Mikhail Mikhailovich had been nothing but loyal to The Chupacabra. He had been his bodyguard, codebreaker, henchmen, and confidante. He belonged to The Chupacabra. Then Mikhail had been caught in a compromising position with his master's wife. Because of that, The Chupacabra made Mikhail pay. Mikhail's oldest son, Yuri, died in a car rigged with explosives meant for Mikhail. The Chupacabra had purchased plans for a powerful bomb to destroy his enemies, but Mikhail stole the plans and vanished.

There had been plans for a second bomb that no one knew about, designed by Goldstein himself. Somehow, those plans ended up in the hands of British Ambassador George Buchanan, and the Russian Empress needed to find him before someone else did.

Today, her meeting with Mikhail Mikhailovich could fix that.

As they approached the door, Marie slightly hesitated for a moment, her stomach churning.

"Minnie, are you alright?"

Marie ignored her sister. She recalled that there were many powerful men who did not want this meeting to happen. "Yes," she finally said, swallowing hard. "I'm fine." A man opened the door and held it open. The women moved forward, entering the threshold.

Konstantin stopped outside the hotel and waited. The sun was hidden behind the clouds, and a blistering wind cut through his cheeks like a dagger. He shivered, reached inside his pant pocket, and pulled out a cigarette case. The smoke in his lungs would keep him warm. He glanced up; a pair of pink ballerina slippers caught his eye. They were in the hands of a red-headed woman entering the apartment building across the street.

Konstantin thought of his mother, her beautiful red curls, emerald eyes, a slender nose, and thin lips. She had been a ballerina herself. She danced for the Imperial Russian Ballet and trained her heart, soul, and body to be the next Prima Ballerina. Her dreams faded into regret when she agreed to be the wife of a Baron—a sadistic, cold-hearted man.

A taxi pulled up along the curb, and Sofia exited the vehicle, followed by Ivan. Her dress looked like it was worth a billion rubles; velvet, sleeveless, mink wrapped around her arms, and loose around her tiny waist. She tossed Konstantin a seductive smile, swinging her fur over her shoulder.

"Shall we go, darling?" she said cheerfully.

Konstantin's heart skipped a couple of beats, and the air suddenly felt very warm. He slipped his cigarette case back inside his pocket and nervously straightened his tie, and cleared his throat. "Of course, my darling."

It was Konstantin who saved Sofia. She had been broken, but he loved her anyway. Broken, somehow, looked good on her, he thought. Sofia thought about where her mother might be at this minute. Somewhere in the city, lounging with the snobbish people in London, gossiping about other aristocrats. She wrote to her mother, Catherine, many times. She had asked about her father and how things were doing in London. There had been no response. Catherine would never forgive Sofia for running away with a common soldier.

Konstantin glanced over at Ivan, who had worn a black double-breasted suit with a checkered tie. He'd looked rather dashing. Ivan thought about Anya, and the image of her sleeping in a hotel room alone, safe and sound, somehow brought great comfort.

"Are you ready, my friend?" asked Konstantin.

Ivan closed his eyes, took a deep, sharp breath, and nodded.

A ball-shaped chandelier hung low from the ceiling. Two round, roman columns stood at opposite ends of the restaurant. Small, circular tables stood in rows, single file, with white tablecloths. The air smelled of dark chocolate, tobacco, and wine.

Marie felt nauseous. She walked quickly across the lobby, arms still linked with her sister. Her black button-down walking boots made loud clicks against the marble floor. A group of high-class women giggled loudly. A stern woman with a sharp nose, who reminded Alexandra of Queen Victoria, lifted her blue eyes from her menu and frowned, rolling her eyes. Businessmen in dark suits huddled together smoking cigars. A German noblewoman ordered her meal in slow, broken English.

Mikhail Mikhailovich had not been to a restaurant since his time in the oligarchy. He picked up a green bottle of champagne and poured some into a tall, slender champagne glass. His bright blue eyes glared down in disgust, trying to summon the courage to bring the glass to his lips and swallow. *It's not vodka*, he thought.

Mikhail shifted his attention from the champagne glass to a small family eating lunch across the restaurant; a father, a mother, one son, and two daughters. He thought of the family he abandoned in Russia; his wife, two sons, and a daughter. It was the life—the man he'd left behind. It was not like he had much of a choice to stay; he'd betrayed the most dangerous man in the world, which made his family a target. He did not leave out of selfishness or cowardice; he left out of love. Keeping his family safe had been his top priority.

Some things are better left unsaid. Mikhail had been forced to do the unimaginable to survive. He had stolen his navy worsted suit with the black bow tie. The man he stole it from wouldn't be needing it anymore. His dark blond hair had been combed over to the left side. Mikhail had turned fifty the day before but looked in his late thirties. He wasn't too tall, about five feet and eight inches, but what he lacked in height, he made up for in muscle.

He finally lifted the glass, brought the champagne to his lips, and took one small sip. Mikhail choked hard. It tasted like sour water. He quickly placed the glass on the table, fighting the urge to gag. His blue eyes scanned the restaurant, stopping on a handsome young lad in a black double-breasted suit. He locked eyes with the young man, who looked about twenty-one. That would be his son's age. Then, reality slapped him in the face. Mikhail's blue eyes widened.

Ivan. *His Ivan.* His baby boy, all grown up.

He choked back an ocean of tears. He felt a large knot in his throat, and his hands became sweaty. He fought the urge to gather Ivan in his arms and hold him. And for a moment, the world came to a complete stop.

Ivan couldn't believe his eyes— a cold, dark memory that used to be his prison came to the surface. Terror tunneled through his body, mind, and heart. His face turned whiter than the restaurant's tablecloths as his heart accelerated, tearing itself apart. He thought that he was about to have a heart attack. The world started spinning, and he found he had trouble breathing. He leaned against a column for support, his vision slightly blurry.

The reality changed, the restaurant, the Metropole hotel, it all disappeared. Ivan was somewhere else now. A memory long tucked away in the back of his mind came rushing to the surface.

Ivan felt a hand lightly press against his shoulder.

"Ivan," whispered the voice of a woman.

Ivan turned his body sharply. Startled, Sofia quickly took her hand away. Ivan locked eyes with the Countess. Her gray eyes were glistening with love and empathy as she slowly placed her hand against his shoulder again. Her touch brought him back to reality.

"Mikhail Mikhailovich."

Mikhail blinked several times, awakening from the trance that had held him prisoner. He arose from his chair and straightened his bow tie, tossing the two sisters a seductive smile.

"Queen Alexandra. Empress Marie," said Mikhail in perfect English. "Thank you for joining me this afternoon."

As Alexandra gazed at Mikhail, her heart skipped a few beats. She pulled Marie close, her eyes beaming with mischief. "This one's mine," she whispered in beautiful, soft Danish.

Marie glared at Mikhail, unimpressed. "He's old enough to be your son," she snickered in German.

Alexandra chuckled quietly.

"Indeed," said Mikhail in Danish. Alexandra and Marie's faces turned as white as a sheet. "Which language would you prefer?" he said apologetically in rapid German.

Marie cleared her throat, slightly embarrassed. "English will do. Thank you."

Mikhail pulled a chair out for Marie. Then again for Alexandra.

A young man with blond hair and brown eyes sat at the next table. He had a square jaw and wore an expensive, blue Italian suit. He slowly pulled out a gun and pointed it directly at Marie Feodorovna. His dark eyes rested on Mikhail.

Gasps and screams echoed throughout the restaurant. Ivan heard a waiter ask another to telephone the police. A group of guests hurried out of the restaurant, while another group intensely watched from a distance.

"What's going on?" asked Ivan.

Konstantin grabbed Ivan's arm, squeezing it tightly. He brought his lips close to Ivan's ear. Ivan felt his heavy breath strike his neck. "If I tell you to run, you will run without hesitation," cautioned Konstantin. He then released his grip, and Ivan took a few steps back. He opened his mouth to protest but then swallowed. "If I tell you to forsake me and save yourself, do it obediently." Konstantin's words were madness, and Ivan's hands went cold at the sound of them. "Lastly, don't do anything you'd regret."

Ivan nodded. Konstantin grabbed a silver platter from the nearest table. He turned to look over his shoulder, glancing from Sofia to Ivan, his gray eyes sending a clear message; follow close behind.

Mikhail dug through his coat pocket, pulling out a pistol. He pointed the weapon at the young man with blond hair. "Put the gun away, boy," he warned. "Before someone gets hurt."

Alexandra jumped from her seat, her blue eyes holding back a flood of tears. "This is treason!"

The young man turned his gaze to Alexandra and tossed her a demonic grin. "I have not committed any treason." He curled his finger around the trigger. "Yet." He aimed his gun from Marie to Alexandra.

Marie felt a burst of anger. Jumping from her seat, she slid her hand inside her expensive coat and reached for her revolver, and aimed the weapon at the assassin. "Get behind me, Alix," said Marie in quick, rapid Danish. Marie placed her arm in front of her sister protectively, her blue eyes fixated on the man.

"You're outnumbered, boy," said Mikhail.

Konstantin swung the silver platter against the assassin's face, knocking him to the ground. The young man tried getting up and reaching for his gun. Konstantin kicked his weapon away, sliding his hand inside his coat pocket for his own handgun. Aiming the gun at the man's thigh, he pulled the trigger. The gun's thunderous roar echoed across the room. People scattered across the restaurant like wildfire, shouting and screaming in panic.

Konstantin gazed at the gaping red pool of blood escaping the man's body and grinned slightly. Konstantin pulled a white tablecloth and tore a thin strip off, wrapping it around the assassin's leg tightly, tying it into a knot. He screamed in pain, trying to grasp what had just happened. Konstantin grabbed him by the collar.

"The police will arrive momentarily. And when you wake up, they will be more than happy to hear your story." Konstantin thrust his fist into the assassin's face, knocking him out cold.

Alexandra pulled her sister close again, her blue eyes fixed on Konstantin. "This one's mine too," she whispered in quiet Danish. Marie snickered again, stowing her gun inside her coat pocket.

Mikhail took a step toward his son, but Ivan moved back. "Vanya," he said his voice shaking, his blue eyes choking back a thousand tears. Ivan stood stiff. He had not heard his childhood nickname in a long time. "How is your mother?"

His mother. Ivan had not thought of her in a long time. There was one memory he could not seem to forget, no matter how hard he tried. His stepfather came home drunk one night and had beaten his mother until she'd fallen on the ground. She arose from the floor, her body trembling. And then Svetlana snapped as she pulled a gun on her husband. Ivan's stepfather wrestled the weapon from Svetlana's hands. Tomas came into the room to protect his mother. For his heroism, Tomas paid with his life. The gun went off and shot him in the head. The sound of Svetlana screams were deafening. She cradled her dead son in her arms and screamed. Svetlana's mind became broken and damaged repair.

"She's dead to me." There was no emotion in Ivan's voice.

Mikhail swallowed hard, his heart slowly sinking. "And your sister?" his father said, with a large lump in his throat, choking on the words.

Ivan didn't answer. He stared at the floor, thinking about Olga. He'd found her dead on the bathroom floor, with an ocean of blood between her legs. She had been pregnant, and Ivan did not know until it was too late. If he had known, then perhaps she'd still be alive.

Mikhail opened his mouth to ask about his other boy, Tomas, but Ivan's silence was enough. Mikhail turned his gaze to Marie Feodorovna and straightened his bow tie. "Your Imperial Majesty. We need to get you and your sister to safety." Mikhail glanced at the unconscious man against the floor. "Before reinforcements come."

Marie glanced at her sister, her blue eyes flashing with doubt. Alexandra locked arms with her, tightly holding onto her younger sister. Marie flashed a slight smile, and her eyes twinkled with kindness and reassurance. She glanced back at Mikhail and tossed him a small nod.

Mikhail took a step forward but felt a firm grip on his left arm, forcing him to stop. Mikhail turned his body around sharply, bringing him face to face with his son. Ivan eyed his father darkly.

"I didn't come all this way only to lose what I came here for," said Ivan, his tone darkened, frustration filling every word. Ivan's eyes moved from Mikhail to Marie Feodorovna, then back to his father again.

Mikhail pulled his arm away from Ivan's grip and, for a long moment, eyed his son carefully. He then sighed heavily. He untied his bowtie from around his neck and unbuttoned the cuffs around his wrists. He walked several steps forward and turned around sharply, flashing Ivan a mischievous smile. "Then, by all means, my boy," he cried enthusiastically, "come along!"

Chapter 9

Operation Slient Bird

Gabriel von der Reis patiently waited for six years. He waited for justice, for peace and closure, for vengeance that was rightfully his. Now he had one more day of staying in the shadows. Soon, they will pay dearly.

Gabriel walked carefully across the roof with his large hands inside his pockets. He stopped and listened. Thunder echoed in his ears. He closed his eyes and inhaled the fresh, crisp air deeply. A gust of cool wind brushed against his face, and he opened his eyes and looked up. Clouds as dark as his mind consumed the sky, traveling over him. A storm was coming to London, a big one. His striking brown gaze glared down at the city. An old woman crossed the street, and automobiles traveled down the road. A young child shined a man's shoes, and a woman window-shopped with her husband.

The woman reminded Gabriel of Adeline. His heart broke at the thought of her. Shopping had been her favorite hobby. She had been his world, his reason to live, breathe, love, and feel. Gabriel would cry if he could but no longer had the tears to spare.

Exhausted, he collapsed on his knees against the roof shingles. He glared at the Arisaka Type 44 Cavalry rifle in front of him, the same kind of weapon his sister had hidden inside her trench coat. If he had half a mind, he would use the rifle to end his own life, but they still owed him blood.

One more day, thought Gabriel. But it sounded more like a silent cry for help than for vengeance. Of course, no one knew the hell his father put him through. For six years, he'd suffered quietly, his mind screaming for relief. It was like sitting alone in the dark, with only his thoughts to keep him company. Just one more day and their debt will be paid.

Gabriel picked up the rifle and opened the chamber. There was only one bullet lodged inside, and that bullet would soon have Beatrice Gilbert's blood on it. He slammed the chamber shut, his finger fidgeting with the trigger as he watched Beatrice Gilbert walk slowly around the corner. He glanced at the golden watch around his wrist. It was a few minutes till noon. Right on time. His finger curled more tightly around the trigger. Gabriel held his breath.

"I see you still wear that watch, son," a deep, flat voice chimed behind him.

Gabriel smelled a strange mixture of cigarettes and something else, something oddly familiar — death. The smell of power, the smell of The Chupacabra.

He lowered the weapon and glanced down at his watch again. It had been a gift from her. His Adeline. The honey blond, emerald-eyed Adeline. His heart broke at the thought of her. Adeline never belonged to Gabriel, but her death destroyed him anyway. She had been in a loveless marriage with a man Gabriel would have once called his brother. He betrayed his friend for ten long years, sneaking around and making love to Adeline, his friend's wife, sharing secrets with her. Those secrets could have easily placed her on the wrong end of a pistol. None of that mattered now, not anymore.

Unlike his younger and treacherous half-sister, who purged herself from pain, his favorite form of self-harm was thinking. He would replay the events inside his head like a broken record, from the moment they met Adeline in that run-down bookshop in Berlin to the moments of her disappearance and death. His hatred and loathing toward his father and sister grew along with his buried pain, both of which he kept hidden.

"What are you doing here?" hissed Gabriel.

"I came to watch the show," retorted his father sharply. "But even if you are half the marksmen you think you are, it still wouldn't be much of a show."

Gabriel felt a rush of anger but handled it well.

The Chupacabra smiled and continued, "I was expecting to see your sister." He then glared at Gabriel in disgust. "This will have to make do, I suppose."

"No," said Gabriel emotionlessly, his deep brown glare challenging him.

"No?" questioned his father. The Chupacabra studied his son and gave him a blank stare. "What do you mean by no?"

"Now that I have come to think of it," sighed Gabriel. "I don't think it's right to kill an innocent woman."

"What?" The Chupacabra took a step forward, his fists balled. It took all the patience he had left not to smash his fist into the face of his own child. "Beatrice Gilbert is not an innocent woman."

Gabriel gave The Chupacabra a defiant grin. "I am so sorry, father," he said slowly. "I don't think I can trust you."

The Chupacabra gave his son a beady glare. "If you don't trust me, then trust this; if you don't kill her, Viktor dies," he said, his voice cold. "Am I not a man who keeps his word?"

Gabriel's stomach twisted. That was a threat. He turned his body sharply. Beatrice was a short, fat woman with gray hair drawn into a neat bun. She wore a green evening gown with an emerald hat. As she made small strides closer to the hotel, Gabriel aimed the rifle and pulled the trigger. *God, help and forgive me,* he thought.

Beatrice Gilbert was dead.

Gabriel glared down at Beatrice's body. He heard gasps and screams followed by police sirens. As thunder rolled across the sky, he turned to his father and asked, "Why did you make me do that?"

"It's just a simple insurance policy, son. It's business." The Chupacabra took a few steps back. His cold, gray stare glared at the brick chimney.

In his head, he counted to the number thirty-three. He thought of the colors green and red; the colors of greed and power. The Chupacabra took pleasure in watching blood drain from a human corpse. He thought of Helen, his trophy. He imagined his fingers roaming her dark auburn hair, kissing her lips, and inhaling her rose-scented perfume. She belonged to him.

It had been that way for the past twenty-five years. Anxiety tied knots in his heart as he imagined the velvet blood leaving the body of his next victim. His heartbeat accelerated, painfully hammering against his chest. He now counted backward from thirty-three.

"So, murder is just a business transaction now?"

The sound of Gabriel's voice pulled him back to reality. The Chupacabra looked at his son, eyeing him carefully. "If you wish to see it that way," he muttered quietly.

Gabriel crossed his arms, raising an eyebrow. "I wonder what Helen would say to this." he sighed in a mocking tone. "Especially on the day when little Henry comes home."

The Chupacabra stepped forward and pointed his finger. "When you have power, you'll do anything to keep it," he hissed. He then took a step back and gazed at his son, disappointed. "One day, you will understand."

"Is that why you changed Grandfather's will?"

The Chupacabra's gaze hardened. He grabbed Gabriel and brought his face close to his ear. "I don't know how you could possibly know about that," he said, his cold voice lowered to a whisper. The grip on Gabriel's arm tightened. "But if you ever speak of it again, I will see to it that you rot in hell with my father."

The Chupacabra released him, and Gabriel glared at his father and took a few steps back. "What did Grandfather ever do to you?"

"That man has done things that you will never comprehend."

"I wonder what is in that will that has made you so eager to change it?" asked Gabriel.

The Chupacabra grabbed Gabriel by the collar and pointed his index finger. "That's none of your concern. If I were you, I would be more worried about myself." He released Gabriel's shirt and glared at him darkly. "That's my final warning. I won't ask again."

"What about Ivan Mikhailovich?"

"Ivan will come to me when he is ready," sighed The Chupacabra.

"Why would he do that?"

"All roads lead to the bank, son," his father answered. He then put his hands in his pocket, walked briskly away, stopped, and turned. He gave Gabriel a forced smile. "I love you, Gabriel," he said awkwardly. "I have always wanted what's best for you." There had been a long pause between the two men. Gabriel gave his father a faint smile. The Chupacabra opened his mouth and continued, "But the next time you defy me, I won't be so forgiving."

Gabriel's faint smile disappeared. As he watched his father walk away, he felt some sort of childhood disappointment emerge from the shadows. "There won't be a next time, father," he muttered under his breath.

It was much easier being hated by John von der Reis than loved by him. At least, when he hated you, there were no expectations, and no one ended up disappointed. It didn't hurt as much either.

One more day, thought Gabriel. One more day.

The Nightingale moved quickly. She deflected his kick, which only grazed her skin, and sent a roundhouse kick into his chest. The soldier lost his footing and fell backward. He quickly picked himself up off the ground and planted his fist into The Nightingale's left eye. She lost her footing, but she recovered her balance and tightened her fist, punching the man in the nose, breaking it. As he screamed in pain, The Nightingale grabbed his neck and rammed her knee in his chest. He pushed her back and delivered a three-punch combination to her face. Blood immediately gushed from her nose. Angered, she released two high kicks right into the man's face, dazing him. She then leaped into the air and wrapped her legs around his neck. It snapped immediately, and he was dead before he hit the ground.

She picked through his pockets and took a golden cigarette case, with two cigarettes left, to remember him by. Inside the case, the name John was engraved, the same name as her father. She also took a black and white photo of a woman the man had in his pocket.

The Nightingale turned her attention to the next thing she was going to take from him; the military truck he'd driven. It was a large two-door, forest green beauty. The back of the vehicle had a large tarp over it and looked as if it could hold about ten people, perfect for transporting Russian soldiers and two royals.

Murder had been the easiest part of The Nightingale's trade. However, living with the blood on her wings had been more than uncomfortable.

She slammed the vehicle door shut, started the engine, and drove to the corner of Whitehall Place and Northumberland Avenue. She slowed the engine to stop in front of the hotel.

In the corner of her eye, dark figures moved quickly down the sidewalk. She turned her head sharply, and her heart skipped inside her chest.

Konstantin.

He'd been the only man she couldn't bring herself to kill.

The Nightingale swung the wheel hard to the left, cutting dangerously through traffic, causing a taxi driver to slam on his breaks. An old woman honked her horn several times while another woman gave The Nightingale a cold glare.

The Nightingale slammed the breaks after crossing the street, and her eyes fixated on Konstantin.

Konstantin's face was stiff and emotionless. Jana Kovacevic. He thought he would never see her face again. Memories rolled across his mind. St. Petersburg. He knew he shouldn't, but he couldn't help but smile.

Sofia entwined her fingers around his. It was her touch that brought him back to reality. She gently tugged Konstantin's arm forward. He took a step but then stopped.

Sofia turned sharply, her eyes consumed with worry. "Let's go, my darling," she whispered in Russian.

Marie clutched her sister's hand tightly, and her bright blue eyes fixed on Mikhail.

"Listen to her," assured Mikhail.

Marie glanced at her sister. Alexandra nodded her oval head gently, and Marie stepped forward but then stopped.

Alexandra turned sharply and grabbed her sister's arm. "Minnie, if we hurry now, we might come back home before teatime," she lied. Marie nodded gently, and Alexandra tossed her sister a pleasant smile, encouraging her to move forward. Alexandra climbed inside the truck behind Marie and frowned.

Teatime wasn't coming anytime soon.

Mikhail turned to his son. Ivan's eyes seemed glued to the sidewalk, and his arms were crossed in front of him.

Mikhail placed his hand on Ivan's shoulder. "Ivan, I am sorry," said Mikhail, regretfully. "I'll explain everything later. I promise."

Ivan gave Mikhail a dark look. He opened his mouth as if to speak and then closed it. There was nothing he had to say to his father. He turned and climbed into the truck, and Mikhail grabbed his arm.

"I am still your father," he said sharply.

Ivan could only glare at him.

Mikhail let go of his son's arm and walked around the truck. He opened the passenger door and climbed inside the vehicle, slamming the door shut. The Nightingale pushed the acceleration forward and swung the vehicle to the right.

"I am going to make this quick," said Mikhail. His hand slipped inside his coat, reaching for his revolver, and he aimed the weapon at her torso. "Why are you here, Jana?"

The Nightingale ignored Mikhail; her eyes fixed on the road in front of her.

"I'm sorry," said Mikhail, his tone heavy with sarcasm. "I don't believe you heard me."

The Nightingale heard the click of Mikhail releasing the gun's safety. She gulped, and her face went a light shade of white. She eyes glanced at Mikhail darkly before setting her eyes back on the road.

"I have some information on Operation Dragonfly," she said quickly.

"Why are you so willing to betray your father?" Mikhail pressed the barrel against her arm and her hands went cold. The Nightingale shut her eyes tight, searching for the right words. She opened them again and swung the wheel to the left.

"I want to disappear for good, Mikhail. You're good at that." She flashed Mikhail a smirk.

Mikhail felt a surge of anger. He wanted to slap that smirk right off her face. He pushed the barrel against her arm, harder. "Why would the daughter of one of the most powerful men want to do that?" he said coldly.

The Nightingale stopped the car in front of a four-way stop. She turned her body to face Mikhail. "You've met my father, Mikhail." She leaned forward; her eyes locked with his. "But I hope you never have the pleasure of meeting my brother."

Mikhail glanced over her shoulder, his blue eyes swimming in curiosity as two men drove up in a 1919 Ford T Coupe. Mikhail's mind told him a story about these two men. The driver was from eastern Europe with dark blonde hair and baby blue eyes that gave his identity away. He was born into a poor, working-class family from the gutter, his only meal often nothing more than table scraps. In the passenger seat was a dark-haired man with a smug look on his face. He had been a German aristocrat, but after the war, his family was left penniless. He reached for something in his coat, his cold dark eyes glaring at the Nightingale.

"Look out!" shouted Mikhail. He covered The Nightingale's head with his arms, forcing her to duck. The sound of the gunshot was deafening, causing her to shut her eyes tightly, and she was sure her heart had stopped.

A bullet suddenly pierced into Mikhail's shoulder, ripping through skin and tissue. He shrieked in pain and breathlessly reached for his gun. He aimed the weapon at the German's heart and pulled the trigger. The German fell dead, blood pouring from his chest.

The driver of the T-Coupe cursed loudly in a Romanian accent, and the vehicle accelerated away.

Mikhail glanced down at his shoulder as a river of blood gushed down his arm.

The Nightingale arose slowly. "Mikhail," she whispered hysterically. "You saved me." She touched his shoulder, but Mikhail winced in pain.

"London isn't safe anymore," Mikhail moaned in pain.

It never was, thought The Nightingale.

Ivan heard the gunshot from the back of the truck. His heart staggered with worry. "What happened?"

Konstantin and Sofia exchanged glances as Marie hung tight to her older sister's arm, fear coursing through her.

"Don't worry," promised Alexandra quietly. "We'll still be home for tea."

Sofia had a terrible idea, and she refused to remain like sitting ducks waiting to be killed. She climbed out from the back of the car, but Konstantin grabbed her hand, his eyes pooling with concern.

"My love, where are you going?"

"I have an idea. You are just going to have to trust me," said Sofia. She smiled lovingly. With her eyes, she kindly told him to let go. Konstantin pressed his lips against her hand and slowly let her fingers slip through his. The Countess dashed around the truck and opened the driver's door. She climbed inside the truck and pushed The Nightingale away from the wheel. "I am driving." Before The Nightingale could protest, Sofia slammed her foot against the gas and swung the wheel to the right.

If her mother, Catherine, refused to give Sofia answers about why her father left, she was going to a place that will. It would be the safest and most dangerous place in the world. *God forgive me,* thought Sofia.

As the truck gunned forward, Alexandra looked at Konstantin, eyes beaming. "If she doesn't come back, would you be interested?" she asked playfully.

Marie glared at her. "Alexandra!" she hissed.

Alexandra let out a loud chuckle. "I don't know why you are so upset, Minnie. You were thinking about it, too." Maria buried her face in her hands.

"Did you get a good look at those men," whispered The Nightingale in beautiful Serbian.

Mikhail sat up straight, fighting through the pain. He looked at her with slightly blurry vision. "Yes, and they didn't work for your father."

Gabriel.

"Why would Gabriel want you dead?" asked Mikhail, reading her mind.

"Because I took away something he loved," uttered The Nightingale. She lowered her head in shame. Her father was a very persuasive man. And with the right motivation, he could get you to do anything, even things you knew you would regret later.

"What did you do?"

"I killed Adeline."

Chapter 10

Operation Safe House

Every city has a safe house. In the far corner of London, there stood such a house. A white brick Georgian home with colossal windows, a wraparound balcony, and a crested roof. A large courtyard outlined with well-manicured hedges greeted visitors, along with a grand fountain displayed in the middle. You see, this safe house just happened not to be so safe. But it would do for now. It belonged to a woman named Elise, who died at the age of thirty-eight. She willed the house to her sister, Helen von der Reis.

Mikhail opened the car door and collapsed onto the ground. The Nightingale climbed out of the passenger door, slamming it behind her. She wrapped his arm around her shoulder, lifting him up.

"You didn't have to do that, Mikhail," she huffed.

"Yes, I did," shrieked Mikhail louder, clenching his teeth in agony.

"You're not my bodyguard anymore."

"Old habits die hard," he grunted.

Alexandra peaked her head through the curtain.

"What's going on, Alix?" whispered Marie, her voice slightly quivering.

Alexandra turned her head, glancing at her sister, her blue eyes swimming in pity. "Mikhail Mikhailovich has been shot."

"Papa," gasped Ivan as he leaped from the truck. As his feet hit the ground, he turned his blue eyes sharply to see two things; his father, clinging to life, and blood—old Russian blood. Ivan felt a wave of panic. It felt like the air had left his lungs. No! Not his father. Not his Papa. There must have been some mistake. His father hadn't been shot. This could not be happening.

He dashed across the yard. "Papa," he said, slightly disoriented.

"This is nothing," scoffed Mikhail. "I've been through worse."

The Nightingale suddenly collapsed under the weight of Mikhail's shoulder, pulling him down with her. Ivan picked up his father's arm and wrapped it around his shoulder as they made slow and steady strides to the Georgian house. Mikhail inhaled deeply, fighting through the sharp pain spreading outward from his shoulder. The Nightingale picked herself up and followed close behind.

Sofia opened the driver's side door, hopped out, and slammed it shut before dashing around the vehicle again.

Konstantin grabbed her arm and swung her around. "What were you thinking bringing us here?" he hissed, his gray eyes narrowed. "Are you trying to get us all killed?"

"I am only trying to help," whispered Sofia. "Please, trust me."

Konstantin released her arm slowly, gazing at her in disbelief. "Who are you trying to help? You, or us?"

"What's that supposed to mean?" she gasped, her eyes narrowing in anger.

Konstantin pointed his finger and raised his voice. "You have this foolish, childlike fantasy that you'll find the reasons why your father left you in this house." Sofia opened her mouth but quickly closed it. "You're not going to find it here, Sofia," Konstantin continued harshly. "Give up this childhood fantasy."

Sofia glared at him darkly and walked briskly to the house.

Konstantin stood frozen to his spot. How could he have spoken to Sofia like that?

Alexandra poked her head through the curtain again, chuckling hysterically.

"What's so funny?" smirked Marie.

Alexandra stopped laughing and let out a deep, heavy sigh. "I have not had this much fun since George was born," she said enthusiastically.

Marie rolled her eyes, laughing on the inside. "George would probably send the royal army looking for us."

Alexandra grabbed her sister by the shoulders, her brilliant blue eyes flashing with mischief. "I have a plan!"

"Oh, dear," muttered Marie.

"We are going to sneak past Mr. Handsome, steal the truck, and gun it back to the palace before teatime!"

Marie slipped her hand through the curtain, fondly gazing at Konstantin. "How are we going to sneak past him? He has the body of a Cossack."

Alexandra paused for a few moments and smiled. "I am a queen. I think I know how to distract a man."

Marie scoffed playfully and pointed her finger. "I don't think you thought this plan through," she muttered.

Alexandra grabbed her sister by the shoulders again, and her eyes narrowed. "Nothing is going to keep me from teatime, Minnie. Nothing!"

Konstantin moved the curtain with his fingers, tossing the two sisters a seductive smile. He offered Marie his hand. "Would Her Imperial Majesty like me to escort her to the safe house?"

Marie scoffed again. "If I had a ruble for every time that I heard that," she boasted sarcastically.

Alexandra chuckled.

Marie gently placed her hand on top of Konstantin's and leaped from the truck. Alexandra squeezed Konstantin's hand tight and followed, and they both locked arms with him. The two Danish sisters and the Russian soldier made slow strides to the safe house.

"Just so you know, I am recently widowed," said Alexandra flirtatiously.

Marie scoffed and rolled her eyes again. "Don't worry, my dear sister. We can share him." Konstantin blushed slightly.

Sofia knocked on the door three times before Helen answered. She wore a dark green dress that fell loosely around her waist, and her bouncy red hair cascaded in waves down her shoulders. Her amber eyes darted from Sofia to Mikhail, then back to Sofia again before they rested on the two royals for a few moments.

Her husband wasn't going to like this.

"Hello, Helen," said Mikhail, cheerfully and exhausted.

"Come in. Quickly!" whispered Helen, her voice quivering in fear.

Mikhail hobbled in, his arm hanging down around Ivan's shoulders. Ivan walked inside the house carefully, guilt stabbing his gut. Konstantin escorted the two Danish sisters inside, feeling Alexandra tug on his arm. Sofia followed him, her clear eyes glued to the ground and her arms folded close to her chest. As The Nightingale put a foot in the doorway, Helen extended her arm out, blocking her.

"Do something with that truck before your father comes and sees it," her stepmother hissed.

The Nightingale climbed back in the truck and parked it in the back of the house behind a barn.

Helen stepped outside briefly, her eyes searching for snipers. She brought her foot back inside and shut the door behind her, locking it. She turned her body around halfway and stopped. As she stared at Mikhail's blood on the floor, flashes of the Great War returned to her. Helen took a step back, her stomach turning.

As soon as The Nightingale stepped back through the threshold, Helen grabbed her by the arm, swinging her body slightly forward. "A word in the kitchen," she hissed into her ear.

Helen had almost forgotten everyone else. She turned and announced, "There is a place to hide in the library. Mikhail knows where it is. My stepdaughter and I will return with bandages." She took a step forward and lost her footing on the blood for a moment. "And someone, clean this mess up!"

The Nightingale followed her stepmother into the kitchen and shut the door behind her. Helen's hands clasped onto a kitchen chair, and she breathed heavily and stared at the floor. The Nightingale placed her hand on Helen's shoulder, but Helen violently slapped her hand away.

"Don't touch me!" she snapped. The Nightingale stepped back, and Helen collapsed into the chair, her heart accelerating. "Are you crazy bringing them here?"

"It wasn't me who brought them here," said The Nightingale quietly.

Helen looked up, and her eyes widened. "It was that woman."

"Who?'

Helen arose quickly and searched the cabinets. "That woman," she began, her eyes searching for bandages. "The one with raven hair. What does she want? Money?"

"I don't know what you are talking about."

Helen ignored her stepdaughter and continued, "I did not want Ivan Mikhailovich here until I was ready."

"Gabriel is willing to make a deal with you."

Helen stopped and turned around sharply. Her eyes narrowed at The Nightingale. "What?"

"I said—"

"I heard you." Helen turned around, facing the cabinets again, and scoffed. "You can tell him that I am not interested."

She would take a bullet than make any deals with Gabriel.

"When we first met twenty-five years ago, you were the most beautiful woman I've ever seen," said a man from behind.

The Nightingale swallowed hard. Her father was home early from the bank.

Helen glanced up. Her husband stood in the kitchen doorway, with his hands in his pockets and a seductive smile on his face. Once upon a time, that gorgeous grin would have worked like a charm. Not anymore.

"And when I met you, I thought you were the most charming man that I'd ever met."

The Chupacabra didn't say anything for a few moments. "May I come in?" he asked quietly.

Helen nodded and handed her stepdaughter the bandages. "Please, go tend to the cat, Jana," she said, referring to the stray gray and black tabby that circles the house, scavenging for food.

The Nightingale rushed past her father and down the hallway. The Chupacabra watched his only daughter disappear into the drawing-room. He wondered how long Helen would play this game and keep hiding whatever it was that she didn't want him to find.

He turned and walked towards his wife. He caressed her soft auburn hair with his fingers and pressed his lips against her cheek, kissing it softly.

Helen closed her eyes, her heart accelerating. "John, what are you doing? We are going to be late," she whispered.

The Chupacabra ignored her and kissed her shoulder tenderly.

"Johnny, stop."

The Chupacabra was surprised to hear that pet name. He smiled mischievously. "I've missed my wife," he said, kissing her lips passionately. "Come to bed with me, please? It could be like it used to be." His voice was low and seductive.

Helen pushed him away from her. "Things will never be the way they used to be!" she said Helen, her tone low and cold.

The Chupacabra felt a flash of anger. "It's been six months, and I have been nothing but loving and patient!" he screamed, his words rattling with anger. "Don't you think the time of grieving for Penelope is over?"

That was the name of her only niece, her sister's child, now dead with her sister. "Don't you dare speak her name!" hissed Helen.

"And don't you dare speak to me like that!" roared The Chupacabra.

Sometimes, when Helen looked at him, she saw her husband. The man she was now looking at was not him. He was a monster.

"I don't have time to argue about this. We are going to be late picking up Henry from the train station," she said harshly.

Helen made light, quick strides to the kitchen door.

The Chupacabra grabbed her arm and squeezed. "Don't you dare walk away from me when I am not done talking to you!"

Helen could feel the weight of his hand crushing her arm. "John, let go of my arm," she pleaded, her eyes flashing with fear. His grip tightened, causing her to squeal in pain. "John, please, you're hurting me!"

The Chupacabra wasn't there anymore. His mind had traveled elsewhere. He was thinking about the bank, Operation Dragonfly, the scandalous letters. His life and ego depended on all of those.

"Johnny!" That name brought The Chupacabra back to reality, and he released his grip on Helen's arm. She collapsed to the floor and buried her arm into her lap defensively.

The Chupacabra glared at his wife. He did not have the patience to be compassionate or remorseful towards her. "Meet me in the car in three minutes," he said darkly.

Helen heard the front door slam a few moments later. She hated him but somehow loved him. However, after today, she wouldn't have to put up with him anymore.

She picked herself up off the floor, made her way to the empty library, and pressed her ear against the bookshelf. She heard light footsteps click across the hardwood floor, and they stopped in front of the hidden door.

There was a secret room behind the bookshelf that her own husband didn't know about. Helen often went there to hide from him on bad business days. She sighed, walked briskly to a desk, and opened the drawer to reveal a revolver. She reached for the weapon and placed it inside a small emerald purse on top of the desk. She then dug through the purse and found a pen, scribbling a message on paper. She hung the purse over her shoulder before striding confidently to the front door.

Moments later, Helen was riding in a taxi with her husband.

"Did you really mean all the things you said in Austria?" asked The Chupacabra.

"I say a lot of things, John," sighed Helen impatiently.

"You know exactly what I mean." The Chupacabra ran his fingers through her hair again and looked at his wife lovingly. "I can't live without you, Helen. I can't lose you."

There once was a time when Helen would have felt the same way. She looked at her husband with no ounce of feeling. *You lost me a long time ago,* thought Helen. "What did I ever do to deserve a man like you?" asked Helen slowly.

"You stole me from your sister." The Chupacabra kissed her lips.

"People make mistakes," said Helen darkly, looking out the window. She noticed they'd passed the bank. They were going the wrong way. "This isn't the way to the train station."

"Helen, we're not just going to the train station today."

"What?"

"Helen, I am taking you to a doctor that specializes in mental patients. His name is Dr. Popov. After he heard that you drove a car into a window a couple of days ago, he wanted to take a look at you," smirked The Chupacabra.

"Take a look at me?" repeated Helen. She slipped her fingers around the car door handle. Nothing was going to keep her from reuniting with her son. Nothing. "Why are you doing this?" she asked her husband.

"Like I said. I cannot lose you."

Helen gathered up her courage and opened the door, half her body leaning out of the moving vehicle.

"Helen!" The Chupacabra leaped forward and grabbed her arm. He pulled her back inside the vehicle and slammed the door shut. "Don't you ever do that again!" he shouted, pulling her into his arms. "I can't lose you."

Helen buried her face into his shoulder and cried, yet she felt unsafe in his embrace.

The room behind the bookshelf had been a hidden part of the Georgian estate. It was a small room made of light green porcelain, decorated with five beautiful plates on each wall. The plates were hand-painted, and they were imported from France. A crystal chandelier hung from the ceiling, which had a breathtaking mural of a woman from the fifteenth century riding on a stallion. The hardwood throughout the room was polished and was a stunning backdrop to the white mahogany furniture.

Mikhail reclined on the sofa after gently removing his shirt, revealing the muscles throughout his stomach and arms.

Konstantin reached his hand inside his coat, pulling out a flask. He handed the flask to The Nightingale. "Are you sure you want to do this?" he asked.

The Nightingale nodded gently, taking the flask from Konstantin's hand. She had dug out buried bullets inside her own body before, and this shouldn't be any different. She dug through her trench coat, searching for something sharp, such as a knife.

Sofia sat alone at the table. She exchanged glances with Konstantin and frowned. They still weren't speaking to each other.

Alexandra tossed a chess board on the table and glared at the younger woman sharply. She said, "Have you ever beaten a queen at chess?"

Marie Feodorovna nervously stood in the corner, with her arms crossed. Her eyes stared at the floor, her mind lost in thought. Ivan gazed at her deep blue eyes. It was like looking into a deep, beautiful ocean instead of pupils. Ivan knew he had seen those eyes before.

"Your granddaughter had your eyes?" said Ivan quietly.

Startled, Marie slightly jumped and gazed at the young man. His brilliant blue eyes stared back. Maria's lips curled at the corner of her mouth. Ivan had, indeed, struck her curiosity. "You knew my granddaughter?" muttered Marie, her voice sounding hopeful. She took a few steps forward.

"Yes," sighed Ivan. "I knew her very well."

Marie took another step forward and asked, "Which one?"

Ivan felt a strange mixture of happiness and sadness. It was a special kind of pain that he didn't want to go away. "Anastasia."

As soon as Ivan said that, Marie felt her heart shatter all over again. She gasped, "How do you know her? How did you meet her? Is she alive?" For a moment, she exchanged glances with her sister.

"Minnie," gasped Alexandra, her voice full of worry.

"It's fine, Alix," dismissed Marie. She glanced at Ivan again. "Please, tell me everything."

Ivan reached inside his pocket. As soon as his fingertips touched the letter, it resurrected memories that made him want to laugh and cry. He smelled her perfume again, and it was as if violets flooded the room. He felt her touch again, her hand wrapped around his, bringing him back to life. He felt her warm lips pressed against his, and they tasted like honey. He closed his eyes, his mind dragging him back through time.

He was somewhere else—someone else.

Ivan was nineteen again. Snow hit the ground, lightly covering St. Petersburg in a thin blanket. He climbed out of a car and walked up the steps of his cousin's mansion. His mind shifted forward in time to that night—the night of New Year's Eve—1916. He stood in the middle of the ballroom.

Music flooded the room, men and women spun around him. He felt like he was suffocating. When he thought he couldn't stand it anymore, Ivan's eyes rested on her for the first time. She wore a dark blue dress and a beautiful smile.

Ivan opened his eyes and smiled, fighting to hold the tears in his eyes. It had all been because of a letter from Russia.

I remember. . .

Chapter 11

Operation 1916

It was around four in the afternoon, on New Year's Eve, in the city of St. Petrograd. Ivan arrived at the home of a woman he used to love. He was greeted by an entourage of servants and led to the dining room. As soon as Ivan walked into the large dining room, he felt oddly out of place. Two chandeliers hung from each side of the ceiling, and the walls were creamy white, with crown molding. The dark oval-shaped walnut table had thirty chairs crammed tightly around it.

Ivan had been asked to wait there. He took several steps forward and sat awkwardly on the edge of one of those uncomfortable chairs. He sipped on cold tea and read the morning's newspaper. He read the propaganda and devoured every word.

Ivan read the palace menu; caviar, lobster soup, pudding, roasted duck, and chicken. Ivan felt a surge of anger and fought back the urge to punch his fist against the wall. How dare these people stuff their faces while the Russian people are starving!

He returned his attention to the newspaper and skipped over to the smut column; the secret lives of the Emperor's four daughters, written by their lovers. As Ivan skimmed through the article, part of him wondered if any of it was true. Then Ivan glared at the political cartoons. There had been a drawing of Tsar Nicholas, and he was clapping his hands joyfully, laughing at revolutionists hanging by their necks. The following cartoon was even more disturbing. Nicholas' German wife, Alexandra, reclined in a bath full of blood with a sickening grin on her face. She said, "If Nicky could kill more of these revolutionists, I could have a bath like this more often."

That made Ivan sick.

"Hasn't anyone told you not to read the newspaper, Vanechka?" said a soft voice behind him.

Ivan lifted his eyes from the paper and looked plainly at the cream-colored wall. No one had called him that name since he was a boy, and it brought back memories that tugged on his heartstrings.

It couldn't be, could it? As he turned sharply, his hand knocked over his tea, spilling it all over the newspaper.

He awkwardly stood up, slightly embarrassed at the mess he'd made. "I like to be well informed," he said nervously.

Svetlana giggled softly. "About what? Gossip or the war?"

Ivan didn't answer. It was both, he supposed. Still, he couldn't believe that he was looking at her again. It had been three whole years.

Svetlana Stepanova had grown into a beautiful, tall, slim lady. Her dark honey hair was drawn into a perfect bun. Her embroidered white dress was loose around her tiny waist, and she had a string of pearls around her slender neck. Svetlana was the younger half-sister of Ivan's cousin. She was the girl who Ivan loved as a boy. He never told anyone, but he used to fantasize about marrying her. But then he grew up, and things changed. He became a Bolshevik and revolutionist. And Svetlana married someone else.

Svetlana sighed and continued, "The only real news we have in Russia is about the war. But even that news is propaganda, and I stopped reading the paper because of it. Besides," She stopped and looked around as if someone were listening. "There is enough gossip that happens around here."

Ivan looked at the tea-soaked newspaper again.

"I'll have the servants clean that up for you," she said.

Ivan gazed at her again and swallowed nervously. Servants, he thought. Ivan would never get used to the sound of that word.

"It took you long enough to come and see me," she said softly. "I was beginning to think you were never coming." She smiled widely and took three steps towards him.

He took three steps back.

Svetlana stopped, and her smile faded. She seemed confused, her face covered in disappointment. Her lips parted a little bit. It looked as if she might say something but didn't.

"I heard that you are a mother now," said Ivan indifferently.

After a few moments, she swallowed and nodded firmly. "Polina is two now. She has hundreds of beautiful dolls and dresses. Anything a girl could ask for." She paused between sentences and fidgeted with her golden wedding ring. "She drew me a beautiful picture yesterday." She gave Ivan a hesitant smile, sadness swirling in her pupils.

"How's Maxim?"

Maxim was Svetlana's husband for the past three years. He'd spent most of Polina's life fighting in the war. Svetlana didn't know if he was dead or alive. She could care less. He sure didn't. They never spoke. The only news she received was from the gossip or from newspapers. It was a marriage of convenience—a financial contract. Svetlana had been used as a pawn, so her family could climb up the social ladder. It wasn't until after Polina was born that she realized her mistake.

Ivan had no idea how miserable he made her. Sometimes, she thought it would have been better if she had never met Ivan at all. Then, she wouldn't have feelings, and perhaps she'd hate herself a little less.

She gave him an unreadable stare and opened her mouth to speak when a man walked briskly through the other entrance of the room.

"Hello. Sorry I am late," announced Gabriel loudly. "I had a late luncheon with my father and his business associates that I couldn't get out of." He strode up to Ivan, his footsteps heavy as he went. "My name is—"

"Gabriel von der Reis," said Ivan, completing his sentence.

Gabriel appeared slightly impressed. He raised an eyebrow. "So, you've heard of me," he uttered proudly.

"Only by reputation."

"You have quite the reputation yourself, Codebreaker."

Ivan gave Svetlana a sharp look. "So, this is why you've invited me here," he said slowly.

Svetlana smiled awkwardly and swallowed. "I really did want to see you again, Ivan," she said nervously. It appeared that she might say something else, but Gabriel cut her off.

"Let's put personal matters aside." Gabriel gave Ivan a warm smile and stepped forward. "I had to meet you. You can help me get what I want."

Ivan looked at Gabriel carefully and took a step back. "What do you want?"

Gabriel's smile faded. "It's about tonight. We need to talk."

Chapter 12

Operation Conflicting Wills

Not far south from St. Petersburg, on hundreds of acres of freshly cut grass, Tsarkoe Selo seemed like it belonged in another realm. Elaborate bridges crossed over small canals. Luscious gardens dotted the landscape, with lilacs and roses blooming in the spring. A replica of a Chinese village shimmered in the sunlight. Nearby, a Turkish marble bath was shaded by fruit trees. In an isolated corner of the park, there was a golden palace, with a tall iron fence surrounding it, guarded by Cossacks and thousands of Imperial guards with bayonets.

Inside the palace, beyond the grand columned ballroom and mazes of halls and corridors, was the left-wing that served as the Romanovs' living quarters. It was complete with a drawing-room, a music room, two studies, a grand library, and an indoor saltwater swimming pool. It was the Tsarina's world, her labyrinth, her prison. She replaced the velvet carpets and curtains with floral wallpaper and filled the room with porcelain pots and vases. She wished her family to live as simply as possible. The most famous room of the Alexander Palace was the Empress' lilac room. The carpet, curtains, and even the furniture were a beautiful shade of light purple. It was a refuge for her from Russia, the servants, and her broken mind.

The Empress' oldest daughter, Olga, was a timid twenty-one-year-old with piercing gray eyes and a slim figure. Her face was round with beautiful Slavic features, and she wore her dark blonde hair drawn back into a tight bun. She wore a light pink chiffon evening dress with a warm blanket wrapped around her shoulders. She leaned against the purple wallpaper while her hand touched the cold glass of the window. Her eyes glared at the frozen world outside the palace and wondered what it would be like not to be a Grand Duchess. She huffed and struggled to keep her perfect composure.

Her mother, Alexandra Feodorovna, quietly knitted in a wheelchair. She was a forty-four-year-old German woman with a stern look. She wore a white puffed-sleeve shirt, a black skirt with a belt around her waist, and pearl earrings. Her auburn hair had traces of gray and white. She lifted her head and narrowed her gray eyes at her husband.

"Anything interesting in the newspaper today, darling?" she asked quietly.

Tsar Nicholas Romanov was a slim, handsome, forty-eight-year-old man, with light brown hair combed over to the side and a dark beard that he kept carefully trimmed. His oldest daughter had inherited his nose, which was small and round. His deep blue eyes were calm and soft. He wore a white uniform, with medals covering his chest.

The Tsar reclined on the sofa, looking at the newspaper in disgust. He glared at the cartoon image of his wife bathing in blood. "Nothing, dear" he lied. He closed the paper and folded it into fourths.

Later, Nicholas was going to find all the newspapers in the palace and burn them before his wife could see them because if she did, there would be no living with her. It would be Anastasia and the fire fiasco all over again. He couldn't have that.

Alexandra gave her husband a testing gaze. "Alright," she muttered. The Empress tossed the yarn and needles onto the carpet and slowly rose from the wheelchair, leaning on the arm for support. As her feet touched the carpet, she felt a sharp pain shoot down her leg. She winced, biting her tongue to keep from screaming. She released her grip on the wheelchair and made slow, painful strides to the sofa. "Hand it over," she demanded.

Nicholas' eyes widened. "Alix, you shouldn't be on your feet," the Tsar said, his voice full of worry.

Alexandra ignored him and took another step forward. "Nicky," she said impatiently. "I am fine. Hand it over."

The Tsar jumped on his feet and took several steps back. "I am afraid, my love, I can't let you do that." He put the newspaper behind his back and tossed his wife a playful grin.

"Nicky, I command you to give me that newspaper."

"I veto that command."

"Nicky, this is not a constitutional democracy."

Nicholas chuckled. "I am the Tsar. I can do whatever I want."

In the corner of his eye, he noticed his daughter looking forlornly through the window. "Olga, you know you don't have to do this."

Olga turned, and her light blue eyes rested on her father. "No, Papa," she muttered, giving her father a loving smile. "I want to do this for the sake of Russia and the monarchy."

Nicholas studied his daughter. Her smile said one thing, but her eyes said another.

Olga sighed deeply, thinking of the immense pain she was under to pick a suitor quickly. She did not love any of them. "How did you meet Mama?" she asked. Although she'd heard the story countless times, it was nice to have a little reminder that even in the royal world, you can still find love.

Nicholas' mind went back in time. It was over thirty-two years ago. Nicholas Romanov was a handsome, athletic sixteen-year-old boy with a charming smile and a wicked sense of humor. He had, somehow, been charmed by the shy, awkward twelve-year-old girl. Perhaps, it was because she made him laugh. Or perhaps, it was because the little German princess wasn't like the other Russian girls.

He didn't fall in love with her that night. It wasn't until her next visit to Russia many years later when she came to see her sister in St. Petersburg. Nicholas had visited his uncle that afternoon when he saw her again. Alix wasn't a child anymore. She was a seventeen-year-old young woman with beautiful, slender features. As soon as Nicholas laid eyes on her, he'd made up his mind. Alix was going to be his wife someday.

"We met the night of her sister's wedding," recalled Nicholas. "She fell in love with me, then. And then one day, your mother wrote me a letter that said she was coming to Russia to marry me."

Alexandra folded her arms and gave him a stern look. She scoffed and pointed her finger at him. "Nicky! That's not what happened, and you know it."

Nicholas gave his wife a wicked smirk. "Well, then, you are going to have to refresh my memory, dear wife."

Alexandra thought about that night. No one thought Princess Alix of Hesse would amount to anything. She was a motherless girl and the second youngest of seven children. Her older sister, Elisabeth, had made a good match with Grand Duke Sergei, the son of the Emperor and uncle to the next Tsar. No one ever thought Elisabeth's baby sister could do any better.

It was crowded on the day of Elisabeth's wedding, and Alexandra's mind was reeling with anxiety. She had hidden in the back of the ballroom to avoid making a scene. It must have been some strange twist of fate that she caught the eye of the heir to the Russian throne.

"We met at my sister Elisabeth's wedding, and we didn't see each other again for another four years. I was visiting my sister in St. Petersburg when you fell in love with me."

"Whatever you need to tell yourself, dear," teased Nicholas.

Alexandra sneered. "Clearly, I married your father for his sense of humor."

Nicholas bellowed with laughter. "And I do recall that you were courting your cousin, the Prince of Wales, around the same time you were courting me."

"Mama," gasped Olga. "You didn't."

"We weren't really courting," muttered the Empress.

"But he proposed, dear," said Nicholas innocently.

Olga covered her hands with her mouth and gasped again, "Uncle George proposed to Mama!"

"Her grandmother, Queen Victoria, wanted your mother to be the next Queen of England," added Nicholas.

"Why did you choose Papa?" asked Olga.

"Because." Alexandra paused for a few moments, hating that her husband would have the satisfaction.

"I fell in love with him," she said slowly.

Nicholas took her to the theater and ice skating. He bought her jewelry, and he even threw a ball in her honor. Alix didn't know she had fallen in love with him. It wasn't until after the party when she realized her feelings for him, too.

Nicholas chuckled. "I told you that she chased after me."

"I almost didn't marry you," Alexandra said with reserve.

Nicholas became quiet. His blue eyes rested on his bride.

Alarmed, Olga asked, "What happened?"

Nicholas and Alexandra exchanged glances.

The odds were stacked high against them. No one approved of the marriage. Nicholas' parents thought it was a bad idea, and they weren't too fond of Germans. Alix's grandmother, Queen Victoria, opposed the marriage too. And she wasn't too fond of Russians either. Perhaps, it was because Nicholas' grandfather proposed to Victoria many years earlier, and she rejected his marriage proposal because they were both in line for their own thrones. Then his grandfather got engaged to another woman the next week, leaving the young Victoria heartbroken and angry. But those were just rumors. Nicholas' mother thought Alix wasn't worthy enough to marry her son, let alone be Empress of Russia. She felt the Russian people would tear her apart. Queen Victoria wanted Alix to marry her cousin, but Alix rejected the marriage proposal. She gave her grandmother an ultimatum: she would be Nicholas' wife or not a wife at all.

It was Victoria who conceded first. Nicholas' parents warmed up to Alix, eventually. Perhaps, it had something to do with Nicholas threatening to shave his head, and become a monk, if his mother and father didn't let him marry the love of his life. Reluctantly, his parents allowed the marriage.

"After your papa proposed—" Alexandra continued.

"Your mama said no," said Nicholas.

"What?" gasped Olga. "Why?"

"I was madly in love with your father, but I didn't want to change my religion," answered Alexandra.

Olga had never heard this before.

Alexandra couldn't stand on her feet anymore. The pain returned, and it felt like her hips were going to crush under her weight. Her hands leaned on the sofa for support as she fought through the pain. Nicholas put his arm around her protectively.

"Can I help you get back to the wheelchair, darling?" asked Nicholas lovingly.

Alexandra looked at Nicholas, her eyes flashing in pain. Her husband had the best intentions, but sometimes, he made her feel like an old woman. The burden of her many pregnancies and arduous labors put tremendous pressure on her sciatic nerve, leaving her with a lifetime of unbearable pain. She'd received a lot of criticism for not leaving the palace for years, but Alexandra couldn't leave even if she wanted to, not with her fragile back and poor heart.

"Nicky," sighed Alexandra. "I don't need your help."

Nicholas tossed the newspaper on the sofa and said, "I wasn't asking." Before Alexandra could protest, he picked his wife up and carried her.

"Nicholas!" gasped Alexandra.

He ignored his wife and set her down in her wheelchair. "You're welcome," he said firmly.

Alexandra reached for her knitting yarn and needles from the carpet and began to knit again. As she started on a new stitch, she noticed Nicholas had sat back down on the sofa again. He stared at her lovingly, and she couldn't even imagine the reasons why he still loved her.

Twenty-two years ago, most people would have agreed that she was a devastatingly beautiful woman. Tsarevich Nicholas seemed to have won the lottery. His bride-to-be had been a slender redhead from Germany, with clear blue eyes and rosy cheeks.

Those were the days when she was young and beautiful.

Now her famous looks have long faded. She celebrated her forty-fourth birthday the previous summer but looked much older than that. Her rich auburn hair had salt and pepper streaks due to the stress in her life. Rumors were going around that she was a German spy plotting to take down Russia. If she were going to destroy Russia, why would she spend ten years trying to bring an heir into the world? And because of the stress, she lost the ability to sleep. Dark bags sagged below her gray eyes. Alexandra was still the wife of the Tsar, but she no longer looked like his bride. And after hundreds of panic attacks, two miscarriages, and rumors of her infidelity, she would never understand why Nicholas still loved her.

Olga walked to the sofa and sat down next to her father. She looked at him, curiosity covering her face. "What made Mama say yes?"

"What makes you think she said yes?" said Nicholas in a joking matter.

"Nicholas, I said yes," protested Alexandra. "My sister spoke with me, and she said that I wouldn't be changing religion but changing how I expressed it."

"After I proposed to her again, she fell into my arms and never left."

"Is this true, Mama?" asked Olga.

Alexandra didn't answer. Instead, she fought the urge to smile.

Olga loved that her parents were in love. It was a rare thing for European monarchies to marry for love instead of convenience. Olga sometimes imagined herself ten years older, with two sons and two daughters, married to the love of her life. If her brother weren't so ill, that could've happened. *Sometimes, the things we want are never meant to be*, she supposed.

Her father said he wouldn't force her to marry, but this marriage would be his insurance policy to save the dynasty. If her brother ever died, Olga's son would be the next heir. This was Olga's choice, of course, and she'd already made up her mind, even if she died inside.

She turned to her father and said, "Do you think that I'll learn to love Karl or Boris?" Karl was a Romanian prince who was after her dowery, and Boris was a Russian Grand Duke with an ambitious mother. Those men frightened her.

Nicholas and Alexandra exchanged looks. Before he could answer, there were several small knocks against the door before it opened slowly.

A woman appeared in between the doorway. She was tall and slim and somewhat boney. Her face had broad features, and her dark hair was drawn into a neat bun. She was wearing a long, wool, emerald coat, and black button-down boots. Her eyes were a light shade of brilliant blue, with a hint of sadness. She looked distantly troubled.

"Aunt Olga!" said Olga cheerfully.

Nicholas appeared somewhat surprised. "I didn't expect to see you today. I thought you were in England with Mama."

Aunt Olga looked at her brother and sighed. "Mama and I got back last night. She's tired from the trip but is very eager to see her grandchildren." Her gaze turned to Alexandra.

"And why won't dear, Old Mother pay us a little visit, then?" asked Alexandra darkly.

Aunt Olga's gaze hardened. "Well, she doesn't feel welcome here. Not with all the dirt inside the palace."

"Is that so?"

There was a long pause. The two women exchanged a few deadly glances. Alexandra looked at her sister-in-law, studying her as if trying to pinpoint her weakness. Aunt Olga stood stiff and emotionless like a soldier. It appeared she was waiting for permission or some sort of a formal invitation to enter.

Nicholas clapped his hands together, breaking the silence. "So, tell us about your stay in England?"

Aunt Olga took a sharp breath and stepped forward, closing the door behind her. She walked to the center of the purple room and stopped. She looked around, masking her disgust. If only her mother could see what her daughter-in-law had done to this place.

The Empress sighed impatiently. "Don't just stand there, darling," she grumbled. "Sit!"

Aunt Olga sat down on a lavender armchair, slightly uncomfortable. She shot Alexandra a sharp beady look. "I heard there might be a royal engagement soon," she said, her vocal cords brittle.

"Perhaps," muttered Alexandra.

The thought of her sweet niece getting engaged to one of those narcissistic maniacs made her blood boil. "How's Alexei today?" she asked innocently.

Nicholas and Alexandra had a dark little secret. And their greatest nightmare was that someone would discover it. Alexandra didn't think that her heart could bear it if someone found out about her son's illness. The image of her dying son clinging to life flashed in her mind. She spent every waking moment at Alexei's side. She hardly slept and barely ate. His fever was dangerously high and wouldn't break. Now physically exhausted and emotionally drained, she'd retreated from her battlefield to her wheelchair.

"I know why you're really here, and my answer remains no," said Alexandra coldly.

"Alix, please. Reconsider," said Aunt Olga calmly.

Alexandra couldn't put her finger on it, but she had this terrible feeling that something terrible would happen that night.

"My mind has been made. My girls will not be going," said Alexandra, struggling through her thick German accent. "Besides, they are behind on their lessons."

It seemed that Aunt Olga had reached a point where her patience was wearing thin. Her mother didn't raise a fool. That was an excuse so that the Romanian prince, what's-his-face, or whoever he was could court her oldest niece! But fortunately, all her nieces had better tastes than that. Her own mother, Marie Feodorovna, pressured her to marry a man she didn't love. And look what happened; the marriage ended in a divorce. And Grand Duchesses don't get divorced. Olga just couldn't believe that they were doing that same thing to her beautiful, innocent niece.

She sighed heavily. "Why won't you listen?" she asked coldly. "Mama was looking forward to seeing the girls at Anchikov Palace this Sunday."

Alexandra stopped knitting and tossed Aunt Olga a piercing stare. "I would remember to whom you speak," said Alexandra calmly. "I am still the Empress."

"And I am the daughter of a Tsar," said Aunt Olga firmly.

Alexandra's gray eyes sent a deadly message; not another word.

"Can I say something?" shouted Olga. "I can speak for myself. I don't feel like going anywhere tonight. I would rather stay home."

Her mother and aunt nodded in agreement.

Nicholas looked at Alexandra, his blue eyes pleading for her to reconsider. Alexandra sighed, trying not to feel too guilty. Her daughters didn't get to leave the palace too often. Tonight, her two older daughters would go to the theatre with Nicholas to see a play, with Olga's suitors, of course. That left her two younger daughters at home, with nothing but each other to keep them company. Alexandra shot her husband a beady glare; *don't look at me like that.* Nicholas' eyes softened. Then, something inside Alexandra melted.

"I will have my lady-in-waiting fetch Maria and Anastasia in the morning."

"Really?" gasped Aunt Olga.

"Don't make me change my mind."

Nicholas got up and placed his index finger over his mouth. The three women gave him confusing looks. He walked over to the door and wrapped his hand around the knob. As he opened the door, his three youngest children fell forward.

As soon as Alexandra saw her only son stumble onto the floor, she stopped knitting. The image of him dying flashed in her mind. She'd never felt so afraid in her life. Last night had been the worst. As she prayed, she helplessly watched her baby boy scream her name, begging her to take the pain away. Before he fainted, he told her that after he died, she wouldn't have to see him in pain anymore. Those words plunged a dagger through her heart. It was a mother's worst nightmare.

She opened her mouth to scold her children, but nothing came out. In fact, it was a huge relief to see that her son was all right.

Nicholas took a step forward, his arms crossed. "And what are you doing out of bed, little man?"

Alexei was a small twelve-year-old boy with blue eyes full of mischief. He had an oval face and delicate features like his mother. But he had his father's wicked sense of humor. He wore a sailor uniform, with his brown hair combed over to the left. He was much thinner than usual because of the recent attack, but he would gain the weight back. The poor boy could not eat very much because of his pain.

The boy smiled at his father nervously. "Can I go with Aunt Olga and my sisters, too?"

Nicholas turned to his wife, and she shook her head in disapproval. He sighed heavily, turning back to his son, and shrugged. "Perhaps next time," he said, frankly.

Alexei picked himself up off the floor and frowned, choking back tears. He never got to have any fun. Not without his mother's approval. It wasn't fair! He slammed the door reluctantly as he left the room.

Nicholas turned to his wife again and whispered, "Should I go talk to him?"

Anastasia picked herself up slowly. "No, Papa," she said dismissively.

She was a short fifteen-year-old girl with dark auburn hair and bright blue eyes. Her heart-shaped face was chiseled with beautiful features, and her nose was small and slender. She had three nasty scars on her forehead, the result of childhood innocence and curiosity, but she hid the injury with thick bangs. She was dressed in a long, blue button-up overcoat with a black skirt, gloves, and boots.

Maria grabbed her younger sister by the hand, pulling herself up. She cuffed her hand over her ear and whispered loudly, "Besides, he is going to that secret stash of chocolates in his bedroom that he thinks no one knows about."

Alarmed, Alexandra raised an eyebrow. "His what?"

Maria giggled. She probably shouldn't have said anything, but her mother was going to find out later; she always did.

Maria was a tall and slim seventeen-year-old with thick brown hair, big blue eyes, and full lips. Her square jawline was strikingly beautiful, and her smile flashed with innocence. Her body was strong and well built, strong enough that she could lift her mother off the ground when she fell. She wore a velvet button-up overcoat, a purple scarf, and very worn black boots.

"Are we really going with Aunt Olga, Mama?" asked Anastasia, her blue eyes beaming eagerly.

Before Alexandra could answer, the door opened again. "Are we ready to go?" said Mitya, the adoptive son of Alexandra's older sister, Elisabeth.

He was a devastatingly handsome twenty-five-year-old with dark blonde hair and striking blue eyes, a long nose, and full lips. He was a tall and muscular man, and his navy flannel suit was well fitted and expensive. His shoes were dark leather.

"I don't feel like it tonight, Mitya," sighed Olga.

Mitya frowned. Olga looked so beautiful, even when she was sad. "Why not?" He took a few steps forward, his arms crossed.

"Because I don't feel like it."

Mitya gave her a mischievous glare. "Oh, you're going."

Before Olga could protest, Mitya pulled her from the sofa and threw her over his shoulder.

Olga shrieked. "Mitya! Put me down."

Mitya ignored Olga and chuckled. "Not a chance. You're going, and you're not leaving me alone with Prince whatever-his-name-is and Grand Duke thorn-in-my-side all night."

Olga looked at her parents, her eyes pleading. "Mama. Papa. Don't let him do this."

"Have a nice time, dear," muttered Alexandra. And if Olga didn't know any better, there might have been a slight grin on her mother's face, and it had also appeared that she fought the urge to laugh.

When Mitya was halfway over the threshold, Nicholas stood up and said, "Oh, Mitya."

Mitya stopped and turned. There had been a small part of him that wondered if he'd gone too far this time.

"I'll meet you in the car," Nicholas finally said.

"I want him to do me next!" whispered Anastasia.

"I'm going first," declared her older sister.

"What makes you think you are going first?"

"I came before you."

Olga glared at her two younger sisters and snarled.

Nicholas kissed his wife's cheek and gazed into her eyes. "My beautiful Sunny," he whispered softly. "I love you."

Alexandra exhaled slowly and quietly, realizing that she'd been holding her breath. "How can you stand to look at me?" she said quietly.

"Because every time I look at you, I fall in love all over again," said Nicholas lovingly.

A small but beautiful smile curled on her lips.

It was a beautiful thing to see Alexandra Feodorovna smile, and even more beautiful to know that Nicholas Romanov was the reason behind it.

"Take care of our girls," she whispered.

Nicholas kissed her hand and promised, "I will." The Tsar followed close behind Mitya and gently closed the door.

Aunt Olga arose from the armchair and ushered her two young nieces out. "Oh, you silly girls! Come along." *Especially before your mother changes her mind,* she thought.

The girls kissed their mother goodbye and followed their dear Aunt Olga down mazes of palace corridors.

Maria carefully eyed her younger sister after noticing a smirk on her face. "What's that look?"

"It's about tonight," answered Anastasia. "I have a plan."

Chapter 13

Operation Mikhailovsky Theater

It was colder than death that night. Snow fell lightly on the cobbled stone path, covering the ground with a thin blanket of snow. The arctic wind felt like daggers cutting across his cheeks and hands. Dmitri Bogrov walked lightly across the Italian bridge over the frozen Griboyedov canal, blowing into his hands and rubbing them together.

Dmitri was a thirty-year-old man from Ukraine with an expensive, hand-sewn gray suit. His black Italian leather shoes had just been polished. The round glasses he wore centered his oval-shaped face and brought attention to his eyes that were darker than coal. His silky dark hair was neatly combed to the back, and his cedarwood and pine French cologne was strong and intoxicating. A Browning revolver was concealed inside his coat pocket.

Dmitri, who spoke German and Russian fluently, studied law and philosophy. And he was one of the Okhrana's top double agents, the Tsar's secret police.

His mission tonight was to kill Peter Stolypin, the Prime Minister of Russia. No mistakes could be made. The Prime Minister had to be dead by midnight, or Dmitri would pay dearly.

He took a sharp left turn and quickly crossed the street. The Mikhailovsky Theatre was enormous and resembled more of a palace than a theatre with its light yellow, rectangular-shaped building with white columns and three floors. The theatre's lights lit up the night like a bright star shining in a dark sea. It was built in 1833, the oldest opera house in St. Petersburg. There were hidden rooms and secret passageways concealed around the theatre, and Dmitri was forced to pick one of them as an escape route. Security was tight that night. Thanks to the theater's special guests that evening, Imperial guards were posted at every entrance and exit. The Tsar and his two oldest daughters were coming to watch tonight's show, *The Tale of the Tsar Sultan*, along with The Crowned Prince of Romania and two Grand Dukes.

There would be nowhere to run.

It looked like the whole city was there that night. There was a long line of taxis and horse-drawn carriages outside the theatre. However, they weren't there to see the show. They were there to see the Tsar.

Dmitri leaned against a theatre pillar as he calmly dragged a cigarette. The warm smoke melted his cold lungs. He inhaled deeply, the intoxicating scent calming his nerves.

He'd never killed before. Not even during his time as a revolutionist, but that was many years ago. He had been arrested by the Okhrana for conspiracy and was interrogated and tortured for many days until he finally cracked. For his punishment, he had been given two choices; become a double agent or face execution for his crimes. He chose to become a double agent and was forced to write a descriptive confession of his treason and sign a repentance statement. The confession would be used against him if he ever betrayed the Okhrana. He was pardoned for his crimes and released to spy on the most dangerous man in the world—The Chupacabra.

After eleven long years of sleepless nights, Dmitri's loyalty was torn. He served two masters. He went deep undercover and spied on The Chupacabra. He discovered deadly secrets and reported back to the secret police. The Okhrana knew about his political crimes and terrorist attacks, and threats before they ever happened. And The Chupacabra knew there was a mole.

There was going to be a manhunt. Dmitri felt betrayed, as again, he was given two choices; murder the Prime Minister before midnight tonight, or

The Chupacabra would torture and kill every single member of Dimitri's family before killing him, too. The mission was suicide, of course, but The Chupacabra knew that.

It was because of the Prime Minister's political pursuits that made The Chupacabra his enemy. Stolypin promoted Russian peasants to become industrious farmers because many Russians lived together and worked on the same land, sharing the work and responsibility. But Stolypin's policy allowed peasants to work on their own land, breaking free from the communes. If his plan succeeded, Russia could turn into a capitalist country, and she would finally catch up with the twentieth century and the rest of the world. As long as blood coursed through Stolypin's veins, the civil war would never happen. The Chupacabra hadn't spent this much money just to see his greatest investment crumble to the ground. Something had to change. An intervention had to be made.

Dmitri looked at his golden pocket watch. If his sources were correct, his target would arrive at the theatre...now. Dmitri stowed away his pocket watch as his dark glare watched a cab slowly drive up the curve. A short bald man with a round body and bushy beard climbed out of the vehicle. He looked to be in his late forties. His waist suit was dark gray, and his black shoes looked brand new.

Dmitri's target had arrived.

Two other men climbed out of the vehicle; a Baran and a General. The Baran was short and fat, with a stern look on his face. The General looked older than the Prime Minister, his face decorated with age marks and wrinkles.

Dmitri tossed his cigarette on the ground and stubbed it out with his foot.

The Baran slammed the cab door shut. And the three men walked inside the theater, gossiping about politics and women.

Dmitri followed and watched them from a close distance. They all made their way into the grand theatre. It was a large circular room with a crystal chandelier hanging from the ceiling and a red velvet carpet. The wooden stage was enormous and looked like it could fit hundreds of people on it.

The Baran and the General made their way to the front row behind the orchestra, and Dmitri sat directly behind them. They were just in time for the show to start.

On the opposite end of the theater, facing the stage, was the Imperial box department. Olga sat on the edge of her seat, slightly slouched. She held a pair of golden opera glasses in her hands, her soft blue gaze staring through them curiously.

Mitya sat directly behind Olga, lightly tapping his hands against her shoulder. Olga slowly turned around in her chair. Her slender lips slipped into a genuine smile, reaching her eyes.

"Do you see anyone we know?" whispered Mitya.

"The Prime Minister is here with his entourage," uttered Olga.

"Where is he sitting?"

Olga handed Mitya the glasses. His blue eyes looked through them, scanning the audience.

"First row. In the middle. Behind the orchestra," whispered Olga.

Mitya moved the golden glasses around the theater, and his eyes stopped on the Prime Minister. Peter Stolypin sat there sheepishly, his eyes heavy and fighting to keep his head up. Mitya gave the glasses back to Olga. "Did you see any beautiful women here tonight?" Mitya's lips broke into a mischievous smile. "I've got my eye on one right now. She is the prettiest girl here."

"Do I know her?" giggled Olga.

"No," sighed Mitya. "She tends to be a little shy in a large crowd like this."

A young woman sat beside Olga, with her posture nearly perfect. She was a tall and slender woman with elegant features. Her piercing gray eyes were hooded, and her deep auburn hair was drawn into a perfect bun. Her embroidered evening gown was satin, and pearl earrings dangled from each ear. She sat there quietly, with her lips pinched closed together. Her name was Tatiana, and she was younger than her sister Olga by almost two years.

"I wonder if Mr. Olga Romanov is here tonight," teased Mitya.

Olga dropped her jaw, speechless and Mitya chuckled.

Tatiana didn't know why, but she wished someone wanted her like Mitya wanted her sister. In fact, Tatiana wanted Mitya to love her as she loved him. She fell in love with him three years ago. It was her birthday, and Tatiana had been walking through the rose garden with her friend, Miss Botkin. She belittled herself that whole afternoon, comparing herself to her three beautiful sisters. Mitya overheard most of it, being just an earshot away. He turned and said that she was beautiful, too, and a one-of-a-kind girl.

After Tatiana heard those words, something melted inside of her. No one, and certainly not a man, had ever been that blunt with her before. It was a terrible pain to want to be with someone, but that someone doesn't want to be with you and wants your sister instead!

Grand Duke Boris Vladimirovich sat in the far back corner of the Imperial box. He was a short and slim man, with dark hair and a thick mustache. He wore a dark uniform, with golden buttons down the middle. Boris was invited to tag along by Nicholas, and he agreed to come. His gambling days were pretty much over as his mother made sure of it. His debts were very high, but a marriage to Nicholas' oldest daughter might fix that. After the play tonight, Boris might even propose.

The Romanian Prince named Karl Hohenzollern sat quietly next to Boris, with his legs crossed. His hair was jet black, and his light gray eyes were colder than ice and went nicely with his dark waistcoat and trousers.

He stared at Olga Romanov, with a smug look on his face1. It was no secret that he was sent to Russia to propose to Nicholas' oldest daughter. A little friendly competition never hurt anyone, except possibly his pride. His mother told him to befriend the competition. Somehow, there was less bloodshed that way.

His eyes rested on Mitya, and his expression softened. Perhaps, it was the wine. But the Romanian prince had an idea. "How about we make a little wager?" he whispered, his accent thick and heavy.

"What?" asked Boris.

Karl ignored that statement and leaned in closer. "Two-hundred-thousand rubles says that he is going to make the first move tonight."

"Are you drunk?" said Boris, sounding half confused and half surprised.

At that point, Tatiana overheard them talking and listened carefully.

Karl gave Boris a blank stare, and then his lips broke into a hysterical smile. "I don't know." He laughed. His trip was supposed to be a diplomatic mission for Romania, and instead, it had been more of a vacation with lots of wine.

Boris thought about it. He would do anything for money. "You're on," the Grand Duke muttered.

Those dogs are betting against my sister, Tatiana thought. If she had half a mind, she'd turn around and say something. That kind of horrendous behavior could not be tolerated! But something inside her made her hold her tongue. Then again, there were no lines she wouldn't cross for her sister. None.

Deciding she would speak up, Tatiana turned around sharply and gave them a dark look. "Call off the bet," she hissed.

Karl looked at Tatiana as if she hadn't said anything at all, but Boris was caught off guard. His eyes widened. "Whatever do you mean, Your Imperial Highness?"

"Don't you 'Imperial Highness' me." Tatiana's glare hardened. "If you don't call off the bet now, I won't give you the antidote for the poison that was placed in your wine."

Boris and Karl chuckled like a couple of hyenas. But Tatiana wasn't laughing.

"You're joking," said Karl, his voice quivering nervously.

Meanwhile, Nicholas sat in the center of the Imperial box, listening to his daughter in amusement. He'd taught her well. He fought the strong urge not to smile or laugh.

Tatiana turned to her father. "Papa, where did you put the antidote?" she asked innocently.

"Which one, Tatya?" her father asked.

"The one you made this morning."

"The one for the vodka, or the one for the tea?"

"The antidote for wine," replied Tatiana, fighting the desire to smile.

Boris had vodka and tea this afternoon, and he fought to conceal the worry in his face. Karl had been drinking wine all day. Some part of him wondered if they weren't joking at all. If they were, he could take a joke as he had a decent sense of humor. *But if they weren't?*

Nicholas gave Karl a mischievous glare. "I can't say in front of the Romanian."

Tatiana sighed heavily. "My condolences, gentlemen."

The play had begun. Olga's gaze stared at the stage, watching the ballerinas spin and twirl. "Shhh!" she hissed. "The play has started."

The *Tsar Sultan* was a tale about three beautiful sisters who lived long ago in a faraway kingdom. These sisters worked in the palace, and one day, the three girls were fantasizing in the courtyard about what life would be like if they were married to the Tsar Sultan. The oldest sister said she'd prepare a feast for the entire kingdom. The next sister said she would weave lovely linen for the whole world. The youngest sister said that she'd give the Tsar Sultan an heir. The Tsar Sultan overheard the conversation, fell deeply in love with the youngest sister and asked her to marry him. After becoming his wife, the Tsar Sultan gave her two older sisters jobs as a cook and a weaver.

The youngest sister gave birth to a strong, healthy baby boy while the Tsar Sultan was away on a campaign. His wife sent a messenger to tell her husband the good news. However, the older two sisters had killed the messenger and replaced him with a man who'd do their bidding. This man brought the new message to the Tsar Sultan that read; your wife has given birth to a little unknown creature.

The Tsar Sultan was horrified. He wrote a letter back to his wife, asking her not to do anything until he returned to the palace. The messenger delivered the letter to the older sisters, and they replaced the real letter with a fake one, ordering their younger sister and her child to be thrown into a barrel and cast into the ocean.

The Tsar Sultan's orders had to be obeyed. The royal palace guards put the youngest sister and her child into a barrel and threw them into the cold, merciless sea. Somehow, the mother and her son washed up on the beach of some deserted island; they had survived.

When the Tsar Sultan's son grew up, he became a mighty hunter, skilled with a bow and arrow. While out hunting one day, he saw a huge hawk attack a beautiful swan. As soon as the hawk was about to murder the swan, the young man shot an arrow at the large bird, killing it instantly. The beautiful swan thanked him and said that she would serve him forever.

The following day, a marvelous city appeared on the island, where there was nothing before. There were bakeries, churches, and houses. The young man walked through the city with his mother, marveling at everything the swan had done. The people had even made the young man their king.

One day, a merchant ship came to the island. Those men belonged to the Tsar Sultan's kingdom. The young king welcomed the men into his kingdom and offered food and drink. He'd bought several items and asked the men to give the Tsar Sultan his respects.

The next day, the ship set sail and left the island. As the young king watched the boat disappear into the horizon, he thought about his father. He couldn't understand why his father would toss him into the sea as an infant. He turned to the swan and told the magical bird that he wanted to see his father, and the swan turned the king into a small bird. The king followed the ship, flying to the Tsar Sultan's kingdom.

The merchants told the Tsar Sultan of their journey and about that mysterious island led by the young king. The Tsar Sultan wanted to see the island and meet the king himself. But his wife's two older sisters convinced him not to. They told him of a rare squirrel that could crack emeralds and sing beautiful melodies. And that was more interesting than some fabled island.

The young king flew back to the island and told the swan what was said. The next day, he woke up and found a squirrel in his garden, cracking an emerald and singing a lovely song. The king ordered a crystal house to be built for the unique and talented animal.

It was sometime later before another merchant's ship sailed to the king's island. The merchants were so mesmerized by the magical squirrel that they couldn't wait to go back and tell the Tsar Sultan about it. As they set sail, the king asked the swan to see his father again. The swan turned the king into a bumblebee. The king took off and followed the merchants to his father's kingdom.

Once the Tsar Sultan heard about the squirrel, he wanted to travel to this magical island. Once again, two older sisters talked him out of going. They told the Tsar Sultan of thirty knights who protected the sea and would be more of a wonder to see than some old island in the middle of nowhere.

The young king flew home and turned back into a man. He told the little swan about the thirty knights who protected the sea. Then, as a big wave crashed against the shore, thirty knights emerged from the sea. The swan told the king that the knights would protect the island now.

Almost a year later, another ship returned to the island. The sailors stared at the knights in awe. They returned to the Tsar Sultan's kingdom and told him about the knights who could emerge from the sea and protect the island. The Tsar Sultan had to see the island now.

Meanwhile, the young king was very lonely. He wanted a wife more than anything, so he ordered the swan to give him one. The swan nodded, and with the flap of her wings, she turned into a beautiful princess. The king took her in his arms and kissed her deeply. He married her that evening by the beach as the golden sunset began to set in the deep blue water.

When the Tsar Sultan arrived at the island, he gazed and marveled at everything he'd heard so much about. In the throne room, the Tsar Sultan saw a woman he hadn't seen in a long time; his wife, the lost Queen. He gathered her in his arms and held her close, afraid to let go. As he cried in her arms, he said that he thought he'd never see her again. The Queen kissed his lips tenderly and said there was someone she wanted him to meet.

Then, the Tsar Sultan realized that the young king was his son.

A grand feast was held throughout the kingdom, celebrating the reunion of the father and son. The two older sisters went into exile, never to be heard from again. And the royal family lived the rest of their days, never separated again.

And that was the tale of the *Tsar Sultan.*

Two hours into the play, intermission was called. Nicholas stretched in his seat and arose quickly. He turned his body sharply around, facing Mitya earnestly. "I am going outside for a smoke. Would you care to join me?" he asked.

Mitya jumped quickly from his seat. "It would be my pleasure."

He then turned, and Mitya glared at Boris, who had his light blue eyes resting on Olga. Mitya knew what he was thinking. And he wanted to punch him in the face for even thinking that way. Mitya glanced at the Prince Karl of Romania; however, his face was unreadable.

Karl stood up and buttoned up his coat before turning to Nicholas and giving a halfhearted smile. "Thank you for the pleasant evening. I am not feeling very well, and I may retire for the night."

Alarmed, Nicholas said, "May I call you a cab or a doctor?"

"No need. But thank you for your kindness this evening." Truth be told, Karl really wasn't feeling very well that night. His mother was coming to Russia, and that woman was half the reason he drank. "Have a good night." he said to Nicholas before turning to leave. As Karl turned the doorknob, he gave Boris a sharp glare.

Boris sighed and rolled his eyes. He turned to Nicholas, "May I smoke with you gentlemen?"

Nicholas and Mitya exchanged awkward glances. "Of course!" exclaimed Nicholas.

Mitya glanced from Boris to Olga and winked. Olga's mouth dropped, and her expression hardened. Mitya grinned playfully, causing Olga to shake her head, her lips breaking into a little smile.

Tatiana cleared her throat. "I need a bit of fresh air," she said quietly. She slowly arose from the chair and turned. As she turned, she tripped over her long dress and lost balance. Her body leaned forward, seconds away from hitting the carpet. Mitya held his arms out, and Tatiana fell into them.

"Are you alright?" asked Mitya.

Tatiana didn't answer. Her heart accelerated. She was lost in his bright blue eyes, trying to find her way out. She noticed that his arms felt strong and muscular. And his face was devastatingly handsome.

"Are you alright, darling?" asked Olga.

Startled, Tatiana stepped back, her light blue eyes gazing shyly at Mitya. Then, she shielded her face. "Pardon me," she said, slightly embarrassed.

She waited for Mitya to move, and he realized that he had been blocking her path and stepped back. Tatiana walked quickly to the door, her face slightly blushed. She opened the door, entered the hallway, and slammed it behind her.

Nicholas patted Mitya on the shoulder and grinned slightly. He made quick, light strides to the door, holding it open for him.

Mitya turned his body halfway but stole one last glance at Olga. She sat on the edge of her chair, looking slightly uncomfortable. Her brilliant eyes begged him not to go. She looked so beautiful, even when sad. Mitya frowned slightly before walking through the doorway. Nicholas gently closed the door behind them.

Olga was now alone.

Tatiana and Mitya chatted in the middle of the hallway about court gossip and a crazy woman Mitya had encountered during his travels. Boris smoked, listening in.

Nicholas found a nice quiet corner to smoke. He hadn't had a cigarette in over an hour. The withdrawals were murder, and his nerves were getting the best of him. He dug through his pockets. There must be one somewhere! He never left home without one. He pulled out his golden cigarette case and opened it. There was one left. He slipped it in between his lips and lit it, taking a long drag.

"I never thought that I'd see you around here again," said a woman from behind.

Nicholas choked on the smoke, and his eyes widened. He'd know that soft voice anywhere. Could it be? "Little K," he muttered. The Tsar turned, clearing his voice. "Mathilde, I didn't know you were performing tonight."

Mathilde Kschessinka was a tall, beautiful Polish woman in her late forties. She had a slender and muscular body, dark hair, and soft blue eyes. Her dress was deep blue and fit tightly around her waist, with big puff sleeves.

She took several steps forward, smiling at Nicholas. "I am not," she said, her Polish accent heavy. "I choreographed tonight's show."

"And I heard that you achieved your aspirations of being a Prima Ballerina. It's a little late, but congratulations are in order."

"Thank you."

Nicholas looked down and noticed a diamond bracelet around her wrist. He took a deep breath and gave her half a grin. "I see you still wear my little gift."

Mathilde quickly glanced down at the bracelet nervously. She was half surprised that he'd even remembered it. She glanced back up and smiled widely. "I wear it every show. It's kind of a good luck charm."

Nicholas remembered the days when he was a twenty-two-year-old, young, and naive Tsarevich, who would rather read a good book than go to parties and talk to women. Besides, he already had eyes on one woman, the German princess called Alix. His father thought throwing a beautiful, Polish ballerina in his face would put a stop to those fantasies. Nicholas did fall in love with Mathilde, but in the back of his mind, he was in love with Alix, too.

Nicholas and Mathilde took many strolls through St. Petersburg together. One summer evening, they passed a jewelry store, and Mathilde commented on the beauty of the diamond bracelet on display in the window. Later, Nicholas bought the bracelet and surprised her at a dress rehearsal with it. Mathilde squealed in delight, and she promised that she'd never take it off. It appeared Mathilde was a woman who kept her word.

"How are you these days?" asked Nicholas, taking another drag of his cigarette.

"I'm doing well," the ballerina muttered. "I have been busy working a lot and taking care of my son."

Nicholas choked on the smoke again.

Alarmed, Mathilde asked, "Are you all right, Nicky?" She shouldn't have spoken to him so informally. It was a force of habit.

"Your son," whispered Nicholas fearfully. "Is he—"

"No, he's not yours," gasped Mathilde. Her voice dropped to a low whisper. "I actually don't know who the father is."

Nicholas took a sharp breath of relief.

The Polish ballerina frowned slightly. Mathilde never had Nicholas' child, despite what the rumors say. But she often wished that she had. She was pregnant with his baby at one time, but that was twenty-two years ago. It was cold that day, and it snowed that morning. The road was covered in thick layers of ice, but it seemed like a fun idea to go out on a sleigh ride. Everything happened quickly. The carriage slid on the ice and flipped over. Mathilde made a hard fall and lost the child. Nicholas was devastated, but Mathilde was relieved. His baby would have ruined everything she worked for. Her life would have been over. The child also would have caused complications in his marriage and her career. It worked out for the best. Her career came first, her family second.

Mathilde glanced over his shoulder. For a small moment, she thought she saw Nicholas' wife standing across the hallway, and she felt a surge of panic. Then she blinked several times and smiled gently. "Is that your daughter?"

Nicholas looked back and nodded.

A long time ago, Mathilde thought that no one would ever love Nicholas more than she did. She was glad to know that she was wrong. "She looks like her mother. She is so beautiful, Nicky." She had done it again. She'd addressed him informally. She tried to hide her embarrassment with a warm smile.

"Thank you," he said softly. Nicholas didn't mind that she called him by his nickname. He wished more people did.

Mathilde took a deep breath, gathering the courage to say things that were left unsaid long ago. "I am sorry that things ended the way they did, Nicky," she said quietly.

Nicholas had proposed to her twice, and Mathilde had rejected him twice. She wanted to be a ballerina, not his wife. Her world would have never been the same. She would have been dismissed as a ballerina and automatically labeled the royal consort. No more performing, no more dancing. She would have been an ornament to be seen but not heard. And eventually, she would have faded away into the background.

But sometimes, she wondered if she had made some horrible mistake.

Mathilde took the news particularly hard when Nicholas told her about his engagement to Princess Alix of Hesse. She wept and wailed like a small child. Nicholas didn't mean to make her cry, and it made him feel more guilty than he already did.

"Well, I am sorry I broke your heart." He said.

In the audience, Dmitri glanced at his wristwatch. It was three hours before midnight. He needed to act. The lives of his family were at stake. He stood up and slipped his fingers inside his coat, reaching for his revolver. He pulled it out and aimed. Shrieks echoed around him. The Prime Minister turned around, his eyes pooling with fear. Dmitri summoned the courage and fired.

The gunshot echoed in Olga's ear, and her heart leaped from inside her chest. She leaned against the balcony, her eyes peering down at the audience, searching for the source of the sound. Her eyes stopped on the body of The Prime Minister. He was on the floor in a fetal position, his chest and gut bleeding heavily. Another gun shot was fired. Olga flinched and covered her hand over her mouth, slowly grasping what had just happened. Terror filled her whole body, and she let out a terrifying scream.

Nicholas heard the shots from the hallway, and terror coursed through his whole body. "Olga," he gasped. He turned the knob and pounded against the door, but it wouldn't budge. Olga was blocking the door. "Olga, what's going on? Why is the door locked?" said Nicholas, his voice shaking in fear.

"Papa, you can't come in. They are shooting!" screamed Olga. She pushed against the door harder, keeping it closed. She needed to protect her father.

Nicholas' heart rate accelerated, the adrenaline pumping through his veins. "Olga, open this door." His fist pounded against the door harder. "Olga, please, open up!" If anything happened to her tonight, he'd never forgive himself. And Alexandra would murder him. He pushed his arm and shoulder against the door, and Olga pushed her hands harder on the other side. But no matter how much she tried, her father was stronger. Nicholas pushed the door open. "Olga," said Nicholas, his eyes flashing with fear. "Are you hurt?"

Terror was imprinted on Olga's face. Her finger pointed down at the orchestra.

Nicholas leaned over the balcony and saw the body of the Prime Minister. As his mind froze in shock, he could only think of one thing; his wife must never know about this.

Chapter 14

Operation Cathouse

It was three hours till midnight.

The youngest Romanov sisters tiptoed quietly across the servants' quarters in their aunt's St. Petrograd palace. Anastasia walked in front, wearing a dark blue chiffon evening dress, with small diamonds dangling from her ears. She had her auburn hair placed in a beautiful, neat bun. Maria walked five paces behind Anastasia. She wore a light pink silk georgette evening gown, with a small pearl in each ear. While their aunt was busy playing hostess upstairs, the two girls were going to have a little fun. The servants' quarters were dark and empty, leaving them alone. Maria bumped into a small wooden cabinet. It made a loud thud. Anastasia turned sharply and placed her finger over her mouth.

"Shush! You're going to get us caught," whispered Anastasia, her blue eyes glaring at Maria. She then turned around and continued to walk forward.

Maria tiptoed faster, trying to keep up with her sister. "Anastasia, this is crazy," said Maria, her voice somewhat half distressed and half admiring.

"I know."

Maria gently grabbed Anastasia's hand, swinging her around as her blue eyes pooled with worry and concern. "This is a bad idea."

Anastasia's lips broke into a mischievous smile. "No. This is a terrible idea." Anastasia turned around again and turned left down the hallway. Maria grunted and followed quickly, struggling to keep up with her sister.

Anastasia placed her hand on the doorknob and turned the handle, opening the door an inch, and Maria put her hand against the door, closing it shut. She stepped forward, and her eyes rested on her younger sister. Anastasia stepped back; her blue eyes widened.

"What will we do if we get caught or if someone recognizes us?" Maria questioned.

Anastasia moved forward again and pushed the door open. "We'll be fine, Mashka," said Anastasia, her voice slightly annoyed. Anastasia walked through the doorway, stepping outside their aunt's mansion. Maria rolled her eyes and followed her sister through the threshold closing the door gently behind her. Her blue eyes gazed at her sister's head. She was about ten paces in front of her.

"Anastasia, wait!" Maria whined. She hurried toward her sister and grabbed her hand again. Anastasia stopped. Her head turned sharply around. "There will be no guards around if something were to go wrong." Maria pleaded.

Anastasia thought about it and shook her head. "No. Nothing will go wrong," she said playfully.

Maria loosened her grip on her sister's hand, her eyes swirling in disbelief. "How can you be so certain?" she asked coldly.

Anastasia smiled devilishly. "Just trust me." She walked quickly around the cream-colored mansion, snow falling lightly around her.

Maria was a few paces behind, again struggling to keep up. "Last time you said those words, you set my hair on fire."

Anastasia chuckled, recalling the memory. She had convinced Maria that she needed to do some sort of initiation for a club that did not exist. Maria lay on the floor with lit candles around her. As Anastasia walked around chanting, her foot accidentally knocked over a candle, setting Maria's hair on fire. "You weren't hurt." Anastasia stopped at the edge of the sidewalk and waited.

"My hair was singed. And Mama had to cut a few inches off."

"It grew back," said Anastasia carelessly.

A black 1909 Renault slowly drove along the sidewalk. The driver was a tall and slim woman with blond hair and light blue eyes. Her face was square, with beautiful Slavic features. Her chiffon dress was black, and a string of pearls dangled below her slender neck. Her name was Miss Tatiana Botkin. She was the only daughter of Doctor Botkin, the court physician.

Miss Botkin stopped the car in front of the curb.

"Hello, Tatiana," said Anastasia cheerfully, opening the door.

Miss Botkin sent her a frustrated glare. She didn't know how, but she kept falling into traps to be a part of Anastasia's crazy shenanigans. "You girls owe me big time," she hissed darkly.

Maria tugged on her sister's arm. "How did you get her to do this?"

"Don't ask," replied Anastasia. She looked at Miss Botkin and gave her a lovely smile. "You look lovely this evening, Tatiana."

Miss Botkin rolled her eyes. "Are you girls ready?"

Maria folded her arms and eyed her sister carefully. "You are not going to listen to me, are you?" she sounded slightly disappointed but not surprised. Anastasia climbed inside the car and smiled at her sister. Maria sighed heavily. "Then I better tag along before you do something stupid without me." She said, climbing in after her sister. As soon as she sat down, the vehicle moved forward.

"I knew you'd come around," giggled Anastasia.

"Oh, shut up!"

Tatiana Botkin's mother and father were once happily married with four children. Dmitri was born first, and then Yuri came along. Then, poor Tatiana was born, the only girl. Then, her brother, Gleb, was born.

Her father got a job working for Tsarina after her old physician died. That was back in 1909. He'd been loyal as a dog since then, working until late at night and returning home early in the morning. He had a couple of hours of rest and returned to the palace. He practically lived there. The job as the court physician was demanding and her father all but ignored his family. Her mother began a passionate love affair with Miss Botkin's German teacher. All the Botkin children knew about it. They weren't stupid. Not every teacher spends the night in their student's home. But they pretended not to notice.

A year later, her mother waited until all the children were asleep and waited up for her husband. Miss Botkin sat quietly on the top of the stairs and listened as her mother told her father that she no longer loved him and wanted a divorce. He begged his wife not to take the children. He said that she could take anything with her. Furniture. Money. The car. But not the children. She left the next day, with a suitcase in one hand and a divorce agreement in the other. Miss Botkin noticed that her mother didn't wear her wedding ring that day. She told the children that she was going on a vacation, then walked out of their lives forever. Miss Botkin was forced to become the new mother. She now ran the household, scolded the boys, and even cooked meals.

After the abandonment of his wife and mother of his children, Dr. Botkin took his children to work with him. The Botkin children became playmates to the Imperial children. Somehow, the Grand Duchesses became her sisters. Miss Botkin loved them deeply, but there was resentment. She was constantly cleaning up after them, lying for them, and covering up for them. Especially for Anastasia, who drove her to insanity most of the time. And that family had stolen her father from her.

Half an hour later, Ivan was becoming agitated. He wore a navy gray double-breasted suit, and he hated every moment. He would have much preferred to walk around in uniform. But Gabriel insisted that he wear a suit.

Music and laughter flooded the room. The noise gave Ivan a headache.

"There you are! I was looking for you," said Svetlana cheerfully.

Ivan turned whipped around to her face. She wore a light purple evening gown dripping in diamonds.

"Svetlana," said Ivan quietly. "You look wonderful."

"Well, so do you," said Svetlana without thinking, then moments later, she wished that she said nothing at all. She put her hand on Ivan's shoulder. "I hate that things must be awkward between us."

Ivan pulled away. He was not going down this road again. "You made your choice. And I made mine," he said darkly.

Svetlana needed her husband Maxim's money to fund the party. And Ivan needed a family. In the end, they both got what they wanted.

Svetlana took a step back, her blue eyes full of regret. "Excuse me." She turned and disappeared into the crowd.

Ivan walked to the center of the ballroom. He needed fresh air to breathe as it felt like the walls were slowly closing in. He felt like a showcase on display. And where was his dear Aunt Vera? She was supposed to be here an hour ago. She had something Gabriel wanted, and Ivan was ordered to get it.

The music and laughter grew louder. That was it. He couldn't wait on Aunt Vera any longer. Ivan went outside to get some air.

A few minutes later, the three young women pulled around the large white three-story mansion with grand columns.

Anastasia couldn't believe her luck. For the first time in her life, she was free. She wasn't a Grand Duchess or the Tsar's daughter. She could be a normal girl for one night. Miss Botkin and Maria climbed out of the car.

"Anastasia, I heard that our cousin, Louis, will be here tonight. And I am going to introduce him to Tatiana!" said Maria.

"What?" Miss Botkin gasped.

"Then, when you and Louis get married, I'll be invited to your wedding. I'd be your maid of honor, and Anastasia would be your bridesmaid. And you'll be happy and have ten children. And you'll have me to thank for it!" she squealed.

"That's a terrible idea!" protested Miss Botkin. "I don't want to be related to your family."

Maria grabbed Miss Botkin by the arm and pulled her close. "Hush. You'll come to your senses."

"How come you get to be the maid of honor?" asked Anastasia defiantly.

Maria put her hand on her hip and smirked. "Because—tell her, Tatiana."

Miss Botkin grabbed her arm and took a few steps back. "No one is getting married."

Maria gave Miss Botkin a sharp look and folded her arms. "If I told you that he was going to inherit a lot of money, would that change your mind?"

Miss Botkin opened her mouth and closed it. Maria squealed in delight. "It's settled then!" Maria grabbed Miss Botkin by the hand and walked several paces, but Miss Botkin jerked her hand back.

Anastasia couldn't bring herself to get out of the car. Fear had suddenly replaced her audacity. All her courage melted away, and she felt as if she were stranded on a block of ice.

"I cannot believe my eyes," mocked Maria. "Shvibzik is frightened."

Anastasia gave her sister a sharp look, her blue eyes narrowing. "I am not!"

Maria saw through the lie and raised an eyebrow.

Miss Botkin had seemed to reach the end of her patience. She opened the car door and gave Anastasia a nasty glare. "I didn't climb out a two-story window, jump over a fence, get chased by a dog, and steal my father's car for you to chicken out now."

Anastasia swallowed hard.

She hadn't been afraid when she played with matches and accidentally set Maria's gorgeous brown hair on fire. Maria was frantic, screaming and shouting, and acting like an idiot. Anastasia rolled in the dirt laughing as Maria jumped into the lake to put the flames out. Nicholas and Alexandra were furious. Alexandra was forced to cut a few inches of Maria's beautiful long hair, and Maria cried the entire time. Anastasia was banished to her bedroom for a week.

Where was her fear when Germany declared war on Russia? Her mother had opened a private hospital at the palace for wounded and broken soldiers. Alexandra thought Maria and Anastasia were too young to become Red Cross nurses. Instead, the two youngest Romanov girls became patrons. The two sisters played board games with the soldiers, read letters to them, and even wrote back to their families. Anastasia and her sister even put on comedy plays in the hospital. The hardest part was watching the soldiers die. Where was her fear then?

Why was she afraid now? The scheme was her idea. But her ideas didn't get extremely far, and by now, she should have been caught and punished.

Miss Botkin's eyes softened, and she sighed heavily. "Sometimes it's alright to be afraid. It means you are about to do something very brave." She reached out her hand towards Anastasia and she took it, smiling faintly.

Ivan watched a beautiful woman climb out of a vehicle and shut the door.

"If I didn't know any better, Tatiana, I'd say that you like me," she teased.

The other woman scoffed. "Well, don't get used to it." The third woman, with brown hair, let out a giggle and the three young women linked arms, lumbering forward.

Ivan's eyes followed the young woman with auburn hair and deep blue eyes. She didn't look much younger than him, but she was much shorter. She looked beautiful. Suddenly, his heart leaped. What was that? That had never happened before. Not even when he was with Svetlana. His palms became sweaty, and his breaths were quicker. Ivan didn't know what possessed him at that moment. He heard himself say, "Hello."

The three women stopped and turned, slightly startled. The young woman with auburn hair smiled gently at Ivan. The two older women exchanged glances, unsure of the situation or the young man. The younger woman whispered, "It's all right. I'll meet you inside."

Moments later, Ivan and the young girl with piercing blue eyes were alone.

As Anastasia looked at Ivan for the first time, she gazed deep into his sparkling blue eyes and smiled shyly. Her heart hammered with a strange mixture of excitement and anxiety. She had a feeling that in a few moments, her life would never be the same.

"Hello," she muttered.

"Hello," said Ivan nervously. He cleared his throat. "What's your name?"

Anastasia smiled again, laughing on the inside. He had no idea who she was. She could have a little bit of fun with this. "That depends. Who's asking?" she replied.

"Ivan Mikhailovich."

"Well, my name's not important right now."

Ivan's eyes widened. "Really?" A woman had never spoken to him like this before. This would be interesting. "Where are you from?"

"Where I am from is not important either."

Ivan couldn't help but smile. It felt like more of an interrogation than a formal meeting. "Are you going to tell me anything about yourself?"

Anastasia folded her arms and sighed. "Well, Ivan Mikhailovich, I am afraid that I can't disclose any information at this time. Good evening."

As Anastasia turned to go find her sister and Miss Botkin, Ivan begged, "Please, don't go."

Anastasia stopped. Ivan sighed heavily and continued, "Will you go on a walk with me? That is all I am asking. I won't ask you any more questions."

Anastasia turned around, facing Ivan. She gave him a playful grin. "Well, Ivan Mikhailovich, I would love to."

Yosef Volkov gently pushed through the crowd. He wore a blue waistcoat and black leather shoes that evening. Yosef worked for a man named Gabriel von der Reis, and he hated his job, even more so tonight. He had disturbing news for Gabriel that could destroy his father's years of careful planning.

Volkov saw Gabriel sitting on the sofa, with his arms around two women. Gabriel wore a gray flannel suit with a red tie. It amazed Volkov how much he looked like the exact replica of his father. Gabriel would shoot Volkov dead for even thinking that. He needed to approach the situation with caution. If word got out that two of Nicholas' daughters were here tonight, there would be a riot. There were too many Bolsheviks here. And far too many royalists. And Gabriel would want blood—his blood—if there were two Grand Duchesses here tonight and he was the last to know about it. No one recognized the Grand Duchesses, not yet. Volkov swallowed at the thought and deeply inhaled. He approached Gabriel from behind and whispered inside his ear.

"Ivan Mikhailovich is on a walk with Anastasia Romanov."

"What?" Gabriel shouted. In anger, Gabriel tightened his thick fingers around the scotch glass in his hand, causing the glass to shatter. The two women shrieked but he ignored them as his attention was entirely focused on Volkov. "Are you sure? Where are they?"

Volkov nodded. "They are outside. Should I alert The Chupacabra?"

Gabriel thought about it as he picked through the tiny fragments of glass from his fingers, ignoring the splatters of blood on his skin. "No. Don't tell my father. Not yet."

Gabriel was lost in thought. Why would Ivan Mikhailovich do that? Unless he had no clue that he was talking to the youngest daughter of the most powerful man in the world. But that would soon change. Gabriel had an idea. It was going to take manipulation, persuasion, and careful planning, but nothing that he had not done before.

"I would like you to watch them. Follow them and report back to me what you see and hear. And only me!"

Volkov nodded. He knew what that meant. Gabriel had a wicked scheme, and someone was going to get hurt.

Volkov followed his orders. He watched the Grand Duchess and the Bolshevik walk close together along the bank of the frozen lake from a close distance.

Ivan and Anastasia walked close together. Ivan was glad to be outside and get some fresh air. Now he could finally breathe.

"Where are you from?" asked Anastasia.

"I am from Yakutsk."

"What brings you this far from home?" she asked curiously.

Ivan stopped and thought about it. He couldn't tell her the truth, that he was recruited by the Bolsheviks and joined their army. That information might scare her away. He had to come up with a bit of a lie, but something believable. "Work brought me to St. Petersburg."

"What kind of work?" she asked innocently.

Ivan paused again. "It's just a boring office job," he lied.

"Tell me about your family." She flashed Ivan an adorable smile.

Ivan tried to mask his discomfort. "I have no family," he said without emotion. "I have been on my own for a while."

Anastasia's eyes softened; her smile faded. "Oh, I am sorry. I didn't know."

Ivan let it roll off his shoulders. "What about your family?" he asked.

Anastasia gave him a sharp glare. Ivan received the message. "I am sorry," he muttered. "I promised not to ask questions."

"My father runs a family business," Anastasia said quietly.

Ivan laughed. "Now you decide to share a little about yourself," he teased. "What kind of business?"

"I can't say," she sighed.

Anastasia walked faster. Ivan sped after her to keep up. Suddenly, she stopped and stared at the frozen lake. She had many fond memories of that lake. Her father liked to kayak during the summer with her and her sisters. Anastasia also liked to swim with her brother. During the winter, her family would ice skate. Though, her family hadn't ice-skated that year due to everything going on with the war and volunteering at hospitals. There had been no time for such things until now. She turned to Ivan and grinned with a devilish look in her eyes. "Do you know what one of my favorite things to do at the lake is?"

"No."

Anastasia stepped onto the ice.

Ivan felt a wave of panic. "What are you doing?"

Anastasia looked at him playfully. "I am going to have a little fun. You are more than welcome to join me." She used her shoes to glide in small circles across the ice.

"Come out of there," begged Ivan.

"Why?" asked Anastasia curiously.

Ivan scoffed. "Because it's dangerous." He extended his hand, but Anastasia ignored him, gliding across the ice. "I mean it. If you fall in, I will have to jump in and save you. And I do not want to do that."

Anastasia let out a contagious laugh. "I think you are scared," she teased.

Ivan folded his arms. "I am not scared."

"Then, why aren't you in here with me?" As soon as she said those words, she slipped and fell on her back, letting out a painful moan. Anastasia tried to get up, but she fell again, this time on her side. She looked at Ivan, her blue eyes pleading. Ivan sighed and stepped onto the ice. He carefully walked a couple of steps and extended his hand to her. As she grabbed it, he fell backward, landing hard on his back. Ivan stared at the dark, starless sky and said, "Do you always bring down men you've just met?"

Anastasia giggled. "Only the handsome ones."

Ivan tried hard not to smile and got up. Anastasia began to slide forward but Ivan stopped her and held her shoulders steady. Suddenly, they both heard a cracking sound. The ice was breaking! She panicked as the ice began to break away from underneath her feet. Anastasia stopped and looked at Ivan helplessly. Then half of her body fell through the ice. The cold water seeped through her dress and shoes.

Ivan slowly picked her up and carried her across the lake, the ice slowly breaking behind him. Ivan set her down on the frosty grass. Anastasia shivered and looked down. Her shoes were missing, and half her dress was wet.

"You're soaked," gasped Ivan. He took off his coat and wrapped it around her shoulders. "I need to get you to Aunt Vera's and get you cleaned up," he muttered.

"Aunt who?"

Before Ivan could answer, he picked her up again and carried her across the grass.

"Put me down!" she shouted.

Ivan ignored her and walked quickly to the sidewalk. "I am not letting you walk on the cold grass without any shoes," he said.

"Please," she begged. "Put me down! I can walk on my own."

Ivan put her down on the sidewalk and pointed to a house across the street. "My aunt lives there. She can get you cleaned up and a fresh set of clothes."

As Anastasia stepped onto the pavement, Ivan grabbed her arm and pulled her away from a speeding truck that was barreling down the road. He then picked her up again and walked across the street.

"Put me down!" she protested.

"Not a chance. This is the third time you've tried to get yourself killed tonight, and I don't trust your judgment."

Volkov stood by a lamp post and lit a cigarette. The smoke helped him think.

Across the street from him was a brothel. It was a large, rectangular two-story brick building with dead flowers in the front. Volkov squinted his eyes. What was Ivan doing? Surely, he wouldn't go inside the cathouse. Especially not with an Imperial Princess. Volkov choked on the cigarette. That's exactly what he was doing. Ivan made his way to the brothel with the Grand Duchess in his arms. Volkov had the strange urge to slap Ivan across the face.

Ivan gently put Anastasia down and she looked around. She'd never been to this side of St. Petersburg before. "Where are we?" she asked.

"A brothel," Ivan said without thinking. Anastasia's eyebrows raised. Ivan thought about his words for a moment. Why did he say that? "It's not what you think," he said awkwardly. "My great-aunt," Ivan cleared his voice, "lives here... and she has something for me." Anastasia shook her head awkwardly. Her lips broke into a smile, and she laughed.

Ivan knocked rapidly on the door.

A large woman with a round body and a fat neck answered the door. Her red dress was as round as her body. Her hair was a light shade of strawberry blonde; however, it was obvious to most that it was a wig. Her wide eyes were green. This woman's name was Vera Mikhailovna.

"Ivan!" the fat woman squealed. She embraced Ivan in a tight hug and squeezed.

Ivan felt as if his lungs would slowly collapse under her firm grip. "Aunt Vera," he said, practically suffocating. "It's good to see you."

The big woman released Ivan from her grip, and he inhaled deeply.

"It's good to see you too!" she shouted cheerfully. She patted Ivan on the back hard causing him to choke on his own air. Then, she noticed Anastasia, soaked, and shivering in the cold. "Come inside, darling, before you catch a cold."

Anastasia followed Ivan inside and Vera closed the door behind them.

The house was out of the ordinary. Pink paint was chipping off the walls, and there were portraits of strange, beautiful women wearing clothes that would make Anastasia's mother blush. The red carpet was old and tattered with holes. The antique furniture was very outdated, with an ancient and musty smell. Anastasia had never seen anything like it.

"Who is this?" asked Vera, with a wide smile.

Ivan opened his mouth to answer and stopped. He didn't know her name.

"Anastasia. Pleased to make your acquaintance," the young woman said quietly.

Anastasia.

That name was forever tied to Ivan's heart.

"What's your line of work, Aunt Vera?" asked Anastasia.

Vera's emerald eyes widened, and she looked at Ivan. "You mean to say that you did not tell her?"

Ivan buried his face inside his hands and shook his head. He was never getting married, and he was going to die alone. He was sure of it.

"Tell me what, Ivan?" said Anastasia playfully.

Ivan didn't answer. He was slowly dying of embarrassment.

"I am an entertainer, my dear."

Ivan flinched.

Anastasia laughed inside. She'd never heard it called that before.

"She is good-looking, Ivan." Vera winked at her grandnephew. Ivan blushed, slightly embarrassed. Anastasia chuckled. "Let's sit in the drawing-room, and I'll go bring us some tea."

Ivan cleared his throat. "Aunt Vera?"

As soon as Vera turned, she noticed motioned Anastasia to follow her upstairs. Vera looked through her daughter's closet and pulled out a plain dress. She put it against Anastasia's body, muttering things to herself, and then put it back. She pulled out a light pink silk evening gown and squealed, "Perfect."

"Thank you." Said Anastasia.

"Did you hear all the juicy gossip that happened about an hour ago, darling?" asked Vera.

Anastasia shook her head.

Vera cleared her voice. "Peter Stolypin was shot and killed at the Mikhailovsky theatre."

Anastasia's face went white, and her hands went cold. Her father and sisters were at that theatre.

"Are you all right, dear?" Vera asked.

It took a few moments for Anastasia to realize that she'd been holding her breath. "Never better," lied Anastasia. "Who killed him?"

"Some Ukrainian named Dimitri Bogrov."

"What became of him?"

Vera thought about it. "Last I heard, Bogrov was on death's row." Vera smiled and leaned forward. "But that's not the best part. The Tsar and his two oldest daughters vanished without a trace."

Anastasia's heart stopped.

"I'll give you some privacy, dear. You can throw that wet dress into the laundry when you are done."

As soon as Anastasia thought Vera was gone, she strode to the telephone and held it close to her ear. "I need to speak to Gleb Botkin, please."

Moments later, Vera stopped in the middle of the stairway. She stared at her nephew, watching him recline on the leather armchair in the drawing-room. "Where did you find that one?" she asked.

Ivan turned his head. "I honestly don't know."

Vera walked over to Ivan and pulled out a bundle of letters, and she tossed them on his lap. "I hope that you know what you are doing, boy," said Vera coldly.

"How much?"

"Let's call it a late Christmas present."

"Come on," Ivan huffed. "Nothing is free with you. What's your price?"

Vera's green gaze hardened. "I want out of this country. A new passport. Identity. I want to disappear," she said coolly.

"What do you want me to do about it?"

Vera cackled loudly. "Now you're thinking like a Bolshevik."

"That's illegal!" Ivan jumped up from the armchair, his index finger pointed at his aunt. "And that was not part of the agreement!"

Vera stepped forward and Ivan took a step back. He could smell the cigarettes on her breath.

"Our agreement was that I steal information for the Bolsheviks from my clients, and you offer me protection, nephew." She rolled that last word off her tongue as if it was a horrible curse.

"What about your daughters?"

Vera turned, her arms folded. She had four daughters whom she loved, but she cared about herself more. "They'll survive without me," she said under her breath. "They always have."

Ivan sighed. "I won't make any promises, but I will see what I can do."

"Thank you, Ivan," she paused, remembering Anastasia was upstairs. "Go check on your friend. I am worried that she is distracted," she chuckled.

Anastasia heard a familiar voice on the phone.

"Gleb... did my father and sisters return home?... no... don't put your father on the telephone... Yes, please ask him... I will wait." Her eyes glared at an old photo album on the bed. "Yes...Gleb..." Anastasia saw Ivan standing in between the threshold of the bedroom doorway. She smiled. "They did!... late this evening?... Thank you so much, darling... I'll see you later... Goodbye."

Ivan entered the bedroom and sat on the edge of the bed. Anastasia suddenly leaped on the bed next to him, landing in the center. The weight of them both caused the bed legs to snap, and it crashed to the floor, making a loud thud. Ivan and Anastasia looked at each other.

"You broke the bed," said Ivan. His voice sounded amazed and horrified.

Anastasia chuckled. "We broke the bed!"

Ivan laughed.

"What is going on up there?" shouted Vera.

"We broke the bed, Aunt Vera!" exclaimed Ivan.

Vera was laughing so hard, her lungs and stomach hurt.

Chapter 15

Operation Kissing Bridge

Time was a cruel and nasty little thing. Last night seemed like a dream. A beautiful, wonderful dream. Ivan made her laugh. She'd never met a young man who could do that before. Eventually, Ivan asked her about her age. Instead of telling him that she was fifteen going on sixteen, she said sixteen going on seventeen. Well, she couldn't tell him the truth. Then, he probably wouldn't want to speak to her at all. He seemed to have bought it.

Anastasia even told Ivan one of the stories she told the soldiers at the infirmary. The tale was about a young and brave boyar named Ivan. An old witch named Baba Yaya sent Ivan on a quest to complete three challenges and find his father.

Before Anastasia could finish the story, it was midnight, and she had to meet her sister and Miss Botkin at the car. But before they parted ways, Ivan made Anastasia promise that she would meet him at the park tomorrow afternoon to finish the story.

Anastasia couldn't sleep that night. She nearly stayed up all night telling Maria about it. Maria threw a pillow at her sister and demanded Anastasia get some sleep. Anastasia rolled over on her side but couldn't fall asleep. Not after such an eventful night.

Now, Anastasia couldn't keep her head up. She closed her eyes and dozed off, letting out a tiny snore.

Maria elbowed her sister. "Anastasia," she whispered. Startled, Anastasia opened her eyes and gasped loudly.

"Are you all right?" asked her grandmother, Marie. Her blue eyes narrowed, covered with curiosity.

Anastasia nodded slightly and said, "I am fine." She fought the urge to yawn, realizing that it was Sunday. They were expected to spend the entire afternoon with their grandmother, with a formal luncheon. But she promised that she'd meet Ivan at the park. Unfortunately, that would mean getting out of the luncheon early with her grandmother, which wouldn't be an easy thing to do.

"You look exhausted, dear," added Aunt Olga. "How late did you girls stay up last night?"

Anastasia and Maria exchange a few glances.

Marie Feodorovna blew on her lemon tea and put it close to her lips. "How is your mother doing, girls? Her health is better, I do hope."

"Mama is fine. Papa misses you, and he talks about you often," muttered Maria.

Marie stirred the tea with a spoon in a small circular motion, and her blue eyes rested on her youngest granddaughter. "Does he now? I would visit more often if it weren't for the dirt I supposedly bring to the palace."

Aunt Olga cleared her throat and muttered, "Mother."

"How's your father, girls?" said Marie, changing the subject before a heated argument broke out.

"Papa is doing well," said Anastasia nervously, glaring down at the cabbage soup in disgust. She couldn't understand how Maria didn't seem to mind the food as she watched her scarf it down. "The Romanian prince arrived last week," she added.

Marie gave a little smile.

Politically, Russia needed an alliance. There were too many enemies near the borders. A Romanian marriage would ensure an alliance between the two nations. Marie didn't trust Grand Duke Boris' mother, Grand Duchess Maria Pavlovna. That woman had always been jealous of her, because she married the heir and Maria married the spare. According to the line of succession, if anything happened to her oldest son and grandson, the throne would go to Marie's youngest son, Michael. If anything ever happened to Michael, the throne would be inherited by Boris. Of course, his mother would have known that. That woman was using her innocent granddaughter to strengthen her family's claim on the Russian throne.

"That's right. I think a Romanian marriage is what this country needs." Maria added.

Aunt Olga almost choked on her hot cabbage soup. "Mama, I don't think we should put too much faith in your matchmaking skills."

Marie raised an eye. "What's that supposed to mean?"

Aunt Olga wiped her mouth with a napkin and tossed it on the table. "I am saying you should stay out of the personal affairs of your children and grandchildren."

Marie frowned. "Are you talking about Peter?"

Aunt Olga felt a surge of anger at the sound of his name. "Yes, Mama. I am talking about Peter."

Marie frowned again and pointed her finger defensively. "It's not my fault that your marriage didn't work out."

"It wasn't a marriage at all!" shouted Aunt Olga, her voice shaking with emotion.

The room became dead silent. No one shouted at Marie Feodorovna; no one even raised their voice. Except for her own daughter.

"For someone who calls herself my daughter, sometimes, you're not very smart."

Aunt Olga drew a sharp breath. "Are you that embarrassed by me? That your perfect daughter's marriage ended in a divorce?"

"Olga, no mother wants to see her child go through a divorce," said Marie dismissively.

Aunt Olga folded her arms. "Papa wouldn't have allowed the marriage," she hissed.

"Your papa—" Marie stopped speaking and looked down at the diamond bracelet around her wrist. It was a loving reminder of her late husband, Alexander. It was his first gift to her. She always wore it as she couldn't bring herself to take it off.

Alexander had been a strong man and a good father. He was an excellent leader but ruled with an iron fist. They were married twenty-eight years. Those were the best twenty-eight years of her life. Those years were full of love and laughter behind closed doors. If she could go back in time or roll back the clock, she wouldn't change a thing. Those years were perfect.

After Alexander died, somehow, a little piece of her died with him. Marie didn't want to get remarried because she didn't want to love another man the way she loved Alexander. And it was much easier to train a cat than a second husband.

Marie was delighted to see Alexander live on through the eyes of her children and grandchildren. All five of her children had strong Romanov features, especially Olga and Nicholas. Maria had Alexander's will and strength, and Anastasia inherited his wicked sense of humor. It was a terrible shame Alexander never met their grandchildren.

"Your papa would have been proud of you," Marie finished.

"Can Maria and I go to the park before it gets too cold?" blurted Anastasia.

The room became dead silent again. The mother and daughter exchanged quick glances. Marie sighed and gave her granddaughter a cold, stern look. Sometimes, she was too much like her grandfather. Anastasia gave her grandmother an innocent smile.

"You and Maria may go, Nastasia. But bring Timofey with you."

Not Timofey.

Timofey Yaschik was a Russian Cossack. He was about forty years old and wore a long, heavy coat, black boots, and a dark hat. He had rows of ammo across his chest, which made him appear to be dangerous, but he was really a gentle giant. His body was slightly round, but all of it was pure muscle. He reminded the Dowager Empress of her late husband in that regard. Cossack was in his blood as all the men in his family were loyal and brave Cossacks. Timofey was not just Marie Feodorovna's bodyguard but a friend and constant companion. All of her grandchildren loved him. They climbed on him and played with him. Timofey also had a wild side that came out when he sensed danger. It came out more often since the war started. Anastasia adored Timofey as well. But he was like the crazy uncle that you never talked about and left behind at home.

By the frozen Neva, there was a little park. As the new year brought a sharp wind, the garden slept. The golden fountain even slumbered. The lilac trees and flowers were captured in a thin layer of frost. Marble statues and Greek sculptures stood watch as if protecting the frozen garden as it slept through winter.

It was sometime in the afternoon, and Ivan waited by the golden fountain. He wore a long, heavy trench coat, but the frightening cold air still burned his face and neck. He looked at his watch. Where could she be?

Timofey Yaschik was alert. His blue eyes scanned the park for signs of danger. He walked closely behind Maria and Anastasia, ready to pounce on any threat.

Anastasia saw Ivan across the park. Her heart leaped! She grabbed her sister, Maria, and muttered in her ear, "Distract Timofey."

"Why?"

"Do it. And I won't tell Papa that you were the one who drank the last bit of plum brandy."

Maria gasped. "You were the one who dared me to!"

"That was before the last shipment of brandy sunk at the bottom of the ocean," whispered Anastasia.

Her sister grunted. "Fine!" Maria turned around and grabbed Timofey by the hand, leading a few paces to the left. "Timofey, I want to show you something over here."

His back now faced Anastasia. "What is it, Your Imperial Highness?" he asked.

Maria had to think of something quick, and it better be good. "It's big, yellow, and blue," assured Maria.

Timofey's light blue eyes glanced around the park. He couldn't find anything that matched the young woman's description. "I don't see anything."

Anastasia mouthed the word thank you, and Maria shot her a sharp look. "It's there," Maria lied. "Just keep looking." Maria watched her sister slowly tiptoe away. Where is she going?

"Now I see it!" exclaimed Timofey.

"You do?" said Maria, sounding more surprised than she should have been. Maria looked around the garden for a big yellow and blue object or figure.

"Yes. That woman needs to see a doctor immediately."

Maria was puzzled. She didn't see a woman anywhere.

Timofey turned around, and Anastasia was gone. He turned his body again, facing Maria. "Where's Anastasia Nikolaevna?"

Maria just stared at him. She didn't know either, but wherever her baby sister ran off to, she didn't want Maria or Timofey to follow.

Timofey searched frantically for Anastasia "I need to find Her Imperial Highness."

Maria had an idea. Anastasia owed her big time.

Timofey walked a few paces forward. Maria ran up to him from behind and jumped on his back. She wrapped her legs around his torso and wrapped her arms around his eyes so he couldn't see. He couldn't believe what had just happened. Neither could Maria. She was supposed to be the angel of her family.

"Your Imperial Highness," gasped Timofey. "With all due respect... what's gotten into you?"

"You're protecting me," promised Maria.

"From whom?"

"You're protecting me from myself!"

She didn't come, thought Ivan. He huffed and walked away, with his hands deep in his pockets.

Anastasia approached from behind and grabbed his arm and cheerfully said, "Where to?"

Ivan turned his head and smiled. "You came."

"Where are we going?" she asked.

"Where would you like to go?" responded Ivan.

"Anywhere! I have never seen the city before."

Ivan raised an eyebrow. He found that hard to believe. "What?"

"My father has taken my sisters and I to the city during his business exchanges," explained Anastasia. "But he's never taken us around the city."

Ivan made a mental note: she had more than one sister. He gave her a sly grin. "Well," he said. He grabbed her hand and pulled her forward. "We are going to change that."

"Where are you taking me?" she asked, her voice racing with excitement.

"You'll see," promised Ivan.

There was a bridge across the Moika river and near the Yusupov Palace. It was a short-arched bridge, made from a granite facing and an iron cast. It was called the kissing bridge.

Ivan and Anastasia hurried across the bridge. Anastasia let go of Ivan's hand and stopped, trying to catch her breath. She hadn't run that far since she escaped French class and her tutor had to apprehend her. After she caught a couple of breaths, she looked around. St. Petersburg was beautiful, with elegant churches and colorful rooftops.

"Where are we?" asked Anastasia.

"We are standing on the kissing bridge," replied Ivan.

"What?" giggled Anastasia.

"Many years ago," began Ivan. "There was a merchant who was madly in love with his beautiful wife. They lived in a tavern nearby called A Kiss. One day, the merchant had to go to war and leave his wife behind." Ivan grabbed Anastasia's hands and pulled her to the middle of the bridge. "They had one last kiss on this spot. He promised to return to her one day and be waiting on the bridge. The merchant's wife waited every night on the bridge for her husband to come home." Ivan looked deep into her deep blue eyes and pulled her hair behind her ear.

"What happened to his wife?" whispered Anastasia, her heart beating fast.

"She died, waiting on a man who never came home. But people say that if you kiss someone you love on this bridge, you will have a long and happy relationship."

Anastasia took a few steps back. "Are you making this up?" she asked, letting out an adorable giggle.

Ivan shook his head. "I would never make something like this up."

"I don't believe you."

"Do you want me to prove it?" challenged Ivan.

Anastasia nodded.

"Then come over here, and let's find out," teased Ivan.

Anastasia suddenly realized that they were somewhere near Yusupov Palace. Her cousin, Princess Irina Alexandrovna, lived there with her husband and small child. If Irina saw Anastasia out and about, she would tell her mother, Aunt Xenia, and Aunt Xenia would tell her husband, Uncle Sandro. Uncle Sandro would then tell Nicholas. And Nicholas would tell Anastasia's strong-willed and iron-fisted mother, Empress Alexandra.

Anastasia walked past Ivan and said, "Nice try."

Ivan couldn't help himself. Better luck next time, he supposed. He grabbed her hand again and hurried across the bridge, making a sharp left down a cobbled road. It took a few moments for Anastasia to realize where they were going to St. Isaac's Cathedral.

Anastasia couldn't stop grinning.

St. Isaac's Cathedral was a granite and marble building, faced with pink and gray stones, with a gilded iron dome. The exterior included Byzantine columns, and the interior was decorated with different precious stones like marble and malachite. The ceiling had depictions of the Virgin Mary and Christ that covered more than eight thousand square feet. The iconostasis was formed in an arch decorated with pillars. The window near the main altar was a stained-glass image of the Resurrection.

Ivan led Anastasia up the spiral staircase. She clung to Ivan's hand tightly, her heart racing. She tripped several times, trying to keep up the pace, and Ivan reconsidered the idea of hurrying up the winding staircase, but they were almost to the top.

Ivan opened the door and Anastasia felt a gust of wind rush against her face. Ivan had taken her to St. Isaac's colonnade. She could see the square, beautiful churches with golden steeples, houses with red and green rooftops, emerald statues in the park, and boats crossing the dark blue river.

"It's beautiful up here," she said breathlessly, her auburn hair dancing in the wind.

Ivan looked at Anastasia, lost in her eyes. *You're beautiful,* he thought.

"I like the view from where I am standing," he said, glancing at Anastasia.

She blushed and wanted to live in this moment forever. Anastasia rested her hands on the rail and leaned forward.

Ivan felt a surge of panic. "Don't lean too close to the edge," he warned. "You are scaring me."

Anastasia blushed again and smiled. "Are you afraid that I might fly away?" she teased.

"No. I am afraid you'll fall headfirst, and I would have to go after you. And I don't want to do that today," retorted Ivan.

"What if I climbed over the rail?" she asked innocently.

"Please, don't," said Ivan nervously.

"All right. I won't do that today." Anastasia leaned on the rail and gazed at the beautiful city.

Ivan rested his hands on the iron rail and said, "How does that story end? Does Ivan, the boyar, find his father?"

"No, he doesn't. He found something better."

"What is it?"

Anastasia glanced at Ivan and smiled. "Write to me at Twenty-four Tchaikovsky Street, and I might just tell you all about it."

Ivan nodded.

It wasn't her own address, of course. She didn't want Ivan knowing that she lived in the Alexander Palace. He might become suspicious, and she couldn't have that. It was the address of Miss Botkin. She would help Anastasia. She just didn't know it yet.

Chapter 16

Operation Bayonet Thief

After Maria basically risked her life the other day so that her sister could have a secret rendezvous with whatever-his-name-is, Marie Feodorovna brought her granddaughters back to the palace herself. She made sure her daughter-in-law knew what kind of mother she turned out to be for those girls. Marie Feodorovna had been so infuriated that not even her own son could calm her down. Marie screamed at her son's wife so loud, the palace staff could hear it from down the hall. For the sake of her husband and children, Alexandra did not retaliate. It had been a terrible shame that Marie never was the mother Alexandra wanted. Alexandra half-expected Nicholas to say something in her defense, but he just stood there astounded. Alexandra understood why. Marie was his mother, after all. Later, Nicholas would tell her that he was mortified for not standing up to his mother. Humiliated, Alexandra had banished Maria to her bedroom for her erotic behavior.

Maria tried to protest, but Alexandra wouldn't tolerate the backtalk. She scolded her daughter and said it didn't matter whose fault it was. Maria was the elder sister; she should have been the example. Maria stormed to her bedroom and locked herself in.

Maria and Anastasia shared a bedroom. The room was over-furnished with floral furniture. The walls were light gray, covered with family pictures and holy icons, stenciled with purple butterflies and roses. The girls slept on thin mattresses on a folded camp bed, covered in blue blankets.

Three days had passed since her restrictions. Maria wrote in her diary, her hand pressed hard against the pen, anger soaking onto the paper. For a moment, she glanced up and looked through the window. She saw Anastasia sneaking around the palace grounds, looking over her shoulder. What was she doing? Then, as soon as her sister thought no one was watching, she pulled a bayonet from a thick bush. *What was she going to do with that bayonet? t*hought Maria.

She sighed and closed her journal. Maria didn't want to know. She couldn't risk getting in trouble for her sister again.

She looked through the vanity mirror and brushed a comb through her brown hair. Suddenly, she heard the door crack. She saw Prince Karl's reflection through the mirror, and he walked in, slightly tipsy.

"Your Highness, this is a surprise," she muttered nervously.

Karl glared at her diary. "What's that?" Before Maria could answer, he took it from her. He started flipping through pages, skimming over the words. Then, Karl had the audacity to throw the journal over his shoulder, tossing it on the floor.

Maria gasped and strode up to him. "I am afraid you have crossed a line, Sir." Maria pointed her index finger to the door. "You need to leave."

"I want you," said Karl, his voice hysterical.

"I beg your pardon."

The Romanian prince strode up to Maria. The Grand Duchess took a couple of steps back, trembling in fear.

"I could have any woman in the world, but I choose you."

"No, Karl. Please, stop."

"I don't want Olga. I want you to be the Queen of Romania." He had her cornered into a wall. She could smell the brandy on his breath and clothes.

"Karl, you're drunk," she whispered fearfully.

He grabbed Maria's hands and kissed them. "I want you to be my wife."

Maria snatched them away. "I said no."

Karl grabbed her waist. "Marry me."

Maria slapped Karl so hard, his head moved to the side. "I said, no," she repeated.

The Romanian felt a burst of anger. "You will regret that, you ungrateful little—"

Maria braced herself for the worst.

"Is there a problem?" said a voice from behind.

The prince turned and his glare darkened. Mitya stood several feet away, his arms crossed, and his face covered in anger.

Karl bellowed, "This doesn't concern you!"

"I am the son of Tsarina's sister. As far as I am concerned, this matter does concern me." Mitya took a step forward, his fists clenched. He fought through the strong urge to cause some sort of international incident.

"Is there a problem, gentlemen?" said another voice from behind them.

Mitya turned to see Konstantin standing there in a Cossack uniform, his hand rested on his sword handle. By the look of things, he was ready for a fight.

Prince Karl cleared his throat. "Not a problem at all," he muttered nervously. "I was returning a book that Her Imperial Highness let me borrow."

Konstantin crossed his arms, not impressed.

"I believe your business here is concluded, Your Highness," said Mitya darkly.

"For now," smirked Karl. He stormed out of the room and went straight to the liquor cabinet, his pride wounded. Konstantin watched the prince closely from a distance, to make sure he didn't do anything else stupid.

After they were left alone, Maria let out a massive sigh of relief. "I hope Olga doesn't marry that toad." Maria picked up her diary and set it on her desk.

"What kind of toad should Olga marry?" asked Mitya.

Maria turned and grinned. "The kind that turns into a prince," she said thoughtfully.

"Those kinds of toads are hard to find."

"Not really. Weren't you a toad once?" Maria asked as she opened the closet and grabbed some yarn and needles.

"I was an ugly toad once until I was kissed by a beautiful princess."

Maria eyed him carefully. "Do tell," she said in amusement, with her arms crossed.

Mitya sat on the bed. "Her and I were children," he began. "I think she did this on a dare. She kissed me and afterward, she ran away screaming."

Maria laughed hard. "She sounds like a smart girl."

Mitya continued, "At first, I was astounded. I thought, *do girls really find me this repulsive?* I wanted to find her and tell her how repulsive she was. Now I look back at it and laugh."

Maria gasped in horror. "Good grief! Are you talking about me?"

Mitya bellowed in laughter. Maria balled her fist and punched him in the arm, and he laughed even harder. *He kind of deserved that*, she though. She then looked out the window and saw Anastasia sneaking around again.

"I wonder what Her Imperial Naughtiness is up to today," said Mitya from behind.

Maria scoffed. "I don't care, and I don't want to know."

Several minutes later, Maria and Mitya began knitting on the floor. Maria was quite skilled with a needle and yarn, something her mother had taught her. Maria had taught Mitya to knit, but he was still learning. Somehow, he managed to get the needle stuck in the yarn, and Maria had to dig it out.

"What are you making?" asked Maria.

Mitya looked at the clump of yarn knitted together and uttered, "It's a deep state secret. If I told you, I'd have to kill you."

Maria giggled and started on a new stitch. "What was all the fuss this morning?" she asked. Mitya raised an eyebrow. "You mean to say you didn't hear?" Maria shook her head.

Mitya sighed. "Prince Christopher of Denmark asked your father's permission to marry Olga."

Maria gasped. "What did Olga say?"

Mitya tried to conceal a smile. "She rejected his proposal."

Now Mitya had managed to get his needle stuck in the yarn again. Maria carefully took the needle out and put it in the correct stitch, prompting him to begin again.

"You seem pleased about her decision. Is there someone else you think Olga should marry?" asked Maria, frankly.

Mitya cleared his voice. "Her Imperial Highness should marry whom she wants," he said nervously.

"My thoughts exactly." Maria stopped knitting and set the needles to the side for a moment, her eyes locked on Mitya. "You have something those other princes do not."

Mitya waved her statement away with his hand, before getting his needle stuck in the yarn again. "Besides a kingdom and fortune to inherit?" he muttered.

Maria shook her head. "You have her heart."

Somehow, Mitya felt a flicker of hope. "How do you know?"

Maria put her hand over her heart and gave him a slight smirk. "I am her sister, and I know these things."

Mitya tossed the yarn to the floor in frustration and let out a sigh. "That doesn't change anything. I am not the son of a King or Grand Duke. I am the orphan boy who was taken in by the kindness of a Grand Duchess."

Maria put her knees close to her chest. "These are unique circumstances. But I will say this; if you allow Olga to marry another man, you'll regret it for the rest of your life."

It was a dangerous little thing when Anastasia got bored. Terrible sorts of things were bound to happen. And a terrible sort of thing would happen, eventually. But not while she was reading stories to her brother as the books distracted his mind from the pain.

The walls of Alexei's bedroom were floral, with holy icons and family photos placed randomly. Every toy an eleven-year-old boy could ask for was placed on a white built-in bookshelf. He slept on a cot with a blue blanket with his name sewn on it. Anastasia sat in a chair as she read, and her blue eyes stopped at the last word.

"What's that look?" asked Alexei.

"What look?" she asked innocently.

Alexei sat up on the bed crisscrossed. He gave his sister a sharp look. "It's the same look you have when you are thinking of something fun."

Anastasia sat on the edge of the chair and flipped to the next page in the book. "Oh," she muttered. "I was just thinking of something." She then gave her brother a devilish look.

"What are you up to?" he asked, grinning mischievously.

"Why don't we get out of here and do something that would get us arrested later?"

Alexei nodded and wondered what he'd gotten himself into this time. He followed his older sister to a small corner room of the palace where his mother would go to retreat. She would spend hours there alone, feeling bad for herself. She'd spent days at a time in this room knitting, reading, and sewing in her wheelchair, fighting through her physical and emotional war. This room was called the purple room.

Alexei stopped outside the door. "Anastasia, we can't go in there," the boy whispered. "That's Mama's special room."

Anastasia cracked the door open and peeked inside. "Mama's not in there, Alexei. Mama is a nurse, remember? She will be at the infirmary all today with Olga and Tatiana. You go inside and get the string of yarn, and I will keep watch."

The string of yarn was for her little trick later.

"No way!" shouted Alexei.

"Shhh! You are going to get us caught."

Alexei threw his hands in the air in frustration. "Why do I have to be the one to sneak in there? This was your idea. You go!" he hissed.

"Because I am the older one. And the older one always keeps watch."

"You made that up," said Alexei coldly.

"And you're not supposed to be out of bed anyway," snapped Anastasia.

Alexei grunted. He placed his hand on the doorknob and inched it open, and it made a slight creaking noise. He quietly walked inside, holding his breath.

Anastasia kept watch. A few minutes had passed. What is taking him so long? He was given one job to cut one piece of string from a ball of yarn, and it shouldn't be taking this long. If she were doing it, she would have been in and out.

"Anastasia!" The Grand Duchess' heart jumped. Anastasia turned, her heart beating a thousand beats a minute. "Explain yourself," hissed the doctor's daughter. Miss Botkin wore a long red coat, with a black scarf, and a velvet hat. She waved an envelope in Anastasia's face.

"Oh, you got my letter." Anastasia snatched it from Miss Botkin's hands and read the envelope. It was from Ivan. She stared lovingly at his handwriting and memorized it. Her heart fluttered with joy. "You will be secretly harboring letters for me from now on."

"I certainly will not. I do not appreciate you giving my address to a complete and utter stranger!" said Miss Botkin coldly.

"Shhh! Lower your voice," Anastasia whispered.

The young woman's face hardened and turned scarlet. "I am telling your father what you did." She turned back the way she came and walked quickly down the corridor. Anastasia had to think of something fast.

"Is that really how you feel?" she called after her.

Miss Botkin ignored Anastasia and continued walking. Fear crept inside her mind. If her father found out about Ivan, the party, the letter, or even the brothel, he would end things quicker than they began. And she'll never see Ivan again. She couldn't have that. She had an idea, but it was a long shot. "What if I told you something that might change your mind?"

Miss Botkin stopped and turned her body halfway. "What are you talking about this time?" she asked impatiently.

Anastasia had to choose her following words carefully, or this whole thing could blow over. "Do I have to remind you of that isolated incident that I am still trying to forget?" She began to move towards Miss Botkin.

Miss Botkin looked perplexed. "What are you talking about?"

"It was last summer... do I have to remind you?"

Last summer was all it took for Miss Botkin to remember. It was June, and Anastasia was visiting the Botkin home while staying at her aunt's in St. Petersburg. She snuck into Miss Botkin's bedroom and started snooping when she heard the bedroom door open, and she quickly hid under the bed.

Miss Botkin locked the door and opened the window allowing a soldier to climb inside. His name was Officer Melnyk. He was tall, slender, and a handsome blond-haired, blue-eyed Imperial soldier. He and Miss Botkin talked for hours, exchanging secrets and kisses. Anastasia hid under the bed the whole time and didn't say a word. When the young man was gone, Anastasia climbed from underneath the bed. Miss Botkin had never been so embarrassed or infuriated in her entire life. Anastasia swore she'd never tell.

"You wouldn't dare!" gasped the physician's daughter.

"If you tell my father, I'll tell yours."

Miss Botkin grunted loudly. She knew Anastasia would do it, and her father would never leave her alone again. And worse, she'd never see Officer Melnyk again. The doctor's daughter groaned again angrily. "Fine! I'll do it."

"Thank you," Anastasia said cheerfully.

"I am not doing this for you," Miss Botkin huffed.

The door to the purple room slowly opened an inch, and Alexei snuck out, closing the door behind him, holding a long string of yarn.

"What is he doing out of bed? Where's my father?" barked Miss Botkin.

"What's going on?" asked Alexei. "I heard shouting."

Anastasia rolled her eyes. "Ignore her. It's that time of the month."

Curious, Alexei tilted his head and asked, "What does that mean?"

Miss Botkin gasped in horror.

"What took you so long?" demanded Anastasia.

A smudge of chocolate was smeared on his chin.

"You found Mama's chocolate stash again, didn't you?" Anastasia pointed to the chocolate.

Alexei grinned and laughed hesitatingly. He wiped the chocolate off with his hand.

"For a scrawny boy, you are such a pig," teased Anastasia.

"What did we need the string of yarn for again?" asked Alexei.

Anastasia's blue eyes lit up. Miss Botkin knew that look. Oh, no. What was she up to this time? Whatever it was, it was nothing good.

"The both of you, follow me," Anastasia demanded.

Miss Botkin sighed heavily. She knew that somehow, she was going to regret this later.

The heir to the Russian throne and the court physician's daughter followed the Grand Duchess outdoor and deep into the depths of Tsarskoe Selo in a woodland area. Anastasia stopped in front of a bayonet tied to a small tree.

"Where did you get that?" asked Alexei, his voice reaching a high note of amazement.

"I borrowed it," said Anastasia proudly.

"You mean stole it," Miss Botkin accused.

"I borrowed it without permission," retorted the Grand Duchess. She then gathered some rocks and placed them inside the chamber. She reached her hand inside her pocket and pulled out a small bag of gunpowder.

"Oh, no!" said Miss Botkin.

"Oh, yes!" exclaimed Alexei.

"Anastasia Nikolaevna, you are going to get us killed."

Anastasia ignored her friend and poured the gunpowder inside the chamber. She shut it and looked at Alexei, smiling devilishly. "Alexei, would you, please, give me the yarn?"

Alexei chuckled and walked toward his sister. He handed her the large piece of blue string. Tatiana Botkin covered her eyes with her hands. She couldn't watch. Anastasia tied the string to the trigger of the weapon before holding it in her hand and moving back carefully. Alexei walked close behind her.

"Tatiana, get behind me," said Anastasia.

The young woman didn't move an inch. Anastasia looked at her little brother. Alexei walked over to Miss Botkin and grabbed her gently by the arm, pulling her behind his sister. They hid behind some trees and ducked down for cover.

Anastasia looked at her brother. "Would you like to do the honors?" she asked.

"Certainly."

Alexei took the piece of yarn from his sister's hand. The doctor's daughter uncovered her eyes and watched as the heir pulled the yarn. The bayonet blew up almost immediately, and the explosion was deafening. It was like a bomb had gone off. The bayonet sailed through the air, cutting the tree almost in half. Miss Botkin was curled up in a little ball, screaming as she covered her ears with her hands. Anastasia and Alexei were curled up, too, only they were laughing hysterically.

"You people are crazy!" screamed Miss Botkin.

"Then, why did you come?" asked Anastasia innocently.

Miss Botkin grunted.

Anastasia sat up and looked at Tatiana sharply. "If you don't tell my father, I won't tell yours." Miss Botkin's eyes narrowed, and she nodded reluctantly. Anastasia helped herself and Miss Botkin off the ground and walked quickly back to the Alexander Palace, with Miss Botkin and Alexei following.

"What are we going to do now?" asked Alexei.

Anastasia thought about the war and her job as a patroness and frowned. "I don't know about the two of you, but I am going to spend the rest of my day at the infirmary."

Alexei turned to the doctor's daughter and smiled innocently. "Would you, please, take me back to the palace, Tatiana?"

Miss Botkin nodded and walked the heir down an old dirt trail back to the Alexander Palace.

Ten minutes later, they were tiptoeing through the throne room, their shoes clicking as they walked along the hardwood floor. The throne room had a golden ceiling and velvet walls. Three steps made of red carpet led to the throne chair, which was golden with a single red cushion, and it appeared uncomfortable to sit on.

Miss Botkin and Alexei heard muffled voices. It sounded like Tsar Nicholas and his advisors. Miss Botkin turned sharply, her heart beating quickly. Nicholas was dressed in a naval uniform, with golden medals across his chest. He was surrounded by an entourage of advisors; six old and round men who looked twice his age.

"Papa!" exclaimed Alexei. He made a dash towards his father. Miss Botkin stepped forward to grab him, but it was too late. The eleven-year-old heir was halfway down the throne room.

"Alexei? What are you doing out of bed?" asked Nicholas. There was concern in his voice, but he was glad to see that his only son was feeling better.

"Papa, what does that time of the month mean?" asked Alexei, his eyes filled with curiosity and innocence.

Did he just say that? thought Miss Botkin. Her father was going to hear about this.

Nicholas' face went white. He cleared his voice nervously. This was not how he planned to spend the afternoon.

Chapter 17

Operation Romania

The hot infirmary smelled like sweat and fear, and stress and anxiety flooded the atmosphere. Dying soldiers occupied every bed, and their screams and prayers could be heard from every corner. Some prayed to live, others prayed to die.

Alexandra and her two oldest daughters were forced to clean up the mess the Germans made. They were nurses, after all.

One soldier with light brown hair and brown eyes had been at the hospital for three days. He arrived earlier that week from the Eastern Front. It was the war zone between the Russian Empire and the Ottomans and Austro-Hungarian Empire. His knee was nearly blown off from a German explosion, and now it needed to be amputated. The soldier was out cold after inhaling a good amount of Diethyl Ether. Tatiana Nikolaevna tied a belt around the soldier's leg, making a tourniquet and cutting off circulation.

"Mama, please, hand me the saw," said Tatiana, her voice reached a high note of urgency.

Alexandra grabbed the amputation saw from the table and placed it in her daughter's hand. Tatiana stared at the blade, and an unwelcome amount of fear entered her. It froze her mind. For a moment, she couldn't think of what to do next.

Alexandra placed her hand on Tatiana's shoulder. "Are you sure you want to do this, darling?"

Tatiana looked at her mother and nodded. She placed the bone saw above the soldier's knee. This was going to hurt her a lot more than it was going to hurt him. She sliced through the skin and blood as she moved the saw back and forth.

Olga Nikolaevna froze. She watched the soldier's blood pour from his wound onto her sister's hands, the floor, and the white bedsheets. She felt queasy and lightheaded, and tears gathered in her blue eyes.

She quickly found her way to the bathroom and locked the door. Her back leaned against the door, and she slowly slid down to the floor. A river of tears streamed down her face. Her hands were shaking as she crawled to the toilet and opened the lid. She wrapped her arms around the cold porcelain as she felt the vomit moving up her throat. It burned its way into her mouth before she emptied her entire lunch into the toilet. She then heard several knocks on the door and her mother's German accent.

"Olga! Please, open the door." Alexandra knocked on the door again. "Please, darling, I know you are in there."

Olga wouldn't budge. She sat on the floor, curled up into a small ball, and continued to cry.

Later that day, Olga took a small stroll around the palace. She wore a light pink dress, loose around the hips, and a string of pearls around her neck. She carried with her a parasol in her hand as the newspaper predicted rain later that day. But that didn't stop her from wanting to take a walk outside. She stopped in the middle of the palace corridor and stared at the window looking at her reflection. Something was boiling inside her, something that was lodged deep inside her chest. She could feel it twist and turn. She was tired of pretending.

She was depressed, and the arsenic was not working. That made her angry. The horrors of war scarred her mind and were imprinted inside her brain. She could see the blood cascade down soldiers' bodies. Every night, screams filled her ears before she went to sleep, and she couldn't escape it. That only added to her anger.

Olga loved her brother deeply. He couldn't help it that he was born different. His near-death experiences had affected everyone. Her parents could not trust him alone for five seconds because he might fall and hurt himself. He was no ordinary boy. Her family revolved around Alexei. If the baby wasn't well, her family fell apart. Alexandra would lock herself in Alexei's room and use all her energy to make her son better, then retreat to her purple room for weeks at a time. Nicholas would lock himself inside his office and not talk to anyone. He chain-smoked and cried because he thought that his son was going to die. Anastasia and Maria would stop smiling. Tatiana would be at Alexandra's side for emotional support. And that left Olga, who hated to be ignored all the time.

She was sick of doctors, and her parents, telling her that she was alright or that everything was just inside her head. She didn't feel alright, and she was tired of pretending that everything was normal. Her country was at war, but everyone ignored the war going on inside her head.

Karl and Boris.

Those men gave her anxiety. She knew she had to get married as that was her family's only option to secure the dynasty. But what did she want? Her heart wanted to fall in love with a man who loved her, with no political gain. But everyone expected her to get married, and soon. Olga didn't want to disappoint anyone, especially her parents. Why did this have to be so confusing? She had a tough choice to pick. Boris or Karl. It was like choosing between two evils. *Which choice do I make?* She thought.

The world drove her insane, her family, the infirmary, her suitors, all of them. She wanted to scream and hit something, to cry until she had no tears left.

Before she knew what she was doing, she raised her parasol into the air and smashed it through the corridor window. Shards of glass flew in every direction and landed on the ground, breaking into smaller pieces. It was a good sense of relief to release all the anger she'd bottled up inside for so long. She raised the parasol in the air again, but this time higher. She smashed another window and screamed with anger. That one was for the anxiety. She raised the parasol in the air once again and shattered the next window. That one was for her power-hungry suiters. She raised the parasol one last time. Olga could see her own reflection in the glass again as she smashed it. That one was for her.

Olga fell to her knees, and she stared at the broken glass, tears welling up in her eyes. Her mind was just as broken as the windows. Tomorrow, she was resigning from the infirmary. She couldn't do it anymore. She was done with her own insanity.

Just done.

That night, unbeknownst to almost all, a Queen traveled from the depths of Romania to Russia. Through her father, a British naval officer, she was the grandchild of Queen Victoria of England. Through her mother, a Grand Duchess, she was the granddaughter of Tsar Alexander II. Through both her mother and father, she was a first cousin to Nicholas and Alexandra. She wore a white dress with embroidered patterns and a large white, floppy hat. Her silky blonde hair was placed in a loose bun. She had a tall and slim body, a long and slender neck, piercing blue eyes, and full lips. Her hands were soft and delicate, but her grip was strong. The Queen was forty-two years old, but she looked much younger than that. Her name was Marie.

Queen Marie stepped off the train with a small suitcase in one hand. Her eight-year-old daughter, Princess Ileana, followed closely behind her. The mother and daughter climbed inside a golden carriage with an enormous white horse. The carriage ride was cold, dark, and rough. Princess Ileana fell asleep during the ride with her head resting on her mother's lap. The Queen stroked her daughter's blonde hair as she slept. Marie realized that tomorrow would be the two-month mark of her youngest child's death. His name was Mircea. He would have been four years old tomorrow. Every moment without that little boy in her arms felt like an eternity. She missed him dearly.

The carriage stopped in front of the Alexander Palace. Marie gazed down at her sleeping child. She shook her gently and Ileana opened her eyes.

"Are we there yet, Mama?" said the child, rubbing her blue eyes.

"We are here," promised Marie.

The mother and daughter stepped out of the carriage, and climbed up the steps of Alexander Palace, Queen Marie's ancestral home. The welcoming was warm. Ileana was offered a cozy bed and Marie was offered some warm food and English tea. The Queen felt right at home.

Twenty minutes later, Marie started to unpack her things. She planned on staying in Russia for a while. She predicted that there would be a wedding soon; a marriage between Russia and Romania.

Marie looked back at her daughter, curled up in a tiny ball, sleeping quietly on the bed. She looked so peaceful. She thought of Mircea again. It wasn't fair. She knew Typhoid was deadly but never imagined her three-year-old falling ill to it. Why did he have to go? She didn't understand. Why did her son have to be the one who died? Her heart shook with grief every time she thought of him. That boy had grown inside of her. That boy was once a part of her. Now he was gone. If one good thing came out of Mircea's death, it was that it made her realize that she wasn't the mother Ileana needed. Marie had been a distant mother. She never nursed her children, and she never held or cuddled them. She did not bond with them after they were born at all. She loved all her children but did not know how to show it. It was easier for her not to.

Marie heard a knock on the door and her heart leaped. As she opened the door, Grand Duke Boris gathered her in his arms and kissed her passionately. She grabbed him by the collar and pulled him into the bedroom. The Romanian Queen closed the door and turned sharply. She whispered, "Are you insane coming here? Someone could have seen you."

"I had to see you. I missed you," he said lovingly. Boris kissed her lips again softly.

"Boris," the Queen hissed. "We can't. My child is asleep."

Startled, Marie heard a small knock against the door.

Boris' heart jumped. If anyone caught him here, his engagement to Olga was as good as gone. "What are we going to do?" he gasped.

Suddenly, Marie grabbed him by the collar again and dragged him to the closet. "Don't make a sound," she warned. She shut the closet door gently.

The Queen went to the bedroom door and cracked it open an inch. "Alix, what a pleasant surprise!" whispered Marie.

Alexandra looked through the door and saw the child sleeping on the bed. "Perhaps, I'll come back later."

Marie opened the door wider. "Nonsense, cousin. I have not seen you in ages," she said cheerfully.

Alexandra walked through the doorway, her gray eyes fixed on the sleeping girl. "You have a very beautiful daughter, Missy," she said quietly.

No one had called her that name for a while. She assumed everyone had just forgotten it. "All of your children are beautiful, too," said Marie.

Alexandra took her eyes off the child and gave Marie a cold, blank stare. Her mind was elsewhere, lost in a familiar world called anxiety.

"What is it, Sunny?" whispered Marie, using her cousin's childhood nickname.

Alexandra stared at Marie, concern covered her silver eyes. "Something has been brought to my attention. I don't know all the details, but Karl has taken a strong liking to Maria."

"That's not unusual. Maria is an attractive girl. I'm sure it's just an innocent flirtation," assured Marie.

Alexandra wasn't sure about that, and something didn't feel right. She frowned and said, "Maria is too young to marry a man as charming and experienced as Karl."

"I agree."

"If Karl were to say something to you about the matter, you'll discourage it?"

"Of course."

Alexandra gave a deep breath of relief and smiled. "That's all I needed to hear you say, darling."

"How has Karl been since his visit here?" asked Marie.

There was a long pause. "Well," said Alexandra nervously. "He was a good houseguest the first week here with us. . ." There was another long pause. "As soon as he received a telegram that you were coming, his demeanor changed."

Marie frowned. "I was afraid of that."

"Is something wrong?" asked her cousin curiously.

"Did you know I was married at sixteen? When I had Karl, I was just seventeen." Marie felt a small amount of anger rise. "I didn't even get to hold him. He was stolen from me."

"By whom?"

"By the late king," hissed Marie, and her voice shook with powerful emotion. Marie balled her fist. She wanted to hit someone or throw something. But she was a Queen. She kept her composure and continued, "The tyrant thought I was too young to be a mother. He took Karl and raised him to be a spoiled palace brat. I gave birth to Elizabeth the following year. But that bloody, old king took her, too. I could do nothing to stop him."

Marie had fought for many years to get her children back. But the king was a stubborn, old tyrant who had no room in his heart to show the young mother compassion. Eventually, Marie gave up fighting. Her children could have everything in the world they could possibly want, but a mother's love was out of the question. Karl no longer wanted it anyway. It stung at first, but Marie couldn't blame him. He had every reason to be angry.

"What did Ferdinand do?" asked Alexandra in disbelief.

Marie wrapped her arms around herself defensively. "Ferdinand? Ha! He was too much of a bloody coward to stand up to his cold uncle." She had little respect and patience for her doormat of a husband, who didn't have a spine to stand up to his overbearing uncle. "But I can hardly blame him!" she cried, her voice cold. "His uncle had crushed the life out of poor Ferdinand."

"The old king is gone. Surely, you can have a relationship now," reassured Alexandra.

"I have tried. I have nothing in common with them. Karl is selfish and out of control, and Elizabeth is shy and awkward. Is it normal not to like your children?"

Alexandra had to give her an honest answer. "Yes. Sometimes my children make me want to pull my hair out. Olga has Granny's temper. Tatiana is stubborn, and Maria is moody. Anastasia is defiant and lazy. Alexei comes up with ways to get himself killed all the time. But that doesn't mean I stop loving them."

"Oh, I love my children so much!" she uttered with a small sniff. "My family is just so broken, and it can't be fixed."

Alexandra gathered Marie in her arms and embraced her. "Can I tell you a little secret?" Her cousin looked at her sharply. "Every family is a little broken. But that doesn't mean it can't be fixed."

Marie contemplated this for a moment. "Thank you," she muttered.

Alexandra squeezed her cousin's hand and smiled.

The two women didn't speak for a minute. Then Marie said, "Sometimes, I am jealous of you and Nicky."

"What?" the Empress gasped. "Why?"

Marie nodded. "Nicky adores you."

"I am more than certain Ferdinand loves you."

Marie scoffed. "Ferdinand is more like a close friend than a husband. We spent the early years of our marriage just learning how to live together. We grew up together." Then, Marie had a mischievous idea. It wasn't pleasant, but it would humor her cousin. "What do you think of Grand Duke Boris?"

Alexandra shrugged and folded her arms. "There's something not right about that man. I don't like him."

Marie fought the urge to laugh or smile. She put on a good poker face. "I have met the man on a few occasions. He's so dull, but he thinks he's so charming and handsome. Truly, he is arrogant and stubborn."

Alexandra nodded in approval. "Good night, darling. Sleep well," she sighed.

As soon as Alexandra was gone, Boris opened the closet. His face was covered with anger and concern. "Why did you do that?" he demanded.

Marie kissed him deeply. "I couldn't resist," she said flirtatiously.

Boris had a difficult time staying angry at her.

Later, Boris smoked a cigarette in the men's parlor. Karl strode in with anger shrouding his face. "Stay away from my mother!" he hissed. Boris opened his mouth to protest. "I know you went to see her tonight. Don't deny it."

"You can't control who your mother sees," retorted Boris.

Karl felt a rise of anger. The Romanian prince lowered his tone, his voice cold and dominating. "Stay away from her. I won't ask again."

Boris chuckled in amusement. He crossed his arms. "Is that supposed to be a threat?"

That remark angered the Romanian more. "If you ever touch my mother again, I'll let the Tsar know about your mother's little secret."

Boris felt his heart stop. "I don't know what you are talking about."

"A failed coup attempt is still treason. I guess since she can't get rid of the Empress by force, she's having you marry her daughter instead."

"How could you possibly know that?" asked Boris, his voice hoarse.

Karl sighed. "You know as well as I that money talks. Stay away from my mother, and I will assure you that your family's dirty little secret remains that way."

"You're lying," muttered Boris.

"You're good at poker. Am I bluffing?"

Boris shook his head. "No, Your Highness."

"Stay away from my mother," Karl warned again.

Mitya, who was listening from behind the door, heard everything.

For a few short moments, he was glad. This was good news. Prince Karl and Grand Duke Boris would be out of the question if that information left that room. There would be nothing standing in the way of Mitya marrying Olga. But did she love him?

Then Mitya felt mortified. He couldn't tell anyone the things he heard that evening. It could destroy the monarchy. What if Mitya told Nicholas the truth? Nicholas trusted him, no doubt. Boris and his mother would be banished for conspiracy. Karl would be sent back to Romania, and Olga could finally be his. But at what cost? Mitya wasn't even sure if she loved him. Would her father even give his blessing? He was born a common boy, after all. If not, then the monarchy would be doomed, and it would be Mitya's fault.

"Mitya," said a man from behind.

Startled, Mitya's heart jumped. He turned, taking a breath of relief. "Nicholas," his voice filled with solace. Nicholas stood frozen, his face covered with concern. "What is it?" Mitya asked.

"We are losing the war to the Germans," he said plainly.

"What?" Mitya had stopped reading the newspaper a while ago. Most of it was propaganda against his family and the war.

"Everything I do and say is being used as ammunition against me," the Tsar whispered. "I fear for the worst."

"What do you mean?" asked Mitya, his voice frightened.

"I believe there are spies in my government."

As soon as Nicholas said that it gave Mitya goosebumps, and it made his skin crawl. "Spies," he repeated.

Nicholas continued, "I believe some of my advisors and ministers have turned against me and sided with the Bolsheviks."

"That's treason," shrieked Mitya.

"I don't know who I can trust anymore. That's why I must go to the front myself. Perhaps inspire the men and win this war."

"When are you leaving?"

Nicholas shrugged. "First, I need to cater to the Romanians until they leave. But something needs to happen, and time is running out."

Mitya stood there in disbelief. "Why are you telling me this?" he cried.

Nicholas put his hand on his shoulder and looked at him intensely. I want you to come with me."

Mitya's heart accelerated, and his breaths quickened. He swallowed hard. The front was a war zone. And how could he leave Olga behind? He loved her more than life itself. His dream was to marry her even if he didn't know if she felt the same way. Mitya couldn't leave without telling her his feelings. And would her father approve? Nicholas had been an uncle, mentor, and father to him.

"I will have to think about it."

Chapter 18

Operation Unfortunate News

It was a cold, wet day in the middle of January. The sky was gray and mournful, but Gabriel loved the smell of rain in the afternoon. He wore a gray trench coat and a dark fedora as he made quick strides down the sidewalk, stepping in small rain puddles. He approached an enormous white mansion with a black iron gate surrounding it. It was the home of a famous politician, who disappeared without a trace. Gabriel predicted that he'll probably read about someone finding his body in the paper any day now. He opened the dark iron gate and closed it behind him. He walked to the door and scraped his shoes against the mat before entering the home and slamming the door shut behind him.

Gabriel walked around the foyer, his light gray eyes searching for his father, but there was no sign of him. He looked in the drawing-room and saw the brown leather sofas, armchairs, and a grand marble fireplace but no sign of his father. He moved to the dining room with the uniquely carved oak table and chairs from Paris but no sign of The Chupacabra. He checked in the kitchen and the patio. Still, he couldn't find his father anywhere. Gabriel sighed. There was one other place he had not checked—the bedroom.

He climbed to the top of the oak stairway to the second floor of the mansion. The first door on the left was the master bedroom. He swung the door open to find his father in bed reading the newspaper. Helen laid on her side, pretending to be asleep. Gabriel should have known.

"Gabriel," said his father impatiently, without taking his eyes off the paper. "What do you want?"

"I need to talk to you," hissed Gabriel. The Chupacabra took his eyes off the paper and gave his son a sharp look. "Alone."

The Chupacabra looked at his wife and ran his fingers through her hair. "You'll have to leave, darling," he sighed. "My son and I need to talk."

Helen sat up on the bed, faced the wall, and stretched her arms. A few seconds later, she rolled off the bed and made light strides past Gabriel, her hands clutched tightly to her scarlet bathrobe. Gabriel quickly glanced at her as she walked by. Helen was more beautiful than he remembered. Her eyes were the color of whiskey, and her silk fawn hair was falling over her shoulders. Her body was slim and slightly curvy, and it took Gabriel a few seconds to realize he was staring at his father's wife. His father noticed, his face covered in disapproval.

As Helen walked past Gabriel, she tossed him a seductive smile before walking through the threshold of the door and disappearing into the shadows.

"This better be good, Gabriel." The Chupacabra climbed out of bed and stretched his arms. He slipped a pair of slippers on his feet and walked over to a small cabinet on the other side of the room. He pulled out a small glass and a bottle of whiskey. He poured the whiskey inside the glass and drank a gulp.

"For several weeks, I've had a man spying on a soldier."

"Why should a soldier concern me?"

"The soldier is Ivan Mikhailovich," said Gabriel nervously.

The Chupacabra choked on the whiskey and gave his son a stone-cold glare. Gabriel expected a stronger reaction from the most dangerous man alive. Instead, The Chupacabra stopped and listened. Now, he had his father's full attention.

"Ivan has been writing to her for weeks now."

"Her?" asked The Chupacabra.

"The Grand Duchess."

The Chupacabra was speechless. A Grand Duchess and a Bolshevik. That could ruin his plans for Ivan, his plan for revenge. If it were any other soldier, he would have him killed on the spot. But for the son of a traitor, he would make a small exception.

The Chupacabra thought of Helen again. She was walking around the house, wearing nothing but a bathrobe. What could she be doing? Anxiety covered his heart. He forced himself to snap out of it.

"Which Grand Duchess?" growled The Chupacabra.

"Grand Duchess Anastasia Nikolaevna Romanov."

The youngest daughter of the Tsar. If The Chupacabra remembered correctly, she was only fifteen, and Ivan was only nineteen. Practically children and easily manipulated.

"You could use the situation to your advantage," said Gabriel.

The Chupacabra turned and smiled proudly. His son had read his mind. "Yes. That is not a bad idea, son."

Ivan could be used as a pawn to get what he wanted—he could still have his revenge. Ivan would weave his way into the imperial circle, gain their trust, and be a part of a family that he'd always wanted. Then, The Chupacabra would take it all away. Ivan needed a firm push in the right direction. The revolution could be used to do that if he ordered an attack on the imperial residence. Ivan would have no other choice but to go to their rescue. It amazed The Chupacabra how much his son thought like him. Somehow, that frightened him, but he'd never admit that to anyone.

"There is also another thing that you should know."

"What is that?" his father asked.

Gabriel looked at his watch. It was almost one in the afternoon. "Ivan is on his way over here right now."

The Chupacabra didn't expect that news at all. He swallowed his whiskey the wrong way and coughed. "What?" he exclaimed.

Gabriel sighed impatiently. He hated repeating himself. He stepped forward with his arms crossed over his chest. He glared at his father. "Ivan Mikhailovich will be here any minute."

Gabriel then left the room and jogged down the stairs. At the bottom of the stairs, he saw Helen sneak into the sitting room. She wore a draped satin dress and a big diamond around her slender neck. He followed her and hid behind a wall.

Ivan Mikhailovich sat on the brown leather sofa. The smell of Helen's lavender perfume filled the room.

Helen's eyes fell on Ivan for the first time and stopped. Her face became pale, and she'd looked as if she'd seen a ghost. For a brief moment, she thought she saw Ivan's father in the sitting room. "Mikhail," she gasped.

Ivan gazed up at Helen, his expression perplexed. "How do you know my father?" he asked.

Helen took a step forward and smiled nervously as Ivan impatiently waited for an answer. Helen cleared her throat. "Your father and I were good friends."

Gabriel rolled his eyes and continued to listen.

"What is your name, Madame?" asked Ivan.

"My name is Hel—"

It was at that moment Gabriel stepped out of the shadows. "I see you met my stepmother," he said.

Ivan tried his best to mask his astonishment. This woman didn't look old enough to be his stepmother. He stood up and cleared his voice, "Stepmother, Sir?"

"Yes," Gabriel explained. "Helen is my father's second wife. The first one. . ." Gabriel had to choose his next words carefully. They weren't allowed to talk about his mother. He never met the woman, but he did know a few things about her. That marriage was doomed from the start. That was what his father got for marrying an Englishwoman. The marriage lasted barely two years, but they courted much longer than that. "Divorced," Gabriel finally said.

Ivan understood.

"Did you bring what I asked for?" asked Gabriel.

Ivan dug through his coat. He pulled out the bundle of letters that his aunt had stolen from one of her clients. He wondered what the letters were for but didn't ask. Bolsheviks don't ask questions because questions often put you on the wrong side of a gun barrel.

Gabriel gave Ivan a demonic smile. "Excellent, my boy," he said proudly. "My father will be with you shortly, Ivan."

"What?"

"Goodbye, Ivan Mikhailovich." Gabriel took one last glance at Ivan before leaving. "And good luck." He would need it. He'd given Ivan an opportunity that a lot of men in Russia would kill for. An audience with The Chupacabra.

Ivan suddenly found himself alone in the lion's den with an attractive lioness. There was a very awkward, uneasy silence. Ivan sat there quietly, fidgeting with his fingers and glancing at his wristwatch occasionally. He was afraid to look directly at her.

Helen had enough of this boyish behavior, but she didn't show it. She gave him a warm smile and touched his shoulder. "Can I get you a drink?" she asked. Her heavily accented voice was soft and soothing, and it was German.

Ivan flinched. He was slightly taken off guard as he wasn't expecting to hear a German accent. He felt uncomfortable associating with her, especially with the war. "No, but thank you," said Ivan awkwardly.

"I promise that I don't bite," teased Helen.

Ivan knew the woman was harmless, but her husband most certainly was not.

"Your accent," Ivan began. "You're from Berlin."

Helen smiled slightly. "Yes!" she gasped. She didn't know a Russian who would have known that. "How did you know?"

"It was a lucky guess," said Ivan quietly.

"Do you speak German?"

"Some. . . My father taught it to me when I was younger, and sometimes he would only speak to me in German. I can carry on a good conversation."

The young soldier and the German woman heard big, heavy footsteps slowly walking down the staircase. Her husband was coming, and Helen was running out of time to warn Ivan of danger. Helen pulled Ivan close and whispered in his ear. "Now and always, don't speak unless spoken to. And don't look him in the eye. At least, not for too long."

Ivan held his breath. What was she talking about? Nothing made sense, and her words were madness. After all, she was married to a madman.

"And don't do anything that could get yourself killed."

The footsteps were getting closer. Ivan felt her grip on his hand tighten. Helen swallowed. The last words she spoke were quiet German. "Wenn Sie jemals etwas brauchen, bin ich immer für Sie da." *If you ever need anything, I am always here to help.*

Ivan nodded but had a million questions that she didn't have time to answer. Helen released her grip and walked backward a few steps.

"Ivan Mikhailovich." The Chupacabra entered the threshold wearing a gray flannel suit and a red tie. That was his trademark these days. He immediately began to circle Ivan, and he had to remind himself that he was speaking to the son, not the treacherous father. "I've heard so much about you and your incredible gift."

Ivan glanced at Helen quickly. He wasn't sure if he should speak or not. Helen nodded slightly, and Ivan cleared his voice. "Thank you, Sir."

The Chupacabra stopped and turned to his wife, giving her a sharp, cold look. Helen understood. Her presence was no longer welcome. She departed the sitting room, but not before getting one last glare at Ivan. Her eyes sent a clear message; be careful.

The Chupacabra circled Ivan again, with his hands behind his back. "I don't know how much my son has told you," he began. "I need you to do something for me. As you are aware, a revolution is about to erupt. An attack of some form will be made on the Imperial family. I need you to do whatever means necessary to protect them."

"What?"

"Then, I need you to stay put and await further instruction. Can you do that?"

"You want me to spy, Sir?" asked Ivan.

The Chupacabra stopped and gave Ivan a heated look. Ivan wished that he had never asked that. It was a stupid question. Of course, he wanted him to spy. "Are you up for the task, Ivan?" said The Chupacabra darkly.

Ivan swallowed hard. His nerves were building up, and he needed to say something before it was too late. "Yes, Sir."

"Good!" The Chupacabra patted Ivan hard on the back. He smiled demonically. "I know you won't let me down."

Ivan's heart accelerated. The Chupacabra wanted him to spy on the Tsar and his family? That didn't make any sense. Ivan gave The Chupacabra a perplexed stare. There was something else that he wasn't telling Ivan, something he was hiding. He didn't know what, but he was going to find out.

"I expect great things from you, Ivan Mikhailovich," whispered The Chupacabra.

Chapter 19

Operation Tchaikovsky Street

Ivan replayed the events inside his head and took a left down Tchaikovsky Street. He didn't understand The Chupacabra's impossible task. Ivan could be killed or arrested. But Bolsheviks don't ask questions.

He looked both ways before quickly crossing the street. He looked for house number twenty-four, and it appeared to be two houses down.

Number 24 Tchaikovsky Street was a charming two-story pale-colored house with a small white fence and a scarlet door and shutters. The flowers planted in front of the house were dead, yet an ivy grew from the side of the house to the chimney. Some shingles were slightly falling off the roof. It looked like a middle-class family lived there.

Ivan quickly approached the door and knocked.

The news about her brother, Yuri, was too hard to swallow. Her broken heart was completely fractured. Her own father didn't even know that he was dead yet. Miss Botkin would have to break the news to him when he returned home tonight. Unless the heir was dying again, or Tsarina desperately needed him for some reason, which was highly unlikely. That would be the second child her father had lost to the war. The oldest Botkin child, Dmitri, had died at the beginning of the war and her father had never been the same. He buried his grief in his work and religion. Miss Botkin and her youngest brother rarely saw him. He was far too busy tending to the royal mess over at the Alexander Palace to console his crying children. Miss Botkin didn't blame him. It was her father's duty.

As she was mourning her brother's death, Miss Botkin heard a knock on the door. She answered it to find a young man on the other side of the threshold.

"Hello, my name is Ivan Mikhailovich. Is Anastasia home?"

The doctor's daughter screamed on the inside. What was she going to do? She couldn't tell him that Anastasia didn't live there or that she lived at the Alexander Palace with her family. Think, Tatiana. Think. What would Anastasia do? Miss Botkin gave Ivan a weak smile.

"Sorry. My sister isn't home now," she said nervously.

"That's fine," said Ivan. He pushed the door open with his hand, letting himself inside the Botkin home. Miss Botkin took a few steps back, flabbergasted. "I'll wait." He smiled slightly, standing inside the foyer.

Tatiana didn't know if she should start panicking or screaming. This was not how she planned to spend her afternoon. But she pulled herself together and said calmly, "Would you like to wait in the drawing room?"

Ivan smiled again. "Certainly."

Miss Botkin made Ivan some tea and poured him a cup. He sat on the clumpy sofa, sipping on the warm tea. She sighed deeply. "I am going to make a telephone call. Make yourself at home," she said politely.

She raced to the telephone and dialed the number to the palace. "I need to speak to Anastasia Nikolaevna. It's urgent!"

The Romanov family sat down at the table for a luncheon with their Romanian guests. Anastasia sat at the end of the table in between her father and Maria, glaring at the roasted reindeer tongue on her plate. Maria took small bits of the tongue, with sadness pooling in her eyes. Nicholas wouldn't allow his nephew to marry his third daughter.

Anastasia pushed the plate quietly away from her. The luncheon was silent and awkward, and everyone appeared to know that the luncheon was an ulterior motive to what would happen next.

The Crown Prince Karl of Romania planned on proposing to Grand Duchess Olga Nikolaevna that afternoon. Everything was planned. After luncheon, they'd take a walk in the park, and at precisely 1:45, he'd pop the question.

The butler entered the dining room quickly and whispered something to the Tsar's ear. Nicholas nodded and dismissed the man. Nicholas glared at his youngest daughter and whispered in her ear. "Anastasia, darling, were you expecting a telephone call from Miss Tatiana Botkin during our luncheon with the Romanian royal family?"

"No, Papa," whispered Anastasia.

Nicholas took a sip of tea. He knew the Botkin children well, especially Doctor Botkin's only daughter, Tatiana. She had been his children's playmate for years, and he watched her grow up. He also knew that she would never call unless it were of the utmost importance.

"Go answer it, darling," said Nicholas quietly.

As Anastasia got up from the table, Alexei exclaimed, "It must be that time of the month again."

Nicholas practically choked on his tea. Olga and Tatiana exchanged awkward glances. Alexandra gave her only son a sharp look. "What did you say?" she gasped.

Alexei looked at his father innocently and pointed his index finger. "But Papa said—"

Alexandra gave Nicholas a cold glare. The message was clear; what exactly did you say to our eleven-year-old son?

Ileana put down her cup and looked at her mother sharply. "Mama, what does 'that time of the month' mean?" she asked innocently.

Karl stopped eating. He just lost his appetite.

"It's a private womanly thing. Now, finish your food," said Marie.

Ileana took another bite of the reindeer tongue.

Alexei appeared confused. "But Papa said it was painful, nasty business."

Olga and Maria were silently laughing while Tatiana looked appalled.

Alexandra looked at Marie, slightly embarrassed. Then, her eyes rested on Nicholas. "You and I need to have a talk with our son later," she said slowly.

Nicholas buried his face in his hands. This was not exactly how the luncheon was supposed to go.

Outside, Anastasia pressed the telephone against her ear. "Hello?"

A loud and hysterical voice screamed into the telephone. "Get down here now. Ivan is here, and he won't leave!" said Miss Botkin quickly.

Anastasia could not help but smile, her heart fluttering at the thought of a handsome young man demanding her attention. Then there was a sudden wave of anxiety. She was anxious to go. If her parents found out, they'd never let her leave the palace until she was thirty. "I can't leave," whispered Anastasia softly.

"What do you mean you can't leave?"

"My family and I are having a luncheon with the Queen of Romania and two of her children. I can't just leave."

Miss Botkin wanted to scream. She'd never been so frustrated in her life. "Think of something, please!" The urgency in her voice made Anastasia's heart sink. "I rarely ask you to do anything, and I'm always getting into trouble with you and covering up for you. I don't know how much more of this I can take."

"Alright, I am coming. I'll be there as soon as I can," sighed Anastasia.

"Thank you." Miss Botkin heard the phone click. She placed the telephone down and sighed deeply.

Anastasia hurried to the dining hall and whispered to her father, "Why don't we entertain our guests with music, Papa?"

"Excellent idea!" the Tsar exclaimed. *Especially since the Romanians looked bored out of their minds,* he thought.

A few moments later, the emperor ushered everyone out of the dining hall. As the last person left, Anastasia grabbed her brother by the arm and whispered, "Do you think you can distract Mama and Papa for a little while?"

A slight smirk appeared on the boy's face. "What are you planning?"

"Please," begged Anastasia. "I need you to cause a huge distraction for a couple of hours."

Alexei nodded, delighted to be of help.

The Russian heir snuck away for a few moments and ordered the servants to have his bicycle built for two waiting for him outside of the music room. He'd need a get-away car, but a bicycle would do. He then rejoined his family and the Romanians in the music room.

The room was stunning, with satin walls with golden motifs. The white fireplace was marble, with a large mirror above the mantle. The wooden floors were polished to a shine, and a crystal chandelier hung from the ceiling. The red-cushioned furniture was antique, but the piece-de-resistance was the grand piano the Tsarina ordered from Switzerland. It was Tatiana's pride and joy, and she would lock herself in the music room and play for hours.

"Play us a song, Tatya!" squealed Maria.

Tatiana looked around nervously. "I don't know."

"I'll play with you," volunteered Olga.

Olga grabbed her younger sister by the hand and strode to the piano. The two sisters sat on the edge of the bench, with their backs straight and arms relaxed.

Nicholas and Alexandra and their other children gathered around the piano to listen to them play. The Romanians sat on the sofa, and Ileana snuggled close to her mother, their hands entangled. Marie wrapped her arm around Karl though he appeared somewhat uncomfortable.

Olga gently pressed her hands on the keys and began to play Beethoven's fifth symphony. Tatiana hesitated and joined a few moments later. Olga played the keys with skill and confidence, while Tatiana played with powerful emotion. As her fingers danced on the keys, you could hear a story. It was a story of love and devotion but also pain and disappointment.

As his sisters played, Alexei crawled under the piano. He pulled out five firecrackers from his pocket and lit them. Then, he crawled out from underneath the piano before they exploded. As his sisters reached the last note, the firecrackers went off! It sounded like small gunshots causing both Olga and Tatiana to scream and fall back over the bench. Tatiana's legs went over her head, and Alexandra fell on the floor, covering her head. The

Romanians ducked behind the sofa while Maria and Anastasia screamed. Nicholas ducked for cover. He thought they were under attack!

Smoke filled the room. Alexei stood in the corner and laughed demonically.

Anastasia thought that might be her cue to leave, so she snuck through the door before anyone noticed.

When the smoke cleared, Olga helped Tatiana regain her composure. Moments later, Tatiana stood in horror as she saw that the explosion had destroyed the entire bottom of her piano. Her eyes rested on Alexei. "I am going to kill you!" she shouted.

"What!" shrieked the Tsar.

Tatiana stepped forward, but Olga grabbed her arm, holding her sister back. Tatiana let out a painful scream. "Look what that beast did to my piano!"

The Romanians poked their heads up, slowly realizing what had just happened. Karl smirked at his mother and sister, his arms crossed. "Finally, something exciting happens around here. I could get used to this," he said in Romanian.

His mother smacked him in the back of the head.

Ileana whispered loudly to her mother, "Let's do that again, Mama."

"Hush!" hissed Marie.

Tatiana sobbed louder in Olga's shoulder.

Before his parents could scold him, Alexei made a run for it. He grabbed Ileana by the hand, and the two royal children ran out the double doors. Alexei mounted on the front of his bicycle and turned to her. The Russian heir quickly said, "Come on, girl. We're going for a ride." Without thinking, Ileana climbed on the back end, and the two children started pedaling through the hallway towards the elevator.

Alexandra and Nicholas hurried to the hallway. They watched their twelve-year-old son and the princess of Romania pedal into an elevator. The Tsarevich let out a demonic laugh as the doors closed.

Alexandra felt a surge of panic. "Nicky! We need to find him before something bad happens," she screamed.

Nicholas hurried downstairs and saw the children pedaling towards the throne room. "Stop those cyclists!" shouted Nicholas.

Imperial guards chased after the heir and the princess. Alexei pedaled faster, turning down a hallway. Eventually, Nicholas hurried after the boy himself.

Marie and Alexandra walked down the stairs, arms locked.

"You know," muttered Marie. "If Karl and Olga don't work out, we can always set up Alexei and Ileana."

Later, the Russian heir was finally apprehended. And after a few small glasses of wine, Tatiana was able to calm down.

Olga received an odd letter from her grandmother. She ripped open the envelope and stared at the beautiful cursive, written on lovely floral stationary.

It read:

Dear Olga,
I hired a private detective to do some investigating on Prince Karl. There are a few things you need to know.

Meanwhile, Anastasia knocked on the door at the Botkin home. Miss Botkin answered the door. She'd never been so glad to see a grand duchess in her life. She pulled her into the house before someone saw her. "I am so glad you are here. He is in the drawing-room," she said quietly.

Anastasia followed the physician's daughter to the drawing room. She saw Ivan sitting on the sofa next to Tatiana's brother, Gleb, and they were looking through Gleb's art book.

Gleb was a year older than Anastasia. He was a tall, scrawny boy with dark hair and green eyes and resembled his father.

Gleb was also a talented artist and as Ivan turned through the pages of his book, he looked like a little boy opening a present on Christmas. Anastasia thought that was cute and giggled.

"Hello, Ivan," she said cheerfully.

Ivan stopped and held his breath. It was her—the beautiful angel. He jumped to his feet and smiled shyly. "Hello, devushka," he said sweetly.

Ivan couldn't peel his eyes away from her, not even for a moment. Anastasia couldn't look away either. It was like they were the last people on earth. Miss Botkin signaled to her brother to follow her out of the room.

Anastasia and Ivan were alone.

Anastasia sat on the sofa with Ivan's arm wrapped around her. They talked and joked around for hours. She learned about his past. He spoke of his father, whom he loved but had deserted him, and his mother, who did her best to raise him alone. He told her about his travels across Russia and the extraordinary people he met. But he didn't talk about his brother or sister. Sometimes he liked to pretend they never existed. He didn't talk about the Bolsheviks either as he didn't want to frighten her. Anastasia spoke about as little of her past as possible; she just listened. She could listen to Ivan's stories and adventures all day.

"You never told me how the story about the boyar ended," said Ivan.

"I didn't?" she asked innocently.

Ivan shook his head. Anastasia rested her head on his shoulder. His arm had fallen asleep a while ago, but he didn't want to move it.

"The boyar never found his father," said Anastasia, lost in deep thought.

"What? Why?"

"Instead, he found something else. He realized that what he wanted was something he already had," she said, lost in thought.

"What was it?"

"Perhaps I'll tell you some other time. I have to go," whispered Anastasia.

"I thought you lived here?" questioned Ivan.

"I do. . .but I have an important train to catch." Anastasia wrapped her arms around Ivan's neck and held him tight. She had memorized everything about him. The smell of his cologne. His firm and loving touch. His cute dimples. She wanted every moment to be photographed in her memory forever. Ivan didn't want to let go either. He wrapped his arms around her back and deeply inhaled the smell of her hair.

"When will I see you again?" he asked helplessly.

Anastasia slowly arose from the sofa with Ivan's hand entwined with hers. She looked him in the eyes lovingly and promised, "Soon."

He gazed into her deep, beautiful blue eyes with a loving sadness, and pulled her in to kiss her. But before he had the chance, Miss Botkin grabbed Anastasia's arm.

"There's no time for that," she retorted. She pulled the Grand Duchess and the Bolshevik outside.

Anastasia slowly let her fingers slip through Ivan's and walked down the street to the train station with Miss Botkin. Ivan sighed and walked in the opposite direction. Did she have to go? His heart missed her deeply already.

And for the first time in a long time, Ivan couldn't stop smiling.

Chapter 20

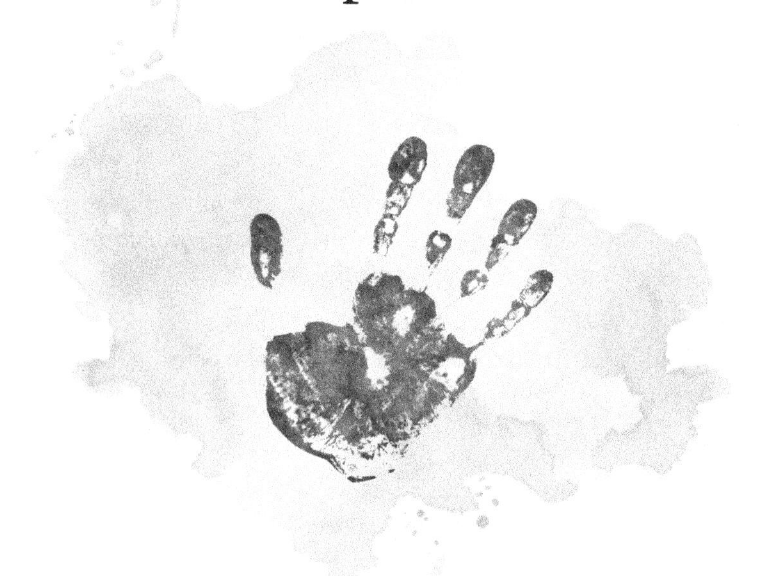

Operation Redhanded

Those firecrackers had ruined Karl's afternoon. Everything was planned perfectly; a lovely luncheon, a beautiful walk in the garden, and a proposal would have put the icing on the cake. Those firecrackers had ruined his day because he helped put out the small fire. That was the last time he tried playing hero to impress some girl. Olga couldn't have been less impressed. Karl shouldn't have to impress a woman. He was the future king of Romania! Women should be trying to impress him. But Olga didn't say a word, nothing at all. It had been several hours since the fire had been put out—several hours of awkward smiles and glances.

They were alone in the purple room. Karl sat in a lavender armchair, with his legs crossed. Olga sat on the edge of the violet sofa, looking slightly uncomfortable. Her mother had been gone for about ten minutes. How odd. Alexandra was the type of woman who wouldn't allow an unmarried man and a woman alone together—unless...

Karl quickly moved to the sofa, sitting directly by Olga. She looked just as surprised as he did by this unexpected decision. Karl grabbed Olga's hand and looked deeply into her piercing blue eyes. He hated this as much as she did.

"Olga Nikolaevna," Karl cleared his voice. "I love you, and I can't live without you by my side."

Olga took her hand from Karl's grasp and gave him a sharp, stern look. "I think what you meant to say was that you can't live without my handsome dowry." Olga's voice was cold and unfeeling.

"No, my darling," said Karl nervously. "That's not true." Karl moved closer and placed his arm around Olga. "I love you more than anything. And I want to spend the rest of my life with you."

"Love me?" repeated Olga.

Karl grabbed Olga by the hand again and squeezed it. "Yes, my love." Karl caressed her face slowly and looked deep into her eyes. "Will you marry me?"

Olga didn't have to think about the answer. She shook her head. "No," she said quietly.

The Crown Prince was not familiar with that word. Did he hear her right? He knew what that word meant and didn't like how it made him feel. The word stung, and he couldn't remember the last time someone had denied him anything.

"I'm sorry," said the Prince slowly. "What did you say?"

"No," repeated Olga.

It stung worse the second time.

Karl arose from the sofa and ran his fingers through his hair, slowly grasping the word. What did she mean by that? Never had a woman told him no before, not even a royal woman. Was this some sort of joke? Karl turned slightly, facing Olga, and chuckled quietly. "You're joking with me, right?" he bellowed louder. "Good one. You almost had me there."

But Olga wasn't laughing. "I cannot marry you," she said softly.

Karl fell back on the sofa, his hand covering his mouth. Many women would kill to be with him and to marry him. But t302his woman wouldn't. "May I ask why, pray tell?"

"You must think of me as some kind of fool, Karl."

"What are you talking about?" said Karl slowly.

"Oh!" roared Olga hysterically. "You don't think I know?" A wet, warm tear slowly rolled down her face. Olga had heard the rumors, and she was done pretending that they weren't real. Her grandmother's letter confirmed it. "Where should I begin? The secret fling you had in Romania."

"That was nothing," retorted Karl.

"Nothing?" she snapped. "You had a child with her, Karl. Then, you abandoned them in the dirt." Her voice was trembling now. "It almost makes me wonder how you would have treated me and our child if we had one."

Karl didn't say anything. He listened to her cold and piercing words. He wanted to say that none of them were true, but he would be lying.

"And your mother-" Olga went on.

Those three words touched a very sensitive wound. "Don't you dare talk about my mother!" threatened Karl.

Olga ignored him. He needed to hear the truth. "You look at her like she is the dirt on the bottom of your shoe. You speak to her like she is a dog. How would you speak to me, Karl?" The Romanian prince flinched. Those words were painful to hear. "The excessive drinking. The partying. Would you still do those things if we were married?" Olga leaned in closer. "You think that I don't notice the way that you look at my sister?"

He almost asked which one but didn't. It wouldn't help his case, and if anything, it would make things between them worse and only prove her point.

"I would rather walk a thousand miles, jump off the edge of the earth, and die a hundred painful deaths than be your wife."

Karl raised his hand to strike her. Olga didn't flinch. She didn't even blink. Karl hesitated as he remembered his place and lowered his hand. He rose from the sofa again and buttoned up his coat. "I didn't know that marrying me revolted you so much. I am going back to Romania in the morning."

"Goodbye, Karl."

Olga heard him slam the door.

Just like that, The Crowned Prince of Romania was gone and out of her life for good.

Olga was now alone in the purple room, and the silence bounced off the walls. Her body collapsed on the couch, and she fell apart, tears streaming down her face. What had she done? Now she was stuck with Boris. Her arms clung to a small purple pillow, and she screamed into it as loud as she could. The sobs that came out of her mouth were uncontrollable. Olga screamed louder before forcing herself to dry her tears. She hoped she hadn't just made a colossal mistake. After she pulled herself together again, she went to find Boris. She found him smoking in the men's parlor. "Boris Vladimirovich," she announced.

Alarmed, Boris muttered, "Yes, Your Imperial Highness."

"Will you marry me?"

Chapter 21

Operation Vienna

It was mid-February. Darya Lisanova arrived in the city of Vienna at nine 'o'clock in the evening. As she exited the train, she looked over her shoulder. She had a strange feeling that she was being watched.

Five minutes later, she met her driver in front of the train station, and he didn't look familiar. He looked twenty years old with a big black eye and a bleeding nose. Where was Maxim, the man who usually drove her places? It didn't matter. His body was probably in a ditch somewhere not far from the city. The driver's nose had not clotted yet; the blood looked fresh, and his eye was swollen. Someone got into a nasty fight. Despite her strong instincts to run, Darya climbed inside the vehicle.

They drove around the city for half an hour. She gazed out the window, watching the buildings glide by. She noticed that they passed the same small bookshop several times. They were going in circles. The anticipation was murder. She was supposed to come face to face with her cold-blooded father any minute now. It seemed like Professor Goldstein wasn't ready to see her yet. Otherwise, this driver wouldn't be stalling.

The driver finally pulled up to the side of a curb. A man in a gray suit and a dark heavy coat climbed into the other side of the vehicle.

His face triggered memories that Darya wanted to remember, and Anna wished to forget. Something inside Darya emerged from the darkness, and terror tunneled through every part of her body. Her heart accelerated. Nowhere was safe. Anna wanted to crawl back into that part of Darya that no longer existed, but it was too late. Her father had already seen her.

He said something to the driver in quiet German, and then the car moved slowly forward. Anna noticed the dried blood on his hands and in his fingernails, which could only mean one thing.

"Where is Maxim?" asked Anna slowly.

He smiled as if Anna had said something amusing.

"What did you do?" she hissed darkly.

Professor Goldstein recalled the events that happened the hour before. Kidnapping Maxim was too easy, and gutting the young man like a fish was more pleasant than he imagined. There was a reason why he was called the Professor. Dissection was his specialty. And this young man worked for a certain Gabriel von der Reis. He couldn't have a man like that walking around Vienna.

"You should have chosen your friends more wisely, Anna! Now, look what happened. Now, look at what you made me do. That man is dead now because of you." He spoke to her like she was a small child. That made Anna angry. He was punishing her for his mistakes again. "What I can't seem to understand is why my own daughter—"

"Don't you dare call me that!" she screamed. "You lost that right a long time ago!"

The mad German doctor slapped Anna so hard that he left a perfect print of his hand plastered on the side of her beautiful face. "How dare you speak to me like that! That's no way to speak to your father. Did you retrieve the letters?"

"No," she said quietly.

There was a deadly silence.

"What?" Professor Goldstein rammed his fist into his daughter's nose, and blood immediately began to gush down her face. Anna was more than certain her nose was broken. "You stupid girl! There will be serious consequences later."

Anna covered her nose with her hand. She knew that she should have put off getting dirt on Prince Karl of Romania and Grand Duke Boris for a later time, but Marie Feodorovna gave her an offer that she couldn't refuse. "Why do you need those letters?" she cried.

"Let's call it a liability."

"Liability," she sneered. "What is in those letters?"

"Oh, it's just a couple of business transactions that I don't want the world to see."

Professor Goldstein needed to hurry. He was running out of time. His life, and everything he had, depended on those letters.

Chapter 22

Operation Elephant in the Room

It was the day before Nicholas planned on going to the front. The Romanians returned home, but not before Karl demanded Maria's hand in marriage. His mother retorted that he would demand nothing. The prince made a huge scene in the throne room, cursing and screaming at his mother and Nicholas came to the Romanian Queen's defense. He reminded the spoiled brat that he was the future king of Romania, so he had better start acting like it. Besides, Nicholas insisted, his daughter, Maria, was just a schoolgirl. Karl didn't like that answer at all. He screamed that if Maria didn't return to Romania to be his wife, he would kill himself. Alarmed, Marie promised her son that he could have one of her ladies-in-waiting as a mistress if he calmed down. The Queen left Russia embarrassed.

Mitya heard the news after his return from Moscow. Mitya and his mother did some charity work for the orphans there. It was a bit of a late Christmas gift.

As soon as Mitya stepped out of the carriage, he hurried through the palace. He hoped that things weren't too late. Mitya found Olga in the music room, playing on the brand-new piano. As soon as he saw her beautiful, angelic face, his heart leaped with joy.

"Olga, I have something that I must tell you," he said enthusiastically.

Olga turned, her face covered with excitement. "What is it, Mitya?"

Mitya grabbed her hands and pulled her close. "There's something that I have been meaning to tell you for a very long time." Mitya held Olga's hands in his palm and smiled. He couldn't remain silent a moment longer. Then he looked down. He noticed a massive diamond ring on her finger. His stomach dropped. "What's this?"

"Boris and I are engaged," she said plainly.

Mitya tried giving her a smile as he struggled not to cry. "Congratulations," he said.

"Thank you," said Olga. "What was it that you wanted to tell me?"

Mitya swallowed hard, trying to get the words out. "I am going to the front tomorrow," he said painfully.

"Oh," she muttered sadly. "Why?"

Mitya couldn't keep his silence a moment longer. He wouldn't be able to live with himself if he didn't tell her at least once. He suddenly grabbed her and embraced her lovingly. His arms moved to her lower back, pulling her closer. Olga noticed that his touch was strong but soft. His fragrance was strong, too and she recognized his scent as French cologne. He had never done anything like this before, but she didn't want him to stop. She felt safe and loved in his arms.

"Olga, I love you," he whispered in her ear. "I always have, and I always will. I hope you and Boris are happy together."

Olga's heart melted. He'd never said those words to her before, and she had no idea that he even felt that way.

Mitya pulled away and kissed her forehead gently. "I am going to miss you so much on the front. Goodbye, princess."

He walked away in a hurry as he couldn't wait to get away from there. Of course, saying goodbye to the woman he loved would be the hardest thing to ask a man to do.

As Mitya walked out those double doors, Olga's heart cried out in pain. It was an aching that did not cease. That had never happened before. Olga sat down on the piano bench and stared through the window. She wondered if the pain would ever stop or if she'd always feel this way. Then tears escaped her eyes. She leaned on the piano and cried. Olga had forgotten to tell Mitya that she loved him, too.

On the way back to the carriage, trying to hold himself together, Mitya bumped into Tatiana. "Mitya, what's wrong?" she gasped.

Mitya took a couple of deep breaths.

"Tatiana, I want you to hear this from me. I am going to the front."

Tatiana's heart stopped. Her face turned white. "What?" Her voice sounded hysterical. "No, you can't leave."

"I am leaving tomorrow morning."

"No. I absolutely forbid this," she cried.

Mitya looked at her in surprise. She had never forbidden him to do anything before. And when a member of the Tsar's family commands you to do something, you must obey. However, in this case, there was a slight exception.

"You can't forbid anything. I was invited by your father." Mitya made his way down the palace corridor, and Tatiana hurried after him.

"No! Please, stay," she begged.

Mitya shrugged it off. "I have made my mind. I am going."

Tatiana grabbed Mitya's arm and tugged it gently.

"Let go of my arm, Tatiana."

"Please, Mitya. Don't go."

"Why?"

"Because I love you!" she exclaimed. She didn't mean for it to come out that way, or at all for the matter.

Mitya appeared surprised and flattered. "Tatiana—"

Tatiana's gray eyes pleaded. "I love you so much, Mitya. Please stay. Don't go."

Mitya sighed heavily. "Tatiana, I am so sorry," he said, his voice shaking with emotion.

Tatiana turned and ran to her bedroom with tears streaming down her face. She slammed the door and screamed loudly. Tatiana crawled to her bed and wailed louder into her pillow. Her heart was breaking. It was a terrible predicament when you want to be with someone so much, but they don't want to be with you.

Later that evening, Marie Feodorovna barged through the palace. She demanded to see her son, the Emperor. The palace staff dismissed her politely. They assured her that he was not to be disturbed as he was in a private meeting. The Emperor's mother did not mind, nor did she care. She insisted that she was not leaving until she spoke with her son. A few minutes later, Nicholas dismissed his advisors and met with his mother in the throne room.

Marie Feodorovna paced the floor, her hands clutching the bundle of letters and documents a little tighter. As soon as she saw her son, the Danish woman shouted, "Nicky!"

"Mama," muttered Nicholas. "What are you doing here?"

"I am disgusted that I cannot come to see my son and my grandchildren without a formal invitation," snarled Marie.

"That's not true," assured Nicholas.

"Not according to your staff!"

Nicholas noticed the bundle of letters and documents. "What's this?" he asked, his voice rich with curiosity.

"It's about Boris and Olga's engagement. There is something you must know," his mother explained. "I intercepted some personal letters and documents, and you must read them."

"Mama, I don't think this is wise—"

"I know you and your sister don't like that I pry in private matters. However, the proof you need is written in ink."

Nicholas ripped open an envelope and began reading one of the letters. It was written in French. The letter was a correspondence between Grand Duke Boris and Queen Marie. They were having an affair! That wasn't even the most alarming part. After he read the last paragraph, Nicholas looked at his mother. "You know what you must do."

The next morning, Olga arose before dawn. She took a cold bath before she took a half hour walk in the park with her father. Next, she ate a small breakfast and a cup of coffee. After her morning routine, she had the strange inclination that she must speak with her much older fiancé, Boris.

Olga found Boris on the balcony, staring into the pond. The balcony was one of the latest additions to the palace. Because Alexandra had a difficult time leaving the palace due to her fragile back, Nicholas ordered the balcony to be built for her, so she could go outside without leaving. It was an elegant balcony that wrapped around the palace. It was more comfortable to be out there since her mother had bought wicker furniture, and she would often sit on the balcony for hours, staring at the pond and the trees.

"Boris," called Olga from behind. Boris turned at the sound of his name. Olga strode nervously towards him, with her arms crossed. "I need to know exactly how you feel about me. Do you love me?"

Boris appeared somewhat surprised. "Yes, of course," he said quietly. "You know I do."

Olga swallowed hard. "Do you love the Queen of Romania, too?" she said, her voice cracking.

Boris' heart dropped. "Where did you hear that?"

Olga shook her head. "It doesn't matter where I heard it. I need to know if you love her."

Boris sighed lightly. His silence gave the answer away.

"When were you going to tell me that you were having an affair and shared a child with her?"

"I didn't know how or when to tell you."

"Were you going to wait until after our wedding?" asked Olga.

Boris shook his head. "I don't know."

"Do you love me, Boris?"

"Well," he uttered nervously. "I love you more like a niece than I do an actual—"

"Lover." Olga had finished the sentence for him, and Boris nodded gently. Olga frowned and sighed. "So, this is a royal engagement?"

Boris looked at her, disappointed. "It shouldn't be like this, but yes."

Olga leaned on the railing and looked at the trees dancing in the wind, wondering if this was how her life was going to be; Boris with a mistress, while she shuts her mouth and pretends nothing is happening. "Boris, what are we going to do?" she asked sadly.

Boris slouched over his elbows and rested on the railing. "You can take a lover if you'd like," he said, thinking out loud. Olga looked at him, appalled. "I am not asking for fidelity. I am asking for loyalty."

"What is loyalty without fidelity?" hissed Olga.

"It's like you said. This is a royal engagement, and it's a small price to pay," said Boris emotionlessly.

"It shouldn't be like this," she snapped.

"It's the way things are," sighed Boris. "Marriage is either a financial or political contract. There are no strings attached in the marital agreement. You and I agreed to this when we agreed to marry each other."

"I suppose so," the young woman muttered.

Suddenly, Boris took her by the hand. "Olga, do you love me?" he said plainly.

"I do."

Then, Boris looked at her in a way he's never looked at her before. "Please, be honest. Do you love me enough to marry me this spring?"

"No," she admitted sadly.

Boris touched her chin, tilting it up. For a small moment, she thought Boris might kiss her. Instead, he said, "You deserve better than this."

"Boris—"

"Don't interpret," he said kindly. "You deserve a man who's going to wake up beside you every morning, love you fully, and give you complete fidelity. That man cannot be me." Boris held Olga's hands again. "You must understand that."

"Boris, don't do this," begged Olga.

"I don't want you to torture yourself more than you already have. If you don't want this marriage, you need to speak now. And I will leave today, and you don't have to see me again."

Olga slowly slid off her engagement ring.

"Keep it," insisted Boris. "It was a gift to you."

Olga embraced Boris in a deep hug, with tears spilling from her eyes. "Thank you for making this easier."

Boris held her in his arms and kissed her forehead. That was the hardest thing he had to do in his life. His mother was going to murder him later. "I am sorry that I couldn't be that man for you, Olga Nikolaevna."

That was the sincerest apology Boris Vladimirovich ever gave.

What about the dynasty? She wondered.

"You'll find that man someday, but something tells me you've already have," added Boris. He kissed her hand. "Goodbye, Your Imperial Highness. It was an honor being engaged to you."

"Goodbye, Boris."

An hour later, Boris had packed his last bag when he heard a knock on the door.

"Come in," he shouted in frustration.

The door cracked open. "There should be enough money in your account to pay off your debts, cover your travel expenses, and get away from your overbearing mother," said the Tsar.

Boris turned halfway and gave a fake smile. "I should be grateful for your kindness and generosity, Your Imperial Highness. But considering the circumstances—"

"Did you mean everything you said to her?" asked Nicholas calmly.

"I did," said the Grand Duke proudly.

Nicholas smiled and entered the room, closing the door gently behind him before making his way over to Boris.

"I know what you must think of me. I must be a terrible sort of man to get involved with—" Boris began.

Nicholas put his finger over his mouth and motioned Boris to follow him. Nicholas made loud, deliberately heavy stomps with his feet and opened the door. Then, he closed it again.

Suddenly, the door to the dressing room opened slowly. Maria, having not noticed her father or Boris, poked her head out.

"Are Papa and Uncle Boris gone?" exclaimed Alexei. "Can we come out now?"

"Hush!" hissed Anastasia.

"I think the coast is clear," whispered Maria.

Nicholas folded his arms in both admiration and disapproval. "You must forgive my children, Boris. They can be nosy little creatures."

As soon as Maria heard her father, she shrieked and slammed the door. Nicholas motioned Boris to follow him again. The two men walked over to the door, and Nicholas knocked lightly.

"Nobody's home. Come back later," shouted Alexei from behind the door.

"Hush!" Nicholas knocked on the door again. "Children, you have two choices. Either you open and let Boris and I in, or I'll you get your mother. And you could let her in."

The door cracked open.

The dressing room was small, with white floral furniture and a red English carpet. The fireplace was ivory with a thermometer beside it to let the servants know if the room was too cold. The walls were covered in watercolors that family members had painted. It appeared that Nicholas' children had used the furniture to make a fort and covered it with sheets and blankets.

Nicholas and Boris crawled through the front to find the floor was covered in pillows his wife had embroidered. There was a stack of books not meant for young minds and a couple of bottles of vodka in the corner.

Nicholas had only one thought; his wife was going to murder them.

Maria appeared to be knitting a new blanket, perhaps for her mother. Alexei and Anastasia sat crisscrossed, smoking, and playing poker in the middle.

"Hello, Papa," said his son cheerfully.

"What is this place?" uttered Boris in admiration.

"We call it: The Secret Society of Naughty Royals," answered Anastasia. "Would you and Papa care to join?"

Nicholas noticed the bottles of vodka. "What were those bottles for?" he asked, sounding alarmed.

"That was part of the initiation ceremony," explained Maria, without taking her eyes off the next stitch. "You have to drink a whole bottle, then say the alphabet backward. It was quite fun. You and Uncle Boris can join. But not Olga, Tatiana, or Mama. They are not invited." Boris laughed and turned to Nicholas. "This sounds exactly like the stories I heard about you, Sandro, and Andrei."

"You and Uncle Sandro did this at our age, Papa?" asked Alexei, his voice covered in excitement and curiosity.

"I do remember a time when you, Sandro, and Andrei snuck out of the palace at night. And the three of you got rowdy at a pub, and a local policeman tried to calm you down. Then, you responded by shoving caviar in the poor man's face!"

Nicholas was horrified.

"Is that true, Papa?" asked Alexei.

"The policeman would have arrested you that night. Then, he realized you were the Tsarevich," added Boris, laughing harder. "And he considered it an honor for you to have dumped caviar in his face!"

Nicholas smiled nervously.

"You are a horrible example to your children," teased Boris.

"Is Uncle Boris not going to be our brother-in-law anymore?" asked Alexei innocently.

Boris stopped laughing.

"No, children, he won't," sighed Nicholas. "It's because Boris has to go to Paris."

"Why?" asked Anastasia, taking her eyes off her cards for a small moment.

Boris had a perplexed expression on his face. "There's something in Paris that I need to do. And I will be gone for a while. But I will miss you all very terribly."

Alexei appeared sad. He looked forward to having a brother-in-law around. Finally, there would have been another man around the house, and not just him and his father. The safety of the men in this family had been compromised, and the women now outnumbered them five to two.

"Can't you just take Olga with you?" uttered Alexei.

"It's not that simple, little man," said Boris quietly. "This is something I have to do alone. Perhaps you'll understand when you are older."

There were a few moments of complete silence before Alexei bluntly said, "Does this have something to do with a woman?"

Maria gave her brother a deadly glare. "Alexei!"

Boris forgave him. The boy asked out of pure innocence. "She was a friend who was special to me, and she left me something in Paris that I must take care of."

"Does it have something to do with a baby?"

Maria grabbed a pillow and hit Alexei with it. "Shut up."

Nicholas looked at Boris nervously. "I am so sorry," he muttered.

Boris let it roll off his shoulders. "I will miss this, actually."

Nicholas had let Boris read the documents full of information his aunt had given him the night before. The documents contained the birth record of his son in Paris and the death record of his child's mother. He read through them thoroughly this morning and sighed in relief when he learned his son was being looked after by his mother's relatives in France. He desperately wanted to see his child. Did he look like him? Did he look like Jeanne? What was his boy like? Did they like to do the same things? Oh, he hoped not.

A few weeks ago, the Queen of Romania wrote a letter to Boris, explaining that one of her children was fathered by him. And that was why she petitioned to divorce Ferdinand all those years ago. He wondered which child belonged to him, though he never asked. It was most likely one of the younger ones.

Nicholas also explained earlier that he knew of his mother's failed coup and his many unpaid debts. The Tsar offered to pay them on the condition that Boris break off the engagement with Olga and leave Russia to find his child in France. Boris knew it was some kind of nice way of banishing him from the country, but Nicholas was more than generous, so he did not protest.

Boris' mother tried to finance the coup because she believed Alexandra was a German spy, loyal to the Fatherland. His mother also didn't like her political views, or her role in foreign and domestic policies. She believed that Alexandra had too much power over the Emperor. And it made her skin crawl that the Tsarina was German. It was Maria Pavlova's greatest wish that Nicholas, his son, and his brother die so that one of her sons could be the next Tsar. Boris didn't need to explain any of this. Nicholas knew it.

Later that morning, Nicholas invited Olga on a walk and confronted her about his worries about Boris concerning his illegitimate child with Queen Marie. Olga then felt prompted to speak to Boris about the matter herself. She could have never broken the engagement with Boris on her own as she loved her family and the dynasty too much. Olga just needed a little push.

When Nicholas walked with Boris to his carriage that was waiting outside to take him to the train station, he noticed that his face showed traces of disappointment and sadness.

"I am not cut out to be a father," he said softly.

"What made you think you were cut out to be a husband?"

Boris scoffed loudly. "I would have made a terrible husband."

"When the time comes, Boris, you may find that you rise to the occasion," said Nicholas kindly. "Goodbye, my friend."

As Boris closed the carriage door, he had a strange feeling that he would never see Mother Russia again.

Chapter 23

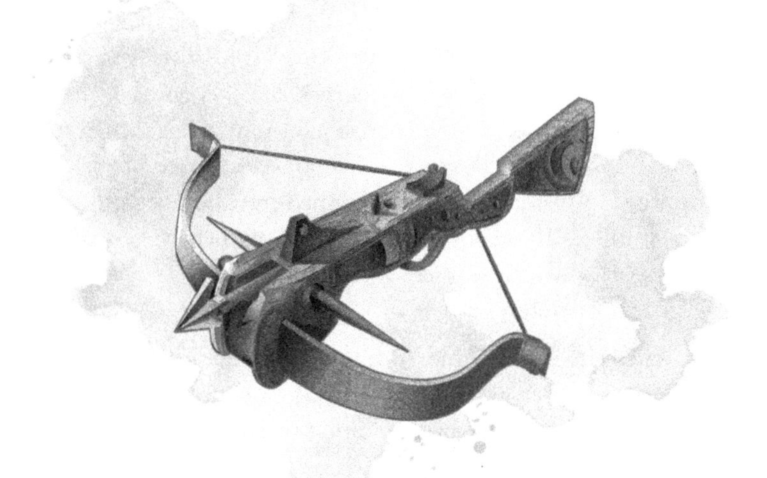

Operation Crossbow

The next day, the Tsar prepared to go to the front. He boarded the train a few minutes after noon. This was his last chance to take back control of his country. Mitya agreed to come along.

Nicholas was terrified for the journey ahead. The front was fraught with the terrors of war and traitors. If Nicholas failed, everyone he loved would pay dearly.

His father's sudden death, over twenty years ago, shook the country. No one was spared from the grief. His mother and sisters couldn't stop crying, and Russia couldn't stop mourning. As the new Tsar, young Nicholas couldn't stop trembling. He used to love trains, boats, and cars. He could read twenty-seven books in one week. He liked science, history and spent hours in the classroom. He wanted to be a soldier. Instead, he became the Tsar. He inherited a world that was stuck in the past.

Europe was changing. Monarchs were handing over power to the people. Citizens were thinking for themselves. Imperialism. Capitalism. Europe was growing. Transforming into something no longer familiar. Not for Russia. Nicholas thought it was best to continue his father's legacy and autocracy. And the communists were giving him hell for it. They always had something to complain about.

Nicholas entered the dining car, working on his fifth cigarette. Chain smoking had a calming effect on his nerves. He was going to be smoking more than usual from now on. He had separation anxiety when it came to Alexei. He had to know if Alexei was alright every second of the day. It was exhausting. The boy was a maniac. He climbed trees, jumped off beds, trying to get himself killed. If Nicholas didn't know any better, he would assume Alexei had a death wish. Other than that, Alexei acted like a normal boy. But Alexei wasn't a normal boy, was he?

Mitya followed close behind him, with his face shrouded in sadness. No one seemed to notice except for Nicholas. A concerned look relaxed on Nicholas' face, his Danish blue eyes beaming with kindness and compassion.

"What's wrong?" said Nicholas in a fatherly way.

Mitya didn't answer. He was lost in thought. There were many things floating around in his brain, Olga being one of the most important and leaving her behind hurt worse than a gunshot wound. At least, Karl and Boris were gone. Nothing was standing in between him and Olga now. Except that Mitya had nothing to bring to the table.

Nicholas had a lot on his mind as well. The war had clouded his brain since it started. His family's safety was a concern as well. If anything were to happen, they'd have to go to England or France. He made a mental note to contact the authorities of those countries immediately. But Nicholas could spare a few moments for Mitya.

"Mitya, something is troubling you. What is it?" asked Nicholas.

Nicholas sat down at a small dining table, and Mitya sat across from him. Nicholas patiently waited for an answer. Mitya was quiet for a few moments longer before he slowly gathered the courage he required.

"I know that I was born without a title, and I have nothing to offer. But I have loved Olga for a long time now, and I love her more than anything now. I want to marry her," he said quietly, his voice shaking with emotion.

Nicholas was quiet, and Mitya couldn't tell what he was thinking which made all the more nervous.

None of that mattered. Nicholas had already made his decision.

"Many years ago. . ." Nicholas paused for a few moments, recalling the events. "Your mother died in childbirth and your father left you. Elisabeth, my wife's older sister, was married to my uncle at the time. They were childless, and they took you in and raised you as their own."

Mitya frowned.

"It so happens that your mother was the heiress to the largest fortune in Greece."

"What?" gasped Mitya. "Why am I just now hearing about this?"

Nicholas lowered his voice, "We didn't want you to grow a big head." Mitya appeared confused, and he still wasn't understanding. Nicholas smiled. "Please, take care of her."

Mitya's heart leaped from his chest. "You mean?" Nicholas smiled again in approval. "When can I marry her?" exclaimed Mitya, his voice full of enthusiasm and excitement.

"You have to ask her first," chuckled Nicholas.

"Where is she?"

He glanced at his watch. "I'm afraid I don't know, but the train should leave right about...now," said Nicholas regrettably as the train lurched forward.

Disappointment covered Mitya's face, but then he had an idea. Mitya ran faster than he'd ever run in his entire life. He bumped into a few tables and a wall, but he didn't care. He didn't even wince in pain. He just continued to run as if his life depended on it. In his mind, it did.

"Where are you going?" Nicholas called.

"I am going to jump off this train," shouted Mitya.

"What!?" Nicholas hurried after him.

Mitya opened the door to the outside. The train began to speed up slowly. But before Mitya could jump, Nicholas grabbed his shoulder, and Mitya turned slightly towards him.

"Please, take care of my family. Now go," uttered Nicholas.

"Thank you," said Mitya gratefully.

"Go! Quickly!" the Tsar shouted.

Mitya nodded and jumped from the moving train, his body hitting the ground hard. He grunted in pain but quickly got on his feet and ran to a black Mercedes someone had parked outside the train station. As soon as he was in, he gunned the stolen vehicle to the Alexander Palace.

Meanwhile, the Romanov children spent the late morning in the formal reception room. The eighteenth-century-styled room was furnished by their ancestor, Catherine the Great, and some of the French tapestries and furniture belonged to Marie Antoinette herself. The walls were white marble, topped with classical designs. The large windows had dark red curtains, with the inner drapes made from delicate lace. A crystal chandelier hung in the center of the ceiling, with a scarlet glass center. A regal portrait of their mother hung between the two doors that led to the reception room. It was painted a decade before by a German artist. Alexandra wore a violet gown, with a diamond diadem, standing in a dim forest. It was Nicholas and the children's favorite portrait of her.

Olga sat at the roll-top desk, already writing a letter to her father. Alexei laid on his stomach, littering the floor with crumbs from the crackers he ate. Maria reclined on a chair, knitting scarves for the wounded soldiers. Tatiana and Anastasia chattered and giggled loudly, which was beginning to annoy Olga.

"It feels kind of strange and empty with Papa and Mitya gone," sighed Maria.

"Mitya was the closest thing I had to a father," said Alexei.

Tatiana raised an eyebrow and folded her arms. "We already have one of those," she said defensively. "And he is a very good one."

"Do you mean brother?" asked Anastasia quietly.

"That, too," the boy teased.

Maria glanced over at Olga, then back at her stitch. "Are you all right, Olga? You seem out of sorts today."

Olga stopped writing. "Mitya said that he loved me before he left."

Alexei nearly choked on a cracker. "What?"

Maria and Anastasia grabbed each other, jumped up and down, and squealed joyfully. Tatiana could feel her heart breaking again.

"How?" asked Maria eagerly

"It was two days ago, in the music room," began Olga. Her words were more than what Tatiana could bear. It was like losing Mitya all over again. "He said that he had something important to tell me. He grabbed my hands and noticed my ring. He became quiet. Then he said that he was going to the front and that he loved me."

Maria and Anastasia squealed louder.

"What did you say?" asked Anastasia quickly.

"I said nothing," responded Olga.

"What?" gasped Alexei. He nearly choked on the cracker again. This would be his chance to have a brother, and his older sister was ruining it for him. "What do you mean you said nothing? You love him, don't you?"

Olga nodded.

Maria squealed playfully. "I knew it! You must go after him and tell him," she shouted.

"The train leaves at any moment," muttered Olga.

"You can still try and catch it," insisted Anastasia.

Olga sighed and smiled. "Alright."

Maria and Anastasia grabbed each other's hands and squealed again. "We are going with you! This is like Romeo and Juliet!" shouted Maria.

Alexei finished the last cracker, and stood up on his feet, wiping away any crumbs on his gray uniform. "This is better than Romeo and Juliet. I need a net and a crossbow!"

Alarmed, Tatiana asked, "Why?"

"Another future brother of mine isn't escaping this time," declared the boy.

Tatiana stepped forward, her arms folded. "I will stay here. Someone has to cover for all of you."

The four Romanovs hurried to the garage, started a vehicle, and gunned it down the long driveway.

Tatiana watched her siblings from the window as they swiftly disappeared. She sighed painfully as her heart shattered inside of her. When she heard footsteps coming from behind, she got startled. Turning sharply, she found Konstantin behind her.

"Konstantin," she sighed in relief. A thought, born out of desperation, filled her head. "Would you do anything for me?" she asked him.

"Of course. Anything."

Tatiana stepped a little closer, her heart aching in pain. For once, she wanted someone to want her as much as she wanted them. She wanted to be desired instead of being rejected. Was that so much to ask? Also, she was tired of being picture-perfect all the time, and the pressure was breaking her. Tatiana wished she could be as brave as Maria and wild as Anastasia. She wanted to be passionate and spontaneous for once in her life.

"If I told you to kiss me, would you do it?" she finally asked.

Konstantin didn't think twice. He wrapped his arms around Tatiana, pulled her in close, and kissed her lips passionately. Tatiana felt fireworks explode inside of her. She never knew that a kiss could be so powerful. For a small moment, Tatiana felt cherished. Then Konstantin pulled away.

"Kiss me again, please," she whispered breathlessly.

Konstantin looked deep into her light gray eyes and caressed her chin. Konstantin kissed her lips softly. A few moments later, he pulled away again. Tatiana fought the urge to cry.

"If I told you to love me, would you do it?"

The soldier nodded.

Tatiana studied him, her heart completely broken. "Then, why don't you?" she asked, her voice shaking with grief.

"Your Imperial Highness-"

"It's Tatiana," she corrected.

"Tatiana," he sighed. "It's because you deserve something real."

Tatiana's face hardened, and she pointed her finger. "I don't need you to tell me what I do and don't need. I can do that for myself." She folded her arms and turned defensively. "What I need is you."

Konstantin grabbed her and cradled her in his arms. He tried to keep his feelings for her bottled up inside for so long, but she was making it so hard. "I will be whatever you need me to be, princess," he promised.

"I need you to be there," she whispered.

"I will be here for as long as you need me to be."

Heading to the train station, Olga passed Mitya in a Mercedes.

"Mitya!" screamed Maria.

Olga slammed on the brakes and made a quick U-turn. Seeing Olga drive by, Mitya slowed his car down and parked it in the grass. Mitya and Olga climbed out of their vehicles about the same time and walked slowly towards each other until they met in the middle of the plush green blades. Olga stared into Mitya's deep blue eyes, her heart beating rapidly.

"I thought you were going to the front," said Olga quietly.

"Something changed my mind."

Mitya watched her eyes to expose her feelings. His heart rate accelerated. "What did?"

"You," confessed Mitya. Suddenly, he grabbed her in a tight embrace. He wrapped his arms tighter around her, pulling her closer. Olga clasped her arms around his neck, tears spilling from her eyes.

"I love you. I am sorry that I didn't say it sooner," she whispered.

A smile spread across his face as he took in her words. His dreams of this moment finally came true. "I love you, too." Mitya then got down on one knee.

The three Romanovs waiting in the car watched in amazement. Maria and Anastasia held hands, holding their breaths. Olga covered her mouth, choked with emotion, her heart beating faster.

"Olga Nikolaevna Romanov, will you marry me?"

"Yes!"

Chapter 24

Operation Abdiacte

The flour was gone.

There were lines of shivering and starving mothers and old babushkas, who had been waiting all night for bread rations. Their skeletal children slept with bloated stomachs. So many were sick and dying. Their husbands wandered in the streets with grumbling bellies and anger coursing through their veins. They were angry at the lack of jobs and resources. The factory workers had gone on strike, and because of that, there were no jobs to support their families, or to put food on the table for their starving children. They were outraged because of the war.

Russian soldiers were forced to charge into battle without guns or ammunition. They were ordered by the Minister of War to take weapons off of the bodies of dead soldiers. Warm clothes, thick coats, and boots were nonexistent. Those boys were running around the battlefield barefoot, wearing thin duffle coats. That was unacceptable. But most of all, the people were angry that the Tsar did not seem to care.

And now that the flour was gone, bread could not be made. The Chupacabra made sure of that.

The Russian people had reached a breaking point. This could no longer be tolerated. Things had to change, and someone had to be destroyed and annihilated.

Riots had erupted in the streets. Crowds of workers and women marched in circles carrying large, red banners that read, "Down with the war! Down with the Tsar! Down with the German woman! Give us bread!" Cossacks were sent to keep the crowd under control, but instead, they sided with the mob. Police were dispatched to arrest the rebels, which made the mob angrier. Women threw rocks and large chunks of ice at them, and the men joined in. Shops and bakeries were looted, police stations were burned to the ground, and prisoners were set free.

The Chief of Military opened fire on the people. Several were injured, and hundreds were killed. It was all done by order of the Tsar.

St. Petersburg was a bloodbath.

The Chupacabra made sure of that, too. He had people preach to hungry souls God's work. With a little bit of money and using the right people inside his pocket, the flour was gone. Soon, the monarchy would be gone as well.

The ministers and advisors knew about the mass destruction for about a week before anyone dared break the news to Nicholas. They tried getting the situation under control as they sent police and Cossacks loose on the angry mob. Instead, the Cossacks turned against them. The police were now just as helpless as the people. Nicholas was kept in the dark about how dire the situation truly was. After plan A and plan B failed miserably, it was time for Nicholas to take the fall.

Nicholas was on his way home from the front. Military officials greeted him off the train and drove him around the front. Nicholas had an awful feeling that they showed him what they wanted him to see. Thousands of soldiers gather to see him, wishing him good health. Nothing seemed too out of the ordinary. Now, he was two days travel away from St. Petersburg. He locked himself inside his office in the Imperial train, not to be disturbed. He paced the floor, chain-smoked, and muttered to himself.

Moments ago, he had received a telegram from his general suggesting that the Tsar abdicate the throne. It was a preposterous idea. It was Nicholas' right to rule. It was his birthright. Tsars were chosen by God to lead and govern Mother Russia. And if he wasn't a Tsar, then what was he? Besides, there were a few small riots in St. Petersburg. Nicholas' government had it under control.

Suddenly, Nicholas received a telephone call.

"Hello, Your Imperial Highness," said the man on the other end. "Do you have a moment?"

Nicholas' heart made quick and steady beats against his chest as he braced himself for what was next. Nicholas cleared his throat, "Yes, I do."

"Good," said the man enthusiastically. "There are a few things that I regret to inform you about."

Nicholas' hand clenched the phone tighter.

The man told Nicholas the truth about the riots and his soldiers. He even said that if things didn't calm down, Tsarskoe Selo might be attacked.

Nicholas held his breath, and it was if his mind froze. He slowly grasped the words from moments before. Riots? Mobs? His family? He didn't understand. Everything was fine a week ago! It had been fine for the past twenty-two years, supposedly.

"Thank you for informing me of the situation," said Nicholas, his voice slightly shaking. "Have a good night." He gently put down the phone.

His ministers had lied to him.

Nicholas asked his ministers for three years how the war was doing. He received the same answers. "The war was fine, Sire." No questions asked, and he took their word for it. How could he have been so trusting? Nicholas asked them how the peasants were doing. "The peasants are doing marvelous, Sire." How could have been so naive?

His soldiers. The thought made him sick. No wonder Russia was losing the war. How could they keep the truth from him?

His ministers had sugar-coated the whole revolution. Nicholas did hear about small riots on the streets and telegrammed The Chief of Military and politely asked him to take care of the problem. He didn't tell him to open fire and murder hundreds of people! This made him look like a monster! His name had, indeed, been through a lot. And after today, there would be no coming back from this. The Cossacks had taken the rebels' side. The electricity and water were cut off in St. Petersburg and his government had collapsed out from under him. Now his family was in danger!

And his children were sick with the measles, leaving them helpless and defenseless.

Nicholas needed a smoke. He lit a cigarette and took a long drag, inhaling the sweet addiction. His blue eyes were glued to a photograph of his wife on his desk. It was a stunning photo of Alix taken after their engagement. Nicholas picked up the picture and smiled slightly. Nicholas was the luckiest man in the world. Alix looked so beautiful—still was. Alexandra was a shy and awkward girl, who had a difficult time carrying on a conversation, but she was his world. Nicholas stared at the image a few moments longer before placing it back down.

There were two small knocks on the door. Nicholas put his cigarette out and hurried to answer it. The Tsar opened the door quickly. "Mama," he exclaimed in relief.

Marie Feodorovna made four quick strides into the study. Nicholas took three steps back, moving aside for his mother. The Dowager Empress stopped in the middle of the room and looked around. The place looked nice and tidy. That was not a good sign. Her son tended to reorganize his study when he was stressed. Her eyes rested on him, and she broke into a smile. "It's good to see you, darling," said Marie softly.

Nicholas frowned slightly. Behind that patient smile and warm gaze, she knew. He could hide it from the rest of the world, but he couldn't hide it from his mother. Something terrible had happened.

"Nicholas," whispered his mother, her voice shaking in concern. "What is it?"

"Do you want to go on a walk?" said Nicholas hysterically. "Let's go for a walk." He took her arm and hurried her out the door.

Nicholas and his mother walked side by side around the train. Silence accompanied their walk, and he could hardly keep himself together. Suddenly, it dawned on him why the train was parked halfway from the front to Tsarskoe Selo. The traitors were using this as leverage against him to sign abdication papers.

"What happened?" his mother asked him.

Nicholas stopped. He couldn't hold himself together anymore. He whimpered as tears filled his eyes. "I have to abdicate!"

Marie gasped and covered her mouth. "What?"

He let out a small wail trying to get the words out. "My family is trapped in Tsarskoe Selo. The children are sick with measles, and they can't be moved. The mob is going to kill them if I don't abdicate." Marie stared at her son, her face unreadable. "I am sorry, Mama. I failed you and the dynasty. I failed Russia."

Marie grabbed her son's hand firmly. "No, you haven't. We can fix this. You can't abdicate if they can't find you."

"Mama, no," whispered Nicholas.

Marie ignored him and continued, "We need to get off this train. We need to go to Crimea. We'll send for Alexandra and the children later," she cried.

Nicholas grabbed his mother by the shoulders gently. "Mama," he said quietly. "It's over."

Marie's heart broke into a thousand pieces. "This is all my fault," she whimpered.

Nicholas shook his head. "No, Mama. The fault is all mine."

Marie scoffed and continued walking forward. "It's your father's fault. He created this." Nicholas walked beside his mother and listened. "He didn't train you on how to rule properly. I fought for you on your behalf. He was so stubborn; he wouldn't listen to reason! If I had known this would happen, I would have taught you myself."

"Why didn't Papa teach me how to rule?"

Marie looked at her son, her blue eyes pitiful. "I don't know. Nicholas, if you do abdicate, who will you be turning power to?"

Nicholas said without thinking, "Michael."

Marie gave Nicholas a sharp look. "Why not Alexei? It's his birthright," she hissed.

Nicholas shrugged and sighed. "It's too complicated, Mama."

Marie scoffed again. "You and your wife spent nearly a decade trying to conceive an heir for just an occasion such as this.".

Nicholas ignored his mother. It was, indeed, the boy's birthright, and it would save the dynasty. But he couldn't give his son the throne. Alexei was too sickly of a boy. Nicholas and Alexandra would be forced into exile, leaving their son with arrogant strangers. Then the boy would be the puppet for the new liberal government. Nicholas had to give the throne to his brother. It was the only way to save Russia, his family, and the dynasty.

"I am giving the throne to Michael."

Michael was Marie's youngest son. He was somewhere in St. Petersburg with his family, and Marie needed to find him before the Bolsheviks did.

"I need to leave," said Marie firmly. "Your brother will be the next Tsar in a few hours, and he may need me."

As Marie left the train, she took one last look at her oldest son. His arms were folded. He appeared to be the most defeated man alive.

"I still love you, Nicky," she said tenderly.

"I love you, too, Mama."

Marie swallowed hard. "Goodbye, my angel. May God be with you." *And may God be with Russia,* she thought.

As the Tsar watched his mother climb into a vehicle, he had the strangest feeling that he would never see her again.

Later that evening, Nicholas greeted two men with a handshake. After a smoke or two and some awkward small talk, one man presented the abdication papers to Nicholas. He stared at the document coldly and signed his signature at the bottom.

It was done.

Nicholas felt a strong sense of relief. It was all over. Nicholas could finally breathe.

Michael read the news in a telegram, and it nearly gave him a heart attack. Did he read that last part right? His brother was no longer The Tsar, and his nephew wasn't going to be The Tsar? Michael was the new Tsar! What was Nicky thinking? Michael didn't want to be Tsar and Nicholas knew that.

Michael knew as much about running a country as Nicholas did. Nicholas also knew that. How could Nicky do this to him? Michael didn't need to be Tsar. What he needed was a strong drink.

Michael drank half a bottle of vodka in one swallow. He then slammed the bottle on the table. His mind was already made up. He was going to abdicate the throne.

Five minutes later, another abdication paper was typed out and Michael sighed it. His signature ended the three hundred and four years of the Romanov dynasty.

Chapter 25

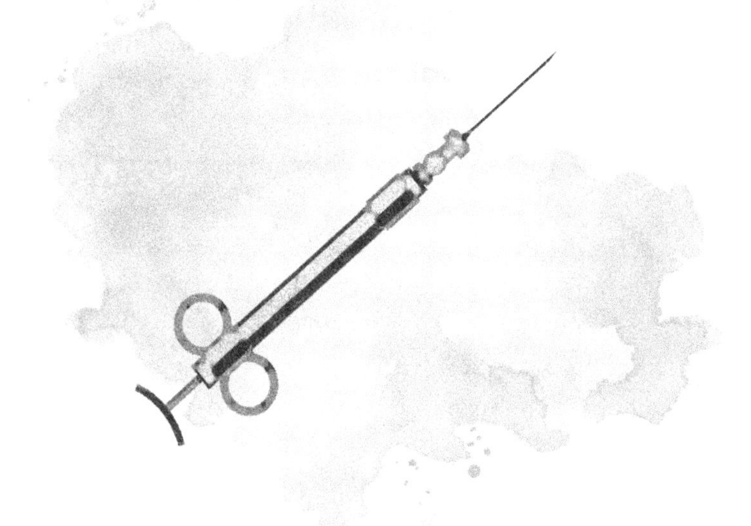

Operation Outbreak

The escape and train routes were cut off. The revolutionists were becoming bolder. They had also cut off the Alexander Palace's electricity, water supply, telegram machine, and telephone. The palace staff had resigned, and the soldiers had abandoned them and left the family unprotected. The children took a turn for the worse and contracted measles. No one had heard a peep from the Tsar. Rumors were going around that revolutionists were going to storm into the palace and lock Alexandra away in prison or the nunnery.

The Romanovs became sitting ducks.

It was Maria who had been Alexandra's savior. She had been the only one of the children who'd not caught the disease. With the power and the electricity gone, the elevator was no good. Maria was forced to step up her game and take on the role of Tatiana. Maria either helped Alexandra climb the steep palace steps or pushed her around in the wheelchair. Her soft-spoken prayers were a great comfort to Alexandra's frail heart.

Alexandra was relaxing in her purple room when a servant handed her a telegram. "It's from your father!" she squealed.

Alexandra's crystal eyes devoured every word of that telegram. For a small moment, there was a genuine smile on her face, and that made Maria happy. But she saw mother's smile quickly fa as she read the last word. Something was wrong.

"Abdicate," Alexandra's voice trembled. "Your father abdicated the throne?"

Maria's quivering lips fought to give her mother a comforting smile. Choking through the lump caught in her throat, Maria croaked quietly, "It's going to be alright, Mama." Her voice struggled to speak. "Papa is going to be home soon, and everything will be alright again."

Maria's smile put a rare grin on Alexandra's face. That made Maria happy. Even for a moment.

"Oh, Mashka," cried Alexandra. She gathered Maria in her arms and whispered lovingly, "What would I do without you, my beautiful darling?" Maria wrapped her arms around Alexandra and cradled her mother.

Later, as Maria walked through the cold, dark palace alone, her arms crossed, and her lips trembling. There was a deep-rooted pain that she'd carried with her for two days that she didn't let her mother see. It was a horrible discomfort in her chest. Her heart was aching and throbbing in agony and. with every step and breath, it grew stronger. Maria wandered inside the purple room and stopped, tears were swelling in her eyes that began to trickle down her face.

That was it.

Maria fell to her knees, curled up into fetal position, and began to cry, and those cries turned to sobs that poured out of her.

How could all this happen? Maria did everything right. She said all her prayers and attended church with her family. She read the bible every day like a good girl. Why was all this happening? Fear pumped through every part of her body. Were those people really going to come and take her mother away? Maria couldn't stand the thought of a life without her mother. It was unimaginable. Was she no longer a Grand Duchess? That didn't make sense! The new reality was hard to swallow, and the others didn't even know about it yet.

Maria wiped the tears from her face and began to wander through the palace again. She found her mother and Dr. Botkin with their patient. Dr. Botkin had packed his bags and camped inside the palace several days ago to care for the Tsar's four sick children.

Dr. Eugene Botkin was a soft-spoken man, with a round body. His thin brown hair and carefully trimmed beard had some gray streaks, and his wide eyes were a good mixture of brown and green. A set of small glasses sat on the edge of his big Russian nose. He wore a dark blue tweed suit dark shoes and a pocket watch chain hung from one pocket.

His own children were still in the city. If anything were to happen to his two remaining children, he'd never forgive himself. Tatiana and Gleb were all he had left in this world. But Tatiana was a smart girl, and he knew she'd keep them both safe.

His wife didn't want to be married to him anymore. She claimed that he was more in love with his work than he was with her, and she blamed him for the marriage falling apart. She left and never came back. She even didn't write. But that didn't matter. Eugene didn't need to hear from her anyway. What made him angry was that she never bothered to visit the children. His wife would send a telegram, announcing that she'd stop by and visit. But she never came. No one did that to his children. No one. He paid her way to Germany and made her swear never to make promises that she couldn't keep with his children ever again. She agreed and took the first train to Berlin, divorced Botkin, and married her German lover.

Eugene had never said anything bad about the woman who gave him his children. Nor did he allow the children to speak ill of her. No matter how much she'd hurt them, she was still their mother, and no magic could change that. They were now stuck with a father who tended more to his job than his own children.

The physician placed his hand on Anastasia's forehead. It was boiling hot. He checked her temperature again. One hundred and three; the fever had gone up one degree. Eugene knew it wasn't looking good.

Half-conscious, Anastasia's whole body throbbed in pain. "Where's Papa?" she grunted loudly. Dr. Botkin didn't know how to answer. Anastasia sat up in the bed. Measles or not, nothing was going to keep Anastasia away from her father. "I need to find him," she said hysterically. "I need to find the train."

"I am afraid that you can't do that, Your Imperial Highness. You are not well," said Dr. Botkin.

The good, old doctor turned his back for a moment to search inside his medicine bag for Phenacetin. The drug should reduce the fever and help her sleep. And finally, he could get some sleep as he hadn't shut his eyes for two days straight because he was busy caring for the little escape artist.

Anastasia climbed out of the bed and collapsed onto the floor.

Alexandra gasped and took a step forward.

Maria grabbed her mother's hand and squeezed it as she knew she didn't have the physical strength to handle seeing that.

When Dr. Botkin heard the big thud, he turned around. "Anastasia Nikolaevna," he said calmly. "I don't know how many times one must tell you to stay in bed."

Something like this did not surprise him. Anastasia tried to escape her sick bed several times a day.

Dr. Botkin lifted her off the floor and put her back in bed. "You need to stay in bed," he said firmly.

"B-b-but." Anastasia coughed ferociously. "I need to find Papa. He is inside the train." She coughed again.

It shattered Alexandra's delicate heart to see her daughter in so much pain, knowing she was helpless to stop it. She rushed to Anastasia's side and stroked her burning face, holding her hand. "Your Papa will be here soon, my love," promised Alexandra but it sounded more like a cry for help.

"When?" moaned Anastasia.

Alexandra looked at Dr. Botkin for the answer, but he didn't have it. The railroads had been cut off and no one was getting in or out of Tsarkoe Selo. Thankfully, the children didn't know that yet. What was a mother to do? She swallowed hard, choking back a million tears. "The train is running a little late, my darling," she lied, her quiet voice shaking. Her heart accelerated, and her hands felt colder than snow. Her breaths were short and heavy. "But he'll be here soon."

Anastasia moaned and groaned, barely awake. "The train is never late," she stuttered.

Gunshots were suddenly heard blazing outside. Alexandra stood frozen in fear, holding her breath. Maria squeezed her mother's hand again and shut her eyes tight. She was sure her heart had stopped. Dr. Botkin's face froze, and his eyes were glued to the floor.

There was a dead silence.

Alexandra exhaled lightly and summoned every ounce of her courage she had left. "I am going outside," she announced coldly.

Dr. Botkin raised his eyebrows. Did he hear her correctly? Alexandra wanted to go outside where there were mad men frantically running around, shooting rifles at one another? She could end up dead—or worse. What would he tell Nicholas?

Dr. Botkin folded his arms and tossed Alexandra an impatient glare. "Your Imperial Majesty, you can't be serious. People are being murdered out there!"

Alexandra's face hardened, and she grunted through her teeth. She made slow painful strides forward, but a sharp pain pierced her side and lower back, forcing her to stop. Alexandra shook her finger at the doctor's face. "Now you see here!" she shouted. "Someone must do something. I am done hiding in here like some sort of coward!"

There was a long pause. The gun shots were getting louder.

"Your Imperial Majesty," pleaded the doctor. "If you die, what use will you be to your husband and your children? I urge you to stay inside."

"I'll go," said a man from behind.

Alexandra gasped in relief and turned to see Konstantin. He had been the only soldier not to abandon them.

"There's one man in St. Petersburg who hasn't turned his back on the Imperial family, yet."

"Who would that be?"

Chapter 26

Operation Roundhouse

Mitya held Olga's warm hand and rubbed his thumb against her knuckles. He looked at his sleeping bride-to-be with love. He hadn't left his chair in over a day as he was far too busy caring for Olga, waiting on her hand and foot.

Suddenly, she woke up for the first time in eight hours. "Mitya," she muttered. As Olga tried to sit up, she let out a ferocious cough.

"You must rest, darling," said Mitya softy.

Olga laid on her back and looked at Mitya. She smiled lovingly. "I had a beautiful dream about you," she whispered faintly. "It was our wedding day. We got married at a church. My whole family and your mother were there. Even Uncle Boris was there." Mitya and Olga chuckled softly. Olga wrapped her hand around his and pulled it close. "My father walked me down the aisle. You looked so handsome and happy. Then you took my hand, and we were married before God."

"That's a beautiful dream," whispered Mitya.

Olga nodded and let out an exhausted moan. "Then we had four children. Dmitri, Misha, Katina, and Elisabeth."

Mitya's heart melted, and he gave her a beautiful smile. "You want to name one of our daughters after my mother?"

Olga nodded again, her eyes getting heavier. "I want to name our first daughter Elisabeth and our first son Dmitri."

"I love that idea," he whispered lovingly.

Olga smiled faintly and drifted into a deep sleep.

Moments later, Mitya heard the door creak and he looked up. "Konstantin Petrovich," he said, sounding surprised. "I thought you left with the other soldiers."

"I could say the same about you." Konstantin stared across the bedroom at Tatiana sleeping on an army cot.

"You stayed for her, didn't you?" asked Mitya in a low whisper.

Konstantin took several steps forward, his grey eyes full of urgency. "I am going to St. Petersburg. I came here to see her just in case--"

Mitya gave him a hesitant gaze. "Just in case of what?"

Tatiana woke up to the sound of Konstantin's voice. She rolled over and muttered, "Konstantin. Konstantin, I need you."

Konstantin hurried over to her. "What is it?"

"I need you to stay with me," she begged.

"I can't right now. I must go."

Tatiana had a confused expression on her face. "What? I don't understand."

"I have to go find someone to help me protect you," said Konstantin tenderly. He reached inside his coat and pulled out a pocket watch with a rose engraved on the golden surface. It had belonged to his mother. It was his most prized possession, but it was broken. The time forever stopped at 5:52, and Konstantin couldn't bring himself to fix it.

And if he died that night, he didn't want the Bolsheviks to have it. He placed it in Tatiana's warm hands. "Keep this safe for me," whispered Konstantin.

Tatiana could no longer keep her eyes open. She fell asleep quickly, her hands still clenching the pocket watch. Konstantin looked at her for a few more moments before he bent over and placed a kiss on her forehead. He turned to Mitya and gave him a letter.

"If I don't come back, will you see that she gets this?"

Mitya took the letter. "You came here to say goodbye." Konstantin's gaze softened, his face unreadable. Mitya put his hand on Konstantin's shoulder. "Be careful, soldier."

"Take care of them. And if I don't come back--"

"You'll come back," retorted Mitya.

It was several hours later, when Konstantin picked up Ivan's trail at a local pub. Someone had seen the lad called Ivan Mikhailovich at a bakery but he didn't find him there, so he kept looking. An old Babushka said that she heard Ivan Mikhailovich was at Bolshevik Headquarters, a mansion belonging to a ballerina named Mathilde Kschenkinaya. Konstantin checked but there was no sign of him. Konstantin finally picked up a fresh scent after bribing some local street rats. He finally found Ivan turning into a narrow alley.

St. Petersburg was in the hands of rebels. Everything had gone according to plan. This organized crime was used for a holy purpose, and all would be forgiven.

Ivan walked through the shadows and sharply turned into a narrow alley. Konstantin turned down that same alley but now Ivan was nowhere in sight. For a moment, Konstantin thought he'd lost him. Then he felt a cold pistol pressed against the back of his neck.

"Who are you?" asked Ivan darkly. "Why are you following me?"

Konstantin didn't flinch. "Put that away before you get hurt." He heard the click of the safety being released. "I said put the gun away," he warned. "I don't want to hurt you."

Ivan was done listening. His index finger wrapped around the trigger.

Konstantin sighed heavily. *Schoolboys never listen*, he thought, and he roundhouse kicked the weapon out of Ivan's hand. Instinctively, Ivan threw a left punch, but Konstantin ducked quickly and gave Ivan an uppercut in the jaw.

"I don't want to fight, Ivan. I came here to talk to you," pleaded Konstantin.

Ivan didn't listen.

Instead, he kicked Konstantin in the gut, knocking the air out of him. Konstantin clung to his stomach in pain, gasping for air. Ivan took advantage of this vulnerability and rammed his fist into Konstantin's face. He fell hard to the ground, blood gushing from his nose. That was the last straw. He charged at Ivan and grabbed held him in a firm headlock. Ivan struggled to get free.

"I don't know what Anastasia Nikolaevna sees in you," grunted Konstantin.

Ivan stopped struggling. Anastasia? Did he hear him right?

Konstantin released Ivan from his tight grip and Ivan looked at him sharply. "How do you know about my devushka?" he demanded.

Konstantin sighed. "There is no time to explain, my friend. Her Imperial Highness is in terrible danger."

Chapter 27

Operation Gunpowder

Ivan locked all the doors, closed all the curtains, and ordered everyone to stay away from the windows. Exhausted, Alexandra felt safe enough to return to her bedroom for the first time in two days and sleep. Maria sketched in her notebook elegantly with her left hand. She portrayed the face of a woman, but drawing was of a girl, standing in front of a mirror. Half her reflection was shattered beyond repair.

"That is a beautiful drawing."

Startled, Maria jumped. Her heart stopped. She took her eyes off her drawing and looked up. The voice belonged to Ivan. "Thank you," said Maria bashfully.

"I didn't mean to frighten you," said Ivan apologetically.

Maria cleared her voice. "You didn't frighten me at all," she said shyly. "It's just with everything going on. . ." Maria's voice trailed off. But she didn't need to say anymore. Ivan understood.

He glanced around the Tsar's grand library. Rare books were placed in display cabinets and mahogany bookshelves. The room was smaller than he'd imagined. A chandelier hung from the ceiling and a marble statue of a renaissance era man stood in the corner. Beautiful antique paintings hung on the walls. Maria Romanov sat by a small wooden circular table at the center of the room. Ivan never in his life would have thought he'd be standing in the Alexander Palace's library. Nor in the presence of Maria Nikolaevna, who was more beautiful than the rumors said.

"Are you all right?" asked Ivan.

Maria slowly arose from the chair. "Yes. Why wouldn't I be?" she said nervously.

"Your drawing said otherwise," Ivan pointed out.

Maria closed her notebook and made quick strides to the white double doors.

"I didn't mean to offend you," he said.

Maria pressed her hand against the doorknob and stopped. Ivan didn't offend her at all. Quite the opposite. Maria was hurt about things that she wasn't ready to talk about, yet. The foundation of her pain was how she felt about her family.

Everything Tatiana did was perfect. She always had the perfect hair, drawn into a tight and neat bun. She had the perfect clothes that were the envy of her friends. Men loved her and women hated her which was obvious to everyone but her. Her sister had the perfect posture and a perfect tall and slim figure. Tatiana spoke perfect English, French, Russian—and German. That fact that she spoke four languages effortlessly infuriated Maria. She tried learning German, but she'd always get harshly corrected by her mother, unlike Tatiana, who earned love and praise for perfect sentence structure. After realizing that she would never master the language, Maria gave up on learning German.

While Tatiana excelled in the infirmary, amputating limbs and sewing men back together, it took Maria all she had to not break down at the hospital. The war hospital gave her nightmares of soldiers dying every night, and she could do nothing about it. Sometimes she'd have dreams about soldiers screaming at her, blaming her for their deaths.

Maria also spent every day silently watching her brother suffer. Alexei was not a normal child, and she understood that. She also watched her mother beat herself up and slowly deteriorate over the failing health of her only son Maria worried about her enormously, and she couldn't imagine a life without her mother.

Maria turned her body slowly, with her notebook against her chest, and her big blue eyes rested on Ivan. She smiled slightly. "You didn't offend me," she said quietly.

Ivan was relieved as he understood that there were some things that Maria would rather not talk about, and he understood that more than anyone. Ivan still wasn't ready to talk about what had happened to his sister or mother.

Svetlana, *his mother,* practically became an invalid after the tragic death of his brother. She was riddled with grief. She ate next to nothing. Even a morsel of food was a battle for her. Ivan even reached the point where he didn't care anymore. If she didn't eat, that was her fault. Svetlana was nearly a skeleton by the time he left home. She rarely slept as imagines of her son's mangled body haunted her dreams. Ivan woke up countless nights to the sound of his mother screaming bloody murder. Ivan had to calm her down, soothe her tears, and often stay by her side until she fell asleep again. Ivan acted more like her father than her son. Svetlana also had no energy to do anything herself; she even refused to bathe herself. To this very day, Ivan thanked God every day that Olga, *his sister,* bathed their mother. Ivan would have never recovered from seeing his mother in the nude.

The doctor prescribed cocaine for depression. Svetlana became irresponsible, irrational, and impossible to live with. She even took advantage of the kindness of her children. And she didn't care.

Olga was the saint who paid a high price to keep food on the table. Olga was beaten, used, seduced, and destroyed by the underworld. If only Ivan knew about his sister's affair with the governor, then maybe she would still be alive today. Ivan also never knew that his sister carried the governor's child inside her.

The governor had an image to keep, the doting husband and father, and a respectable leader in the community. Olga's child would have destroyed him. The governor paid Olga five-thousand rubles to get rid of the problem. It was like sending a lamb to the slaughter.

How could she take that blood money? Didn't she know the abortion could kill her? Olga wanted a few children of her own someday. That was her dream, and now, it was gone. How could she do it? Ivan would never know for sure.

It was a Sunday afternoon when Ivan returned home from his apprenticeship with a painter. He found Olga on the kitchen floor in a fetal position. He felt a surge of horror as he watched blood pour from her in between her legs. Her face was warm and feverish.

Olga heard Ivan's footsteps and looked up. She screamed to the top of her lungs, "*It was a girl!*"

The abortionist botched the abortion.

His sister was giving birth to what was left of the baby: the head. Ivan helped deliver it. He'd never seen a woman give birth before. Ivan almost fainted when he saw the head come out of the birth canal. And his poor sister was in so much pain, he wanted to take the pain away. After his niece's head entered the world, he carried his sister to her bedroom. He then sent a telegram to the nearest doctor, who was two travel days away.

Ivan did his best to nurse his sister back to health until the doctor arrived, along with consoling her uncontrollable sobs and tears. Ivan sat by her bed until Olga fell asleep before he spent all night scrubbing the blood and the remains of the child off the kitchen floor. He then buried her tiny little head outside.

The next morning, Ivan found Olga dead on the bathroom floor. The image was haunting. Her face was lifeless but somehow full of emotion. It became hard for Ivan to swallow. It was like all the pain in the world rushed through him, somehow causing him to lose his balance. His body hit the bathroom wall with a hard thump.

What was happening? This couldn't be happening. It had to be a dream. A horrible, horrible nightmare that he was going to wake up from any minute.

Ivan tried to stand but lost his ability to stand and his knees hit the floor. His voice whimpered her name and begged her to wake up. Olga never did. Ivan gathered his sister's body in his arms, and he sobbed uncontrollably. It took all Ivan had not to start screaming the day of her funeral. That was the worst day of his life.

Svetlana was no help. Her words were like a blade that jammed inside his heart. It wasn't like Ivan didn't understand. He knew his mother was in pain, too. She lost two husbands. Her first husband had abandoned her and her second husband had a little too much to drink after he killed Ivan's brother. He was found face down in the snow the following day, frozen to death. The pain nearly destroyed Svetlana. But she didn't have to take it out on her son.

After his sister's death, Ivan left home and took the first train to Moscow. It was harder leaving his mother than it was staying with her. He must be a horrible son. Who would care for her? But as soon as he boarded the train to Moscow, all his guilt somehow faded away.

"I know why you are here," said Maria quietly.

Ivan snapped out of his trance. She did? How?

Maria smiled again as if reading his thoughts, and she motioned Ivan to follow her.

Ivan followed closely behind her, walking through miles of mazes and double doors. Maria stopped unexpectedly in front of two white doors, and she turned and placed her index finger above her lips. Ivan had the funny feeling that they weren't supposed to be there.

Maria cracked the door open to peek inside. "Anastasia? Anastasia?" she whispered. When Ivan heard that name, his heart leaped for joy. "Anastasia, are you in here?" Maria pushed the door open.

The bed was empty. Anastasia was nowhere in sight. Neither was Dr. Botkin. He must have retired to his bed. The poor man must have been exhausted.

"She's gone!" cried Maria. She walked to the center of her bedroom.

Alarmed, Ivan quickly followed Maria inside and closed the door. "Gone," repeated Ivan, "What do you mean gone?"

Maria ignored him and began pacing the floor. It was all her fault that Anastasia was gone. Maria should have been there with her, instead of drawing away in her sketch book. Anastasia must have taken advantage of Dr. Botkin's absence and escaped. But how? Her sister was somewhere out there. Lost and confused. Sick with the measles. She could be anywhere. She could be with anyone. Doing anything.

"Gone... my sister is gone...," muttered Maria hysterically. "She's gone." The thought made Maria's heart twist into strong, unbreakable knots. Her breathing accelerated, and her hands were slightly shaking, although she tried to fight it.

Ivan grabbed Maria's hands gently, snapping her out of her trance. "Your Imperial Highness," he said calmly. "Look at me."

Maria stared into the depths of Ivan's sparkling blue eyes. There was something soothing about them. Something magnetic and mesmerizing.

"Breathe with me." He said, and they both inhaled deeply and exhaled. Inhaled again and exhaled. Inhaled and exhaled.

Maria somehow felt better.

"I thought your sister was sick," said Ivan softly. "How could she escape?"

"She is sick." Maria looked over Ivan's shoulder and noticed something odd about the window. It was wide open. The window was never open. Anastasia must have climbed through to get outside. "Ivan—the window!"

Ivan darted toward the window and looked through it. It was dark and cold outside, and the sounds of the gunshots were deafening. "Anastasia must have climbed through," said Ivan. He stuck his head further out the window and looked straight ahead. Anastasia was somewhere out there, and he needed to find her before someone else did. Ivan placed half his body out the window.

"I am going with you," declared Maria.

Ivan looked back and shook his head. "No. It's too dangerous," he retorted.

Maria folded her arms and glared at Ivan darkly. "She's my sister, and I wasn't asking for your permission," she said coldly.

He sighed heavily. Why did women have to be so stubborn?

Ivan crawled the rest of the way through the window first and looked around. It seemed like it was safe enough for the Grand Duchess. Ivan held out his hand, and Maria grabbed it. She stepped through the window and jumped down. Ivan pulled out a small pistol and handed it to her. Maria swallowed hard. The man couldn't be serious. Grand Duchesses don't hold guns.

"You might be needing it," promised Ivan.

Maria swallowed hard again and shyly took the pistol. She'd never held a gun before as her mother said it was too dangerous, and it was a little heavier than she imagined.

Ivan pulled out his own revolver. "This is how you take the gun off safety, Your Imperial Highness—." He began showing her how he maneuvered it.

"It's Maria," said Maria quietly. "My name is Maria."

Ivan paused for a few moments, grasping her preferred informality. "All right, Maria." He continued showing her how to releasee the t safety and how to put it switch it back. Maria stared and nodded that she understood.

“Try to stay behind me at all times. If I tell you to run and save yourself, you need to do it,” whispered Ivan.

Maria took her first step forward. There was no going back now, but she felt that she didn't need to fear nor worry. Ivan would protect her. He wouldn't let anything happen to her. But who would protect him?

As her sister and Ivan made their way from the palace, Anastasia was darting through Tsarskoe Selo, dodging bullets. Her heart was beating out of her chest. She thought she needed to hurry and find her father's train before the Japanese found her. If the Japanese got to her before her mission was complete, all of Russia's secrets would die with her. Anastasia hid behind a tree, where she was sure the Japanese would never find her. *They'll never dare look here,* she thought.

Anastasia looked up at the sky, and in her fear, she hallucinated that a dark storm cloud had conjured up a German plane. The pilot drove the plane right towards her. She ducked down for cover and began to scream loudly.

A man pulled her off the ground and she punched and kicked, screaming louder.

“Anastasia, please,” pleaded Ivan.

“Get away from me! Get away from me!” shouted Anastasia hysterically.

“Anastasia!” shouted Ivan.

She stopped struggling. That voice was familiar. She gazed up into a pair of soft, ocean-blue eyes. Those were familiar, too. She couldn't remember where she'd seen them before. Did she know this man somehow?

Ivan placed his hand against her face and caressed her hair, and his touch felt like silk against her skin. “It's me,” he said softly, lowering his voice.

Anastasia touched the side of his face delicately. “Ivan?” she whispered. “You're so handsome tonight. I always like looking at your face.” She sounded very drunk, but she wasn't.

Ivan blushed.

Meanwhile, Maria wanted to vomit. Did she say what she thought she just said? Maria was embarrassed for them. Who in their right mind would say something like that? But Anastasia wasn't in her right mind, was she?

“I am so sorry,” whispered Maria, so low that only Ivan could hear. “It's the measles. She's been delusional lately.”

“I can tell,” said Ivan quietly.

Anastasia couldn't contain herself much longer. "Kiss me!" she shouted. She leapt forward but Ivan put his hands in front of him and quickly stepped back.

Maria grabbed Anastasia by the hand. "It's time to go back inside the palace, Nastasia," she said playfully as if she were speaking to a small child.

"No!" Anastasia snatched her hand from her sister's grasp. "Ivan and I were going to get married!"

That was news to Ivan.

"But you and Ivan can't get married right now," said Maria in a child-like voice.

"Why not?" pouted Anastasia. "We were going to honeymoon in Paris."

Ivan grabbed Anastasia by the hand and smiled playfully, fighting the strong urge to blush again. "Because we need to play a game first."

"What kind of game?" she gasped.

Ivan had to think of something quickly. "The game is called *Let's go back to the palace.*"

Anastasia's eyebrows raised, and her eyes lit up. Her voice broke out into hysterical giggles, and she clapped her hands together. "I love that game!" she squealed.

Ivan smiled. Her excitement was kind of adorable.

Anastasia grabbed Maria's hand and darted towards the Alexander Palace. Maria looked back at Ivan and mouthed the words thank you.

As Ivan stepped forward, he felt the barrel of a gun against his shoulder. Maria looked back, her blue eyes shaking with horror. A tall, broad-shouldered man with a tattered uniform and dark animal-like eyes was glaring back at her.

"Run!" shouted Ivan. Ivan slammed roundhouse kick into the man's gut, causing him to grunt and stumble back.

Maria stood there, frozen in shock.

"I said run!" screamed Ivan louder.

Maria snapped out of her daze and grabbed her sister by the hand and took off running for their lives.

"What are we doing?" asked Anastasia.

Maria turned her head slightly, her heart beating out of her chest. "We're playing a new game called *Run and Try Not to Get Killed!"*

"Oh, I love that game!" said Anastasia enthusiastically.

Ivan's brutal kick knocked the rifle away from the man. But the soldier got up and swung his fist at Ivan, hitting his jaw. Ivan grunted loudly, the pain drilling through his chin. He stepped back and punched the man twice in the face and then kicked the soldier hard in the right leg. There was a sick cracking sound. The Hungarian screamed in pain and stumbled to the ground. Ivan picked up the rifle and placed the barrel against the man's head.

"Who sent you?" he said darkly.

Once they reached the palace, Maria swung the double doors open, her hand still locked with her sister's, and hurried they inside their bedroom. Anastasia followed closely behind her sister like a child would follow her mother. Maria led her sister to the small army cot in the corner where she hopped onto it and giggled like an infant.

"Sit there and be still," demanded Maria, pointing her index finger at her sister. Anastasia giggled again louder. "And be quiet.

Anastasia nodded her head.

Maria turned her back, and her eyes rested on Doctor Botkin's medicine bag.

"Where's Ivan?" asked Anastasia quietly, her voice slurring through the words.

Maria ignored her sister and slammed the window shut, locking it. She opened the doctor's medical bag and dug through it.

Anastasia climbed off the army cot and peeked under it. "Ivan," she whispered loudly. "Are you under there?"

Maria found a large syringe and filled it with four hundred milligrams of Barbital, a drug that put people to sleep. It should do the same with Anastasia. Part of her doubted that it was the correct amount needed to put her sister to sleep. She was always such a nervous wreck when it came to working at the infirmary. Maria turned, facing her sister with the syringe in her left hand.

"Mashka, we need to find Ivan. We were supposed to get married after the game," pouted Anastasia like a child. Then, she noticed her sister holding the syringe. She took several steps back, her eyes widened. It must be some sort of deadly poison! It appeared that her sister was trying to murder her!

"You're not going to use that on me, are you?" she said nervously.

Maria took several steps forward and grabbed her sister's arm. Anastasia reacted on instinct, and she kicked her sister in the shin hard. Maria hopped on one foot, grunting in pain.

"Why did you do that?" screamed Maria.

Anastasia crossed her arms, defensively while Maria glared darkly at her sister. Anastasia looked at the double doors and then back at Maria.

Maria let out a sharp breath as Anastasia made a run for it towards the double doors. She tackled Anastasia to the floor, and the two sisters tumbled around the room, knocking over picture frames from the dresser. Maria put her sister in a leg lock and held down her arm. Anastasia grunted and flipped Maria off her body, kicking her. Maria yelped as she toppled over, her fingers losing grip of the syringe. Maria jumped on her feet. They locked eyes, their hearts racing faster. The two sisters glanced at the double doors.

Anastasia made a break for it again. Maria chased after her and grabbed her leg, dragging her sister across the floor. Anastasia kicked Maria in the face with her free leg causing Maria to let go as she shrieked in pain. Anastasia ran several steps forward and placed her hands on the doorknobs. Maria jumped on her sister's back and clung to her tightly. Anastasia took several steps backward, struggling to maintain her balance before slamming her sister's body against the wall. Maria shrieked and let go. She saw the syringe on the floor and grabbed it. As soon as Anastasia thought she could make a break for it again, Maria body slammed her sister against the floor. Anastasia struggled while Maria held down her arm and quickly injected the drug inside her body.

Anastasia felt a slight pitch in her right arm and flinched. She snatched her arm away from her sister and stared at her forearm in horror. "What did you do?" she gasped quietly.

Maria ignored her sister and walked quickly toward the double doors, slamming them shut and locking them.

Anastasia banged her fists against the doors. "Let me out! Let me out now!" she screamed.

Maria clutched the gun Ivan gave her in her hand. What was she doing? This was crazy. Grand Duchesses don't shoot guns, and holding one was next to inappropriate. But she knew that as of a couple hours ago, Maria Nikolaevna was no longer a Grand Duchess of Russia. She could be anything that she wanted to be, and she could go anywhere that she wanted to go, with her mother's permission, of course.

Maria closed her eyes. She swallowed hard and slowly gathered up what little courage she had left. It was like leaping off a high cliff into some deep and unfamiliar water. There was no going back. Not to the way things were. Her heart beat faster as she opened her eyes and took several steps forward.

"I'm coming, Ivan," whispered Maria.

The Hungarian was out cold, but he wasn't dead yet.

Ivan was searching for whatever the soldier had on his person. Any scrap of information. No money. No pistol. Not even identification. It was like the man didn't exist. Finally, Ivan did find something. A piece of rumbled paper with random numbers. It was written almost like a letter. Ivan knew better. It was a code. A cleaver, ingenious code. Ivan turned and examined the numbers on the page: 112 364 375 986...

As Ivan was digging through his pockets, the Hungarian woke up from his sleep. He reached for the concealed knife hidden in his boot.

Then a deafening gunshot went off.

Ivan jumped. He turned sharply and glared at the Hungarian soldier. A big, gaping red hole was in the center of his hand. He dropped the knife and screamed in pain. Ivan turned around again to see Maria Romanov holding the pistol in her hand, her bright blue eyes shaking with horror, her.

With her lips trembling, Maria aimed the gun straight at the man, the pistol shaking in her hand.

Ivan walked slowly toward Maria and reached out to lower the pistol. "Maria," he whispered softly, with concern.

Maria blinked her eyes several times, awakening from some sort of trance. "Ivan?" she whispered, her voice caught into a tight knot, her hands uncontrollably shaking. Ivan held her in his arms, and she buried her face inside his shoulder.

"It's all right," whispered Ivan. "It's all right."

As Ivan held Maria's shaking body in his arms, Konstantin made slow and heavy strides toward them. He held a rifle he had stolen off a dead body.

"I'll take care of the problem," said Konstantin emotionlessly.

Maria heard him release the safety. "What's going on?" she asked, with a hint of worry in her voice.

Ivan didn't answer. He grabbed Maria by the arm and walked quickly in the direction of the Alexander Palace. Maria looked over her shoulder and saw that Konstantin was getting closer to the defenseless man lying on the ground, with his hand bleeding out.

"What's he going to do?" Her tone was a little higher, shaking with emotion.

Konstantin aimed the gun at the man's head. Maria turned back, breaking from Ivan's grip as Konstantin pulled the trigger. Maria watched the man fall dead, blood and brain matter splattering from his head. Maria let out an ear-splitting scream. Never witnessing death before, she fell to her knees and sobbed.

Maria fell to her knees and sobbed. Ivan held her in his arms again, rubbing her cold shoulders.

"Shh... Shh," his lips uttered. "We need to keep moving." He lifted Maria back on her feet. She walked beside him, making her way slowly back to the palace.

Ivan followed Maria to her bedroom again through the endless mazes of the palace. She unlocked the double doors and the two Russians walked through the threshold. Ivan stopped in the middle of the room and was relieved to see Anastasia sleeping peacefully in her bed. She looked like an angel. Ivan couldn't look away.

"Thank you for helping my sister," whispered Maria. Ivan gave Maria a small smile. Maria couldn't stop thinking about how she saved Ivan's life, or about the Hungarian soldier and his death. Maria sniffled again. "I must find you an army cot to sleep on," she said quietly. "I'll be right back."

As soon as Ivan thought Maria was gone, he tiptoed to Anastasia's side to get a better look at her. He held her hand and pressed his lips against it tenderly. Ivan let go, but suddenly, she grabbed his hand back.

"Ivan, my love," whispered Anastasia cheerfully.

Without thinking, Ivan Mikhailovich sat down on the edge of the bed and stared into Anastasia's face. Anastasia sat up and looked around. Maria was nowhere in sight. But Ivan Mikhailovich was in her bedroom, looking at her in a way any girl would envy. Anastasia smiled angelically as she kissed his hand softly.

"Ivan, I have something important to tell you," she said slowly.

"What is it?"

Anastasia sniffled. "I lied to you. I am fifteen!" she cried.

Ivan ran his fingers through her hair and looked at her pitifully. "I know," he said Ivan plainly. He wasn't stupid, after all.

"But I will be sixteen in June. I am sorry that I lied to you. Will you forgive me?"

Ivan didn't even give it a second thought. "Of course."

"Will you promise to stay, Ivan?" she whispered hopefully.

"I will stay for as long as you need me here," promised Ivan.

Anastasia gave him a faint smile, her eyes getting heavier. "Will you, please, watch me sleep tonight? I feel safer with you here."

"I am not going anywhere."

Chapter 28

Operation Foxtrot

It was midnight in St. Petersburg. The English ambassador, George Buchanan, woke up to the telephone chiming into the darkness. He was a lean man in his late sixties, with thin hair and a sharp nose. The ambassador forced his aching body out of bed and slowly walked to the telephone. He let out a yawn before he answered. The message on the other line was quite clear; The Chupacabra was on his way.

Fear pumped through every part of his body. The plans were in danger. If The Chupacabra found them in the ambassador's possession, George was a dead man. Or worse. Merial. His precious, sweet Merial. His only child. Though she hadn't been a child in a long time. Merial was his unmarried thirty-one-year-old daughter, who since recently, been living on her own. She was all he had left in the world. And if anything happened to her, George would never be able to live with himself.

The plans needed to leave the house tonight. But how? He could always call Merial. Although, she could get killed out there. And George promised himself that he wouldn't contact Merial before their rendezvous in London. Was there any other way? There was no one that George could trust other than Merial.

The ambassador hesitated. He must be a horrible father. He dialed the number and heard the telephone ring.

"Hello?" yawned Merial.

"Merial, I need you to come over to the house now," demanded George.

There was a long pause.

"Why?" asked Merial, her voice laced with exhaustion.

George felt a surge of frustration. "There's no time to explain. I need you now!"

George hung up the phone and sighed. When did he become an old, grouchy man? The ambassador sent a telegram to his contact. The message contained only one word: Foxtrot. She'll know what to do. In fact, she was the one who suggested this backup plan. She must have known this would happen.

George wasted no time. He dressed in his flannel suit and started packing. Russia was no longer safe. George knew the coup and the revolution would happen. No one had listened to him, though. Now, look what happened. Bolsheviks. Anarchy. Disorder. It frightened the ambassador. What terrified him more was what they were calling the new government: the Provisional Government. George also knew that the government would fall just like the last one. And he didn't want to stick around and find out what would happen next.

Half an hour later, George heard a small knock on the front door. He cracked the door open to see Merial standing there. She was a short woman with a husky body, round face, and deep blue eyes. Her long blonde hair was drawn into a messy bun, and she wore a long army trench coat and boots.

George grabbed his daughter by the arm and quickly pulled her inside. He slammed the door and locked it.

"Can you explain to me what is going on?" asked Merial coldly. There was no mistake in her voice. Merial was angry. Of course, her father couldn't blame her.

Merial looked around the drawing room. There were two suitcases packed and ready to go by the sofa. And two travel documents laid on the table. Merial turned to her father, her eyes shaking with fear. "Papa?"

George placed an envelope into Merial's hands. "Follow the directions on the cover. Don't look inside," warned George.

"Papa, what's going on?" asked Merial quietly, her mind swirling with millions of unanswered questions that only the man in front of her could answer.

"We're leaving tomorrow morning."

"What?" asked Merial.

"It's not safe anymore," said George sharply.

Someone suddenly pounded against the door. George's heart felt as though it had stopped, and he swallowed hard. He opened the door to the coat closet.

"Into the closet," he whispered, sounding hysterical.

Merial stood frozen in fear, her mouth gaping open, staring at her father as if he were a man with two heads.

"Now!" hissed George.

Merial jumped and slowly walked inside the coat closet.

"Not a sound," her father warned before gently closing the closet door. He walked quickly to the front door and unlocked it.

Gabriel von der Reis stood at the doorway. He wore a Bosworth sack suit and black shoes, with a dark tie. His arms were crossed, and an angry expression rested perfectly on his face. Gabriel always looked angry. In fact, Gabriel couldn't remember a time when anger didn't pump through his blood. But this time was different. It was anger laced with a seething disappointment.

George gave Gabriel a blank stare. And it took a few more moments to realize that he was trembling. He tried masking his fear with a pleasant smile. "It's good to see you, Mr. von der Reis," he said, fighting to hide the nervousness in his voice. "How could I help—"

"Quiet, old man!" shouted Gabriel. He pushed the door open, knocking George's old and brittle body into a wall, as he invited himself inside the Buchanan home. The ambassador wanted to say something but held his tongue. No one argued with Gabriel von der Reis. No one.

Instead, George remained silent. He quietly shut the door and followed Gabriel from a safe distance. There was something not right about that man. Something evil. Gabriel knew too, only he embraced it. Gabriel tore other people down to build whatever ego he had left back up. His frustrations had beat him down to a pulp. He did not know how to express his emotions anymore. It was the memory of Adeline that made Gabriel cling to whatever humanity he had left.

Gabriel stopped in front of the coat closet and looked around sharply, his arms folded close to his chest. His cold gray eyes scanned the home as if looking for something of value. Gabriel turned and screamed louder. "Where is it?"

He took a few steps forward, causing the old ambassador to move away, falling onto the sofa. George swallowed, his face as white as a ghost. He must play his cards wisely, or these cards would be his last.

"I'm afraid that I don't know what you are talking about," said George, his voice slightly brittle.

A wave of anxiety overcame Gabriel. The anger nearly drove him into complete insanity because he didn't exactly know what he was angry about, but things weren't going according to plan. It was problems like this which pushed Gabriel over the edge and the edge was out of his comfort zone. The edge wasn't where Gabriel belonged. No one understood that. His hands were twitching and his face turned to scarlet as he raised his voice.

"I know you have them!" Gabriel's vocal cords were shaking with anger. "You better hand them over to me now, old man. Or I will tear this place apart brick by brick until I find those—"

"Play nicely, Gabriel," said the deep, malevolent voice of his father. "We don't want George to get hurt."

"Mr. von der Reis," said George nervously. "What a pleasure it is to have you in my home."

"I know." The Chupacabra closed the door gently and made heavy strides into the drawing room. He noticed the suitcases and travel documents, and he turned to George and tossed him a devilish grin. "Leaving Russia so soon, George?"

George cleared his voice. "Well, you see," he began. "My health is failing, and the warmer weather would do me some good."

"I see." The Chupacabra stared at the hardwood floor. He was lost in thought. He traveled deeper down his imagination every day, creating unbreakable webs of obsessions. He thought about Helen. The Chupacabra needed her, and he needed to know exactly what that woman was hiding.

The Chupacabra had his secrets, and Helen didn't have any at all. That was their marriage. Ever since Ivan Mikhailovich came that day, Helen had never been the same. Her touch had been different. Her hands were cold, and her blue eyes were softer. Her waist became thinner she hadn't been sleeping for longer than two hours at a time. Something was terribly wrong. And The Chupacabra was going to find the source and snuff it out of existence. If another man were involved, he would kill him. Helen belonged to him and only him. He'd rather see her dead than in the arms of another man.

His son, Henry, was becoming an absolute disgrace and disappointment. He was too weak and soft like his mother. That was an embarrassment. Henry didn't know the first thing about the family business. Instead, Helen thought it best if Henry received an education in a boarding school somewhere in Canada. Henry knew how to play the violin and piano with great skill. The boy could speak four languages fluently: German, French, Italian, and English. He had perfect grades and conduct, and his teachers loved him. Henry said he wanted to become a doctor. The Chupacabra had failed him as a father! It was about time that Henry left that boarding school and came home. He hadn't seen his son in five years, and he wasn't even sure what the boy looked like anymore. It would give them time to catch up and get reacquainted. And finally, The Chupacabra would get to teach his son the family business. His mother wouldn't like it, but The Chupacabra cared very little of what Helen thought.

He thought about the revolution. He obsessed about those who owed him blood and lots of it.

The Chupacabra shook his head, snapping out of his daydream. "George—I heard that your old pals, the Romanovs want to go to England."

It was like the air was kicked out of George's gut. How could he have known that? That was top secret information, and only a few people in the world knew about that. Of course, George couldn't escape the fact that The Chupacabra was everywhere.

"I am afraid that I cannot let that happen, George," taunted The Chupacabra.

When George spoke, his voice was hoarse. "Why?"

"You see," The Chupacabra continued. "The Romanovs need to stay in Russia because that's good for my business. And you are going to help me do just that."

George glanced over to Gabriel. He stood quietly in the corner, with his arms crossed and his lips pushed close together. Even he looked shocked but fought to hide it.

"They can't stay in Russia," exclaimed George, his voice shaking with emotion. "The Bolsheviks will tear them apart! They'll be killed." Chupacabra let out a wicked laugh. "That's the idea, George."

What The Chupacabra was asking George to do was evil. Unspeakable. Nicholas was his friend. How could he ever forgive himself if he betrayed him?

"I won't do it."

A wicked grin appeared on The Chupacabra's lips. "You have a beautiful daughter, George. It would be horrible if anything were to happen to her, right Gabriel?" The Chupacabra slightly turned his head toward his son. George glared at Gabriel, who had that same evil grin as his father. The Chupacabra scowled at George and stepped forward. George stepped back, falling into the sofa again.

"Let's not forget that the bank can take repossession of your house in London. And I could also pull a few strings, and your pension would be discontinued," said The Chupacabra coolly. "Shall I continue?"

George had heard enough. Choking back tears and accepting defeat, George uttered the words, "What would you have me do?"

"I think you know exactly what you need to do, George."

George needed to go to the English king and beg him not to let the Romanovs into his country. How could he live with himself after that? Nicholas was his friend, and he was the only one in Russia who'd ever listened to his ideas and what he had to say. How could he betray him?

With a heavy heart, George stared at the floor and said darkly, "Very well."

The Chupacabra patted George on the back hard. "I am glad we had this little chat, George." The Chupacabra then showed his way to the door.

Gabriel suddenly looked at the coat closet and began walking toward it. George held his breath as he watched Gabriel place his hand on the doorknob.

"Gabriel! Come!" shouted his father. Gabriel glared at The Chupacabra in disgust, and then tossed his eyes to George. His message was clear; you are hiding something, and I will find out what. Gabriel followed his father back to the car, slamming the front door on his way out.

George let out a breath of relief.

Merial cracked open the door, peeking her head out.

"You can come out, darling. You are safe now."

Merial quietly shut the closet door and walked quickly to her father. "Papa, who were those men?" whispered his daughter, her voice shaking with fear and worry.

George's heart was beating faster, and he fought to catch up with his breathing. A few moments ago, he wasn't lying. His health was slowly deteriorating, and his medicine was wearing off. George could feel it.

"Bad men. Very bad men, and that's why we need to leave," whispered George.

"How will I know who's the contact?" asked Merial.

George didn't know how to answer that. Revealing the identity of his contact would place Merial in extreme danger. The fewer people that knew her identity, the better.

"You'll know," muttered George.

Merial quickly made her way to the front door.

"No!" shouted George. Merial stopped and turned sharply, her eyes shaking with fear and uncertainty. "Go out the back door. It will be safer."

Merial turned around and quickly made her way through the kitchen with her father following. As her hands turned the doorknob, George grabbed her arm. Merial stopped, half her body outside the door.

"Try not to be seen by anyone. And if anything goes wrong, run. Run as fast as you can. And don't look back. Follow the directions on the cover of that envelope and..." George's voice cracked, and tears swelled his eyes. These were the words that he rehearsed in his head a thousand times and prayed that he'd never have to say them. "And you'll be safe. Be brave. I love you."

"I love you, too," said Merial lovingly, as if this were the last time that she'd ever say those beautiful words. Merial's heart was racing. She felt like a character in one of her books!

She took off, disappearing into the shadows.

Helen risked her life and freedom to retrieve those plans. And by some miracle, she was able to escape the clutches of her obsessive and controlling husband for a few moments.

She had recently received a telegram from Mr. George Buchanan as she prepared for bed. Helen acted on pure instinct. She locked herself inside the bathroom and climbed out the window, leaving the bathroom light on. Now she shivered in the cold, waiting patiently in the dark in front of the post office.

Henry turned eleven years old last week. And that was another birthday—another year—without him. It was torture. Henry was away in boarding school in Canada but not by choice. Helen vowed to do everything in her power to make sure that Henry turned out nothing like his insane, sadistic, murderous father. Helen also saw what John did to Gabriel and Jana. That wasn't going to happen to her son. Not if she could help it. And if living apart would do just that, then so be it. It wasn't fair that Helen couldn't see her son because of his father's selfishness. Henry must hate her. Helen wouldn't blame him if he did. Helen hated herself for it, too. She sent her little boy away before she had a chance to say goodbye.

However, John wasn't always a monster, or perhaps he was just better at hiding it now. John was gentle and a reasonable man when she met him. He was a wealthy bachelor who bought her cars and diamond jewelry. Helen fell in love with the idea of being Mrs. von der Reis. It was very easy to say yes to that marriage proposal.

After their wedding day, John was never the same. Something snapped. John started speaking to her like she was a dog. He threw pots and pans at her and flipped tables over. He punched the wall next to her several times, just avoiding her face. Suddenly, it was her fault that he couldn't control his temper. John denied arguments, agreements, and conversations they had. He forced her to question reality and her sanity. He gave long speeches on her errors. He used emotional blackmail to punish her for her mistakes. He locked her in that big mansion all day, isolating her from her friends and society.

John was unpredictable. Helen had no idea what kind of mood he'd be in when he returned home from his errands. Helen was forced to ask permission for everything; how she spent money, her whereabouts, and her diet. John read her private letters and diary. There was no privacy and no boundaries. Nothing was sacred. Helen didn't even know if she loved John anymore or hated him.

Helen also hated the woman that she was forced to become. She was on her guard every waking moment, and that drove her insane. She did not know all the reasons why she became so defensive. But the bottom line was that John wanted Helen all to himself. Helen had John's first wife to thank for that as she had abandoned him and Gabriel. John had never been the same.

There was only so much that a woman could take before she's pushed over the edge. The hardest part wasn't staying in the marriage. It was leaving.

Helen knew she couldn't stay.

After tonight, Helen was done. As soon as the plans were safe, she was going to take her son and leave. Maybe that was more of wishful thinking. But after tonight, her dreams would be falling into place. She had to be patient.

Something caught Helen's eye from outside. It was a figure of a woman darting along the sidewalk from a distance. No one was out this late at night. Not if they weren't drunk and this woman did not appear intoxicated, she seemed worried. And she looked as if she was in a hurry to get somewhere. That couldn't be Merial Buchanan, could it?

Helen walked quickly across the street and darted toward the woman and tapped her on the shoulder.

"Excuse me," said Helen in a heavy German accent. "Are you here for your foxtrot lesson?"

Alarmed, Merial raised her eyebrows. Could this be the contact that her father spoke of? "Who are you?" whispered Merial.

Without even thinking, Helen said, "My name is Charlotte Bismarck." Helen was lost in thought. Why did she just give a stranger her mother's name? She couldn't use her own name, because of course it might get back to her husband somehow. Helen couldn't have that. She'd never hear the last of it. Helen continued, "Did you bring your payment?"

Merial dug through her coat and reached for the envelope. Merial stared at the writing. One of the words in the instructions was indeed foxtrot.

Could Merial trust a German? There was a war going on, after all. Merial stared into Helen's soft loving eyes. She didn't seem threatening. She appeared harmless. Helen gave Merial a gentle smile, and finally, Merial gave in. She handed over the envelope.

"It was nice meeting you, Miss Buchanan!" said Helen cheerfully. "Have a good night. She turned and walked quickly in the opposite direction.

Merial continued down the sidewalk, slowly taking in everything that had happened tonight. How odd. Merial did not remember giving that woman her name. She stopped and turned around to confront the German woman about it, but it was too late. She was gone.

Several minutes later, as Helen was moving quickly through Ploshchad Square, she felt a cold pistol being pressed against her shoulder.

"Hand over those plans, or I'll splatter your brains against the pavement!"

Chapter 29

Operation Codebreaker

Two days later, Nicholas returned home, embarrassed and disgraced. He arrived at the palace in the late afternoon, and he was shocked at how dead and emptied it felt. He'd never seen it like this before. Everything appeared to be just as he left it

Nicholas was different now. His thin hair was falling out, and his blue eyes were bloodshot. He was seeing streaks of grey in his full beard. Abdicating was the hardest thing he had to do in his life.

He walked through the cold, empty halls of his home, passing portraits of his Romanov ancestors who appeared to be staring down at him in shame. He stopped in front of the picture of his late father. That man would be rolling in his grave after what Nicholas had done.

His blue eyes were covered in tears. He needed to see his wife before he saw the children. They had already been through so much, and Nicholas needed to see Alexandra before he could face them. What would happen to them now? He just robbed his own son of his birthright. What kind of father does that? Alexei was born to be Tsar. What had he done? The grief was still sinking in.

Nicholas found Alexandra in Maria and Anastasia's bedroom. Maria lay unconscious on the bed, dying of measles and double pneumonia. Alexandra sat on a chair beside the bed, hunched over, holding her hand, and praying. His darling appeared exhausted.

Nicholas knocked gently, and Alexandra turned her head. As soon as she saw her husband, her heart leaped for joy. "Nicky!"

Nicholas strode to her. She slowly rose from the chair, wrapped her arms around his frame, and squeezed tightly. Nicholas put his arms around her waist. His heart broke in half, watching their child clinging to life.

"Nicky, I missed you, my darling," whispered Alexandra lovingly into his ear, tears falling from her eyes.

Nicholas kissed her hand softly. He opened his mouth to say something, but there was a large lump lodged in his throat. He couldn't utter a single word. He swallowed hard and looked at his wife, his vision blurry. He opened his mouth again and said, "Not as much as I missed you, Alix."

Nicholas and Alexandra went to sleep early. Alexandra lay in bed with Nicholas's head on her chest, weeping like a child. "I still love you, Nicky," she reassured lovingly.

Nicholas kissed her hand softly. He wanted to say something, but there was a large lump in his throat. He looked at his wife, his vision slightly blurring. He opened his mouth, feeling the tears building up again. "I love you, too, Sunny," he sniffled. His head was pounding because of all his crying, and so he continued resting his head on Alexandra's chest, listening to the calming sound of her heartbeat. His weeping continued as Alexandra rubbed his back in a circular motion.

"Do the children know?" asked Nicholas suddenly.

"Yes," said Alexandra quietly.

"How much do they know?"

"Not much at all."

"How's Anastasia?"

That Alexandra did not know. She'd been caring for Maria for the past two days. Now she felt like a horrible mother as she had neglected the other children to care for her sick daughter. She had heard from Tatiana that her youngest daughter had been acting kind of strange since that young man came along. Alexandra hadn't seen much of Anastasia today and assumed that she and Alexei were probably somewhere causing mischief that she'd punish them for later.

Nicholas had known about Anastasia's young man for weeks. At first, he thought it might be an innocent flirtation but now he wasn't too certain.

"Our little Anastasia is too young for boys, Alix," said Nicholas inexpressively.

Alexandra had read his mind. "What do you want to do, Nicky?" she asked.

Nicholas' eyes were getting heavy. "For now," he yawned heavily. "I want to rest."

The former Tsar opened his eyes two hours later. He laid in bed, chain smoking as he rehearsed a thousand different ways to break the news to Ivan.

Nicholas had been nineteen once too. When his mother told him to do something, he made sure to do the opposite of that. Especially when it came to his Polish dancer. For her, there was no line he wouldn't cross just to see Mathilde again.

At that thought, Nicholas felt a wave of anxiety. What was he thinking? Ivan wasn't going to stay away from his daughter just because Nicholas asked. He knew that. He once was a stubborn young man.

If only he could change a few things. Like the time he forced Mathilde to move out of her father's home because Nicholas had bought her a better one in St. Petersburg. However, it was more for Nicholas than it was for her. That shame would forever haunt him, and it was very disrespectful to her father. If he could take that back, he would.

Nicholas suddenly had a brilliant idea. He was going to tell Ivan all the things that he wished Mathilde's father had spoken to him all those years ago. Now, if only he could find the courage to do it.

Several minutes later, Nicholas walked outside to the garden. His deep blue eyes gazed at Ivan who was sitting on a bench, sketching in a book. The boy looked deep in thought, his hand moving the pencil gracefully across the paper.

"Hello," said Nicholas softly.

Ivan did not recognize that voice. He averted his eyes from the paper and looked up.

Nicholas took a sharp breath and continued, "My name is Nicholas Alexandrovich. It's nice to meet you."

Ivan's heart nearly jumped out of his chest. Nicholas wasn't just the former Tsar; he was Anastasia's father! He wasn't at all what Ivan imagined. He wore a plain soldier's uniform with black leather boots and appeared to be an ordinary man. But still, this man was Anastasia's father. Ivan wanted to get up and run.

"Hello, Sir," said Ivan nervously.

Nicholas smiled patiently with his eyes, his hands behind his back. He walked a few paces, passed Ivan, and turned around sharply. "Please, walk with me."

For the next few minutes, there was an awkward silence between the two men. Ivan nervously walked beside the former Emperor of Russia. Nicholas didn't say much of anything. He was far too busy formulating not only what he'd say to the boy but how he would say it. Ivan didn't say anything at all. He thought about running away from there.

Suddenly, Nicholas stopped. His blue eyes were filled with urgency, and Ivan could only imagine what the Tsar was going to say next.

"I've made many unforgivable mistakes as a man. And because of that, I've lost the throne and the people's respect. The only thing that I have left is my dignity and my family. As a father, I refuse to remain silent again," said Nicholas quietly.

Ivan appeared puzzled. His mind was racing with questions.

Nicholas noticed this and continued, "Anastasia's mental, physical, and emotional well-being is a delicate constitution. My daughter is naïve and unfamiliar with the ways of men. You understand, don't you?"

Ivan's stomach dropped to the ground. Unfortunately, Ivan did understand.

Nicholas gently placed his hand against Ivan's shoulder. The Tsar's touch was softer than Ivan expected. It was kind and firm. It was the touch of a father. "If you care about my daughter," sighed Nicholas, his eyes pleading with Ivan to stay away, "you will do the right thing."

Did Nicholas not know what he was asking Ivan to do? It was unthinkable. Ivan loved Anastasia more than he ever loved anything in his entire life, and he couldn't stay away even if he tried. However, Nicholas knew precisely what he'd asked Ivan to do. It was better this way. It would not only protect his family and Anastasia, but it would also keep Ivan safe from harm.

Ivan didn't want to, but he nodded firmly.

Nicholas smiled with his eyes again and patted Ivan on the shoulder.

"Thank you." Nicholas let out a breath of relief. "Have a nice day."

Ivan felt a hole open in his heart as he watched the former Tsar walk away.

Chapter 30

Operation Forbidden Love

March was reaching the end of winter and Maria's fever grew worse. Her earache turned into an ear infection that had made her nearly deaf. Her bronchitis turned into pneumonia and the pneumonia turned into double pneumonia. Her fever spiked up to one hundred and five degrees.

Maria was dying.

She asked to see her baby sister one last time.

As soon as Anastasia heard the news, she hurried to her sister's side. Maria's face was white, her pupils dilated. When Maria saw her sister, she tried to pick her head up and cried, "Nastasia. Nastasia."

Anastasia strode to the chair by the bed and whispered, "I am here, Mashka. I am here."

Moments later, Maria closed her eyes and drifted to sleep.

Anastasia noticed a little book of poems on the nightstand. She opened the book to today's date and started to read it:

Blue is the raindrops that fall from the sky. It's a small box that you are trapped in and cannot find a way out. Blue is lost hope. Blue is a twisted playground of death, the heartless monster who separates families. Blue feels like broken ribs. The pain rips through your soul every time you see his face. Blue is someone who wandered deep in the dark and cannot find a way out. Blue is a traveler, struggling to keep climbing the mountain.

Blue is confidence, leadership, and ambition to succeed. Blue is a warrior who puts up a good fight. Blue is wisdom. It's an untamable spark of hope every time you see his face. Blue is daring dreams. It's an unseen hope, the roots buried deep in your heart. It's fairies dancing in the sky. It's unicorns galloping in the wind. Blue is cotton candy at the circus. It's a caterpillar breaking out of the prison it created, waiting to show that world that it can fly. Blue is flowers blooming from the coldest winter, to show the world how beautiful it is. Blue is the greatest symphony the world has yet to hear. Blue is my childhood, slowly fading away.

"Olga wrote that," said Maria, suddenly. "She read it to me earlier today."

Anastasia reread the phrase out loud, "The pain rips through your soul every time you see his face. Maria," she gasped, "she's talking about Pavel."

Maria let out a heavy cough. "Didn't he marry a woman named Olga? Wasn't she one of Mama's ladies-in-waiting?"

Anastasia nodded. "He did," she recalled. "We went to the wedding before the war, remember? Olga was upset, and she was in the back of the chapel, trying to stop herself from crying."

"It never would have worked out. Pavel was much older than her. Olga was just fifteen," muttered Maria.

Anastasia nodded. "She was still upset."

Maria put her hand over her mouth and let out a nasty cough. "There were rumors about the day."

"What rumors?"

Maria shrugged. "I probably shouldn't say. I heard it from Tatiana, who heard it from one of Mama's ladies-in-waiting, who heard it from someone else."

"Please, tell me, Mashka," begged Anastasia.

Maria sighed heavily. She supposed she couldn't let this secret die with her. "There was a rumor going around that Mama encouraged the relationship between one of her ladies and Pavel. Apparently, Mama was afraid that the flirtation between Olga and Pavel was becoming more than an innocent thing."

"What?" gasped Anastasia, her blue eyes filled with curiosity.

"It's just a rumor," Maria reminded her sister. "Don't mention it to Olga either. It might hurt her."

"I won't say anything," promised Anastasia. A few moments of silence passed between them. "Ivan's been avoiding me."

Maria's eyes widened. "What?"

"Everything is so confusing," she said in frustration. "Last week, he was avoiding me. When I tried to talk to him, he'd walk the other way, ignoring me. Then he left the palace three days ago and didn't say goodbye. Did I do something wrong, Mashka? He's breaking my heart."

"You didn't do anything wrong, Nastasia. Although," Maria cleared her throat, "while you were sick with the measles, you did tell him that you were going to marry him."

Anastasia gasped. Her face appeared flushed. "I did? That is so embarrassing."

"Then you said you wanted to honeymoon with him in Paris." Anastasia's face turned bright red. Maria laughed loudly. "Then you said that you wanted to kiss his handsome face."

"I think that I am going to dig a hole and die now."

Maria laughed again. Then she became quiet. She appeared to be in deep thought. "You didn't do anything wrong. Men are so complicated, and sometimes women spend more time thinking on about men are thinking than men do actually thinking." The two sisters laughed. Then it became quiet for a few moments. "It will all be over soon," whispered Maria. "I had my last rites after supper tonight."

Anastasia grabbed Maria's hand. "Don't you dare talk like that. Don't you dare quit. You keep fighting this, Mashka. You have always been a fighter. You always fought for other people. For once, fight for yourself. You have never let anything beat you before in your life. Don't start now. This family still needs you." Tears flooded Anastasia's eyes. "I still need you."

Tears swelled in Maria's eyes. "Oh, Nastasia!" she cried in pain. "It hurts so much."

Anastasia stroked her warm, sweaty forehead. "I know it hurts. Believe me, I do. But you have to keep going. You have to keep fighting."

Suddenly, Anastasia heard small knocks against the door, and she got up to answer it.

"Who is it, Nastasia?" Maria turned and looked at her sister in disbelief.

"It's Ivan," said Anastasia, in astonishment. Anastasia gave Ivan a stern look and whispered, "How were you able to get back in? Everyone in the palace is now under house arrest."

Ivan didn't answer. He used his position to pull a few strings, but he couldn't tell her that.

"Why were you avoiding me?" she asked, crossing her arms defensively, waiting for an answer.

But Ivan wouldn't answer. Instead, he said, "Can I come in?"

Anastasia poked her head out in the hallway and looked both ways. She then grabbed him by the collar, pulling him into the room. "You better start explaining yourself," she demanded as she shut the door.

"I don't think it's a good idea to see each other anymore."

"You came all this way to tell me that?" she asked painfully. "Why are you doing this? Was it something I said or did?"

Ivan shook his head, fighting to hide the pain in his eyes.

"Is it because I am ugly?" said Anastasia quietly.

How could she say that about herself? She was the most beautiful girl in the world. That was what he wanted to say. Instead, Ivan uttered the word, "No."

Anastasia thought about it. "Did my father speak to you?" she said, her heart beating louder.

Ivan's silence answered everything.

"I-I," her voice was cracking. "I can't believe this!" Anastasia turned and covered her mouth.

Ivan grabbed her arm. "Anastasia, it's better this way," he said calmly. "No one will get hurt."

"Really? It's a little late for that," hissed Anastasia.

Ivan couldn't bear this a moment later. He began making his way to the door.

"After all these months, after all that we've been through, don't you know how much I love you!" Anastasia wailed.

Ivan wanted to say that he loved her, too, but didn't. Instead, he kept walking.

Ivan still couldn't believe that he'd done that to Anastasia. He went straight to the home of his Aunt Vera, who was finishing up packing for Switzerland. After he explained what had happened, she smacked her nephew hard on the back of the neck.

"For such a clever boy, sometimes you can be quite stupid."

A few days later, Anastasia received a letter from Vera Mikhailovna that said:

Dear Anastasia Nikolaevna,

I knew who you were the moment I saw you. You have Romanov eyes. I'm terribly sorry about what has happened to you and your family, dear. I continue to pray for your health and safety.

I am leaving the country soon. Before I go, there are a few things I need you to know. My nephew is a very complicated man. His father abandoned him. His brother and sister died unspeakable deaths. And his mother went insane. Because of that, Ivan became very angry and bitter. He doesn't trust easily. He believes everyone has an ulterior motive to achieve something, or someone might abandon him later. He has lost hope that there are still good people in the world.

After he met you, darling, my Ivan has never been the same. He is smiling again. He is happy again. He is a kinder and gentler man. He has become more forgiving. I know that you have your reasons to be angry, please, don't be angry with him forever. There is nothing Ivan *wouldn't do to protect you. I know whatever he did, dear, it was out of love. It was for your own protection. There is nothing my nephew wouldn't do to protect you. Because he really loves you, darling.*

Best Regards!

Vera Mikhailovna

Aunt Vera left for Switzerland the following day. Ivan knew he couldn't live with the guilt anymore, and he drove directly to Tsarkoe Selo. Because of his connections, the guards let him in.

Ivan found Anastasia in the music room. Upon hearing his quick footsteps, Anastasia looked up, and saw Ivan. He stood before her as his blue eyes pleaded for forgiveness. He grabbed her by the hand and squeezed gently.

"It took everything I had in me to stay away from you, but I can't do it a second longer. I love you more than I have loved anything or anyone in my entire life. And I am sor—"

Anastasia cupped his face in her hands and kissed him passionately. Ivan put his arms around her back. "I love you, Ivan Mikhailovich."

Ivan held her in his arms, and he wasn't ever going to let her go ever again. "What are we going to do, Ivan?" whispered Anastasia, her head on his chest.

Ivan did not know. If the Bolsheviks found out, there would be serious consequences. They could both be shot or far worse. If her father found out, there was no telling what he might do. Ivan gazed into Anastasia's eyes and smiled lovingly. "We'll figure something out. But I am not going to let anything bad happen to you."

For the first time in weeks, Anastasia felt safe and loved.

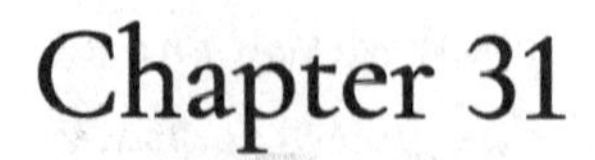

Chapter 31

Operation Canary

Gabriel could not wait on Helen forever. He drove to his father's private home in St. Petersburg, with anger burning inside of him. It was the anger that kept him alive long enough to live another day, and it was the anger that made Gabriel survive.

Gabriel entered his father's home with his revolver at aim. After what happened to Adeline, John von der Reis deserved this and much worse.

You see, Gabriel and Adeline were lovers. Adeline planned on escaping her husband, a man that she did not love, to run away with Gabriel. Adeline had written a letter to Gabriel, explaining that she was expecting his child. But Gabriel received no letter as it was intercepted by his father, The Chupacabra. He had written Adeline back, pretending to be Gabriel. He told her that he never loved her and wanted nothing to do with that child. When Adeline's husband found the letter, he threw her out into the streets, and she disappeared.

The Chupacabra also wrote a letter to Gabriel, pretending to be Adeline. The Chupacabra gave Adeline's actual letter to The Nightingale. She kept the letter for years before she felt guilty enough to hand it over to Gabriel. To make it up to him, The Nightingale and Gabriel went to Germany to search for Adeline. But when they got there, it was too late. Adeline was gone now, and Gabriel held his father and sister responsible for her death.

Gabriel found his father inside his office with his back turned, facing the window, glaring out into the cold world. It was now or never. Gabriel took a step forward.

"I'd think very carefully before pulling that trigger, son. Someone might get hurt," smirked The Chupacabra.

"Why not?" asked Gabriel quietly.

The Chupacabra turned, facing his son for the first time in weeks since the encounter with George Buchanan. The Chupacabra smiled wickedly. "Don't you want to know what happened to your son, Gabriel?" said his father slowly.

"My what?"

His son? Gabriel couldn't believe what he was hearing. That would be impossible. Adeline and Gabriel had always been more than careful. Gabriel couldn't have a son.

The Chupacabra continued, "That woman died in childbirth as I understand."

That woman. Gabriel wanted to pull the trigger and watch his brains splatter across the floor. That woman had a name. Adeline. She was beautiful and intelligent. And that man took her away from him.

"No. Adeline was never pregnant. She did not die in childbirth. She died of pneumonia," retorted Gabriel.

"Is that what they told you?" taunted The Chupacabra. His father let out a wicked chuckle. "I thought you were smarter than that, son." The Chupacabra took several steps forward. "No. It was childbirth."

"Why are you telling me this?"

The Chupacabra smiled. "Because, if you ever want to see your son alive, you'll do exactly as I say."

Gabriel's mouth dropped half-open, and his cold eyes widened as the world crumbled around him. He was not able to move. Gabriel experienced a new feeling. It was strange and powerful. The fear of his child's life felt like running until he was all out of breath. His father had to be lying. There was no way that Gabriel had a child. But what if his father was telling the truth? Gabriel could not take that chance.

"What will you have me do?"

The Chupacabra smirked. "I want you to come to Berlin with me."

Before you read another word, you need to sit down and take a couple of deep breaths. Nothing I can do or say will prepare for you what's next.

This part of the journey ends with a poor, old midwife named Johanna.

Johanna was a seventy-eight-year-old German woman from Berlin. Her dark gray hair was drawn in a tight bun, and her golden spectacles sat on the edge of her hooked nose. Her face was round and gentle, with light, crystal-like eyes. Johanna wore a long black dress that day, with a silver chain hanging below her neck. She lived alone. No husband and no children. She rarely had any visitors. Most of the time, it was some young lad selling something useless. So, it was no surprise that she heard a small knock against the door that morning. She could have pretended she wasn't home, but they might simply come back later.

Johanna ignored it and continued breakfast.

There was a pounding against the door again. This time louder.

Johanna answered it, and that would be the last mistake of her life.

A few minutes later, the poor, old German woman would be entertaining some unexpected house guests; John von der Reis and his son.

The Chupacabra stood in the middle of the kitchen, with his arms crossed. He appeared impatient. He wore a flannel suit and a dark coat, and his cold eyes were fixed on the woman. Gabriel sat at the table, sipping on honey-flavored tea. He wore a dark suit with a torn-out trench coat. He was very anxious that morning but hid it well.

"Then what happened?" asked Gabriel impatiently.

Johanna poured herself some tea, swallowing hard. She sat down at the kitchen table and took a small sip. She was nervous. Gabriel had a reputation, and his father had an even bigger one. Johanna looked at the floor, twiddled her thumbs, trying to remember the events of that night.

She'd delivered almost four hundred babies in her day. The stories that woman could tell you! There was this one night when a mother of three went into labor. At nine centimeters, her pain was excruciating. She desperately moved all over the bed, writhing in agony. Johanna could tell that this mother was starting to panic and did her best to help her through the last part of labor. Johanna was kind but firm. She calmly asked the mother to lay back down. The mother seemed to respond to Johanna's soft voice, and as she forced herself to breathe evenly, her cervix reached ten centimeters. Johanna told this woman that it was time to push, and a healthy baby girl was born that night.

After that birth, Johanna got a telephone call. Another mother was in labor. It was Helen von der Reis. Johanna made a big mistake going to Mrs. von der Reis. Her career was never the same. She retired early because of that night. Never in her life did she think she'd repeat the details to anyone, especially to Gabriel von der Reis and his father.

Gabriel slammed his hand on the table, causing Johanna to jump and shriek in horror. "Tell me what happened!" shouted Gabriel.

"I went to d-d-deliver the b-b-baby. Frau von der Reis gave birth to a boy that night."

That would be Gabriel's half-brother, Daniel. He was born dead. His father was away on an extended business trip when Helen went into labor. The funeral was short, and Helen didn't have time for grief. She buried the baby in a small tomb in her family's mausoleum. Some information was linked to him that Ivan Mikhailovich shared the same birthday with his deceased half-brother. Gabriel did some investigating, which led him to his brother's tomb. After receiving permission from the city of Berlin to open the crypt, he found there was no body. His brother was not buried there. His constant search led him to a woman named Johanna.

The Chupacabra listened to everything carefully, thinking of ways to murder the poor woman when all this was over. "Where was the child born?" he asked quietly.

Johanna swallowed hard. "I don't remember," she muttered.

Gabriel slammed his fist on the table harder. "You better try to remember like your life depends on it!"

Johanna jumped again, trying to hold back tears. She closed her eyes and tried to picture the house. It was a gothic mansion, surrounded by a wild garden on the outskirts of Berlin. The woman who owned the beautiful manor must have known Helen very well. A relation perhaps.

"I don't remember," repeated Johanna, lying to protect the secret.

Gabriel's face hardened, and he flipped over the table. The teacups and sugar went flying. Johanna screamed in terror, covering her face with her hands.

"You must remember something," said Gabriel, his cold gray eyes flashing with impatience.

"The woman who owned the house had long blonde hair with a scar on her neck."

Alarmed, The Chupacabra asked, "What did the scar look like?"

Johanna closed her eyes tight, trying to imagine it. "It's four small marks, I think they were from a dinner fork," she said.

There was only one woman alive who fit that description. It was the woman who The Chupacabra loved and somehow destroyed. It was the woman who hated Helen the most.

Her name was Gertrude Hahnsburg.

That name awoke memories. The Chupacabra needed her like a car needed an engine to start. He was addicted to her. But then he simply got bored with her. Gertrude changed somehow, or maybe it was him that had changed. The idea of her was no longer fun. Gertrude was no longer exciting or new to him. Then Gertrude's nineteen-year-old sister, Helen, returned from Paris. Suddenly, he wanted Helen. And he was going to do anything to get her.

"What happened next?" asked Gabriel quietly.

Johanna paused for a few moments, recollecting the moments she tried pushing out of her memory for almost two decades.

"Frau von der Reis seemed nervous or scared that night. I thought it was the nerves of a new mother, but I was mistaken. A man came to the house."

"Who was he?" asked Gabriel calmly.

"I don't know. He was Russian."

That could be Mikhail Mikhailovich, thought Gabriel.

Anger passed through The Chupacabra as he popped his knuckles and balled his fists.

"This man appeared to be her lover. He was very affectionate with her."

Gabriel's father had heard enough. He pulled out his gun and pointed it at poor Johanna's chest. He pulled the trigger. Johanna didn't have time to scream before her body landed on the floor, with fear imprinted on her face. Johanna, the German midwife, was dead.

Gabriel glared at his father in horror. "She wasn't finished yet!" he shouted.

The Chupacabra stowed the weapon. "But I was done listening," he hissed.

His father began pacing the kitchen floor, muttering nonsense to himself. It must have made sense to him but it didn't make any sense to Gabriel. After a few moments, The Chupacabra couldn't contain himself anymore. He picked up a wooden chair and threw it across the room. He tore open cabinets, pulling out glass and cups, smashing them on the floor. It was like something had taken over. The Chupacabra couldn't stop. He pulled out silverware from drawers and threw them on the floor. He took picture frames and smashed them, and he punched a hole in the wall.

Then the Chupacabra stopped and looked around. The tiny, over-furnished apartment was a mess. His eyes stopped on Gabriel. His son stood across the kitchen, with his arms folded. He appeared disappointed. But that would be an understatement.

"If you are done with your tantrum, are you ready to have a civilized conversation?" said Gabriel calmly.

The Chupacabra took several heavy breaths, his heart rate decreasing in rhythm. "Do you think it's true?" his father asked quietly. It was paranoia, and it got the best of him every time. Gabriel had never seen his father quite this way before. He appeared helpless and defeated. Although, The Chupacabra would never admit defeat.

"Do I think Helen gave birth to Ivan Mikhailovich? I don't know," said Gabriel.

The Chupacabra's heart hammered against his chest. His voice was shaking as he tried to get the words out. "H-how c-c-could s-s-he do this-s-s-s to m-e-e? How c-c-could she b-b-be like—"

"How could she be like my mother?" Gabriel finished that sentence for him.

His father looked at him and paused. The Chupacabra walked towards his son with deep emotion in his cold eyes. The Chupacabra raised his hand.

For a moment, Gabriel thought his father might hit him. Instead, The Chupacabra put his hand on his face.

"Oh, my boy," he cried. "Some days, I am very proud of you." The Chupacabra gave his son a slight smile, then it faded. "And other days, you really disappoint me."

Gabriel didn't take offense. Somehow, it was his father's strange and twisted way of saying that he loved Gabriel. Even if he didn't show it or never said it, it was there but twisted up. Gabriel didn't mind. He was used to it.

The Chupacabra paced the floor, stepping over broken glass and Johanna's dead body. He began to mutter things to himself again.

"I was a good husband to her." He sounded hurt and half hysterical. It was like he was reliving his ex-wife's abandonment and betrayal all over again. "I gave her everything she wanted. I gave her a house. I gave her shoes. . . dresses. . . jewelry. I gave her you. That wasn't enough. I wasn't enough!" The Chupacabra turned to Gabriel again, his gray eyes flashing in pain. "She left me. And she left you."

The Chupacabra didn't usually speak of Gabriel's mother much. It awoke a sense of betrayal that was too powerful to understand. Gabriel had never even seen a photograph of his mother. He wasn't even sure what she looked like, and he wasn't even sure what her name was. His mother left when he was too young to remember. It was all for the best though. He wouldn't want to remember something like that. He was sure this very moment that his father would want to forget. If Gabriel hadn't had a long string of nannies to look after him, he probably wouldn't have survived.

"The way you treat Helen now, I can't imagine how you must have treated your first wife. I imagine not very well," said Gabriel bluntly. "Women don't just leave."

The Chupacabra turned sharply and gave Gabriel a murderous look. "Watch it," he threatened. The Chupacabra made three steps forward, and Gabriel took three steps back, challenging him with his eyes. "Be very careful what you say next, son."

"It's no wonder Helen had an affair."

The Chupacabra's cold gaze hardened, flashing with anger. "You shouldn't have said that," he sighed. "I want you to watch Ivan Mikhailovich for me—if you want your son back."

Gabriel felt a surge of panic. "You said—"

"You shouldn't have defied me," shouted The Chupacabra. "Now I have another task for you: watch Ivan Mikhailovich from a distance. If you serve me well, I will give you your son back. Do I make myself clear?"

Gabriel felt a tight knot in his throat. He wanted to punch something until his fists bleed. He should have kept his big mouth shut. "Yes, sir," he said quietly.

The Chupacabra pointed his index finger. "And nothing that was said leaves this room."

The Chupacabra opened the front door. He was running late for another business transaction, and he couldn't be late.

Gabriel looked at Johanna's dead body and said, "What about her?"

The Chupacabra turned halfway and looked at her as if nothing had happened. "What about her?" he repeated grimly.

"We can't just leave her here," said Gabriel.

The Chupacabra sighed heavily. "We can't just take her with us, Gabriel. We're not savages."

"Of course not," scoffed Gabriel quietly.

The Chupacabra left the modest home and climbed inside a waiting cab.

"I'll take a different cab, Father."

The Chupacabra appeared surprised. "Why? What are you up to?"

Gabriel sighed and gazed down at the sidewalk, thinking about the woman Johanna might have called Gertrude. "There's something I must do."

"Be careful, my son. Berlin is a dangerous place." As soon as The Chupacabra shut the car door, the vehicle accelerated. If he ever saw his dear wife again, he would make her wish that she was never born.

Gabriel climbed in the next cab. The driver drove to a gothic manor on the outskirts of the city. The mansion was dark and beautiful, surrounded by exotic plants and green bushes in the shape of animals. The roof was uniquely slanted, with dark bricks barely hanging on.

Gabriel knocked on the door. A forty-eight-year-old woman answered. She was a tall, thin woman, with an hourglass figure and amber eyes. She had short, bouncy blonde hair that fell below her shoulders. Her full lips were crimson, and her cheeks were rosy. She wore a white blouse and a gray tie, with dark pants that fit her perfect figure. There was a cigarette between her fingers. The woman named Gertrude took a long drag.

"Look what the cat dragged in!" she said cheerfully. She put her hand on her hip and gave Gabriel a seductive smile. "I was wondering when a von der Reis was going to walk through my door again." Her smile faded, and she gave Gabriel a suspicious look. "Did my sister send you?"

Gertrude was just as beautiful as her younger sister, Helen. But it was a different type of beauty. Helen was dark and mysterious while Gertrude had a sweet and innocent demeanor. But she was far from it.

Gabriel gave Gertrude a charming smile. "No. I am not here on Helen's behalf."

Gertrude's red lips broke into an angelic smile. "Good," she said Gertrude, her voice sounding husky. She held open the door for Gabriel and gave a loving grin. "Come in, boy."

Gabriel walked through the door. The house was magnificent. There was an oak staircase leading to four different floors. A crystal chandelier hung from the ceiling, and a red Persian carpet lay in the hallway. A private collection of rare and exotic paintings covered the walls. Helen's sister had seemed to be doing very well for herself.

Gertrude took another drag of her cigarette and stared at Gabriel a moment longer. "Tea? Gin?" his step aunt asked.

"Tea would be nice."

Gertrude walked to the lady's parlor, swinging her hips. Gabriel followed close behind, his eyes admiring the satin walls. Gertrude poured Gabriel a cup of imported tea from Asia. Gabriel took a sip, reclining on a leather armchair. He thought carefully of what he was going to say.

"How's Margaret?" asked Gabriel.

"My perfect and overachieving sister-in-law?" smirked Gertrude. She stared out the window and took another drag, trying to mask her disgust. "Margaret has never been the same since her daughter, Adeline, died. The last time I heard, she left her husband and fled to Switzerland with her lover. But you didn't hear that from me," she chuckled.

Gabriel took another sip of the Chinese tea. "How did Adeline die?" Gabriel wasn't stupid. He knew it wasn't childbirth.

There was a deafening silence.

Gertrude put out the cigarette and walked to an antique liquor cabinet. She opened the drawer and pulled out a cigar case. "Why are you here,

Gabriel?" she asked. She slipped the cigar in her mouth and lit it. "It was about to drink my imported tea," she said slowly.

"You're the only woman I know with blonde hair and a scar like that on her neck."

Gertrude glared at him and sat on the leather sofa. "Yes, one of my previous lovers had a very jealous wife, and she didn't take kindly to me. What's it to you?"

"I have a little mystery to solve," said Gabriel in a conniving way.

Gertrude kicked off her black shoes and reclined on her side. Her red lips smiled seductively again. "Do tell."

"As I understand, Daniel was born in this house."

Gertrude's smile faded. She put out the cigar. "You were going to discover the truth someday."

"How much is the truth worth?" said Gabriel emotionlessly.

"How much do you think betrayal is worth?"

Gabriel thought about it. He walked to the case of cigars and opened it. "How about we make a deal?" Gabriel slipped the cigar in his mouth and lit it. He coughed several times and continued, "If you tell me what I want to know, I owe you a favor."

Gertrude laughed wickedly. "A favor from a von der Reis. That sounds expensive."

"Do we have a deal?"

"I believe we do."

Gertrude closed her eyes, and her mind returned to that awful place. It was the place that made her vulnerable. The anger and jealousy resurfaced, and it took all she had in her not to hit or throw something. It wasn't fair that things ended the way they did. Although, nothing ever is fair.

Gertrude and John von der Reis were once in simple terms engaged. At least she got to keep the ring.

"Your father and I were thick as thieves," she said quietly. "Then. . ."

Gertrude leaned forward and buried her face in her hands. Then, he tricked Gertrude into getting an abortion and married her sister. Not a day has gone by that she hasn't missed that baby. He promised that he'd marry her, and he promised that they'd be a family. What a beautiful lie that was!

"You don't have to tell me what he did to you," said Gabriel.

Gertrude looked at Gabriel. He looked like his father, but he wasn't at all like his father. Gabriel wasn't a good man, but he wasn't a bad one either. Gabriel had some sort of light that didn't exist inside his father. Gertrude gave him a small smile.

"Right," she muttered.

No matter how much she tried to hate John for what he did, somehow, she still loved him. Now, even more than she did all those years ago.

"My baby sister showed up at my doorstep in labor. I let her in and called a midwife."

Gabriel looked surprised.

"Whatever differences my sister and I have, I am not a cruel woman," said Gertrude calmly.

Gabriel took a long drag of his cigar. "The midwife said that a man came for the child that night."

"Yes," she recalled. "A man did come to take the child away. I asked her what her husband thought of this. She said that he didn't know because he wasn't the father," smirked Gertrude.

Gabriel choked on the cigar smoke and cleared his voice, "What? Why would Helen tell you that?"

Gertrude had a wicked smile. "I can be very persuasive."

Gabriel nodded. That confirmed his suspicions and the midwife's story.

"The child's father was not Mikhail Mikhailovich," she added.

"Who is the father?" asked Gabriel quietly.

Gertrude's smile faded.

For a second, it appeared that she might rethink the whole situation, and not tell Gabriel at all. Instead, she leaned in closer. Her red lips were so close to his face, he could feel them. What she said next changed everything Gabriel thought about Helen, and of course, Mother Russia herself.

CPSIA information can be obtained
at www.ICGtesting.com
Printed in the USA
LVHW101533090522
718289LV00006B/289